Told You Twice

Told You Series #2

Kristen Heitzmann

Print Edition

bHd Books

Cover photography by Jessica Lovitt

Dedication

To Jessie and Darius whose love for each other spills joy into the world

"Yes, I'm meeting them, Jeffrey." Would the world wobble on its axis if just once someone didn't feel the need to check up on her? It had been years since she needed checking, and she didn't want to think about that now that things were going so great.

Alexis hunched over her phone so she wouldn't bother the other subway travelers. Some had headphones and only a handful were staring—most with more interest than irritation—but she didn't like to be annoying. A passing train on a parallel track drowned out her fiancé's response. "I'm at the station, Jeffrey. Have to go." She would have added, "Love you, bye," but didn't want to holler that.

She slipped the phone into her jeans pocket and moved with the crowd of professionals, sightseers, and regular people through the resplendent Grand Central Terminal. Outdoors, with the noise and smell of traffic, she followed Forty-Second Street to the New York Public Library. The Beaux-Arts edifice was beautiful, historical, and dazed even avid readers with its sheer magnitude. Yet here alone, among the world's great libraries, anyone could walk in and request a book without needing permission to use the library. She loved that, among so many other things in this crazy great place she lived.

She leaned against Patience, the marble lion on its pedestal across from Fortitude, and watched for Devin Bressard, the cousin she hadn't seen in too long. She'd thought him so mysterious, even had sort of a crush, but in a cousin-y way. Now he'd married the romance novelist Grace Evangeline and that was beyond exciting. Yes, there'd been the scandal when they got pregnant before the wedding. Because Grace's brand promoted courtship and marriage—the power to say "not yet"—she'd taken fire for that.

She expressed sorrow for failing but refused to regret her baby girl, Mattie Angelica. Grace came through that ordeal more genuine than ever. Almost two years later, the Grace Evangeline Babies line was nearly as popular as her themed weddings, but neither as popular as the novels they sprang from. Alexis could hardly wait for Grace to finish speaking in the library. She and Jeffrey hoped so much for Grace Evangeline to plan their wedding and write their story. Her fists did a little dance at the thought.

Devin hadn't sounded too sure, but something giddy—actually giddy—bubbled up, though giddy was not her normal mode. In fact, giddy started with Jeffrey. So much had started with Jeffrey.

At last she saw them coming through the left-hand arch—Devin dark and lanky with golden-haired Grace almost as tall in four-inch wedges, carrying Mattie in her arms. The adults formed a complementary study, while the child broke the plane in a golden ratio of artistic composition. She wanted to cry, "Freeze," and snap a picture to work up on canvas. Instead she pushed off the pedestal and hugged her cousin, while sneaking a peek at his glamorous wife. Yeah … she'd be getting that inside scoop.

Devin released her. "How you doing, Exi?"

"Exi?" Grace asked.

"When I was little I couldn't say Alexis," she explained. "It came out Exi and kind of stuck."

"I like it." Grace shifted her toddler and held out her hand. "It's so nice meeting you. I was surprised to learn Devin has cousins who weren't on our wedding list. I suspect it was because I had no family coming, and he didn't want his side of the park to cave in."

"It was limited seating on both sides." He motioned them down to the broad sidewalk surrounding the complex. "There's only so far you can extend before people think your invitation grasping."

Maybe, but she would have gone in a heartbeat.

"Exi's mom is Eddie's second cousin, which makes us … some cousin variety, which I won't work out since you Southerners lump all the first, second, and thrice removeds into a single term anyway."

As they circled toward Bryant Park, Grace raised her chin. "I'm born and raised in Georgia but a New Yorker now like you—only with better connections."

"Yes," he muttered. "NYPD *loves* you."

"And the FDNY."

"Even the ones who haven't rescued or arrested you."

Grace tsked. "That was a false arrest, as you know, since you were handcuffed right beside me."

Exi stared. "I never heard about that."

"The commissioner quashed it." Devin avoided a gob of something on the sidewalk.

"More embarrassing to them than us," Grace said.

Mattie stretched to tear leaves from a dangling branch and examined them like a miniature botanist. Exi looked from her to Devin, the resemblance uncanny. "You really are the dad—not that there was any question," she told Grace in a rush. "But Mattie looks exactly like him."

Devin flat-toned, "She has her mother's nature." He replaced the leaves with a loopy lamb from the bag over his shoulder.

"No offense," Exi told him, "but that's a good thing. No brooding."

Grace choked a laugh.

"Not that brooding's bad. I'm sure it's all deep thoughts and stuff."

"And stuff." His eyebrows hitched up.

They moved into the shaded walkways of the verdant park that smelled of grass and blooms, of eateries, and the surrounding city. The noise of traffic and population muted just a little. Devin had suggested this location so they could fit their discussion into Grace's tight schedule. Aware of that, Exi took a breath and dove in. "What do you think of our idea?"

"Well, that's straight to the point." Grace set Mattie down beside a flower bed.

"Sorry. Jeffrey says I'm always six steps ahead of myself."

"Scarily similar to someone else I know," Devin muttered.

"Jeffrey's your fiancé?" Grace followed Mattie as she bounced the lamb on some flowering kale.

"Yes. He's the one who suggested we have a Grace Evangeline wedding."

Grace gave her husband a pointed look. "I like him already."

"I adore your novels and the whole courtship concept. And Jeffrey's onboard all the way."

"Bless his heart. Tell me about him."

"Oh. Wow. Where to start?"

Devin said, "How'd you meet?"

"It was sort of an interview."

"Did you throw tea in his face?"

Her laugh burst out. "No. But I've watched your gif about a million times."

"I'm not thrilled that Grace tossing tea in my face is memorialized forever."

"It's not her tossing tea. It's you wiping and wiping your face. Hilarious."

"Great."

"He only wiped it once," Grace said. "The gif repeats."

"Yeah. So funny."

"Please go on," he intoned. "I can't wait to hear."

Exi tucked her hair behind her ear. "I just moved back five months ago and was looking for work. Jeffrey needed commercial art done for his PR firm and took a look at my portfolio."

"Graphic artist?" Grace asked.

"That's my undergrad degree, something sort of practical. But I love painting so I went for a master of fine arts." Following Mattie's curious path, they wended through a spindly forest of green tables and chairs haphazardly lining the walk.

"Did you get the job?" Devin guided Mattie away from the furniture and toward the lawn.

"His sales team preferred someone else's work. But that's cool, because he asked me out and wouldn't have if we worked together. He'd never mix personal and professional."

"Sometimes the opposite works out." Devin brushed Grace's back.

"I get that, but being in PR, Jeffrey's cautious of anything remotely compromising."

"And he wants a Grace Evangeline wedding?" Grace probed.

"Absolutely. He's so impressed that you didn't change your message to justify what happened."

Grace relaxed her shoulders. "Sounds like you found a special guy."

"So special. It's still sinking in."

Devin said, "You've only known him five months?"

"I knew after five days." She turned to Grace. "Was it that way for you?"

"Took me five minutes. Then Devin opened his mouth."

Exi snorted. "So you threw your tea and swept him away."

Grace slid a look at her husband. "In a manner of speaking."

"It's not like that with Jeffrey. We get along so well it's as if someone matched us up point by point." She talked about him during their walk through the park, then finally sighed. "I'm really lucky."

"He's the lucky one," Devin said and sounded like he meant it.

Grace carried her tuckered daughter as Devin maneuvered them along the sidewalk toward home—watchful of careening bike messengers, dog thieves, and fans-turned-stalkers. He'd learned that from her. With Mattie's moist head snugged into her neck, Grace nudged her husband. "You're thinking something. What is it?"

"I'm wondering whether Jeffrey turned her work down so he could ask her out."

"Really?"

"You saw what a knockout she is."

Alexis did have the biggest hazel eyes and such a genuine smile. Devin was probably talking about the rest of the package. Though petite, Exi's wedding gown would require shoring up her own had not. "Can hardly blame him. You know how it is to be felled at first sight."

"Don't I ever."

"But?"

"If it's true, he should say so. Not put it on his sales team."

"What, 'I know you need the job but I'd rather date you'?"

"I don't mean right at that moment."

They entered the building.

"Hi, Vince." Grace gave the doorman a bright smile as he walked them to the elevator and pushed the button.

"Have a great day, Grace. Mr. Bressard."

Devin got in and hit the floor button.

"That's funny, isn't it?" Grace said when the doors closed.

"What?"

"He still calls you Mr. Bressard."

"He calls everyone by their surname. Except you, apparently."

She snuggled her sleepy daughter. "Why is Jeffrey bothering you?"

"Just seems he'd have told her, now that they're engaged. But you saw her. She completely believes it."

"Maybe it's true."

"Sure. Just like your plot devices."

She clicked her tongue. "I'm sure Exi's smart enough to know if she's being played."

Devin slid her a look.

"Not smart?"

"Hard to say. She's always been like a pet, cute and a little uncontrollable."

"Devin."

"She doesn't wet the floors, but she'll get into everything and make a mess of it."

Grace rolled her eyes but actually found it sort of funny. "You can ask Jeffrey when we meet him."

"I intend to."

Shifting Mattie, she leaned against him. "Is this like a big-brother thing? Because I kind of like it."

"It's a something-removed-cousin thing. Because Exi isn't the best judge. I told you, she's like a puppy all wiggles and charm who doesn't see the truck coming."

"She seemed very sharp to me."

"Yeah, well …"

She sent him a death ray. He pulled her into his arms.

"You're squishing your daughter."

"Is she complaining?"

"No. She likes it. But only because she thinks she belongs against your chest. I told you taking her out of her crib every time she fell asleep was a bad idea."

He peeked down at Mattie's pearly toothed grin. "She seems none the worse for it."

In fact, she thrived on her daddy's attention. And why not? Their little minx had channeled so deeply into his heart it reshaped around her. Grace soaked them in. Mattie's eyes had settled between Devin's stormy gray and her own ocean blue. He swore his daughter's moods drove the color one direction or the other, and he had a point. Right now they were clear, coral-reef turquoise.

Several days later, Exi stared up at her cousin's shiny building rising like a jewel amid the older East Village structures. It tickled her to recognize the influence of Piet Mondrian in its design. Though the artist never used the subtle blue and green tones of the glass on this structure, the lines and segments were there. She went inside and told the doorman Grace and Devin Bressard were expecting her.

His face lit. "You know Grace?"

"I just met her, but Devin's my cousin."

"And you're?"

"Alexis Murphy."

"Sure, I got your name here. Let me get the elevator."

"Thanks."

She rode up, and Grace let her into their condo in the clouds. Well, not like actual skyscrapers, but high enough for an unobstructed view through floor-to-ceiling windows. It looked like a picture postcard out there, and a high-rent fishbowl in here. Don't gape, she told herself.

Grace said, "So glad you're here, Alexis. Jeffrey coming separately?"

"From work."

"Would you like a glass of wine, Coke, or sweet tea?"

"Tea sounds great, though I doubt I'll be dousing Jeffrey."

Grace poured. "You never know what might come in handy."

Grinning, Exi accepted the glass, then took a swallow. "Wow. That's sweet."

"If it doesn't stand and salute, I've failed my grandma's recipe." Grace tipped her head. "Want something else?"

"No, it's good. Just takes you by surprise." The second sip wasn't such a shock. "Thanks for inviting us over. I don't know why I'm nervous. Jeffrey's won my family so completely they'd choose him if it came to taking sides. I have no reason to think Devin will be different."

"He sets a high bar."

"Yeah. Takes an act of God to measure up."

Grace arched her brows. "Do all your family feel that way?"

"Maybe just me. And it's not his fault. He's just, you know, up there himself." Exi looked around. "Like this place."

"His uncle Robert gifted the condo before he died. Took a long time for Devin to feel at home."

She could imagine. "Robert was sort of odd with all those big talking birds. He brought them around in a travel cage."

"That's not so odd."

"But they had conversations in Robert's voice like, 'How do you love me?' 'Let me count the ways.' Then all this loud smooching."

Grace bit her lip. "You're making that up."

"I swear on Sister Monique's toe." At Grace's stare, she said, "The principal—Sister M—wore Birkenstocks under her habit. She had this gnarly toenail, so swearing by it is like wishing-to-die."

Grace pressed a hand to her chest, laughing.

"I'm not lying. Ask Devin. She was old when he was there."

"Devin attended parochial school?"

"You don't know?"

"He's not that forthcoming with his personal history." Grace took out a container of cut vegetables and arranged them on a platter.

"Jeffrey tells me everything. He's so transparent and personable. The opposite of Cousin Robert, who liked birds better than people. Except Devin. They were the brainiacs." Exi ran her hand over the butter-soft leather couch. "He made heaps of money but had to be lonely, don't you think?"

"It appears the men in this family do just fine in solitary situations. Might be intellect. I had to train Devin to think with half his brain." Grace pinched off a leaf from a celery stick. "Anyway, they were together at the end—Devin, his uncle, and the birds. Maybe that was just right."

Exi nodded. "Would you rather know you were dying or just have it happen?"

"I'd like time to make things right with people." Her voice had a tiny catch.

"What could you have to make up for?"

"Everyone has something."

"I wrote the book on that. Only not literally since you're the author." She moved along the kitchen counter and studied a photograph. "Is that Cousin Eddie?"

"Devin's dad, yes. And the rabbi he plays chess with."

"I didn't know he played."

"Moshe doesn't think so either. The only time Eddie won, he had a heart attack."

"The rabbi?"

"Eddie. He's had three that led to a double bypass."

"Oh no. I've been farther out of the loop than I realized."

Grace nodded. "We're awfully worried, but he seems stronger since the surgery."

"I hope so. He's such a nice guy. Do you believe in auras?"

"I'm not sure how you mean that."

She studied his face in the photo. "Like in art when people have halos. I doubt some painter decided to circle the holy ones."

Grace turned to look at the photo with her. "What does that have to do with Eddie?"

"Haven't you seen his glow?"

"I've seen his goodness."

"Exactly." This sip of tea electrified her teeth, and she guessed she'd had enough sugar for a while. She set the glass on the gray stone counter. "What about the opposite? Have you felt a creepy vibe around people sometimes?"

"You have a discerning spirit."

"Maybe now, but I've made errors in judgment. More than my share. Until Jeffrey. Now I've got it figured out. Finally."

"Oh?" Grace toweled moisture off the faucet.

"You'll see when you meet him. He's so … right for me."

"That's great."

"Especially when I've made a practice of wrong for me."

"Sometimes it's hard to tell."

"Not as hard to tell as to resist. I'm a sucker for hard-luck boys who just need love."

"I take it Jeffrey's not that."

"Anything but. He's smart, successful, and knows exactly what he thinks. There's hardly a ripple of uncertainty in anything he does, while I get tangled in all the possibilities."

"I thought you were matched up on every point."

Exi swiveled the cafe stool. "We're not the same, but complementary. He fills my gaps."

"I see. Will you pursue your art career when you're married?"

"I want to." Exi bit her lip. "Right now I share a studio with a bunch of others in a co-op gallery, but I haven't had much time to paint. Between Jeffrey and working at MoMA—"

"The Museum of Modern Art? That sounds important."

"I'm just a guest assistant, but, with my degree, a real position might open up. The problem is, while I really want to be painting, what I see there doesn't inspire me. Not that it's bad, it's just not me. I used to have ideas sparking all the time, but now I wonder if that magic is gone."

"I hope not."

"I entered the MFA program with adequate skills, but my adviser all but shot down my direction. She said we have cameras to record reality and my representational bent should be used to send a political message or have shock value or both."

Grace frowned. "I believe art should evoke a response but doesn't have to be shocking. Art being political makes me cringe. Why not beauty for beauty's sake?"

"She said the important markets want jarring not pretty, stark not joyful. To be considered relevant I should paint dead people in bathtubs or heaps of garbage."

"Reminds me of a caustic poet I'd rather forget."

"One instructor suggested I try that in abstract with high saturation color. Let people think they see a dead body in a bathtub, but distort the lines and make the colors pop."

"How'd that go?"

"Better. I painted Jeffrey that way."

"Dead in a bathtub?"

"No." Exi giggled. "Bright and abstract. He hung it beside his wall-mounted TV. But I'm not really satisfied. I feel like—I don't know—I have a long way to go or maybe I'm not going the right direction at all. I wish I could afford to explore it."

"Sounds like you could have used that graphics job."

"Yeah." She shrugged. "But that's okay. My favorite part of graphic design is illustrations. I've done a number of those, especially children's books."

"I'd like to see them sometime."

"Oh?" Exi whipped out her phone and opened the gallery, taking just a second to guess which images best fit Grace's personality, then chose the line-drawing figures with curlicues and watercolor washes. "Ta-da." She slid her phone to Grace.

Grace swiped from one to another. "I love that whimsical look."

"Thanks." Exi retrieved her phone. "So, have you considered our request?"

"When I meet Jeffrey and get a feel for your wedding I'll know if there might be someone better."

"There's not. And no one else can write the book."

A lock of hair came loose from Grace's casual updo. She tucked it behind her ear. "I have proposals lined up with my publisher, so I don't see a different novel happening."

"Please, Grace. Jeff will be so disappointed."

"Jeff will?"

"It was his idea. He said you could use our names and everything."

Grace collected herself. "I create fictional characters and put a note in every book that any resemblance to anyone is strictly their imagination."

"Couldn't you make an exception? Name us something else if you want."

"Forgive me, Alexis, but how much story could you two have in the five months you've known each other?"

"There have been a lot of things. Like our meeting. What if they'd accepted my portfolio and we could never have gone out?"

"What if," Grace murmured.

"And then there's his family. They thought he would marry a medical intern he was dating. Hey, she could be the adversary. She still calls and tells him how sorry he's going to be."

"She threatens him?"

"No. For passing up the best thing in his life, blah, blah. Would you ever do that?"

"I can't imagine."

"Except you did stalk Devin until he saw the light."

"Did he say that?"

"Oops." Exi covered her mouth. "I think he meant that to stay between us."

"He calls it stalking, but it was research."

Exi giggled.

"How does Jeffrey react to her calls?"

"He's nice, tells her she's as great as she thinks she is."

Grace's eyebrows rose.

"Well, not in those words. Anyway, Kendyl would not have stayed home with their children."

"I don't suppose you go through medical school if that's your plan. What about you?"

"Jeffrey can support us, but I hope to make some headway with my art. If I can paint I'm happy to be home."

"You've never lived with a toddler."

Exi grinned. "Good point. I'll need a designated studio since Jeffrey wants to start a family right away."

"Do you?"

She shrugged. "It worked for you guys."

"As the world knows, we started our family prematurely."

"But look how happy you are. You said in that interview, God makes even our mistakes shine."

"I don't recommend making them on purpose."

"We won't, but you could put anything in the book. As long as it works out."

Grace rested her palms on the counter. "I put my characters through an awful lot before they triumph in the end."

"Go ahead. I can take it."

"But none of it's happened to you, Exi. It wouldn't be your story."

"I like that."

"What?"

"You called me Exi."

"Oh." Grace added a Crock-Pot of artichoke dip to the veggies. "Devin does, so it's in my head."

"I've always gone by Exi, and I sign my art X-E, but Jeffrey thinks it's babyish." She scooped dip with a carrot. "Mmm. That's good. Anyway it's fine to call me Exi, only not when Jeff's here. And don't call him Jeff. I keep slipping, but he doesn't like it.

"You can't be Exi and he can't be Jeff. Got it."

"Does that sound weird?"

"It sounds as if you know what Jeffrey likes."

"That's one reason we get along so well."

"As important as his knowing what you like."

"Right. You really understand people, Grace. It's why your characters are so believable."

Grace added pita wedges to the platter. "It's about motivation. You can understand a lot if you get down to that."

Exi studied this woman her cousin had lucked into. Grace's surface sparkled like a bubbling brook. But, like her novels, there was so much happening underneath. "I bet you and Devin have interesting conversations."

"And survive them."

Exi laughed. Grace had been fun to watch in TV interviews. She was even better in real life. "So maybe ours isn't a long story. It could be a novella."

"More like flash fiction."

Exi laughed full out. "Add whatever you want to the story. Just make it kind of about us and Jeff will be happy."

"As I said, I don't write real people. I'll explain that to Jeffrey when he gets here."

A blaring noise made Exi jump. "Is that a fire alarm?"

"Probably another glitch in the system, but we can't take the chance." Grace rushed for the door. "Mattie's with our neighbors and loud noise scares her." In the hall, she practically ran for the stairs.

Exi rushed after. At least their dash was down.

2

At each floor, people entered the stairwell. Exi couldn't keep up with Grace, but it didn't matter. They were all going the same way. Except, at the third floor, Grace pushed through the door into the hallway while everyone else continued down. Reaching the door, Exi hesitated. No New Yorker who'd lived through 9/11 didn't tremble at the thought of building fires. But she went after Grace and saw her reach an open condo door where two stunning blondes held a hysterical Mattie.

"We told her you were coming!" the taller one hollered over the alarm, the sound of sirens outside, and Mattie's wailing.

"Thank you." Grace grabbed up her child. "It's all right, baby. Mama's here." Grace looked ashen, which was weird if she didn't think the emergency real.

Exi held the door open as the four of them rejoined her at the stairs, and they continued down. Wholly focused on her child, Grace made no introductions, but the bobbed blonde spoke over the din. "I'm Cate. This is my sister, Mia."

"Are you models?"

Cate hooked her arm through Mia's. "Used to be. I do some still, but mostly we head up Grace Evangeline Merchandising."

Mia said, "I'm trying out clothing designs on Mattie for the new toddler line. She's such a little elf, I can't get enough of her."

"Mia's an amazing designer," Cate said. "The wedding gowns are her line also."

"Oh, the Mia gowns." Exi got excited. "I'm having a Grace

Evangeline wedding, so you might create my gown."

Mia cocked her head. "I've already designed gowns for each theme. Which one are you using?"

"Mine is going to be custom."

The sisters glanced at each other and said in tandem, "Really?"

"Yes. I'm Exi, by the way." She probably should have said Alexis, but whatever. "Devin's cousin."

"Oh." The women lit up. "We knew Devin long before Grace," Cate shouted as they passed an alarm.

"Funny those two together, hmm?" Mia reached for the lobby level door. "Did not see that coming."

If Grace was hearing any of this, she gave no sign. In the lobby, the doorman hurried over and escorted her and Mattie through. Because she was famous? They spoke briefly, then he went back to attending the crowd.

Out on the sidewalk Mattie stopped crying, though her little body shuddered. Grace seemed just as shaken. What was the deal?

"Ms. Evangeline?"

Grace turned to a burly firefighter whose five-o'clock shadow turned his whole neck blue. "Tony. You're East Village now?"

He puffed his chest. "I transferred with my promotion."

Grace beamed. "Good for you."

"Glad you used the stairs." He winked and pulled on his helmet. "Got to go."

Mia said, "He must be the one who saved her from that broken elevator."

Exi looked at them blankly.

"Oh-ho-ho," Cate laughed. "We will fill you in." They looked as eager to tell as she was to hear.

But then Devin strode up all dapper in a sport jacket and slacks. He frowned. "Again?"

"Afraid so," Grace released her daughter into his arms. "I'm sure it's still that glitch."

"Yes," he spoke dryly. "The glitch that never existed before you moved in."

What did that mean?

Grace rolled her eyes. "He thinks I make stuff happen by just being around."

"Being around and *imagining* things."

"That doesn't mean I cause it."

"And yet …" He indicated the crowd on the sidewalk, then turned to the rest of them. "Exi, Cate, Mia. Doing okay?"

"I got my exercise." Exi wiggled Mattie's high-top sneaker. "These look good for marching."

Mattie pressed the side of her head against her daddy. It was fairly heart melting to see them together.

Only now did Grace seem calmer. "We should hire someone to get to the bottom of it."

"For all the good that would do."

"Devin." Grace folded her arms, piqued.

Finally the firefighters came out and announced the building was clear. They didn't say false alarm, but apparently it was as Grace and Devin suspected. The disgruntled crowd moved, but reentry would not be quick.

Devin pursed his lips. "Should we go out instead?"

"Dinner's in the oven."

"Right." He nodded, then realized something. "Where's Jeffrey?"

"He's coming from work," Exi told him.

Grace checked her watch and the street traffic. "He must have been held up."

"Maybe." Exi clasped the back her neck. "He runs late a lot."

"That's surprising for a public-relations person."

"No one minds."

"No one says."

Exi raised her brows.

"Do you like waiting for him?" Grace reached for the door as those in front filed in.

"Not until he gets here. Then I'm so glad he came. Everyone

feels that way."

"So he gets a pass?"

"I guess so." She followed them through the doors into the packed lobby. People on lower floors were taking the stairs. Cate and Mia said they'd do the same.

"Thank you so much for keeping Mattie together until I reached you," Grace told them.

"You know we'd keep her forever if you didn't notice her missing," Mia said.

Devin nuzzled his daughter. "You just want to dress up our baby doll."

"True," they called back and left.

Back inside their condo, Devin carried Mattie off for an early bedtime. The episode had drained her.

"She doesn't need to eat?" Exi asked.

"Cate and Mia fed her. They can't resist." Grace seemed wrung out herself.

"Are you all right? You look a little rattled."

"Is it obvious?" Grace drew herself up. "I don't want Devin to see."

"You hid it when he joined us." She'd mistaken Grace's calm. "What's wrong?"

"It's residue from that gunman incident. Loud noise. Mattie in danger. I don't know if I'll ever stop replaying it."

"Devin doesn't understand?"

"Oh, he understands. Too well. It upsets him."

"They got the guy, right?"

"Yes. But Devin hates that it still affects me. Mattie wasn't born yet, but I think the gunshot left an impression, because she overreacts to loud things."

"That's rough."

"Just as well Jeffrey's late. Gives me a chance to compose myself while Magic Daddy soothes his little girl." She released a slow breath. "Thanks for letting me say it out loud. I feel better."

A knock sounded on the door. When Grace opened it, there was Jeffrey with his cadmium yellow hair and viridian green eyes. Not really of course, but since painting him in the high-saturation hues, Exi saw him that way in her mind.

He strode in as always, on top of the world. She could never put her finger on how. He just commanded every room he entered—in a good way. He handed Grace one of two spring-mix bouquets.

"Grace Evangeline. You need no introduction, but I'm honored to meet you."

"The pleasure's mine. Come on in."

Exi beamed when he gave her the second bouquet. Thoughtful man. She gripped his arm. "So, Grace, here is my awesome fiancé, Jeffrey Young." She rose on tiptoes and kissed his cheek.

"You have a fan," Grace said. "That's clear, even in the limited time Exi's had to tell us about you."

"I'm the fan here tonight. I'll try not to embarrass myself."

Exi thrilled that he'd kept the focus on Grace. He always knew exactly what to do.

"Thoroughly enjoyed your televised wedding. Just the right notes."

"Thanks. Would you like some wine?" She held up a choice of white or red.

"No, thank you."

"Sweet tea, coke, or water?"

"Perrier?" He looked toward the Sub-Zero refrigerator.

"Just flat, I'm afraid, but filtered."

"That'll be fine, thanks." He looked around the place. "Very nice."

Grace served him his beverage and a timer went off. "Excuse me a moment." She tended something Italian that filled the kitchen with a rich, tangy aroma. "I thought we'd mingle awhile, but it's so late this is almost ready to serve."

"That's no problem," Jeffrey told her.

"Well, that's good." Grace placed the steaming pan on the

Thermador range and removed her oven mitts with no visible annoyance over his tardiness.

Relieved, Exi brought Jeffrey through the main room to see the view.

He murmured, "Must be more money in theater than I realized." Over his shoulder, Jeffrey said, "I wouldn't mind talking to you and your husband about any public-relations needs you might have."

"That's nice," Grace said, "but Devin's perfect, and my publisher takes care of me."

"Keep me in mind if their hands get too full." He winked. "You've made the news with regularity."

"Only good news from now on, I hope."

Devin came out from Mattie's room with a measured smile. Before Exi could introduce them, Jeffrey walked forward, hand extended.

"Jeffrey Young. Quite a fan of your work."

"Thanks." Devin shook his hand. "And you're in PR. That must be challenging."

"And rewarding." Jeffrey told him about his firm and some of the clients. Before the conversation got too thick, Exi said, "I love this song," and rocked a little air guitar to Brad Paisley and Carrie Underwood's "Remind Me."

Devin grinned. "Still playing?"

Jeffrey turned with surprise. "An instrument?"

"Three actually. Before settling on art, I planned to be a rock star."

"She had a garage band," Devin said. "Not that bad either."

She braced her hips. "Slay me with faint praise, why don't you?"

"You were fine on the instruments, but that singer …" He wobbled his hand.

"That singer's my roommate, Treya."

"Has she improved?"

"Not by what I hear in the shower." She laughed. "We knew she was off key, but she put on such a show people came to see us anyway."

Jeffrey looked bemused. "What do you play?"

"Guitar, keyboard, and sax."

"I'd like to hear you."

"Oh." She slumped. "I would, but the boyfriend who hit me stole my instruments when I pressed charges." Jeffrey looked like she'd just spoken a foreign language. Yeah, TMI. "Made it easy to decide on art. I love both and choosing might have killed me."

"Do you struggle with decisions?" Grace's face said she'd rather pursue the assault revelation, but she allowed the redirection.

"No, I typically make the wrong ones. Or I did." She smiled at Jeffrey. "Now I'm cured."

He winked encouragement. "You don't give yourself enough credit. Like anything, it's a process."

One of the best things about Jeffrey was his positivity. He and Devin discussed confidence and optimism. Listening to them talk, Exi didn't know why she'd been nervous to introduce them. She should have stayed in touch, but Devin got so important, she'd been afraid to seem like a hanger-on. Now she could see he was simply her cousin, talking to her fiancé.

Grace invited them to take a seat at the table by the windows. Instead, Exi helped her serve. The food looked and smelled great. How long had it been since she ate something someone put as much effort into as she did her own cooking?

"This is very good." Jeffrey praised the eggplant parmigiana served with asparagus and crispy baguette. "Eggplant is not easy to get right."

"Do you cook?"

"No. But I've had enough bad eggplant to say that for a fact."

"A compliment from a connoisseur."

"Merely an aficionado."

"Alexis mentioned you particularly liked eggplant. This is one of my favorite recipes."

"A good recipe still needs expertise to pull it off."

"I guess that's true for everything." Grace smiled.

"Yes. Which is why we've come to you for our wedding and novel. Why not the best at both?" Jeffrey was the right blend of confident and deferential. He might just convince her—

A cry from Mattie's room had Grace on her feet. "Excuse me."

When she had resettled her daughter and returned, Jeffrey said, "Motherhood comes naturally to you."

"It's the most natural thing."

"Not often for women with your kind of career."

"Well, Devin's here when I'm not, and we have friends and family to fill the gaps."

Jeffrey turned to Devin. "You ever wish for a nine-to-five, man-of-the-house job?"

Devin's fork paused. "I prefer my dawn-to-dawn, man-of-the-house job."

Jeffrey's smile showed dimples in both cheeks and chin. "Of course."

"Speaking of jobs"—Devin set his fork down—"Exi tells me you almost hired her."

"Oh. Yes. Alexis has a strong portfolio. But the sales team makes the final call. Unfortunate, though it worked out better for us." He turned his smile on her.

"Way better."

Jeffrey laid his hands beside his plate. "So that brings us back to our Grace Evangeline wedding and novel. Have you …"

Grace explained her writing schedule and that she didn't use real people.

"But this is a perfect opportunity."

"It is?"

"Through us you can restore the lost faith of your followers."

Grace tipped her head. "How so?"

"Because we'll do it. Just like your fictional characters, we'll do this right without—well, for lack of a better word—failing. We'll prove your concept isn't a fictional device. And we'll get out there and talk about it."

Grace opened and closed her mouth.

"It's a win-win for everyone."

"I see. Well, that's an interesting thought." Grace looked at Devin, then back to Jeffrey. "I'll take your plate if you're finished. I have fruit for dessert."

Exi cleared the other plates, joined her in the loft-style kitchen, and whispered, "Do you think Devin likes him?"

"What's not to like? He's very personable." From the refrigerator, Grace took out kiwi and berries in cobalt-stem dessert dishes. "Mind grabbing that cream?" She indicated a bowl of silky cream sauce laced with honey.

"The thing I miss most from Georgia is peaches," Grace told the guys as she set their desserts down. "No matter how they look in the markets here, I can't bear to serve counterfeits. So glad Devin understands."

"If I'm in peach withdrawal, I can walk up the street and get one."

Jeffrey dipped his spoon into the cream. "Or Grace could bend her standards."

Exi caught her breath.

"Last time I did that, the whole world heard about it."

That got a laugh, and Jeffrey was smart enough to leave it alone.

Grace loaded the dishes while Devin saw their guests out. Exi had offered to help, but Grace told her she knew the Bosch's idiosyncrasies. Mostly she'd sensed her husband's reluctance to tarry with Jeffrey. When he joined her in the kitchen, she started the wash cycle, then turned into the bend of his arm. She found a light tone. "Sister Monique?"

His brow lowered. "If you follow that with *toenail*, I'll lose your excellent meal. And that would be a waste." He brought his mouth to her neck. "You okay?"

"I'm fine."

"And … did you like him?"

"As I told Exi, he's personable. Polite. He brought flowers, which people don't often think of anymore. Oh." She looked at the vases on the counter. "Alexis forgot hers."

Devin clasped her elbow. "Polite, personable, and what?"

"Oh, maybe a little opinionated?"

He nodded. "Go on."

"Exi thinks he hangs the moon. We should be happy for her."

"I am. In the past, she attracted less savory sorts."

"So she said, though she doesn't seem that way."

"As an early bloomer, she didn't know how to dial down the sex appeal."

Grace sobered. "I hope no one acted on it."

"Your silence as a thirteen-year-old makes me realize it's probably more prevalent than we know."

Grace rested her hands on his chest. "I don't believe Jeffrey's a predator. I think he has strong opinions, but they're not bad in themselves. We probably agree with most."

"Oh? You wish for a man-of-the-house, Grace?"

"Any manlier, you'll be swinging from vines."

He looked over his shoulder. "Probably could hang one in this open floorplan."

"Me, Jane?" She arched her eyebrows.

He kissed her, then held onto her chin. "Can we talk about the elephant now?"

"The one named failure?"

"That's the one."

"I think he means it sincerely. Exi says he's always looking for ways to help."

He narrowed his eyes. "It didn't offend you?"

"Do you know how many people think they would have done better in our shoes?"

"Maybe, but—"

"Lots of them would have."

"Still . . ."

"My own family won't talk to me. At least Jeffrey thinks positively."

Devin frowned. "You're not considering it."

"No. That's not how I work. But I don't think Jeffrey's sinister for thinking of it." A knock came at the door. Grace said, "I bet that's Exi."

Sure enough his cousin came in, looking chagrinned. "Forgot my flowers."

Grace rubber-banded the stems in a plastic bag with a small amount of water and handed them over.

"Thanks. I didn't want to seem unappreciative."

"Of course not. Thank Jeffrey again for mine. That was nice of him."

"He's that way," Exi beamed, then waved good-bye.

Devin closed the door. "What do you want to bet he sent her back for them?"

"You have no reason to think that. If I forgot flowers you gave me, I'd go get them without being told."

"Well, if he's that nice, why is she selling him so hard?"

Grace took a moment. "If I had to guess, it's because your opinion matters."

"Oh yeah?"

"In fact I don't have to guess, because Alexis said so."

He leaned his back to the door and folded his arms. "I'm supposed to like him?"

"You have no reason not to. I don't know what it is with you thinking the worst of people."

"I don't."

"Bo Corrigan? You went on about him to the day he stood up with you at our wedding."

"I never said anything untrue. And you asked me to include

him."

"But see, Devin? Look at your face. Listen to your tone. Your acceptance bar is so high no one measures up."

"And you see good in people where there is none. Even violent criminals."

"People are more than their bad choices."

He ran a finger along her jaw. "Let's go back to the 'Me, Jane' part of this conversation."

She bit a smile. "I will. But if we're going to plan their wedding, you have to find a way to get along."

"I always get along. And what's this *we*?"

"She's your cousin."

"Who wants a Grace Evangeline wedding. *Your* website. *Your* plans—"

"Custom, Devin. Not a plan based on my already published novels, created around my already written heroines. This would be their happy story and their names in a novel."

"You're kidding."

"I wish I were."

He slid his hand down her arm. "Tell her no. You'll help with the wedding, but no book."

"Except it's Jeffrey who wants it."

Devin took that in. "Jeffrey wants to appear in a romance novel? By name?"

"Exi said so."

"I thought he was pushing for her sake."

"Nope."

He cocked his jaw. "I'm going to have to chew on that awhile."

"Maybe I could chronicle their story as a wedding gift, for just the two of them."

"Exi would love it."

"And Jeff?"

He frowned. "I'm still chewing."

She took his hand. "Come on, Tarzan. We can worry about it

tomorrow."

"Grace ..."

"Don't give that man's remark another thought. I think he's green with envy." She tugged him off the door. Devin's acclaim in his chosen profession spoke for itself. While he wasn't arrogant, he and everyone else recognized his gifts. She had to wonder why Jeffrey Young had gotten under his skin.

3

In her glorified closet of a bedroom ten days after the dinner party, Exi squeezed her rib cage to keep from squealing into the phone when Devin said, "We'd like you and Jeffrey to be our guests at the anniversary performance of *Windows and Doors* opening on Broadway. There's a cast party following."

Yes, yes, yes! She cleared her throat. "We'd love that. I'll ask Jeffrey, but yes. Thank you."

"My pleasure. Grace is texting you the details."

"Okay." Unbelievable how great her life was going. A perfect man, an awesome family, Grace planning her wedding and *maybe* writing the book.

When she told Jeffrey she'd be happy with a custom wedding planned by the queen of wedding romance, he said, *That's fine, Alexis. But anyone can plan a wedding. Only Grace Evangeline can write the novel. It's really the point.*

She would try again to convince Grace—at the anniversary performance? Hands clenched at face-level, she danced in a circle. Not only had she never seen the play, but the cast party too? She let out a whoop—a little one, but her roommates looked up from watching TV.

"Why you dancing in circles, girl?" Treya crunched a popcorn.

She told them.

"*Windows and Doors*?" Suz gasped. "I love that play."

"You love who's *in* that play. Don't lie." Treya pushed her shoulder. "You've seen it five times for who's in that play."

"Who?" Exi said.

As Suz fixed her with owl eyes, Treya clamped the microbraids covering her head. "Don't tell me you've been back for months and not seen your cousin's hit play."

Exi shrugged. "How hard have I scratched to make rent? Even same-day seats are too much."

"Hello." Suz knocked on the wall. "Jeffrey Young? Man with a paycheck. Date night?"

"Jeffrey's not a theater buff." He'd been polite saying he liked her cousin's work. Thankfully Devin didn't ask for details. Although Jeffrey probably had answers ready. "Want to hear the rest?"

Her friends looked at each other. "Nah."

She folded her arms. "Then I won't tell you I'm invited to the cast party afterward."

Treya looked at Suz's face and bent double with laughter. "You're slaying her, girl."

"Why?"

"Suz can't speak. She's jelly that you're going to party with her heartthrob." She tugged her shirt in and out in a magnified heart thumping.

Exi folded her arms. "Who's the heartthrob?"

"Bo Corrigan," they said in chorus.

Exi waited for more.

Suz circled her hand. "Giorgio spokesmodel. Times Square spectacular. Ringing any bells?"

"Afraid not. Jeffrey doesn't like the commercialism of Times Square. Too many tourists."

"Jeffrey's got good points," Treya said, "but you need to lighten him up."

"Hey." Suz propelled herself off the couch. "If he won't go, can I?"

Exi turned to Treya. "You too?"

Treya groaned. "I'm flying out to see Val's baby."

"That trumps a theater production. And whoever this Giorgio-spectacular guy is."

Suz hyperventilated in protest.

"What do you want me to do if Jeffrey accepts the invitation?"

Her friend pressed her forehead to the doorframe. "Shoot me?"

"I'll call him now and see how long you have to live."

Suz laughed against the wood.

It took only seconds for Jeffrey to say, "Of course we go. It's an opportunity. We give a little, they give a little. That's positive motion. Way to go, Alexis. You are really something."

She started to say accepting the invitation wasn't giving anything on her part. It was a big fat receiving something.

But he said, "Sorry, I have to go," and the call ended.

She turned sad eyes to Suz. "Would it save a bullet if I try to get three tickets? And another invitation to the party?"

Suz squashed her face into the doorframe and slid her a look. "I'd stammer myself stupid if I met him in person. I'd rather keep believing Bo really is Peter and imagine I'm Angel."

"Umm …"

"In the play. You'll see." She released a long sigh.

Treya rolled her eyes. "Get a grip, Suz." Then to Exi, "Your cousin's hot stuff. I'd get me some of that if Grace Evangeline hadn't snatched him up."

"He's old." Suz pulled her creased face free.

"Not that much older than her man." Treya pointed. "Besides, I like experience."

"Um. Guys? It's my cousin you're discussing."

"I'm not related." Treya swept the backs of her fingers down her svelte mahogany self. "In case you can't tell."

Exi shook her head at how little the three of them had changed since being best friends in high school. "And by the way, Jeffrey's just old enough to be established. There's a whole lot to be said for that."

"He's a sweetie," Suz said.

"And a charmer," Treya added.

"Yeah." Exi glowed. All was good.

The anniversary performance of *Windows and Doors* went as flawlessly as the first, but in this six-hundred-seat Broadway theater it shone. Grace beamed at Eileen, the producer who'd all but forced her collaboration with Devin. "Did you ever imagine this?"

"It's exactly what I imagined." At seventy-six, Eileen radiated beauty, class, and indefatigable zeal. Former stage star and current glitterati, she joined the actors for their bows as if she'd never stopped treading the boards.

Grace leaned into Devin. On the opening night she'd been awash with so many emotions. Watching that first performance, they'd been watching themselves played by Bo and Louisa. Now, as then, she rose with the audience in standing ovation, caught Bo's eye, and shared his triumph. Would they have this success without his skill as an actor, his name as a draw, and his willingness to take it on for far less money than he'd been worth? From that first rehearsal to now, he'd given nothing less than his utmost.

Grace glanced over her shoulder to Jeffrey and Alexis, several rows back and a few seats over. Devin had thought sitting separately would let them experience the show unencumbered by expectations. Maybe he was right, but she would have liked to see Exi's expressions. His cousin met her eyes now and squeezed her fists together in glee. Jeffrey applauded magnanimously.

She'd have to wait to hear their opinions since they took separate town cars to the party afterward. Eileen gave the club carte blanche for anyone connected to the show and guests. There was something to be said for connections that ran generations deep—even if those progenitors had been smugglers and rakes and probably still were.

As Grace finished a conversation with the stage manager, Bo came up and clinked his champagne flute with hers. "One year on the Great White Way, Grace."

"It's like a dream." And Bo looked dreamy himself. She might be the only one who knew that underneath his nightmare-you'd-love-to-love facade breathed a tortured thespian of the purest kind. Well, *pure* probably wasn't the word for Bo, but people had no idea how he suffered for his art. She only knew because he'd let her see the real man—whether she wanted to or not.

"You made this happen, Grace, you and Devin."

"And the rest of you."

He nudged her arm with his. "I told you we'd make magic together."

"I'm sure this is exactly what you meant. Are you tired of playing Peter yet?"

He shook his head. "Every time there's something, some nuance …" His eyes got a faraway look.

"That's what makes you great."

Striking a rakish pose, he scanned the private club room, then froze like a hawk siting a mouse.

"What?" Grace startled. For all she knew Bo was still a target for the criminals who came after him and found her instead—or he was in some new trouble. Her heart galloped.

"Who is that?"

She followed his gaze and relief rushed in as adrenaline seeped out. "Oh, that's Exi."

"Like Sexy?"

"Alexis. She's Devin's cousin."

Bo cursed.

"What?"

"He won't let me within ten yards of her."

"A hundred. She's engaged to be married."

"To whom, pray tell?" He dragged *tell* at the end like *Downton Abbey*'s Lady Crawley.

Grace pointed to Jeffrey, with his burnished hair and ingratiating stance.

Bo located him. "Why?" He loaded *why* with such ironic disdain the single syllable resonated.

Grace bit a laugh, knowing she shouldn't. "He has good manners."

Bo formed a wolfish grin. "If that's it, I'm golden."

Grace touched his forearm. "If you know what's good for you—"

"When has that ever been the case?"

"Devin has power in your industry."

"Not as much as Eileen. In New York anyway."

"Yes, but she's in both your corners."

His grin spread with smug assurance.

"I'm not going to argue. Just ... Exi's a nice girl."

He made the sound of a cat on the prowl, then laughed. "I can handle a nice girl."

"Well, she can't handle you."

"Grace, I'm a changed man."

"You look like a leopard to me. I recognize those spots."

He got serious. "Have you met Eileen's brother?"

"Liam O'Hare? No, why?"

"Let me just say, if I mess up before he's paid off, I'll take myself out."

She pushed his arm. "Come on."

He held her eyes.

"Well, I'm happy you're reformed, but Exi's engaged. Did you miss that part?"

"I don't miss a thing." As he moved away, he swept a fresh flute from a waiter's tray.

"Oh boy," Grace breathed. "Exi, use that discerning spirit." Bo was not the devil Devin thought him, but he could raise hell and make it look like heaven.

In a club that screamed old money, Exi conversed with Louisa Bourne, the sultry actress who played Angel in Grace and Devin's play. Just past Louisa's shoulder, she caught sight of her smoking-hot counterpart—who seemed to be coming their way.

Louisa turned. "Is that for me?"

Bo Corrigan bent and kissed Louisa's mouth. "That's for you.

This … is for you."

Exi's breath stopped. She took the champagne that she'd been avoiding since it made her bubbly and thought of Suz's stammering-herself-stupid remark. A squeal rang in her head. "Thanks."

"Any time. Exi."

Her mouth fell slack. Louisa drifted away. Bo smelled as good as he looked. Giorgio? She resisted pressing in and breathing deep.

"You okay?" His regular speaking voice had a rich timbre, deeper than the high notes he sang. Probably an incredible range the musician in her wanted to test.

"Yes."

"Good. We better get all our talking in before your cousin breaks us up."

He thought Devin a greater threat than Jeffrey? A quick glance showed her fiancé looking as if he'd enjoyed the performance as much as he said. She drew her eyes back to the sun for more scorching. "Why would Devin do that?"

"He thinks I'm bad."

"Are you?"

"You watched me tonight. What do you think?"

"Oh. Wow. Where to start. Okay. You were amazing. I never cry at movies, never. But I practically sobbed out loud. I mean seriously, I held my chest to keep it in."

His eyes drifted down. Exi braced for his remark. He would think it flattering. She'd pretend it was.

Bo raised his eyes. "The script gives us so much to work with. Your cousin's a prig, but a walking genius nonetheless."

Her mouth pulled into a goofy smile. "I think Grace brought a lot to it. I could hear her voice in there."

"He made it raw. She kept it bearable."

"That's it exactly!" She beamed at their mind-meld.

He glanced past her and held out his flute. "Here's to meeting you." He clinked hers with a ping and walked away.

From behind her, Devin said, "Don't play with that fire, Exi."

She turned. "Oh, Devin. *Windows and Doors* was … I can't even express how great. Bo says you're a genius, and I believe it."

"Bo said that?"

"A genius and a prig. What exactly is a prig?"

Devin laughed. "Someone who feels morally superior to others. And in Bo's case it's true."

She looked where Bo had joined a vibrant older lady. "Who's he talking to?"

"That's Eileen O'Hare, the original producer. All this was her brainchild. When he's finished there, I'll introduce you."

Bo wasn't kidding. Her cousin did think him bad—for her at least.

"Here you are, Alexis." Jeffrey joined them. He and Devin shook hands, and the comments her fiancé made demonstrated the attention he'd paid to the show. She smiled as she listened, then glanced over her shoulder and saw Bo watching. He raised his flute the tiniest bit. Her heart kicked. Oh. Wow.

Bo watched Exi leave with her well-behaved fiancé. Grace didn't think that much of the guy, but Exi did, or she wouldn't be engaged. How did a dud like that make a woman like Exi want to spend her life with him?

"What's turning 'round in that bonny head, Bo?"

His eyes slid to Eileen. "That's something I haven't been called."

"I'm feeling my Irish roots."

He dragged a hand down his mouth and jaw. "Devin's cousin."

"Oh, Alexis is delightful."

Alexis? No, Exi, definitely.

Eileen huffed. "Too bad she's fallen for that schmoozer."

"What's his name?"

"Jeffrey Young. He doesn't know the first thing about theater and cares even less."

He hadn't spoken with the man, which was surprising since the guy made the rounds like a glad-hander at a rally. "Exi liked our play."

"She loved it. And not only the play I imagine." Eileen repositioned herself. "So what will you do now?"

"About what?"

"The firecrackers that went off between you."

"I have that effect." He bit his lip. "Sadly, your protégé warned her off me."

"Admirably protective. That's Devin's role. What's yours, I wonder?" She slid her arm into his. "Take me home, Bo. It's long past my bedtime."

He walked her out and had the valet bring the car. When it came, he helped Eileen into the passenger seat of her 1933 Rolls Royce Phantom II Continental Barker Sedanca. Getting behind that wheel turned the blood in his veins to quicksilver, as if he melded with the black feline body, the chrome trim and grille. Sometimes he gave Eileen rides to remember. But fatigue cloaked her now, so he sailed her galleon over smooth seas and docked it in the garage someone had portioned out from the street level of her four-story Gramercy Park townhouse.

His money was on the rum runner. Lots of secrets could be transferred inside what might be the sole private-dwelling garage in this part of the city. The only person who knew the gate code besides the housekeeper, Eileen, and himself, was Devin Bressard. No—check that. Eileen's brother, Liam, had access.

Liam, who could have arranged Sergei Karkov's accident after Grace's nearly fatal encounter with one of the Russian mob leader's enforcers. Law enforcement didn't even blink at Liam after Karkov's body was recovered, but did that rule him out? Bo's chest tightened at what might have happened to Grace and to Mattie inside her. Karkov's gunman had been after him, sent to make a point. He'd found Grace, and the trauma brought her baby too soon. Another band squeezed his chest. Was atonement even possible? Devin didn't think so.

Bo went around the car for Eileen. Seventy-six was not old, but she looked her years tonight. Too much champagne maybe. He effected an upper-crust British accent. "Come along, Mum. I'll put you to bed."

"Would you be minding your manners now?" Eileen shot back. "I'll not have a bloody redcoat in my chamber."

Laughing at themselves, they went inside. He didn't go into her chamber, now or ever. Sondra managed the house and had the training for any medical or personal assistance Eileen might someday require. He climbed the stairs to the fourth floor, which the grande dame had converted to an apartment. Up until Grace had her baby, the woman lived alone. Then she'd found it convenient to repurpose parts of the townhouse to suit her schemes.

First a nursery for Grace and Mattie that encouraged a reconciliation with Devin. Now a reckoning with Liam O'Hare for Bo Corrigan. He meant what he told Grace. It was get his act together or wish like hell he had. At twenty-eight, he was seeing the light.

4

"Sleeping like an angel," Grace murmured when Devin joined her in Mattie's room after their long night out. "Do you think she is one?"

"Ask me in fourteen years."

"We'll be lucky to get that without a rebellious hiccup or two."

"Coming from you."

"She'll have a high opinion of herself, coming from you."

They slipped out, and Devin closed the door. "I hope she gets the best of both of us."

"We better save something for the next ones."

"Next ones?" He tipped her chin up.

"You don't want an only child, do you?"

He frowned. "What if they're not as great as she is?"

"Coming from you?"

"I'm serious. She's so …" He choked up, then cleared his throat.

Grace loved that sensitivity Mattie brought out in him. He might not be biologically connected to the man who found him on his doorstep, but he'd absorbed Eddie's heart.

Devin drew her in with an arm around her waist. "Did you enjoy yourself tonight?"

"So much. It's everything I envisioned the night I—"

"—threw tea in my face?"

"The night of the incident we're not talking about." She gripped the ends of his tie and let her hands hang from them. "I thank God for you, and that Mattie's doing so well."

"Is she?"

"For coming so early? She's amazing."

He frowned. "When I think of you and that gunman and Bo—"

"We're all here, safe and sound." She let go of the tie and spread her hands on his chest. "This is a good night. Don't let anything trouble you."

"Too late for that."

She searched his face.

"I caught Exi with Bo."

"Caught them? You mean talking?"

"Talking leads to trouble. Bo's her particular brand."

"Devin …"

"And Bo's trouble can get you killed."

She swallowed. Time hadn't tempered Devin's grievance with Bo. It might be getting worse. Her husband had been on another continent when the attack happened, but the knowledge of it ate him. He imagined and even dreamed of her huddled on her kitchen floor one gunshot away—

She wasn't over it either. "Bo didn't know they'd come after him that way."

"He was hiding out at your place."

"It's over." She brought her hand to his cheek. "He's doing the right things."

"Because he's in a cage. Might as well be house arrest. Liam O'Hare has eyes and ears in every club, gambling hall, and most of the private homes and businesses in the entire city."

"Exaggerate much?" Her hand slid to the crook of his shoulder.

"Bo's behaving because he has to. Let the jackal loose, and watch how long the fix sticks."

"I think he's showing restraint and responsibility."

"Restraint? Ha. Certainly not in the attention he gave Alexis."

"Is she Alexis when you're mad?"

"I'm not mad." He clasped her wrist. "But Bo shouldn't come on to a woman who's engaged to another."

"You don't even like Jeffrey."

"I think he's smooth, has an agenda, and probably wants to ride your coattails to a TV talk-show career. But Bo is Bo. And the more Eileen spoils him the more Bo he gets."

"There you go, being jealous of the little brother."

"Grace ..."

"You have a blind spot for Bo Corrigan. He's made strides you won't acknowledge."

He expelled a harsh breath.

Grace trailed her fingers along his jaw. "Exi's smart and discerning. Let her find her way."

He clearly didn't like it but tipped his head into her hand. "I'll try."

And he would. Whether he succeeded remained to be seen. Nothing stuck harder to her husband than his own opinion—especially about Bo.

Suz and Treya had crashed before Exi got home. She had no hope of sleeping when she kept picturing Bo raising that flute—what, one centimeter? *Here's to meeting you.* It was probably all he meant. Nice meeting you. Have a good life. But his eyes ...

She curled like a cat in her microsuede mamasan chair and replayed the night all the way through. The Broadway show, better than she could have guessed, the party amazing. Seeing Grace and Devin glitzed up and distinguished. Meeting Bo and feeling like all her senses were statically charged—even now just thinking it. She quivered.

Her conversation with the star had hardly blipped Jeffrey's radar. He was too excited about the contacts he made. *People in the limelight always need PR. This was a positive night, Alexis. A gesture of goodwill yielding fruitful possibilities.* When she raved about the play, he said, *As these things go, it was probably top-notch. I can see why people go for it.*

And you? she'd pressed.

I think real life has enough drama. It's complicated and fascinating. Why cloud things up?

It was a legitimate position. He got the appeal, just not for himself. That was so Jeffrey, to break it down, understand his own feelings and accept other people's. He didn't drink alcohol or caffeine but only judged people whose excess hurt others—like drunk drivers. Positive and commanding, without the macho connotation, he had nothing to prove. How many people could say that? She closed her eyes as contentment settled in. Maybe she would sleep right here.

She jolted awake, grabbed her phone so it wouldn't wake her roommates, then saw it was nine thirty a.m. "Hello?"

"Alexis." Jeffrey sounded weird. "Where are you?"

"I'm home, why?"

"Don't panic, but your mother's fallen down some stairs."

"What?" She shot up. "How come … wait a minute. How do you know?"

"Your father called."

"Is she okay?"

"I don't have specific details. I'm on my way to get you. And we'll get the answers there."

"My dad—Joe called you?"

"Alexis. I'm going to be there in twenty minutes. It sounds as if you just woke up. Why don't you use the time to get ready?" His reasonable tone cleared her head.

"Okay." She showered, dressed for work, then called her dad's cell phone. "Dad, what happened?"

"Didn't Jeffrey tell you?"

"He said Mom fell down some stairs."

"Subway stairs. She's at the hospital. I asked Jeffrey to get you."

"Why did you call him at work instead of telling me?"

"I thought you'd want him here. Honey, your mom's banged up pretty bad."

Her throat constricted. "How bad?"

"They have her in X-ray now."

Exi pressed a fist to her sternum. It wasn't that she wouldn't have called Jeffrey. She might, probably would have. But shouldn't that be her decision? She wouldn't have asked him to leave work. She could get herself to the hospital—unless her dad thought it so bad she would fall apart.

Okay, they might have thought that from experience. She'd only had five months to show them her wiser, more resilient self. Of course, Jeffrey had been part of those months. Now it seemed he had form-fitted to her family and become the go-to for an emergency like this. Something was seriously wrong with that.

Jeffrey texted that he was circling the block so she should come out. Rushing down her stairs, she pictured her mother falling, and, in spite of her new toughness, tears were streaming by the time she got into her boyfriend's hybrid.

"Your father said you'd be upset, Alexis, but let's wait until we have the facts."

His tone or the feeling of collusion set her off. "Wait to be upset? My mom is in X-ray after falling down steel-and-concrete stairs. I think worry is a normal reaction."

"Of course it is." He took her hand and drove with the other. "But X-rays are standard procedure. And they rule things out as often as not. Let's hope for the best."

Hope was good. She could do hope. She calmed, but it was a false reprieve. X-rays showed a linear skull fracture, broken collarbone, and shattered wrist. In the curtained cubicle, Exi wiped fresh tears. "I'm so sorry this happened, Mom. How can I help?"

"Flower shop," Rhonda said. "Need sh-omeone ..." It had to be good she was talking and recognizing them. So what if she sounded drunk.

"Don't worry about your store, Rhonda," her dad said. "It can close awhile."

"Water."

"You want water?" Joe looked around for a cup.

"No, Dad. She means someone has to water the plants, arrange the cut flowers, keep the displays in order. You can't just close her store with live plants and perishable inventory."

"Ex-shie."

"I'll do it, Mom. I can cover my shifts at MoMA for a few days. People always want more hours."

"They're talking surgery," Joe said. "It's gonna to be more than a few days."

Exi glanced at Jeffrey, standing with arms folded, while her family talked. Any minute now, he would ease into the conversation and direct them. Before he could, she said, "I'll quit and run Mom's store until she's up to par."

"Alexis." Jeffrey unfolded his arms. "You'll have to give notice. And what about your position working into something substantial?"

"That isn't as important as this. I know Mom's shop better than anyone besides her. I worked there all through high school." She stroked her mother's arm. "It's not as if she can train someone."

"Then cover some shifts, but let's talk before you do anything radical."

"Radical? My mom's flower shop is not a bomb factory, so I don't think I'll be on any watch lists if I make a decision for myself."

"What's this about bombs?" Her brother Sully came in wearing his police uniform, dark waves awry from the hat he removed, the only blue eyes in the family awash with worry.

Exi gritted her teeth. "Nothing about bombs. I offered to run Mom's shop until she can."

"Never sure with you, Mitten." He tugged her hair in passing, then bent and kissed his mother. "How you doing, Ma?"

Her eyes welled. "Mmm okay."

Jeffrey spoke calmly. "I know you want to help, Alexis, but major life decisions shouldn't be made under duress."

Her dad nodded. "He's right, honey. We don't want you losing your job."

"It's an entry-level position that pays no more than fast food."

She took her mother's hand. "Please let me do this. You can pay me less than you'd pay someone else."

"If that's your pitch, is it any wonder you haven't found a six-figure job?" By his grin, Jeffrey meant it as a joke.

But because something really had gotten into her, she said, "I'll do it for free, Dad."

"And how will you make rent?" Jeffrey asked, and Sully eyed her quizzically.

"I'll move home."

"And leave Suz and Treya in the lurch?"

"We'll pay you." Joe held up his hands. "If you insist on this."

"I do. Mom will be much more peaceful. Won't you, Mom?"

Jeffrey seemed to think aliens had replaced her brain with a weird, disruptive one.

"It's the best plan for the situation, Jeff—rey," she quickly added, but the damage was done. She had dissed him, and they both knew it. "Jeffrey, everything you've said is right. But families aren't corporations." She looked at her mom and dad and brother. "I have to bat for the home team."

"I only want you to make the best choice."

"And what do you think that is?" Better late than never.

"You could request a leave of absence. That way your job might be there when you want it back."

"Good idea," Joe said.

"It's a great idea," Exi agreed. But any applicant could step in and take her place. And someone would.

Grace paused, her fingers on the keys. When she was on a roll writing, she didn't usually answer calls but took this one. "Good morning, Eileen. How are you?"

"You must be writing well."

"I am, why?"

"It's two thirty in the afternoon."

"Oh." She looked out the windows and saw the afternoon slant of sunlight. "Well, Devin and Alison took Mattie to the botanic garden. I lose track when I'm all alone."

Eileen clicked her tongue. "What a shame his mother can't see the beauty."

The assault that blinded Alison was beyond tragic, but Grace said, "She can smell and feel and breathe it."

"Yes. They say other senses take over. But I'm so visual I'm not sure I could bear that."

Incomprehensible how Alison bore any of what happened to her. But Eileen didn't know those details. "She does the best she can." Having Devin's mother back in his life, as well as Eddie, was such a gift.

"So Devin's out and you're home writing," Eileen mused.

"He worked a good part of last night. He's funny that way."

"That's theater in his blood, the music of the night."

Grace smiled. Plenty of that around here.

"Why don't you and your family come for dinner Sunday. Oh, and bring Alexis. I had such a nice chat with her at the cast party. I think she liked our little play."

"We're still pulling her out of the clouds." Grace laughed. "Thanks for the invitation. I'll let Devin know and ask Exi. I imagine she could use a break." Since she had wanted to check in and see how Exi's mother was doing, Grace made the call right away.

Exi squealed when she heard Eileen's invitation. "Sorry! I'm working on holding those in."

"Don't do it for my sake. The world could use more glee."

"Okay." Exi laughed. "I would love to come, and Mom's one long-term employee works only Sunday so that's perfect."

"Good. Devin will pick you up."

"I can train to East Village."

"Okay. We'll go together from here to Eileen's. Now tell me how your mama's doing."

"Devin told you the fall caused a stroke?"

"Yes, I'm so sorry."

"They caught it right away and limited the damage. The doctor thinks she'll get her speech back, but she's so frustrated. I try to guess what she wants to say, but people keep telling me to make her do it."

Grace said, "You must be such a blessing."

"I wish I could do more."

"This is a lot to deal with. Fears for your mother, running the flower shop, and planning a wedding. A break might do you good."

"I'll look forward to it, that's for sure."

Alexis didn't ask to bring her fiancé, so she might need more breaks than one.

Devin came in and carried a tuckered tot to her crib. Grace waited for him in the library that held both their desks and a zillion books.

After his lingering kiss, she searched his face. "What's wrong?"

He blew out a breath. "There was a girl about Mattie's age at the reflecting pools."

Grace smiled. "Did they play?"

"Yeah. Sort of. Grace, the girl was talking. Words. Lots of words. And some together."

She swallowed a lump. "That varies so much. It doesn't mean a thing."

"Yeah, I know. I just thought, being yours, she'd have some purple prose by now."

Grace pulled his face down close. "Being yours, she's learning the dictionary first."

He gripped her elbows and raised her to her feet. "Come on. I'm feeling like a nap."

"I didn't write all night."

He nuzzled the indentation beneath her ear. That was the spot that resulted in Mattie. A sound came from her throat. So much for word count.

5

"Epic . . ." Exi stared at the elaborate four-story townhouse when Devin keyed the code to open the gate into Eileen's Gramercy Park driveway. Which unit is hers?"

"It's all hers," he said.

"The whole building?"

"Mmhmm."

Exi took in the surroundings as Grace got Mattie out of her car seat. Even the traffic flowed politely in this neighborhood. She walked with them to the cut-glass doors. When Devin rang, a woman who wasn't Eileen admitted them to a foyer that looked like a museum.

"Sondra, this is my cousin Alexis," Devin said.

"Welcome. And here is our little treasure." The woman reached out, and Mattie went from Grace's arms to hers.

"It's been a while since she saw you," Grace said. "You might not get loose all night."

"Am I complaining? Nope, nope." She tapped the toddler's nose. "Eileen's expecting you in the parlor. I'll bring Mattie when she wants me to."

"Huh," Devin said. "No stranger anxiety here."

"And why would she?" Sondra raised her chin. "I knew her before you did."

He cocked his jaw. "Thanks for the reminder," he said to her square shoulders as she made a meaningful retreat.

Devin strode in as if he belonged here, Exi thought, then realized he did. This was his life, Eileen his friend. And Grace's. Her own feet faltered. What was she doing here?

Grace touched her arm and whispered, "I know how you feel. But Eileen's the same woman you met at the party. She liked talking to you so much, she wanted you to come. That's all there is to it."

It seemed Grace was as good as Jeffrey at defusing her anxiety. Exi entered the parlor and clapped her hands together. "Oh, oh, oh. I had a dollhouse with a room like this. I feel like I shrank and climbed inside."

"You can't go back to yesterday, because you were a different person then."

She jerked her head toward the voice and saw Bo Corrigan standing at the window in faded jeans and a tailored white shirt, open at the collar to show his ropey neck. "What does that mean?"

"Wisdom from the Cheshire cat, or maybe its grin. From *Alice's Adventures in Wonderland*. You shrank, and now you're here."

"I don't—"

"'—want to go among mad people? You can't help that. We're all mad here.'"

Eileen pointed. "'How do you know she's mad?'"

"'She must be. Or she wouldn't have come here.'"

Exi laughed. "I love that story."

"That's it, Eileen," Bo said. "We're *Alice in Wonderland* tonight."

"Oh goodie. Who am I?"

"Queen of Hearts, of course."

"Off with her head."

"Not yet. It's such a nice head."

"That's not in the book," Devin said.

"It's all public domain. I can do what I want with it." He sent Devin a challenging stare.

Devin moved in and kissed Eileen on both cheeks. "You've had your fun, now—"

"Don't be a spoil sport or I'll make you the White Rabbit. You'll dash around all evening, crying, 'Oh dear, oh dear, I shall be late.'"

Devin formed a flat smile. "If we're all in, then I'm the Caterpillar."

"Perfect." Eileen patted his arm and turned. "Bo?"

He mussed his hair. "M. Hatter, of course."

"And Grace?"

Bo cocked his head. "Ah, Grace. We're down to grim choices, I'm afraid."

"I'll be her sister."

"Nice try, but she never enters Wonderland. You must be the Duchess with her squalling baby."

"Let's keep Mattie from the pepper, shall we?"

Exi groaned. "I don't know the book like the rest of you."

Bo waved a hand. "If you're ever in doubt, the Caterpillar on the mushroom will *feed* you a line. He's a director, you know."

"I don't think—"

"'Then you shouldn't talk.'"

She whooped. "I love that line. I think it when people are being really stupid."

Bo got the most incredible expression. She couldn't tell what changed, but it was electrifying.

He said, "What else do you remember?"

She crossed her arms. "I'm terrible at this, really."

He moved toward her. "'Just begin at the beginning and go on until the end.'"

She stared into his eyes. "King of Hearts?"

His smile caused a meltdown.

Devin gripped her elbow and turned her away. "Just say 'curiouser and curiouser.' When's dinner, Your Majesty?"

Eileen said, "Shouldn't we have cocktails?"

"Alice is only seven."

"Oh no, I'm grown-up Alice."

Bo crooned, "Grown-up Alice likes martinis?"

"Uh oh." She bit her lip.

He cocked his head. “What?”

“Appletinis … or … chocolate?”

The corners of Bo’s mouth quirked up. “I know for a fact the Dodo has Godiva liqueur in the kitchen.”

“You won’t get Sondra to stutter,” Devin said.

“Watch me.” Bo went out and came back with the gray-blonde woman and a bottle of chocolate liqueur.

Sondra said, straight-faced, “D-d-do you want this, Alice?”

Devin cast his face to the ceiling. Exi gave her head a vigorous nod.

Grace said, “Where’s my squalling baby?”

The Dodo answered, “In her booster chair, finger-painting p-p-pudding.” Sondra left with a backward glance at Devin.

Taking the chocolate martini Bo mixed at the marble minibar, Exi could not remember when she’d enjoyed herself so much. Oh, yes she could. Watching Bo in *Windows and Doors* and falling, falling into this wonderland.

Bo considered Grace a benevolent angel. She saw through his every facade—a feat, because he only had to imagine something to become it. Across Eileen’s table, she was watchful. Not for his sake, but for the spot of sunshine on the other side of Devin.

She can’t handle you, Grace had told him, but she was wrong. The person in jeopardy was inside himself. Unlike Grace, who was immune on every level but friendship, Exi pulsated with him.

His theatrics entertained her, but she stayed real. He’d never seen a real girl before. Even Grace had her theatrical side. But this one seemed freshly formed from the Creator’s clay. Like Adam, Bo wanted to discover her, name her, have her. Shockingly that last was least.

She was not for taking. She would be won or never known. He became Romeo at Juliet’s balcony: *But soft, what light through yonder window breaks?* The thing that fascinated him in Grace was just as strong in Exi. In a word … purity. It confounded him. How could purity be claimed—and preserved? His gaze dragged to Devin, talking to Eileen. He, of all people, had found a way. Yet now he was the gatekeeper.

Bo startled when Grace said Jeffrey. His eyes moved to Exi, who looked surprised as well.

"I'm sorry, what?"

"I asked how Jeffrey's doing with you working at your mom's store. You said he wasn't for it."

"He wasn't sure I should. It's a lot more hours than I had at the museum, plus I help Dad out in the evenings. But Jeffrey understands it now."

Bo lifted his martini glass. Over the rim, his gaze touched Exi's. *Her eye discourses, I will answer it.* Opposition rose from Devin, caution from Grace. Amusement in Eileen as her scheme played out. She had dropped them like players into this scene where no one had read the script.

He said, "How did your mom fall?" Now they had a reason to engage—that didn't include Jeffrey.

"One of those wacky accidents probably, but she can't tell us. She was talking at first, just kind of slurred, then a bleed from the skull fracture caused a stroke. Now she can't speak." Her eyes teared up.

Devin put an arm around her shoulders. Bo imagined him Juliet's murderous relation, Tybalt.

Exi said, "They postponed her wrist surgery until the head wound stabilizes, and now there's stroke rehab. I don't see her being able to manage things for a long time." She turned to Grace. "Do you think we should consider a different wedding date?"

Yes, Bo said, but only in his head.

Grace told her, "You haven't sent out save-the-dates, so you surely could. What does Jeffrey think?"

"He said if we do, it would give you more time to write the novel."

"I'm confused why he still thinks that's happening."

Bo said, "Novel?"

Exi explained.

He slid a look at Grace and held in a belly laugh.

Exi said, "I told him we haven't had enough turmoil for a Grace Evangeline novel, but he isn't sure why mayhem makes for a good story."

"Yes, well everyone has their opinions on that." Grace gave Devin a pointed look. "But the fact remains that without conflict there's not much story."

Devin slow blinked. "Internal conflict is just as compelling."

In his current condition, Bo had to side with Tybalt.

"We don't have that either," Exi said. "I think we're too perfect for each other."

Grace gave him a direct eye message, but Bo still said, "What fun is that?"

Amazingly, Devin didn't disagree. Exi looked at her cousin.

He shrugged. "I haven't experienced perfection."

"But you and Grace are."

"Crazy in love? Sure. Perfect? Not a chance."

"Devin drives the curve up. I'm just normal."

"Normal you're not."

Exi squeaked, literally squeaked, and the sound hit his ear like fairy dust.

"That's just like the repartee in your books." Her eyes shone like something from another world.

Grace shrugged a shoulder. "I inspire him."

Bo looked to his own inspiration. *O, speak again, bright angel.*

Bouncing Mattie in her lap, Eileen said, "What do you think, Bo?"

"I find perfection insipid."

"And what do you recommend?"

"Dump him."

Exi's mouth fell open. "Dump Jeffrey? My family would rather have him than me."

Then they were lunatics. "'Deny thy father and refuse thy name. Or be but sworn my love—'"

"Hold it. Stop." Devin glared. "Quit filling her head with nonsense."

"It's no more than the rest of you are saying."

"We're talking about rescheduling," Grace said, "not cancelling the wedding."

"Keep the wedding and lose the groom."

At Eileen's raucous laughter, Mattie put fingers in the grande dame's mouth—something he never thought he'd see.

A storm touched Exi's brow. "Jeffrey's … great."

"Of course he is." Grace reached past Devin and patted her hand.

Devin stayed mute, but his expression begged to differ. An ally? Never. Disliking Jeffrey would not mean support. Tybalt he remained.

Exi intended to take the subway back to Brooklyn, but Devin dropped off his wife and daughter and rejoined the glaring scarlet taillights and eye-squinting headlights. The harshness was exacerbated by Godiva-tinis, she guessed, though she hadn't stammered once. Don't let it be said Alice can't handle her licker. She giggled at her own silent pun.

"Were you going to your place or Joe's?"

"Mine. I've hardly been there. Dad, the master plumber, can handle everyone's emergencies but his own. I introduced him to a pot the other night and explained it was good for more than catching drips."

Devin grinned. "Can your brothers help?"

"Sully's the only one who hasn't married and moved away, and he thinks pizza and pistachio ice cream cover the five food groups."

"Same old Sully."

She adjusted her seatback to a better angle. “Eddie’s been great.”

“He has?”

“He and Dad hang out watching sports and being regular guys, you know? Your dad makes people feel good by just being there.”

“Eddie Bressard, the should-have-been priest.”

“For real?”

“That was the plan until I showed up.”

“Why don’t I know this?”

Her cousin shrugged. “It was between us.”

“Is that why he’s not with your mom?”

“That’s complicated.”

She blew through her lips. “I know complicated.”

Devin changed lanes and sped up. “Things are difficult right now, Exi. I hope you can hold tight and not let all of this derail you.”

“Derail me how?”

“You had a direction. Now it seems you’re wavering.”

“You mean Jeffrey?”

“Primarily. I’m afraid tonight might have messed with your head.”

She drew one knee up on the seat. “Why don’t you like Bo?”

“Who says I don’t? He was in our wedding.”

“He must have messed up, then. You couldn’t be more abrasive.”

“Oh, yes I could. Ask Grace.”

Picturing the tea-swabbing gif, she couldn’t argue that. But the tension across the table at Eileen’s had been palpable. “Well, anyway, Grace likes him.”

Devin’s jaw rippled. “You have a man who’s respecting you and your values. Bo *non est hominis.*”

“Okay. Wow. Must be serious if you’re resorting to Latin. Why is Bo not that man?”

“He thinks he gets whatever he wants by being Bo Corrigan. If I’d known he would be there tonight, I’d have …”

“What? Refused to bring me?”

“It was disingenuous of Eileen not to mention it to Grace.”

"I had loads of fun."

"It's always entertaining. But Bo is one pitfall you don't need."

She huffed. "Has it occurred to you—or anyone—that I'm actually an adult?"

"I know you are, Alexis." He looked at her.

"Then what? I'm stupid? Naïve?"

"No. Well … maybe where Bo's concerned."

She pulled her knee in tight. "I finally got out from under my brothers. I don't need another."

"Okay."

"Okay?"

"I'll get off your case." He signaled and juked another lane change.

"Just like that?"

His head lolled to one side. "Exi …"

"Okay. Good. It's just Jeffrey usually has twenty-four points to make before he concedes. Every one earnestly intended to help me see another side of things."

"I don't doubt it."

She chewed her lip. "But you and Bo think—"

"Don't put me and Bo and *think* in the same sentence." He cast her a quick glance. "You decide if Jeffrey's your future. No one else matters."

"Would you say that if we were discussing Bo Corrigan?"

Again that ripple in his jaw. "Yes. Your decision, regardless."

She lowered her knee and raised the volume when "Jar of Hearts" came on Pandora. "I love this song. It's so great the way she sees through the lies and it's 'No way are you getting me back, Jack.' That takes more guts than you think." By Devin's expression, she might be slurring just a little.

"I guess it does. Too bad she fell for the loser at all."

Exi shrugged. "Better late than never on the getting-it bus."

"Yes, it is." His sincere tone suggested she'd struck a chord with that one.

When Devin stopped in front of her building, she said, "I liked it tonight, being in a book. Acting parts."

"Watch out for theater people. We're all mad."

She laughed, but it was Bo's voice she heard as she climbed out. He might be mad, but at least he wasn't perfect. She reached the door and waved, then hurried into her place.

"So, dish." Treya dragged her inside as Suz shut the door. "You snuck in and out after your cousin's play and cast party and hardly been seen since. Now we're all together, and you're going to tell us about Mr. Sexy Pants."

Exi choked a laugh. "Please don't resurrect that."

"Why not?"

"Umm … we're eight years past high school? I'm having a hard enough time getting my family to realize I'm not the baby any more."

"That's what you get for being born after all those brothers."

"Don't talk about brothers," Suz snipped. "You're probably in love with them too."

"Now that would be gross," Treya said.

"What? My brothers are great."

"But they're brothers. And I know them like brothers."

"Okay, you have a point." Exi slipped her purse from her shoulder and moved into their cozy nest. So the walls were stained and the ceiling cracked. So the radiator clanked and there was always a faint scent of cooking gas. Being here with her friends made it home.

"It's Bo we want to hear about," Suz said. "Bo Corrigan."

Exi's heart fluttered like a bird but she pushed it back down. "He's funny."

"Funny?" Treya looked exasperated.

Exi described the *Alice in Wonderland* improvisation. "Devin said the housekeeper wouldn't stutter like the Dodo in the story, remember? But when Bo came back with her, she completely played the part."

"You're surprised?" Suz thrust her hands out. "Have you seen the guy?"

"I'm trying really, really hard not to look at him that way since I'm *engaged* to Jeffrey."

Treya sucked her lips between her teeth as if she was trying really, really hard not to say something to that.

"Come on, guys. I've made some dumb mistakes, but the only heart broken was mine. I wouldn't hurt Jeffrey that way."

"Okay." Treya flopped down on the tattered couch. "But remember, he broke up with Kendyl to be with you. So he knows how it is."

True. Exi's mind slid back to Eileen's amazing home, to the five of them around the table, to Bo's eyes on her. Then it went to Devin's warning. No mystery where that came from. Given her past mistakes, he had reason to worry, except for one thing. "You know he's famous, right? Giorgio spokesmodel, Broadway star?"

"Yeah, so's your cousin, so what?" Treya pulled off her socks and winged them to the stacked washer-dryer unit at the end of the kitchen. They struck the dryer door and slid to the floor.

"So I can't even get a good-paying job." As Jeffrey had not failed to remind her. "I'm a girl from Flatbush who lucked into a guy who makes everyone happy. The last thing I should think about is trouble on two legs like Bo Corrigan."

"Two fine legs." Suz sighed. With her million freckles and auburn hair, Suz looked more Irish than Exi, whose slightly olive skin came from her Bolivian great-grandmother. And Suz had the Celtic angst down pat, though as far as anyone knew it wasn't in her genealogy.

Exi had to ask, "Are you still pretending he's Peter and imagining you're Angel?"

"No, that stopped when you met him. Now he's real."

He was real. Acting formed a second skin but the man inside was real. Devin's words were like an angel on her shoulder. *Don't play with that fire, Exi.* While in the other ear, came, *Be but sworn my love …*

6

Grace was waiting up when Devin got back. He would need to decompress after Bo. Did Eileen realize the conflict she stoked between those guys? Certainly. Her steel on steel applied to lives as well as art, but Devin's jaw would ache tonight if he didn't release the tension she saw there.

He set his keys in the art-glass bowl and raised his eyes. "Mattie sleeping?"

"Soundly."

He started for the master bedroom.

"Would you like a glass of wine?"

He paused. "Not really. Had my fill with dinner. Had my fill of lots of things."

"Meaning Bo?"

"What's he playing at? Exi's nothing to him. Why's he messing with her head?"

"Why do you think she's nothing?"

"To *him.* He runs through women like booze, intoxicated then thirsting for the next drink."

Grace couldn't deny it, but, "Isn't that for them to decide?"

Devin folded his arms. "For the first time in her life, she's thinking smart, setting limits. Bo thinks limits exist to be pushed."

"He pushes limits because he's afraid he's a fraud."

"He is a fraud."

"You're wrong." Grace moved to him. "Eileen sees it, why can't you?"

"Sees what?"

"He's consumed by his art. Not the ads and commercials, but acting, Devin. In the same way you are driven to excellence, so is Bo. It's never good enough. Today's success is something to lose if the next performance isn't better."

Devin frowned but didn't argue.

"How many times has he played Peter? One year on Broadway and eight months getting there. He said every time he does there's something, some nuance that makes it fresh. Don't stand there and tell me you don't recognize that."

"I've never had anything but praise for his work."

"I'm talking about him, the man inside the actor, the drive that makes his acting more than anyone else playing the part. His gift brings tears to my eyes. But it doesn't just happen. He suffers. He taunts himself with failure."

Devin held her stare, absorbing the words. The tendons in his throat worked. "It doesn't make him a better person."

She expelled her breath. "And what, in your mind, would?"

"I didn't mean it that way."

"Yes, you did. You sit in judgment of him the way my folks do of us. If I were a better person I wouldn't have been an unwed mother. We all make mistakes."

"Bo is a walking mistake. He has more talent than any actor I know. But his life's a mess, and I don't want it hurting Exi the way it hurt you and Mattie. My little girl doesn't talk. She might be on a normal course if that goon hadn't tripped your labor before she was ready. Don't tell me that isn't true."

"I don't know when she'd have done anything if she came full-term. But I know Bo hurts over what happened. He'd do anything to change it."

"That's what you have to say?" Devin's teeth aligned. "It isn't enough to be sorry after the damage is done. I want him stopped before he wrecks Exi too."

"You think I'm wrecked? Mattie?"

"I know you have nightmares. I have nightmares."

"It was awful. But Bo didn't plan it. Bo didn't shoot at me. He was trying to get things together. He still is."

"He can do it without Exi."

She raised her chin. "That's not your decision."

He stared long and hard, then strode to the library and closed the door. Maybe he'd work on his novel or the new play he'd started storyboarding. Maybe he'd sleep on the couch. She hadn't intended to fight, but he needed to hear what she'd said.

She crossed her arms defiantly. "Lord, that man has a heart of stone for Bo. Could you soften it up before things get really ugly? Because I'm afraid where it might go, and I clearly don't have the words."

The day after her devious dinner party, Bo strolled with Eileen in the private and coveted Gramercy Park. He'd told her his plan and excused it with, "Our understudy knows the part."

Her hand tightened on his arm. "Entitled brat. We've done well to keep him out of the limelight this far."

Bo gave her a wry smile. "Understudies exist for this."

"Not for treason."

"Treason to guest star in a musical for two weeks?"

"You've already played Monty Navarro, murdering the gentry. Why do it again?"

"I know the part and play it better than either of their understudies."

"Don't bore me with the obvious."

"*Windows and Doors* can spare me for two weeks. I'm owed more than that contractually."

"Don't annoy me with facts."

He laughed. "You're in a mood. But I'm doing it anyway. My good friend wants a vacation. I feel like a change. I can take his place for two weeks of singing and dancing and disposing of my aristocratic relatives."

She raised her face to enjoy the splendor of sunshine after rain. "Are you inviting someone to watch?"

No surprise she guessed that, cunning old gal. "I might, but that's not all of it." He moved her around a spilled soda foaming on the walk with a wasp greedily taking its pleasure. "I think Exi would enjoy it."

"Yes. She and Jeffrey can have a date night."

"Witch."

Eileen snickered. "All right. Make your play. You already ruffled feathers."

"Some feathers need ruffling. Even favored sons."

"Green isn't your color. And I'm not limited to one pet." She leaned in. "I'm a connoisseur of talents."

"Flattery will get you dinner."

"I have a date already. We should circle back so I can dress for it."

"Am I to know my usurper?"

"You are not."

Fine. Let Eileen keep her secrets. It was Exi's secrets he wished to probe. The mystery of Jeffrey. Exi was far too bright to buy his plastic act. There must be something else.

"Yes," Eileen murmured beside him. "She is a puzzle."

"You are a witch pulling thoughts out of my head."

"No, Bo. It's all writ large on your face. Your exquisitely expressive face."

"Can you explain Jeffrey?"

"Yes. He's the right kind of man. If I'm guessing, I'd say Exi has a history of the wrong kinds."

The thought speared.

"She's working very hard to believe she wants that to change."

He swallowed. "Maybe it should."

"Then why play Monty Navarro?"

He grinned. "Why not?"

"There's my incorrigible rake."

"Now, Eileen, you know I only ravish maidens and eat children."

Her laugh rang out as he unlocked the gate and locked it behind them. His neck prickled, and he looked down the sidewalk one way, then the other. In the normal stream of pedestrians, one bony-faced man with odd tattoos eyed them, then moved on.

Bo frowned. "You know him?"

"No," Eileen said.

"Not one of Liam's guys?"

"No. Why?"

"Weird vibe."

She raised her eyes to him. "You want protection?"

"What?" He cocked his head. "Why would you jump to that?"

"Never hurts to be careful."

"Careful isn't crazy."

"Hmm." Eileen's hand shook when she tucked it once more into the crook of his elbow. That shifted his attention back to her. He considered asking what was up with the tremors but refrained. She'd say something when she wanted to.

After seeing Eileen inside her door, Bo took out his phone and told his agent he would accept the guest role he'd secretly engineered with his friend. He did feel like a change, nothing long-term, just a chance to get Peter out of his head for a little while. He didn't want to think about Devin and Exi at the same time.

Exi crawled out from behind the plant stand that held Madagascar jasmine along with ferns that required misting. The hose had kinked right where she had to crawl on the floor to unbend it. She pushed up to her feet and fished the nozzle out from between the shelves. Now when she squeezed, it sent out a fine mist. "There you go, plants. Happy refreshment."

"Ah, Juliet, if the measure of their joy be heaped like mine—"

She spun, almost spraying Bo Corrigan before she released the lever. "What are you"—her heart thumped with more than surprise—"how did you find me here?"

"Grace told me."

"She did?" Exi hung the hose and wiped her soiled hands down her apron. "Does Devin know?"

"I'm going with … no."

Exi grinned.

"Nice shop."

"It's my mom's. She's had Every Bloomin' Thing forever. So many loyal customers keep it going she says she can't ever retire."

"Is she any better?"

Exi sighed. "Not that I can tell. I wish I had a key, like Alice, to just unlock the door. If you knew how many words are getting all clogged up …" Her eyes welled.

"It's hell, to want to change things that can't be changed—not by you anyway."

His voice had lowered as if it came from deep inside. She blinked tears that clung to her lashes. "You understand."

He studied her for three long beats, then said, "I lost my sister."

A ball of sorrow formed in her chest. "Oh, Bo. I'm so sorry. Was it an accident?"

He picked up a stack of gift cards and fanned them. "Bone cancer."

She pressed a hand to the ache. How would she feel losing a brother? "I can't imagine how hard that must be. Were you close?"

"She was the most consistent person in my life." He replaced the cards. "At twenty-eight she got the diagnosis. Three days after her twenty-ninth birthday she died." He swallowed. "Here I am, twenty-eight, and none of the bad things I do to myself seem to have any effect."

"You can't think that way. It's okay to be healthy, talented, and—yeah—freakin' beautiful."

That got his attention. "Bonny to beautiful. Should I be worried?"

"Bonny?"

"Eileen was feeling Irish."

"Is she your aunt or something?"

"I wish. I might stand a better chance against Devin in this showdown."

"Showdown?"

"Do you think he'll let me see you without a fight?"

She blinked. "Do you want to?"

The smile he formed sank right into her. "I'm standing here in your flower shop, Exi."

"Because you need flowers?" She cocked her head.

His eyes got smoky. "What do you like?"

"I can't think of any I don't."

"I'll buy them all for you."

"Psh. Do you know how long it would take to restock inventory and how unhappy everyone coming in to an empty store would be? Plus where would I put them? I live in a hamster cage. And my roommate, Suz, has allergies. She'd sneeze herself into next week." Exi pinched a brown petal off a hydrangea.

"How about dinner instead?"

She gulped. "I can't do that. You know I'm engaged."

"What if you shouldn't be?"

Her pulse quickened. "I'd have to decide that without … provocation."

"Am I provoking you?"

"It might provoke Jeffrey."

"Might?"

"Well, I don't think he gets provoked. But he would tell me all the reasons it's foolish to spend time with you when nothing can come of it."

"That's the flaw in his logic."

"Bo."

"Starting Monday, I'll be performing *A Gentleman's Guide to*

Love and Murder."

"A different play?"

"A musical. Wickedly clever with some very fun tunes. Grace saw it last year when I guest performed Monty Navarro—the role I'm playing again. That's why she told me where to find you. She thinks you'll enjoy it."

"I'm sure I'd love it." She squeezed her hands closed at her sides, wanting to say yes, needing to say no.

"Tell me which night, and I'll have two tickets for you. You can bring Jeffrey or anyone you like."

"You'd give Jeffrey a ticket?"

"This show's a little madcap. He might like it even more than the play."

Words caught in her throat. She hated telling him Jeffrey hadn't cared one way or the other for the play. She suspected he would find a musical ridiculous. Yet it seemed dishonest to leave Bo with the wrong impression. "My friend Suz—with the allergies—loves you in *Windows and Doors*. She would come in a heartbeat. And my other roommate, Treya. She's sort of crushing on Devin but thinks you're really hot." What was she saying!

He picked up a gift tag, turned it over and wrote a number. "You can reach me directly with this. Let me know if you need two tickets or three."

She took the card from him. "Just to see the show?"

"If that's what you want."

A sigh got out before she caught it.

He pulled a slow smile. "We can leave it open-ended."

"No. I mean … maybe …" She pressed the card with his number over her mouth to stop its motion.

"If that becomes yes, we'll go clubbing after. You and your friends or fiancé. He might make some contacts at my clubs."

A sound of pure embarrassment came from her throat.

Bo took the hand holding his card and brought the fingers to his lips. Not a kiss. Just contact. "Until then."

She was shaking when he left. Okay. Whoa. She hadn't done anything wrong. And she didn't plan to. She called Jeffrey and got his voice mail. "It's me, um, Alexis … obviously. So, Bo Corrigan is playing in that musical *A Gentleman's Guide to Love and Murder.* He has two tickets for us if you'd like to go. It's only for the next two weeks, so if you want to, let me know which night."

She hung up and called Grace. "I'm so sorry to bother—"

"I had a feeling I'd hear from you." A smile came through in her voice.

"Bo wants Jeffrey and me to see his show."

"You and Jeffrey?"

"Well, two tickets. Or three. Jeffrey or my friends."

"It's a very fun show. Jeffrey's so knowledgeable I bet he knows all about it."

Exi ground her palm into her eye. "The thing is, he's not really into theater. He thinks real life is interesting enough without make-believe."

After a moment Grace said, "Isn't he the one who wants a novel?"

"Oh. Yes. But I think he's seeing that as real life … since it's us."

"He should get a biographer then. That's the right form for it."

"I know. But he really wants you. You or nothing."

"Hmm. Well, I hope you'll both enjoy the show. Bo hits all the right comedic notes. He sings wonderfully—and looks great in costume."

Exi groaned.

"What?"

"Would it be really bad if I take my friends? Suz loves him in *Windows and Doors.* And Treya's up for anything."

"Why would that be bad?"

"That I'd rather see it with people who love Broadway and … all."

"All being Bo?"

She stretched her fingers over her other eye. "He included clubbing after."

"Jeffrey doesn't club?"

"It's not his thing."

"Exi, what does Jeffrey do?"

"He likes eating out and watching basketball. He especially likes reality TV and talk shows. That's how he knows about you."

"Not from my books."

Exi waved to a customer coming into the store, a browser apparently, so she didn't end the call. "I don't think he's read any, but you talk about them. On my résumé I had Devin down as a personal reference. Jeffrey asked if my cousin was your husband. He saw both of you during the, you know, scandal."

"I see."

"On our first date, he said he was interested in courtship, like your books. I told him your stories had changed my life. It was one of those points of connection where I thought, wow, how cool is that? And when he proposed—"

"He said, 'Let's have a Grace Evangeline wedding.'"

"He did! And then he said, 'We could have her write a novel about us, and put our wedding in.' It was so … earnest. He means it, Grace. He hasn't pushed one boundary. He *set* the boundaries."

"That's very honorable."

She swallowed. "So how wrong would it be to go clubbing with Bo, when—" She choked back what almost came out.

"When what, Exi?"

The customer drifted back out the door. She might have made a sale if she had engaged, but the turmoil inside needed resolution. "When he's Bo."

"Are you attracted to him?"

"Is there a woman alive who's not?"

"According to Bo, I'm it."

"Really?"

"Yes, but I was into Devin. Are you into Jeffrey?"

She pressed a hand to her heart. "Jeffrey's great. Everyone thinks so."

"Exi, I'm going out on a limb here to ask why you think that."

"That people like Jeffrey?"

"Yes."

"Well ..." She frowned. "They say so. My family and friends, you guys ..."

"Would it surprise you to know Devin's not sure?"

"About Jeffrey? It's Bo he doesn't like." She flipped the closed sign and locked the door.

"He likes Bo. There's just an issue he needs to work through."

"Why doesn't he like Jeffrey?"

"I think his jury's out."

"Oh." She breathed. "Jeffrey will convince him."

"But that's not what I asked you."

Exi swallowed. "I'm really happy to have him. I think passion will come when the courtship ends."

"It might. But the point is to fall in love all the other ways first. If you're doing that, then watching Bo perform, and even clubbing with him, won't change how you feel about Jeffrey."

"Even if I attend with Suz and Treya?" Exi grabbed a cloth and gave the counter a furious wipe down.

"Once you're married, it's best to avoid any tempting situation. Before that, as long as you exercise good judgment, it might be instructive. Especially since you jumped so quickly into this engagement."

"Jeffrey couldn't wait to ask. I was so surprised. It was sweet and romantic, just like *The Bachelor*."

"Does Jeffrey watch that?"

Exi pulled the money drawer from the register and moved into the office. "He says it's a good people study. Like you, he's always looking for the meaning, the motivation. It helps in his business."

"I guess it could."

"He'd be surprised Devin has doubts." Exi tried not to ask, but couldn't help it. "Do you?"

"I think you have an awful lot to deal with. It doesn't hurt to take a step back and breathe. Any season can create a beautiful wedding. And you really, really want to be sure."

Ending the call, she wondered how much more of a sure thing Jeffrey could be. Sincere, thoughtful, committed. He took her seriously and listened, even if he also had other thoughts on a matter. He was successful and knowledgeable, made good decisions and treated her with respect—maybe a little condescension at times, but she'd shown less than her best side lately.

As she boarded the subway, Jeffrey returned her call. He said, "I'll go if you want to."

"Do you want to?"

"I've been honest on the subject. But if it makes you happy—"

"I could go with Suz and Treya, if you'd rather." She gripped a pole in the semicrowded car and waited for his answer.

"We haven't had much time together. But it isn't really meaningful, watching a performance. It's more about the people on the stage than each other. So why don't you and your friends go."

"You don't mind?"

"Why would I mind you doing something you enjoy?"

"You wouldn't. You're not that way." He cared about her happiness—unlike losers she'd fallen for before. Those men didn't know the first thing about respect or generosity.

She did wish Jeffrey hadn't said this was about the performers. She wished it wasn't about Bo. She closed her eyes and pictured him in the flower store. *What do you like?* That was a loaded question if she ever heard one.

The night at Eileen's he had gone in and out of theatrical roles, but at the store all that fell away. He shared something painful to meet her in the helplessness. No one else had done that. Her friends were sympathetic, but he'd given her empathy. He hadn't acted like his pain was worse—though it was. Little clues told her even more, like "the most consistent person in my life" and "all the bad things I do to myself." He wasn't over it. He was approaching the age his sister died and might not know how to live past it. That was huge and scary, and she had no idea how to help.

But she wanted to.

Okay, she said it. She wanted to know Bo Corrigan. Zero chance that meant the same thing to him. But it didn't stop her. And she didn't know what to do about that—or Jeffrey.

Grace was right. No matter how cool a wedding plan they came up with, it was a lifetime commitment. She didn't want her story to be Grace's first tragic ending.

7

Bo's mouth twitched when he saw the caller on his Apple Watch. He needed to limber up for the musical performances but raised his torso from his outstretched legs on the workout floor and answered with a touch. "Hi, Exi."

"Oh. Yeah, it's … I guess you know it's me."

"Cute Facebook pic."

"On the balance beam?"

"Striking quite a pose."

She made a noise. "It's Throwback Thursday. I got bronze in my age bracket. But I didn't think about the picture coming up on everyone's phones and stuff."

"Only people you're connected to." He drew up a knee, rested his forearm, and studied her.

"Are we connected?"

"Must be. You're on my Apple Watch right over my pulse. Should I check my heart rate?"

"Um …"

"Add me to your contacts and I'll come up on your phone."

"That might not be the best plan. With Jeffrey, I mean."

"Add me and delete him."

"Bo, I …"

"Don't fret, Juliet. No pox on your house today. Are you coming to my show?"

"Three tickets Friday night?"

"Does that three mean roommates, or has Jeffrey grown two

heads?"

"Stop it!"

He laughed. "Tickets and clubbing?"

Her voice got small. "Yes?"

"No question."

"Okay. Yes. We'll see you Friday for it all. I better get off now."

"Parting is such sweet sorrow." He twisted to stretch the other side of his back.

"I better find some CliffsNotes."

"Let's go out. I'll recite Shakespeare and explain it."

"We can't go out." Her strongest voice yet.

He rose from his stretch. "Are you playing the friend card? Because Grace holds the only one."

"We can't be friends?"

"Want me to lie?"

"I guess not."

"Then no. Jeffrey's courting you. I want to do the same."

A pause. "I'm confused."

"Two suitors." He put his legs together and leaned forward.

"Did you say suitor?"

"What's Jeffrey?"

"My fiancé. We're engaged."

Still baffling, even with Eileen's explanation. "I accept the challenge."

"I'm planning our wedding."

"Grace is planning it. You're choosing a groom."

"Like *The Bachelorette?*"

Bo hissed.

"What?"

"Fie on that abomination."

Exi laughed and kept laughing. "You're on opposite sides of that island."

He pressed a hand to his eyes. "Tell me you don't watch that one too."

"Jeffrey uses the shows as research for PR."

"How likely are you to desist once he's out?"

"That's cocky."

"Never again?"

"Never watch TV?"

"Only skip the brain-sucking shows that ape entertainment."

"I don't speak your language."

"Programs where fake people pretend to be real."

"Not everyone is you."

"If you can't think, don't act."

Another bout of laughter. Her unrestrained hilarity kicked his pulse rate higher. She would enjoy the musical. And he would drink her enjoyment to the dregs. "Exi …"

"I have to go. But thank you for the tickets and all. Oh—how do I get them?"

"I'll bring them to you." She might have argued, but he ended the call. He couldn't remember the last time he needed excuses to see someone. Well … since Grace. And they'd ended up friends. Not happening with Exi.

He wasted no time getting there. As he walked into her store this time, he held the trio of tickets like a bouquet. Her face lit when she saw him. Always a good sign. As they converged, he breathed her in. She smelled like her merchandise, blossoms and earth. And that's how she was, he thought. Not just the pretty surface, but the nourishment, the grounding.

She thanked him for the tickets. "I'm still pinching myself. I already got to see you onstage. I hadn't watched a single production before that. And here I am again. And it's from—you know—you. I'm blabbering."

The corners of his mouth twitched.

"Jeffrey says—"

"Uh-uh. That name's verboten."

"It is?"

"I get to form my own impressions. Untainted by the *other.*"

"Jeffrey's the other?"

"Tssss."

"Sorry. But I've seen myself through his eyes for six months and …"

"Forget that."

"Forget?"

"How do you see yourself?"

"That's the problem. It's like my art. Unfocused. Scattered. My family says I'm this, my friends say I'm that, and don't get me started on what guys think."

He ran his eyes over her. "Why does any of that matter?"

"Because … well … how can it not?"

"Who looks at you from the mirror?"

"On a good hair day?"

He laughed with her, then grew thoughtful. "What do you see inside?"

"Just kind of a mess."

"How is that possible?"

She blinked at him. "I don't get the question."

"You have this brilliance. Brilliance and solidity at once. How can you not see that?"

"You're imagining things."

He shook his head. "I'm an expert. I know what I see."

"Is that a good thing? Your expertise? Cuz I've sworn off that kind."

"Can't undo the past. There's only forward."

"Yes, but people don't change. I've learned that in spades."

"Forget what you've learned. Let's start fresh."

"Like I was born yesterday? No way. I learn from my mistakes."

"Let me prove myself without anyone else's baggage." He held out the tickets.

Biting her lip, she took them with tentative fingers.

Why did so little call for a victory march? Might it be, at long last, he would learn humility?

Sitting with Suz and Treya in a different theater, Exi felt her life expand. Bo brought something raw to *Windows and Doors*, but in this musical he was hilarious and so talented she could hardly take it. Jeffrey might find it pointless, but her friends were equally mesmerized.

At intermission Treya said, "I didn't think anyone could be as flexible as you."

"Bo's more agile than flexible."

"You're both bendy."

"I guess." Exi tucked the hair behind her ear. "He laughed at my balance beam picture."

"Your Throwback Thursday?" said Suz.

"He called it cute, but I could hear laughter in his voice."

"That's not the same thing." Treya jabbed her. "That means he thinks you're cute and funny."

"I think he's cute," Suz said.

"And funny," Treya added.

In this show he was both. The wounded man from her mom's flower shop had disappeared. Same with the contemplative one who delivered the tickets. This Bo radiated charm and, frankly, sizzled.

"Sexy Pants," Suz breathed.

"Stop it." Exi pushed her. The lights flashed for people to take their seats, but since she and her friends hadn't left theirs, Exi just settled into the velvety cushion for more entertainment. She hadn't expected the love story between Bo's character, Monty Navarro, and his longtime flame, Sibella, to be so sensuous. How would it be if Jeffrey was here? Awkward.

Grace said this could be instructional, but as Exi sank into the show she cared less what anything meant than how it felt. That could be trouble, she knew. Jeffrey would say the experience created an emotional connection to the performers. She guessed there wasn't a woman in the audience who wouldn't make herself the heiress or the vixen, even if Bo was a murderer seven times over.

She giggled, and it was as if Bo heard. Their eyes met. Was it only a second? He winked, and the song went on. Suz and Treya expelled their breaths. No talking her way out of that. When the show reached its crazy end, Exi launched to her feet, clapping with all her might. Bo rose from his first bow and held her eyes until he went down again. Then the rest of the audience got his attention.

Treya elbowed her. "He wants you, girlfriend."

In a phone call today Grace had said, "Just remember Bo's an actor … and a flirt. Have fun, but keep your head."

She'd had so much fun her stomach hurt from laughing, but the actor on the stage had nowhere near the impact of the real guy, so Jeffrey would be wrong. It wasn't the experience. It was Bo.

They went backstage with passes, and he introduced the cast. The actor playing all the dying D'Ysquiths was hilarious, the women talented, but Suz only had eyes for Bo. Exi's heart squeezed.

"So let me get this straight"—Treya braced her hips—"both women saved your homicidal buns?"

He pulled a slow grin. "I was innocent."

"Of that last murder. What about the rest?"

"Oh, the English have such a tradition of killing for advancement, why not for laughs?"

Suz beamed her agreement.

Exi said, "My stomach hurts from laughing." She looked at all of the actors. "Do you get sick of hearing how good you are?"

"Yes, it's painful," the heiress said, tucking her arm through Bo's. "Our normal star originated the role, but this stand-by comes in and knocks them *dead*." She got the laugh.

Bo said, "I have a car outside the stage exit. The driver's watching for you. As soon as I'm cleaned up and changed we can go clubbing. If you're still interested."

Her friends left him no doubt. He winked. "Don't let Exi back out." His conspiratorial tone had them vowing support. Exi rolled her eyes. As if she wasn't the one who got them here.

It was a limo, of course, that smelled of leather and cologne.

Maybe the driver's, since it wasn't as nice as Bo's. Settling in, she said, "I need to know you're going to be all right, Suz."

"I'm living the dream."

"That's not reassuring."

"But it's true. If I pretend I'm dreaming, I won't faint or do anything stupid."

Exi gripped her shoulders. "He's just a guy."

"To you."

"Help me out, Treya." She beseeched her friend to speak reason.

"Here's what she's saying, Exi. You got the real relationship going. Suz is in a dream."

"As long as it's imaginary, I'm fine clubbing with the man who just performed for hundreds of people and looks like every fantasy I ever had."

Exi groaned.

"Suz, you got to tell her you'll cut that out when she and Bo get together. She can't have you salivating when they're married."

"Wait. Stop. What are you talking about? I'm engaged to Jeffrey."

Just as she said it, the driver pulled open the door and Bo slid into the seat across from them. "I propose a ban on that sentence tonight. All in favor …"

Both her friends said, "Yes."

"The yeses have it."

Exi laughed in spite of herself. "Fine. But it's true."

Before he could shush her again, two more men got in. Bo introduced Tobias, a strapping stage manager from Jamaica, and Eric, an assistant director everyone called Swede. "All right if they join us?"

What was he going to do, put them out if they said no? Three guys for the three of them. Convenient. But it would be nice to talk to Bo without worrying about Suz pining or Treya getting crazy ideas to liven things up. There was no telling what she might say when the mood struck her.

Best take control of this now. Exi asked the newcomers about their jobs and responsibilities. Drama had never been her thing so this whole world was new. Devin said Bo was only interested in himself, but as she conversed she felt his focus on her like sunlight though a magnifying glass. Much more and she'd be cinders.

Even though the line stretched for two blocks, they went right in at the first club, where Bo's celebrity caused a stir. He took her hand to keep her close in the undulating crowd. Exi looked back to make sure the others followed.

"Don't worry," Bo spoke into her ear to be heard over the music. "The guys know where we're going."

His hand felt hot. Grace said Bo brought to mind that Terri Gibbs song about the devil with blue eyes and blue jeans. And there was Devin's, *Don't play with that fire, Exi.* Yeow.

They went through a door guarded by a bald guy who forgot to stop growing. Exi pressed against Bo as she passed.

"He's a pussycat."

"I think he eats his young."

Bo laughed low. "Just don't jump his line."

"Okay."

He grinned. "I wasn't instructing you, only ... never mind."

"What?"

"You're so literal." They wended around people and tables.

"Well, if you weren't instructing me, you're the only one. Everyone else thinks I need a keeper." This room of the club had a live band and she could feel the energy.

"Do you think so?"

"No."

"Then why choose one?"

"I'm not."

"Really?" He arched a brow.

She frowned. "Jeffrey respects my decisions."

"When they match his?"

"Not only."

A waitress came through to where they stood. Bo said, "Chocolate martini?"

No, she liked those too much. "Just Chardonnay." In little bitty sips.

That seemed to amuse him, but he ordered their drinks and returned his attention. "You were saying?"

He still wanted to hear? "Jeffrey didn't want me taking over Mom's shop."

"Why not?"

"I had to give up my job at MoMA, but honestly it wasn't that great a position. Jeffrey thought I acted rashly, in the heat of emotion. People always think that because, well, it's usually true. Except lately I've tried really hard not to do that. It's just … I knew what Mom needed. Then she had the stroke, and it wasn't even a question anymore, so I'm glad I made the decision when I did."

"And Jeffrey?"

"He gets it."

Bo studied her. "Is getting it enough?"

"Shouldn't it be?"

"What about understanding why you needed to help like that? Or feeling the same way?"

His words caused an uncomfortable sensation, but it seemed an unfair assumption. "We're two different people. I can't expect him to think or feel the way I do."

Bo shrugged.

"What?"

"I'm picturing the scene. Hospital chaos. Your mother's pain and distress. You hurting for her, seeing a way to help. That ray of light in the storm clouds, maybe just a glimmer, but reaching, grasping before it disappears and the chance is gone."

His voice resonated the angst of that moment. She was right back in it. Her throat ached. "We were all doing our best."

His stare deepened. "You're as good an actor as I am."

She wanted to argue, but was he right? She habitually pretended things were the way she wanted them to be. It wasn't wrong to assume the best. But sometimes it was stupid. "It isn't acting, it's believing. I believe in people until they prove me wrong."

"That's rare." He clasped her elbow.

"Is it?" She searched his face. "It seems the least we should do."

"Should." He huffed. "When does *should* come into anything?"

"It comes into everything. With its evil twin *shouldn't.*"

Bo threw his head back and laughed.

"What?"

"You are so refreshing." He ran his other hand down her arm and sobered. "What if I told you you're my Sibella?"

"The bad one?"

"The one Monty Navarro will kill to have."

"You'd kill Jeffrey?"

The waitress brought her wine and an amber liquor in a highball glass for Bo. Exi sipped her cold, crisp Chardonnay as he drank his, their gazes locked. He hadn't answered.

The liquor—or something—made his voice husky. "Sibella should not have married Lionel. It was all wrong and she knew it. But she couldn't take a chance on love and settled for security."

"That's not what I'm doing. Jeffrey's a good person. He has a lot to offer … besides security."

"Though it's not in the script, I imagine there were times Monty considered adding Lionel to the kill list."

"You're freaking me out. I thought that was all for laughs."

Bo tipped his mouth sardonically. He leaned close and sang, "My Sibella …" in a key that matched the slow dance instrumental the band was playing. Bo circled her waist and they moved together. His voice resonated in her ear, a microcosm of the theater he'd filled with its sonorous tones earlier.

She swallowed. "I shouldn't do this."

"It's only a dance."

"I should have brought Jeffrey."

"But you didn't."

"He doesn't like theater."

"Hmm." He nuzzled her ear and murmured, "Only bad TV."

Refusing that bait, she tipped her face up. "I'm not a cheat. I know how that feels and I won't do it."

"Who could ever cheat on you?"

"You'd be surprised."

"I'd be stunned."

She took another cool sip and they swayed. There was hardly room to do more, and that was good. No doubt Bo could out-dance anyone there, and she'd performed enough gymnastic floor routines to guess how good they'd be together. She cleared her throat. "Why not the heiress?"

"Hmm?"

"Why Sibella, not Penelope?"

"Penelope wins his heart. Sibella inhabits his soul. He can't be without her. Didn't you feel it?"

He'd made it palpable and still did. She got drunk on the feeling. "Bo."

"I won't overstep."

"But I could. I'm the one with someone else."

"Trust me."

"Has that ever been a good idea?"

His eyes hooded. "There's always a first time. Will you be my first?" He ran a finger down her cheek.

"That's … honest." Or what she really meant … tempting.

"I'll never lie. That's a promise." He swallowed, the Adam's apple rising and falling.

The temperature ratcheted up. She realized her friends hadn't joined them.

When she looked over her shoulder, he said, "They must have stayed in the outer ring. It's a brighter energy."

"Then why are we in here?"

"Kory's guarding the door."

"Do you need guarding?"

"Doesn't hurt." He ran all his fingers down her neck.

A shiver ran through her. "I can't see you like this." She should leave it at that, but her mouth added, "not unless I talk to Jeffrey. I loved watching you tonight, but I can't do this." That was the biggest lie, because this was exactly what she could do. How her heart broke every time.

He leaned back holding her hand as if the moment were choreographed. Maybe it was.

"Is this an act?" she breathed.

"You tell me."

"I wish I could tell the difference. But as I said, that's my downfall. Believing." Wanting and believing.

His brow furrowed. "Sometimes the line blurs."

"Between acting and real life?"

He nodded. "It's … porous."

She'd seen him cross the barrier like water through a sieve.

"Thing is, even when I'm acting, it's real. Maybe more than when I'm not."

"So on the stage, with Sibella, that was real?"

He blinked. "In that moment it was real."

"That's why people are spellbound. Because you're not acting. Even something so zany, Bo Corrigan disappeared, and Monty loved Sibella."

"You get that?"

"Not sure how but, yeah, I get it."

"What does that make me?"

"Amazing."

He stepped toward her. His eyes had a liquid quality, like mercury. Wasn't that what made the hatter mad?

"There you are," Treya said. "We made the whole circuit before they guessed you were in here."

When Exi turned to Bo, he mouthed, "They knew." But did that make it better or worse?

The rest of the evening, she kept her friends close. Bo played the demigod for adoring crowds, safer by far than in those early moments. When the night finally ended, Exi nearly sleepwalked into bed … and dreamed.

8

Grace pushed Mattie in her stroller along the East River Promenade, eager to catch up with Exi on more than one subject. But first things first. "Did you like *A Gentleman's Guide to Love and Murder*?"

"Like it?" The sky clouded over and began sprinkling by the time Exi exhausted that subject.

Grace pulled the canopy over Mattie and kept walking. If the rain got heavy she'd extract the umbrella from the nifty stroller pocket, but for now it was refreshing. "I've seen that show with the original lead, and he's very good. But I watched it first with Bo and have to say he brings something special to the role. I think he's hungrier for Sibella."

Exi coughed.

"Are you okay?"

"Yeah. Just breathed in wrong."

"Did your friends enjoy it?"

"Suz is crazy about Bo onstage. Treya preferred clubbing. She hit it off with a Jamaican stage manager."

"Tobias?"

"Yes."

"He's wonderful." Grace maneuvered the stroller around a branch on the sidewalk. "So you went in a group."

Exi nodded. "Most fun we've had together in ages. It's funny how you can room together and hardly see each other."

"Even married, it seems we're always fighting for time together.

I'm getting ready to tour, and I don't know how I'll stand it. Devin and Mattie are going to join me at intervals, but as much as I used to love these tours, now I'm just hoping I'll survive." Her heart ached thinking it.

"Touring means a new book?"

"In the romantic thriller line."

"I can't wait to read it."

"Thank you."

"Grace … you really aren't writing one about Jeffrey and me, are you?"

"I'm really not. Sorry."

Exi toyed with the zipper on her hoodie. "Maybe that's good."

"Oh, believe me it's good. Travail is better in books than life. I'm not saying Devin's right about my imagination, but …"

"You have had a lot of stuff. Some not so good."

Grace grimaced. "Better all around to steer clear of my fiction in your real life."

Exi bit off a hangnail. "I'm thinking of asking Jeffrey for some time."

Grace studied her. "Because?"

"You and Devin both said we rushed into things."

"That's not exactly what I said. And if Devin did, you have to take his protectiveness into consideration."

"I know." She rubbed a raindrop from her nose.

"Want the umbrella?"

"No thanks. I'm fine."

She didn't look fine. "Exi, is it Bo?"

"No. I mean … anything that makes me wonder should be investigated right?"

"Sure."

"I think it started at the hospital with my mom. It seemed like Jeffrey didn't care."

"I'm sure that's not true."

"Are you? Because, Grace, I'm not. When I told Bo about my

Mom's struggle, he hurt with me. But Jeffrey just tried to organize things, to herd me in the direction he thought I should go."

"Well, he's a fixer."

"Right. I get that. And I like it. Kind of. I feel secure."

"But?"

"Do you know what Bo said when I told him I couldn't stand her suffering? He said that's hell, to want to change something you can't. He got it. He's been there."

"He has?"

"With his sister."

Grace looked at her for more.

"You know."

"I guess I don't. Even though he lived with me, there's so much about him I don't know."

"He lived with you?"

"That's not the relevant point—unless you're Devin. Bo crashed on my couch for a while. But I don't know anything about a sister."

"She died."

Grace stopped the stroller. "How?"

"Bone cancer."

"Oh, how sad."

"What's that thing where you feel bad you're alive when someone else isn't?"

"Survivor's guilt."

"Right. I think Bo has it."

Grace thought of the shadows she'd seen in him, the destructive behaviors. "That would explain some things."

"He really never told you?"

"He really never did. But I was pregnant and afraid people would find out. Bo was dealing with his own stuff, and those kinds of things never came up. I'm glad he told you. I won't pass it on."

"Not even to Devin?"

"Devin hasn't gotten over Bo endangering Mattie and me."

"Bo did?"

"I won't air that dirty laundry. I'm just saying I don't discuss him with my husband unless I have to."

"I've never thought Devin vindictive."

"Which Devin do you know?" Grace arched her brow.

"One who got me out of scrapes when I was little."

"He's that too." Grace pulled the canopy back as the sun came through the clouds. Mattie grinned up at her, then pointed eloquently forward. They got moving.

Exi said, "Maybe Jeffrey is perfect for me, but I need to be sure without …"

"Jeffrey selling you?"

"Yeah." Her voice got small.

"He should understand if you ask for time. There's a lot in your life right now."

Exi grimaced.

"What?"

"I think I have to tell him about Bo."

Her heart sank. "Exi … did something happen?"

"No."

"Bo didn't put the pressure on, invite you to his place?"

"Nothing like that. Why?"

"With Bo I always expect a full-court press."

"Well … he wants to court me."

"Court you? When I said *full-court—*"

"Like Jeffrey. He said two suitors. I said like *The Bachelorette* and he pretty much gagged, but that's what he meant."

"He wants a competition with Jeffrey for you?"

Exi nodded.

"Hmm," she breathed. "How do you feel about that?"

"I don't know."

"Would Jeffrey continue if you break the engagement and two-time him?"

Exi buried her face in her hands. "It sounds awful like that."

"But he's a fan of that show."

Exi groaned. "I don't know what to do."

"If you have doubts, you need to tell him that much."

"He'll want to know what they are."

"Naturally. Are any of your doubts not named Bo?"

"None are named Bo. He just opened my eyes."

Grace knew how persuasive he could be. "It's easy to point out someone else's faults. And Bo's very skilled at seduction."

"Do you think that's what this is?"

That didn't require an answer. Exi stared at the river, consternation in her face.

Grace sighed. "I will say, he's handling himself differently than I've ever seen before." Hope flooded Exi's eyes. She might be farther gone than she realized. "But, as Devin says, you won't be the first costarring in his bedroom."

She flushed. "I can't throw stones at that glass house."

Grace held her eyes. "And Jeffrey?"

"We were seeing courtship as a chance to do things differently this time. Like that entertainer and his wife? I can't think of their names but they have a show—"

"Let me guess, Jeffrey's a fan."

"Yeah. I mean he only found it when we decided to try courtship." Exi avoided an old couple with walkers.

"Exi, is there anything Jeffrey hasn't learned from a TV show?"

"He didn't learn his profession there. His graduate degree is more useful than mine. He's very good at what he does, and TV helps, so …" She shrugged.

Grace nodded. "We all get inspiration somewhere. How can I help you in all this?"

"Would you tell me if I'm making a mistake?"

"It's hard to speak for someone else. But I do think honesty matters." When a pigeon landed on the sidewalk, Grace lifted Mattie out to chase it. "Asking for time isn't breaking the engagement."

"If I see Bo it is."

"Are you going to?"

Exi drew her shoulders to her ears. "I'm sure you think it's because he's sexy and gorgeous and talented."

"He's all that."

"But … remember when we talked about sensing things? I think he's in trouble."

"He's paying off his debt to Eileen's brother, and I don't believe Liam O'Hare is the ogre Bo makes out."

Exi stared at her, confused.

"That wasn't what you meant." When the bird flew, Grace led Mattie back to the stroller.

"I think his trouble's inside. I feel like he needs me."

"Oh, Exi, that's a dangerous road."

"I know. I've taken it."

"That's why Jeffrey's such a relief?" She buckled Mattie back in.

"Jeffrey's confident and capable."

"And there's a good chance he won't break your heart."

Exi shot her a look, then sighed.

"Is that because you don't love him?" She hated to be the one spoiling Exi's illusion, but perfection didn't exist.

"That's what I have to find out. But don't you think I should?"

Grace fingered her earring. "This is what writers call a plot twist. It's almost always a good idea."

Exi groaned. "I'm getting that story after all. It just might not end with Jeffrey."

"Don't jump to conclusions. He could surprise you."

"You think?"

"Honey, I'm married to the biggest surprise of my life."

Exi had just turned the shop's sign to open when a floral delivery van pulled up.

"This is a first," the man said, "delivering flowers to a flower shop."

Exi looked at what he held out. "What is it?"

"Probably says there."

She slipped out the spiked tag. "Albuca spiralis." She laughed at the onion-type leaves that corkscrewed out from the base.

They wished each other a good day, and she carried the plant to the counter before reading the card. *Since you wouldn't let me buy your inventory, I found you something new. Bo.*

Her heart jumped. What a funny plant, and she'd never seen one. The tag said it bloomed vanilla-scented flowers, but right now the leaves were putting on their own show.

"What's that?" Jeffrey said, coming in the door.

"Something different." She held it up with one hand and slipped the card into her pocket with the other.

"Looks like someone used a curling iron." He bent and kissed her cheek. "Are you trying out new things?"

Oh, boy, was she. "Some." She set the plant on the counter. "I'm glad you're here, but actually why are you?"

"I have a meeting nearby and thought I'd see how you enjoyed your evening. You didn't answer my text."

She took her phone out and checked. "Sorry. I had it off while I walked with Grace this morning." Given its troubling nature, she'd wanted an uninterrupted conversation.

"Change her mind yet?"

"She only writes novels. If you want your story, you need a biographer."

His brow furrowed. "I want our story."

"That's what I meant. She said that's a biography, not fiction."

"I know what a biography is. I want her to novelize our story."

"Well, she won't." Exi cleared her throat. "And I need to talk to you."

He checked his watch. "Okay, shoot."

"It might take more of a window than you have."

"What is it, Alexis? I have time."

"Okay. It's about time, sort of. I need some."

"Well, of course. We've hardly seen each other."

She silently groaned. "That's not what I meant. I think we should give ourselves more time to see if this is really what we want to do."

"This … what?"

"This engagement." Her stomach hurt.

His face went through shades of puzzlement, confusion, and incredulity with a thin wash of hurt. "You're breaking it?"

"I don't know. I think we rushed in and I need to be sure that we should, that we want to marry."

He pushed his hands into his slacks pockets. "I see. Well, you're taking me by surprise, but I'm sure there's a solution. Will moving the wedding back be a good start?"

"Yes, but, Jeffrey, someone else wants to see me too." There it was.

He frowned. "Who?"

"Bo Corrigan."

"Who's that?"

Amazing. "He stars in Grace and Devin's play."

"Oh, that one. Kind of a pretty boy."

Exi bit her lip. Calling Bo freaking beautiful hadn't sounded at all like this.

Understanding dawned in his face. "That's who you watched last night."

She nodded.

"And he wants to see you romantically." His tone had an edge she couldn't fault.

"He said *court.* Like you."

The green eyes sharpened. "He knows you're engaged and wants to try for you also."

She slid the ring from her finger. "If I see you both, the engagement is off. But I totally get it if you walk away. I wouldn't do it in your place."

He took the ring and studied it. "Well, you're not me. And the engagement is … paused." He put the diamond in his pocket and met her eyes. "We can manage this."

"We can?"

"I don't see much of a threat, frankly." He drew himself up. "He'd have some flash points, but when you're talking futures and lifetimes, and what I believe we have, then no, I don't."

Not even close to how she'd behave in the reverse scenario.

"Alexis, I do have to go. I was supposed to be there already. But I don't want you to worry. We can weather this. Don't let it add to your concerns." He bent and kissed her on the lips, squeezed her shoulder, and walked out the door.

She released a slow breath, surprised and … humbled. Had she made a terrible mistake?

Her phone vibrated and she checked the notifications. A text—from Bo. *Busy?*

She texted: *Not too. Thank you for the crazy fun plant. I love it.*

He texted a grinning devil emoji. *Can I come in?*

What?

The door opened. Oh. Wow.

"I guess you told Jeffrey. He looks like thunder."

"No. I told him, but he's okay with it. He doesn't think you're a threat."

Bo cocked a brow.

"I said I'd understand if he dumped me, but he's not concerned. You only get flash points."

"*Flash.*" He gave her a devastating smile, Jeffrey apparently no concern of his either.

She wasn't sure what to make of it. Two confident men posturing?

"What do you do here?" Bo looked around. "How does a flower shop work?"

She followed his gaze. "Well, I've already watered and pinched off old blooms and dry leaves from the potted plants. Between customers I'll arrange cut flowers. Mom does custom bouquets and centerpieces. She gets the particular flowers someone wants and complements them with her own accents. I have a bunch of orders."

"Can I watch you?"

She blinked at him. "Arrange flowers? It's not that interesting."

"How will I know if I don't see it?"

"I think you can imagine."

"Imagining you is perilous. Better give me reality."

Okay then. She swallowed. "It's a simple job, but there is technique, and you have to have an eye for placement. Also a delicate hand for cutting. If you crush the stems, they can't draw water and they'll wilt too soon. And there's weird stuff like cauterizing poppies with a candle before putting them in water but that's way more than you need to know."

"You just told me several things that prove it's not that simple."

A guy came in and went to the wrapped roses stocked near the door. He chose red and brought them to her. She cheerfully checked him out, hyperaware of Bo taking it in. Seriously, what could be so fascinating?

When the customer left, he said, "You're not a red-rose woman."

"How do you know?"

"When he picked that bouquet your face said *typical.*"

"It is the most popular choice."

"You're not roses or carnations."

"I like both well enough."

His eyelids lowered. "You're sweet peas and lavender."

Her mouth fell open. "How do you know sweet peas?"

"A neighbor grew them all over her fence. Do you have any?"

She shook her head. "Lavender maybe, but no sweet peas."

"Can I make something?"

She looked into his face, puzzled by the request. "You want to arrange a bouquet?"

"For you." Again that silky voice. "Show me how?"

It took a second to decide he meant it, though she'd be a long time wondering why. "We can't use the special-order flowers unless I have extra."

He pocketed his hands. "Let me see my choices."

Jeffrey was so nice about bringing flowers, but she could not imagine him arranging them. That wasn't a bad thing. But neither was this. She brought Bo to the cold storage in the back.

He asked about one after another, looking at her, then studying the blooms. Warmth kindled. When had anyone paid this kind of attention to what she did and what she was like? It didn't even matter if he got the flowers right.

"The ginger flowers." He pointed. "And that lavender. Whatever you said these are and that stuff."

"That stuff is bells of Ireland. It's a good choice putting greens with blossoms, and it gives height to your arrangement." She gathered three purple lisianthus and the pink ginger flowers. He really couldn't go wrong because she was crazy for all kinds of blooms.

"Add a couple of these." He chose two ivory gardenias. "And this." A creamy yellow ball dahlia.

They went out to the design table already prepared for cutting with centerpiece bowls and vases at one end, wired picks and other tools arranged accessibly. It amused her how seriously he took the instruction, scowling at his less than perfect efforts. Twice she broke away to wait on someone. The second time she came back, he held out the lopsided bouquet in a vase with flat floral marbles.

"Told you this wasn't simple." He looked crookedly at his final product as if wondering which of them was at fault.

She looked from it to him. Had any bouquet ever meant so much? This man was more dangerous than last night's seducer. "Thank you." She took the vase.

He pulled out his wallet.

"You can't pay when you did all the work."

"Your materials and gift … such as it is."

"No, Bo, really. I love it too much to let you pay."

He pushed his tongue to the side of his mouth. "There's logic in that somewhere."

She gave him a look that said *duh.*

"Then are you free tomorrow night?"

"Sunday? I'm visiting Mom at rehab and cooking at my dad's."

"Can I come?"

"To meet my parents?"

"You can tell them I'm a friend if you don't want to explain the rest."

She couldn't think straight when his eyes looked like that and his sharp jaw and …

"I could come in disguise."

"Why?" She sounded breathy.

"To avoid disappointing Jeffrey's fan club."

She huffed a laugh. "They'd see through."

"Not me."

"Yeah, well, I can't pretend at all. Saying you're a friend will stretch my abilities." He arched a brow, and she realized what she'd said. "I mean …"

"I know what you mean. No friend cards here. But it might not be the best time to explain the arrangement. Let's wait until your mom can scold me."

Her heart rushed that he thought that would happen. "I hope it's soon."

"So do I," he double inflected.

She thought of Grace's warning with a pang in her chest. "Are you seducing me?"

"Courtship leads to something, doesn't it?"

"Marriage. At least that's my plan with Jeffrey. If we do this, I need to—we need some boundaries."

He ran a finger along her cheek. "Put forth thy statutes."

"Well." She cleared her throat. "Jeffrey—"

"Not his rules. Ours."

She drew a breath. "No touching."

"Right." He laughed, then sobered. "Really?"

She nodded.

"Is that possible?"

"I don't know."

He lowered his hand. "Proceed."

"Well, that covers, um, kissing and nuzzling."

He groaned. "I knew not thou meant the Puritan courtship ritual."

"I want to know what I think of you, and I can't do that when it's all feelings and sensations."

"Then, sweet love, heart and body will yield to the mind until its hunger be satisfied."

"Right. I think. Do you have stipulations?"

"Be but sworn my love—"

"I can't. I won't. Jeffrey gets a fair chance."

He eyed her. "Done. Upon thy terms is now a bargain struck. I would seal that with a kiss upon thy hand, if t'would not violate my vow."

She couldn't stop a giggle.

He said, "What time Sunday?"

She gave him Sunday evening's schedule.

"I'll need your address."

With equal parts excitement and fear, she gave it. *Don't play with that fire, Exi.* Oh, shut up already.

Bo walked to the door. The look he sent over his shoulder made everything she'd said about not touching irrelevant.

9

As the town car pulled out, Bo shook his head. No touching? He tried to remember any conversation with a woman without some contact—even Grace. He should have listened to Jeffrey's rules. They were clearly different because that guy kissed her before leaving.

He blew out a breath. She'd been with Jeffrey half a year. Her friends had told him that much. He treated Exi well, way better than lousy choices she'd made before. But Jeffrey's ring was off her finger. Bo pressed his tongue to his side teeth with satisfaction.

He could handle her boundaries. He only wanted time with Exi, doing anything—as the flowers proved. Crazy how much he wanted that, as if getting it now was crucial. He tapped his fingers on his knees. No, he wasn't patient. But this felt different. A sense, not of doom exactly, but kismet. Why had she come into his life right now, this way, the sight of her like a bolt between the eyes? What was different? The question stayed with him into the night's performance and shaded it.

He sensed Sibella as more than a siren he desired. She was the woman he'd imagined being with forever. The awareness brought a new energy and awakened something deeper, a longing to be known. Not merely recognized, but known as he hadn't been since Barb, who saw him as a person, not a commodity.

Barb had never looked at him with awe. She had mocked and provoked and loved him. She'd been his advocate, his comfort, his best friend. Was it any wonder he refused other women that role? Until Grace. Her friendship had surprised and puzzled him. He'd only begun to explore that when the attack all but wrecked things. Now, that hung over them. Especially with Devin.

His mind went back to Barb. He wished he could ask her what she thought, wished he could hear her voice on any subject. Not the wheezing voice at the end, but the commanding, zany, artful projections. Most of all her frank, "It is what it is, Bo. What are you going to do with it?"

Instead of going home or partying after the performance, he found a place to sit alone, a hazardous place to hurt. Far beneath the bridge, water shimmered with the light of moon, shore, and drifting barges. He let the memories come.

His sister was no beauty. Her dad must have been summarily unattractive, since their mother had a striking if not lovely appearance. His father had clearly been a looker, though they'd never seen either. His mother, a psychiatrist, had two liaisons that resulted in children and an indeterminate number that didn't. She chose Barb's dad for character. Bo's, well that was obvious. And hadn't her genetic engineering worked out exactly as she planned?

Poor Barb. If she had looked even a little like their mother, people might not have asked, *Are you really his sister?* If he'd been less self-centered, people might not have said, *How can you be Barb's brother?*

Those differences had no impact on their relationship. Solidarity fed their affection. From his earliest memories it was Barb, not any of the nannies and certainly not their mother, he had looked to for assurance. Barb suffered her needy brother with patience and humor. She got him acting, something she loved more than anything. Her talent was off the charts, yet they never gave her lead roles.

"I don't care," she said and meant it. "The supporting roles are far more challenging and way more fun." She proved it over and over by making the pretty stars insipid.

He tried to follow her footsteps but landed the lead every time. Barb found endless amusement in that. "You're a better actor than your face, Bo, but no one's ever going to see past it." And here he was playing Monty Navarro when he hungered to play all the dying relatives.

His tortured portrayal of Peter in *Windows and Doors* was the closest he had come to something vital. Tears turned the river lights to starbursts when he imagined Barb watching him play the complicated role. She should be here. She should be alive, his amazing sister, doing greater things than he. What cruel fate had chosen between them?

Night wind blew in his face and crawled down his shirt collar. Dark water flowed beneath. Darker thoughts churned inside. A sound penetrated. A vibration in his pocket. He opened the text from Exi.

The plant is a hit. Mom's laughing. Hope you don't mind I brought it to her room.

He texted back: *Happy for that. Why are you there so late?*

Mom tried to get up and tripped. Needed stitches.

Sorry to hear it. And because he couldn't resist: *Jeffrey there?*

No.

Was he?

No. And she added: *I haven't told him. He's tired of hearing every setback.* After a second: *Maybe I just think that.*

Or maybe she didn't want Jeffrey there. *Can I see you?*

Two seconds. Three. *When?*

Now. He shivered, waiting for her answer.

Where?

Not on the edge of a bridge in the dark. He typed: *Eileen's?* That sounded better than "my place."

Okay. I'll borrow Dad's car. He's spending the night in Mom's room.

And where would she spend the night? Bo cautiously climbed to safety and left the bridge and the haunting thoughts behind.

Exi arrived in yoga pants and a gray hoodie. He had opened the gate from the house for her to access the driveway and now he opened the house door. He wanted to hug her, but they'd struck a bargain, so he said, "How is she?"

"Upset with herself. Dad told her the matching head wounds

could start a trend. She wanted to sock him, but her eyes were laughing."

"They have a good marriage."

"The best."

He ushered her into the parlor where they'd played Alice. It was so formal it might stop him laying hands on her, though not—with his emotions raw—from wanting to. Sex as tonic. Sex as balm. Sex to forget. Sex to live again if only in those moments. "Tell me about them."

Exi unzipped the hoodie to reveal a stretchy yellow tank. No way would he keep his promise if they shared the sofa, so he took a chair across from her. "Have they been together long?"

"High school sweethearts. Neither went to college. Dad got vocational training and apprenticed as a plumber. He worked really hard, long hours. He's a master now with his own company. Mom's probably had three dozen jobs, mostly temp positions. She took anything reasonable that allowed her to be home when we got out of school and stockpiled her earnings to open a store."

"Couldn't she get a loan on your dad's income?"

"She wanted to do it herself. They married so young it was her independence, I think."

"I see why she wanted you in there."

Her eyes watered. "Right?"

"Are you their only kid?"

"I have four older brothers."

He raised his eyebrows.

"All but one are married and live at least a few hours from here—which is good since they're bossy and opinionated to the max."

"You're the baby."

She groaned. "I hate when people say that like it's some excuse."

"I was youngest too. Barb had me by three years."

"Bossy?"

"No. She was cool."

"Barb and Bo. What's your middle name?"

"Matthew."

"And Barb's?"

"Marie."

"I can see why neither of you went by your initials."

He loved that she said whatever came into her mind. "Wonder if our mother analyzed that."

"Analyzed?"

"She's a shrink, specializes in eating disorders, body image, and body integrity identity disorder."

"Um …"

"People who think certain body parts aren't theirs and want them cut off."

Exi's face twisted. "Really?"

"Imagine looking at your arm and not knowing it's yours." He stuck out his leg. "What is that thing doing there?"

"Does she help?"

"It's a body mapping disorder. If the brain doesn't recognize the limb, the best you can do is convince the person it doesn't have to be removed."

She looked horrified. "How common is this?"

"Six percent of her clients, and she's a world-renowned expert. The majority of her practice are girls who see fat on a skeleton."

"I don't suppose that's much easier to cure."

"Cure? No. But control. She's very good at controlling things."

"What does your dad do?"

He scratched his jaw. "No clue. Barb's my half sister, technically. We never met either dad."

She looked as if that was a loss. Maybe it was. But not one he felt.

"Faye Corrigan bred for results. One kid with character, one with looks."

"You're not without character, Bo."

A wry smile. "Yet you automatically assumed me the second."

"Well, duh."

Heat surged between them. This was where he would move in, raise her to her feet, and invite her upstairs. Forget the rules he'd agreed to. They'd be so good together. But then Eileen came through the door.

Exi startled. "Did we wake you?"

"I'm old, dear. I don't sleep. Bo, fix us each a chocolate martini."

Exi said, "I have to drive home."

Eileen covered her surprise with, "At this hour? Better use a guest room."

"I have my dad's car."

"It's the weekend. How early can he need it?"

"If my mom were well, church at seven thirty. But he won't go without her."

At the marble minibar, Bo mixed two drinks with Godiva liqueur and one dry with an olive. Eileen's hand almost missed the glass he offered, which was odd since she didn't seem tipsy. He sat with Exi and studied the older woman.

"What inspired this tête-a-tête in my parlor at midnight?"

Bo smirked. "Sounds like Colonel Mustard in the library with a dagger."

"Where's the body?" Eileen chuckled.

"No body, just an accident." Exi told her what happened with her mother at the rehab center.

"Is that the best facility?"

"It's where the hospital, or I guess maybe the insurance, sent her." Exi took a sip.

The same beverage the other night had made her silly. Too bad he couldn't explore where this one might lead.

Eileen left that subject and probed, "I didn't hear you come in after your performance, Bo."

"Missed curfew, Mum." He took a drink.

"If it doesn't concern Liam, I don't need to hear about it."

Truer than she knew.

"Now, I'll take this to my room." She brushed away their invitations to stay. "I got what I came for." Her sly wink said it wasn't the martini.

As Eileen left them, the clock chimed twelve. Again the sense of urgency coiled in his belly. All these hours he could have with Exi if he hadn't struck that bargain. Her skin called to him. Her hair and those eyelashes. Most of all her essence, that part of her that shone even now in the dim room.

She took another swallow and settled her glass on her thigh. "I want to know more about Barb, but I don't know if I should ask or if you'd rather not."

Grief crashed in and stole the moment. "I haven't talked to anyone about her."

"Not even Grace?"

He shook his head.

Exi flushed. "Um … it accidentally came out this morning. I thought for sure you'd told her. I'm sorry."

He sipped. "I'm not sure why I haven't." More accurately why he had told Exi. "But it's okay. What do you want to know?"

"Anything. What was she like?"

"Incredibly cool. Funny. When I was five she decided we were going to have a circus. She had all her friends come with their younger siblings and painted them as the different animals. She would play the human roles, tightrope walker, stunt rider, fortune teller, anything absurd that occurred to her."

"What were you?"

"Ringmaster. I wanted to be a lion, but she said, 'Bo, you're the star of the show.' And that's where it started."

"Acting? Or starring?"

"I guess both. There hasn't been much of one without the other. Barb was my instructor and my inspiration. She molded me through her own innate talent. She was also a genius at costuming. That's how I learned disguise. Right now I could be an old hag or a homeless junkie. If you passed me on the street, you'd walk right by."

"No way."

He nodded.

"Prove it."

"No props or make up? It'll have to be the junkie." He saw the moment his transformation stunned her, and all he'd done was adjust his clothing, posture, expressions and motions.

"Stop. Please."

He did.

"That was horrible."

"Sorry." He reached out, then planted his hand back in his lap. He imagined a force field around her. Don't touch—or die! He laughed inside his head.

"What?"

"You make me smile."

"How?"

"Just being here, being you. Now it's my turn. Tell me something."

"Like what?" She took another drink, and he wanted to taste it on her tongue, the chocolate and the vodka.

"What do you like to do?" Besides drive him crazy.

She shrugged. "Paint, draw, play music."

"Like stream it?"

"Like guitar, sax, keyboard."

He searched her. "For real?"

"Except I no longer have the instruments."

"But you play. Three of them."

"Not like recording studio. Just garage band."

He took out his phone. "Are you on YouTube?"

Exi groaned. "Treya uploaded us, but it's not something you want to see. Seriously. She can't stay on key. I mean, not like people who have no ear, but she goes flat a lot. And we're all just, you know, kids."

"What do I search?"

She rolled her eyes. "Ankle Bracelets."

He raised his brows.

"We thought it made us bad, like jewelry and criminals? Those locators you wear on bail?"

"I get it." And there she was with her short punk hair nailing a guitar intro in an actual garage. He brought up the volume. A beanpole Hispanic handled drums, and Treya started singing ... worse than Exi gave her credit for.

On the sofa, Exi pressed her hands to her ears. "We didn't have good sound equipment or monitors or anything."

Yet she rocked that guitar. "What songs had sax?"

"You're a masochist?"

"I don't care about the others. I want to see you playing it."

She said, "'Harden My Heart,'" into the sofa's upholstery.

He listened all the way through, falling harder for this girl with every note. They were a notch above high school band, but Exi played with style and confidence. That teenage girl was inside this woman, gripping her head in embarrassment. Even that spoke to her depths, knowing they'd been less than perfect when the others seemed oblivious.

"I wanted to play drums but Arturo owned the set. He said he'd know if I touched a drumstick. Which he didn't, because I did mess around with them when he wasn't there."

He turned off the phone and studied her. "Music and gymnastics."

"I quit gymnastics in sixth grade."

"Why?"

"I got distracting body parts. It's hard enough to develop early without bouncing in your leotard. And when you're nicknamed the 'student body' ..."

How could he not look? "That's a compliment."

"Not at eleven when it's obnoxious classmates saying it."

"Their opinion made you quit something you excelled at?"

She shrugged. "I just happen to be bendy."

She was killing him.

"I mean, sure, I thought I'd be chosen for Cirque du Solei."

"Not the Olympics?"

"Without the awesome costumes? And flying wires?" She gave a little laugh. "But I found another dream."

"Rock star."

"For a while. I'm kind of all over the place."

"Is that bad?"

"Most people have a direction, don't they? Like you with acting. My brother Sully knew he'd be a cop when he took our Uncle Deke to kindergarten career day. Two of my other brothers are plumbers like Dad. The last was a fiend for fishing and has a charter boat in New England. All stuff they chose and stuck with, not … careening from one interest to another."

"You think it's a fault to be multitalented?"

"When nothing goes anywhere." She drew her knees up and curled into the curve of the sofa. "So, do you not know your dad at all?"

Clearly finished with the spotlight. "Not even his name. According to my mother, they agreed to that up front."

"I don't understand."

"That's your first mistake, trying to understand Faye Corrigan."

"What's she like?" Exi licked chocolate martini from her lips.

Oh, the effort it took to resist following suit. "Highly respected in her circles."

"And?"

"That's all I know. In addition to clinical hours, she lectures and presents at symposiums all over the world. We were raised by nannies. Private schools, camps, organized youth vacations."

"You're like an orphan."

"Please sir, I want some more?" His falsetto was weak, but Exi caught the reference to *Oliver*.

"You're breaking my heart."

"I never wanted for anything. No neglect or abuse."

"Love?"

It hit him again. “I had Barb.”

“But you lost her.” Tears jeweled those excessive lashes.

Sorrow sprang up like a ravening wolf. Barb had come too close and been too far tonight. “Crying breaks the rules.” He drew Exi into his arms and stroked her hair.

She slid her drink glass onto the table and curled her hand around his side. “I should be comforting you.”

“You are.” He breathed in the almond scent of her hair, reveled in the feel of her. What would it hurt to hold her, kiss her, take her to bed? She could keep her stupid arrangement with Jeffrey. This was his place, his rules. It would take so little to convince her. He felt it even if she wasn’t aware. But he also felt her trust. And that was what he’d asked for, was it just last night?

No one had gotten inside him like this, not even Barb. This … this could tear apart his entire act. It could shred every disguise. Exi reached in and pulled the real man out, whether she knew what she was doing or not. Even worse, he wanted her to. He was coming apart.

“Sorry for that.” She sniffled and drew back. “I’m oversensitive.”

“Says who?”

“Everyone. You should hear my brothers on the subject. And now my dad calls in a support team before giving me bad news. Everyone knows I’m a mess.”

“What would it take to clear that message and start fresh?”

She blinked. “Clear it?”

“A soft heart is not a detriment.” Though attentive, Barb had not been soft. He could have used more softness somewhere along the way.

“What about a runny nose and drippy eyes?”

He pulled a tissue from a filigree container and Exi used it, then curled it into the palm of her hand. He said, “There’s a trash can under the escritoire.”

“The what?”

“That little decorative desk.”

"Oh. Thanks." She discarded it and came back to the sofa.

He said, "I want to amend the rules."

She rubbed her palms along her thighs. "How?"

"A time limit to no touching."

"How long?"

"One minute." He grinned at her expression. "One month." He made the word come out.

"Then what?"

Oh, his mind. "Then we can touch in platonic ways."

"Like hugs?"

"Like."

She pulled a crooked face. "One month to think about you?"

"Too long?"

"Hmm-mmm."

"Was that no?"

She giggled. "I think my mouth is numb." She looked down at her nearly empty glass. "Should I really stay over?"

Yes, with me. "Eileen's not short of rooms. In the morning you can return the car and spend the day with me."

"I thought you wanted the evening."

"It's my only day off. I want it all."

"Devin said that about you."

He tugged a lock of her hair. "Your cousin has a jaundiced eye."

"Yeah." She yawned. "Even Grace says so."

He took in her sleepy condition with warmth. "Staying?"

"Hmmm. Okay."

He couldn't imagine anything more adorable than she looked in this moment. He'd gone for sultry, sexy, hot, arctic, and even hard as nails. Who'd have thought adorable could ever be this devastating?

10

Exi slept in a nest of down. She woke and stretched and practically purred in Eileen's posh guest room. Her own mattress would feel like a bed of nails after this, but no help for that until she married Jeff—she jolted up as yesterday poured into today. She had told Jeffrey about Bo, had ended the engagement … or sort of. He was giving her time. He was letting her see Bo. See Bo! She jolted again.

Now she remembered last night, his bleak eyes when she first arrived, when he talked about Barb and his family that wasn't even a family. Little by little the shadows had passed as they talked. And when he listened to her awful music? Okay, not awful, but bad enough. His expression when she peeked through her hands had been engrossed.

She'd gotten silly. Her defenses were down. He hadn't taken advantage of that, hadn't broken her trust. And she did trust him, more every minute they spent together. The more she learned the more she liked. The more she got to know, the more she wanted to. Had she been this hungry for Jeffrey? She couldn't remember. She'd been flattered, impressed, interested. But hungry?

When Jeffrey learned she had that band he said he'd like to hear her play sometime. Bo dug in right away, even when she warned him. Yes, he laughed, but it was enjoyment. He liked what he saw and wanted more. Bo Corrigan with talent in every cell. She should be humiliated, but that look on his face watching her play the sax …

And don't get started on the flowers. When Jeffrey came to the store, he never even looked around. It was irrelevant to him. She mattered. She knew that. But not the things that mattered to her. Was it unfair to think that because he never made her a wonky bouquet? He always brought flowers, way more than lots of people bothered to do. Jeffrey was a good guy.

So how was she supposed to do this? She scratched her bedhead and yawned. One minute at a time. She hadn't planned this predicament, but she was in it. She rose and showered and got into the same clothes she'd worn over. She'd have to change for church, but maybe she could have a quick bite first. As she headed downstairs she smelled something that could be waffles. Sure enough, Sondra opened a Belgian-waffle iron and removed a crisp golden disk to a plate, which she set before Eileen.

"I see you took my advice and stayed." Eileen motioned for her to sit. "Sleep well? Or hardly at all?"

"I slept like a baby on a cloud." Exi took the seat.

"A pity." Eileen quipped and spooned strawberries onto her waffle.

Pity? Exi caught her meaning and bit her lip. "I hope you don't mind I used a room on the second floor. Bo said—"

"I don't mind." Eileen looked past her. "You're up early, Mr. Corrigan."

Exi turned. How long before the sight of him stopped joggling her insides?

"Never slept."

"At all?" Exi's heart sank. She must have been no comfort to him.

"Theater people often don't," Eileen shifted her gaze from one to the other. "Too many juices flowing."

He shot a dark look at Eileen, then graced the room with his smile. "'But, soft! what light through yonder window breaks? It is the east, and Juliet is the sun.'"

She smiled back. "What do I say?"

"Your line is, 'Wherefore art thou Romeo?'"

"Why would I ask where, when you're here?"

"*Wherefore* means 'why.'" He slid a chair out and sat.

"I'm asking why you're Romeo?"

"Yes. Because he's Romeo Montague, Juliet can't have him."

"Why not?"

"The Montagues and Capulets are sworn enemies. Haven't you read the play, or seen it?"

She shook her head. "We studied *Hamlet* and *Julius Caesar*, but the nuns didn't teach the romances. Sister Ag would have died of embarrassment."

Bo stared at her, that mercurial light in his eyes again.

"What?"

"He's imagining you in Catholic school plaid," Eileen said.

Bo spoke flatly. "If you don't behave, I'll take Exi and go."

"Not yet." The waffle Sondra set in front of her caused a Pavlovian response. She reached for the syrup. "I do have to leave, but I can't pass this up. Thank you."

With a nod, Sondra poured batter for Bo's waffle.

Eileen said, "Misbehavior is the consolation for getting old."

"You're not old and you never behaved." Bo poured coffee from the carafe.

Eileen chortled. "I saw no need."

"And have no regrets."

"No life is lived without regrets."

"Don't I know that," Exi said. She spread her hands when they looked at her. "What? I'm trained to regret."

"Then why behave at all?" Eileen arched her brows.

"Well, I don't regret everything, just what isn't—you know—right and good."

"What do you say to that, Bo?" Eileen prompted.

He kissed Sondra's knuckles when she put the waffle before him. "When I'm bad it's very right, very good."

Nightclub Bo was back. "Devin warned me about that."

He turned to Eileen. "Let's knock him off her shoulder, shall we?"

"Never. He's the perfect foil."

Bo bared his teeth.

Exi swallowed a syrupy bite. "What is it with them?" she asked Eileen.

"Two sides of the same coin."

"Devin and Bo are the same?"

"Not the surface, but the undercurrent? Certainly."

Bo said, "Grace calls us two tortured thespians."

"Devin's tortured?"

"You note she didn't question my side of the coin?"

"Yes." Eileen's eyes sparked with mischief. She pushed her plate away, hardly touched. Sondra removed it with a frown.

"I only mean …" Exi searched for a way out. "Devin's so together and professional and …"

"That's his surface," Eileen agreed. "Underneath he's a mess. Only not as much now that he has Grace. I'm eager to see how you transform the dark twin."

Exi searched her, puzzled.

"She means me," Bo said, though his gold-streaked hair shone in the morning light.

Exi shook her head. "I'm out of that business. It never works and I end up sobbing my guts out."

"So you have Jeffrey"—Eileen raised her teacup—"who won't break your heart."

"That's what Grace said. Why do people think that?"

"Hearts are resilient." Eileen covered her hand with a papery palm. "It takes passion to break one."

Exi frowned. "I'm not passionate about Jeffrey?"

"Are you?"

She thought of the presence he brought to a room, the way her spirits rose, his patience and understanding. "I think so."

"Thought and passion don't coexist," Bo said.

She turned. "I don't feel right discussing him with you, or the other way around. If we're doing this, I have to keep you separate."

"What is it you're doing?" Eileen asked.

"We're courting her." Bo said it as though it were a normal thing.

"Two boyfriends?"

"Bo says suitors."

"How divine." The older woman sat back. "I'll enjoy the spectacle."

"There won't be one," Exi said. "This is a civil contest."

"Is that so?" Eileen's chuckle filled the room with doubt.

"I can't speak for Jeffrey"—Bo waved a hand—"but I've pledged civility."

"And a fine actor you are."

He slow blinked.

Exi used her napkin. "Thank you for breakfast and letting me stay the night. But I really have to get to church." She needed grounding in a big way.

"Haven't you missed?" Bo checked his watch. "You said seven thirty."

"Two more chances including tonight. If I make it this morning, I won't need that option."

"Then let's go." Bo rose.

"You're coming?"

"Unless you think holy water will steam off my forehead."

She'd have to give that some thought.

"Come on. I've never been. It should be interesting."

And how.

Bo waited outside Exi's apartment when she ran in to change, partly because he didn't feel up to her roommates' fawning, and partly because Exi said it would be awkward showing up in last night's clothes with him in tow. The explanation was simple, but believable? He wouldn't buy it. So he waited in the car, seat back, arms folded, eyes closed.

Reliving last night, he had a thought. He took out his phone, did a search, and placed an order. Way better than crazy plants, and he'd get to enjoy it too. Exi wasn't shy, not with him anyway. Even if she was rusty, she'd get it back. She had music inside her.

After a while, Exi climbed back in, nice but casually dressed in capris and a coordinating top. He hadn't even asked if his jeans and T-shirt would do. Both were J. Crew, classy casual. But he had imagined church attire staid and stuffy. Admittedly his experience was nil.

The thought of something brand new with this brand new person was the closest he could imagine to a new beginning. The trustworthy Bo. The Bo that didn't touch … yet. But he could talk. "How are you always so fresh, so bright, like those ginger flowers?"

"It's just me. I like mornings. I like new days." She hit the turn signal and maneuvered through the intersection.

"This is all different. I've been submerged in theater, in theater people. I can't remember when it wasn't the air I breathed."

"With gills."

He looked her way.

"Sorry. You said submerged so I pictured you under water. It's an artist thing."

"You're into art too?"

"It's my MFA. I told you I'm all over the place."

She had a master of fine arts? "I think it's epic. My single focus … sometimes I feel like it's killing me. Like I'm not allowed to be anything else."

"It's where you've experienced success and acceptance. Especially from your sister."

Mention of his sister caused a pang, but he appreciated her talking about Barb without restraint. "Her passion certainly transferred."

"You must have fed on her approval, if she was the only one giving it."

"Oh, everyone gave it. The nannies fawned. Even Faye gave me everything I wanted—or demanded. We were never introduced to the evil twin *shouldn't.*"

"How did you not make terrible choices and end up in jail?"

He shrugged. "It wasn't an appealing thought."

"I'm so impressed with that after some morons I fell for."

He studied her. "Why?"

"What?"

"Why did you fall for losers?"

"I have a weak spot for strays and misfits—not you!" she almost hollered.

He laughed. "You're so painfully cute."

"I think it's what I told you. I believe in people." Her face fell. "But then they prove me wrong. I'm not stupid about it. When the one got violent, I was out of there."

His eyes narrowed at the thought of someone hitting her. "Did you have him arrested?"

"Yeah, but he got bail and stole my instruments. He'd already sold them off when the cops questioned him. Talk about a talented liar. He got a fine and anger-management course. I got rid of him. So it all worked out."

He almost told her what he'd ordered, but he'd wait to see her eyes when it arrived. He carried the pleasure of that thought as they approached the beige, castle-like church with bells ringing in the tower, its spire shining in the morning sun.

The minute Exi entered, people of multiple ethnicities swarmed her. "How's your mother? Dad holding up? Sure wish he would come without her. Miss seeing them in their pew."

Bo watched Exi soak in their concern and comfort like a rose in dry ground until she bloomed. Finally, she turned and said, "This is Bo. It's his first time."

"At our church?" one matron asked.

"Any. I was formed by a believer in nonbelief."

"Wait till we get our hands on you," an elderly black man with random yellowed teeth cackled—yes cackled.

"Janjak. Don't scare him out the door." The plump white woman leaned in and asked, "Do I know you?"

Bo said, "I'm sure I'd remember."

"Oh." Her cheeks pinked with pleasure.

This was where he'd move Exi through them, except he couldn't touch. So he waited until she went into the inner sanctum or whatever the part with pews was called. She dipped her fingers in a water bowl and dabbed herself four times, then glanced back.

"I'd better not risk it."

She grinned. "We could use the baptismal font for exorcism."

"At least you didn't say circumcision."

Her eyes widened. "Stop."

"Or what? Someone will take a ruler to me?" He slacked a hip.

"Can you behave?"

"That's the question."

She shot a warning glance but kept walking.

"How far up are you going?"

"Worried?" Cute that she turned the teasing tables. She stopped at the third row, went down on one knee, then moved into the pew.

He followed her in and studied the altar in front with a gold part above that held a cross on which a dead man hung by nails. Jesus, he supposed, the guest of honor with his thorny crown and bleeding side. "If there's an altar call, I'm not going forward."

"There isn't."

"If they start waving snakes, I'm out of here."

She looked perplexed. "No snakes. Sheesh. And you can wait here through communion." She slid to her knees on a thing made for that.

He stayed seated and took in his environment. Eileen had pegged it with her Catholic uniform crack, but seeing Exi in this milieu brought a dimension to her he'd never expected. And yet … maybe he had. Was this what made her seem so fresh and new? Purity. There was that thought again. He should run, but he wanted to stay, wanted to see, hear, touch …

His mother treated sex like any clinical aspect of human nature. He used it like everything—to feel good. And share those good feelings. He made a point of that. By Exi's remarks, he guessed others had not been generous with her. The desire to change that hit like a freight train—unchurchworthy to say the least.

They rose, singing, as three kids and the priest came forward in gowns. Not the right word, he was sure. "What's he wearing?" he whispered.

"Vestments," Exi whispered back.

This was like a foreign country with its own customs. It seemed ancient and majestic, yet accessible. Faye had sent her offspring to many parts of Europe and Asia for their development, but never Israel or Rome—Faye's antipathy to Christianity and its roots. When Barb found Jesus, she never let on to their mother. He found out accidentally when he walked in on people laying hands on her and praying in the cancer ward.

Even then she said, "It's my thing, Bo. Don't pretend for my sake. I'm so tired of fakers."

And here he was, faking it bigtime. His talent for mimicry got him through the sitting, kneeling, and gesturing. He listened to the parts read aloud. He'd heard Bible readings at one of the camps Barb requested that included morning and evening prayer—something his mother hadn't realized until they were home. She'd written a letter, as he recalled. Not a nice one.

They came to a part where everyone shook hands. Exi's was strong and shapely, her tendons defined. Gymnast, musician, artist. So much talent, compassion, and sex appeal, he didn't want to let go. Then he saw people hugging and took a chance. She looked startled, then hugged back.

"Peace be with you, Bo."

Wouldn't that kick all?

He watched her take communion with something like awe. This was wrong. He shouldn't be here, feeling like this about her. By the end he felt scalded but at the same time salved. No wonder people feared religion.

As they left, Exi was surrounded again. Faye sneered at what she called salt-of-the-earth people. He didn't feel like sneering, but he needed out. In the parking lot, Exi surprised him by slipping her hand into his. He glanced behind them. "Won't they think you're cheating on Jeffrey?"

"They haven't met him."

"He doesn't come with you?"

"He's happy for me to attend."

"But ..."

"It's not real to him the way it is to me."

Don't pretend for my sake. "Let's introduce him to Faye."

It took her a second to recognize the name. "Your mom?"

"She's a cougar. With the right type."

"Jeffrey's her type?"

"He isn't yours."

"Bo." She tried to take her hand away.

He held tight. "No backsies."

"Backsies?" She cracked up. "I haven't heard that since third grade."

"What nun taught you that year?"

She rolled her eyes. "You'll only laugh."

"I want to know. I want to know everything." So badly it seared.

Grace took Eileen's call as Devin lay on his back on their living room floor, balancing Mattie on his upraised arms and hands. She could picture Eddie doing that with toddler Devin since it seemed to be a rite of passage for fathers and their offspring. At first Mattie was too afraid to stand upright. Now that she knew her daddy's arms would hold secure, she loved it almost as much as he.

"How are you, Eileen?" Grace moved into the bedroom to change out of church clothes.

"Feisty, thank you very much. I want to talk to you about a

project I've come across. I think it has potential but could use your spark."

"Oh, Eileen, I'd love to say I could take a look, but my plate is so full I don't dare. Plus I'm leaving on tour in a few days, and that's going to be an ordeal in itself." She slid her Versace heels to the partitioned closet shelf.

Gales of high-pitched laughter suggested Devin had stopped balancing and commenced tickling his daughter. Leaving those two was going to kill her.

"Well, maybe we can talk when you get back. You wouldn't have to work with this person, just tell me what's missing."

"You don't want to ask Devin?"

"It's already skewed his direction, with a fraction of his finesse."

"Sounds a little dreary."

"Yes, rather."

"Then why touch it?"

Eileen sighed. "Just a feeling."

"Well." Grace exchanged her skirt for lightweight leggings. "I'll make time when I get back."

"That would be lovely. On another subject, what do you think of Bo and Alexis?"

"In what way?"

"They just left to spend the day together. I can't help thinking she's exactly what he needs."

Funny how her husband thought the opposite. She felt conflicted answering. Exi might be what Bo needed, but was the reverse true? "Are you playing matchmaker?"

"Me?"

"You only toy with the ones you love."

Eileen laughed. "You're sounding like Devin these days. Give Mattie a kiss from Nana Eileen."

"I'll give her two. And we'll talk when I'm back."

Grace hung up, leaned against the closet shelves, and breathed the cedarwood that kept their clothing fresh. Bo and Exi. How did she feel about that? "Lord?" she murmured. But she knew. He had it under control.

Her Dad had his company van and told Exi she could return the car this evening. So she and Bo grabbed deli sandwiches and went to Prospect Park in Flatbush, one of her happy places.

He slid her a look. "You're taking me to the zoo?"

"Want to?"

"Why do I think even that would be amusing with you?"

"Because I'm fun and funny?" She arched a brow. "But no, I thought we'd picnic."

"And recite Shakespeare?"

"That would be you. Recite and translate." They strode toward the meadows where others enjoyed the beautiful day. Three guys and a teenage girl were playing Frisbee with a chocolate lab wearing a yellow kerchief. The girl's toss overshot, and Bo stomped it, then sent it soaring straight to her with a swift flick of his wrist.

"How did you do that?" Exi shook her head. "I cannot, for the life of me, throw those straight."

"Sure you can."

"Nope. And you'd be joining the long line of instructors, starting with my brothers, who were certain they could teach me."

His mouth quirked. "Hopeless, huh?"

"Beyond hopeless."

He spread his hands. "It's not a necessary life skill. And I'm glad to know there's something you can't do."

"There's so many things, don't get me started."

"Like what?"

"Can't write a story. Or an essay. Term paper? I did a happy dance for a C."

Mirth filled his eyes. "What else?"

"I can't whistle. I mean I can manage a windy cave, but no tune. I squeak a mean grass blade though."

His mouth twitched. "Who needs to whistle when you play a killer sax?"

"Kill-your-eardrums sax is what my brothers called it."

"They have no ear."

She shrugged. "It's painful hearing someone learn an instrument. Do you play anything?"

"No."

"Your voice is amazing."

He reached toward her, then withdrew his hand. She wondered if he knew how many times he did that. She wondered if she was glad he stopped himself.

When he veered toward a smaller field separated by a fringe of trees, she said, "Don't want to be seen?"

"I'd rather not attract a crowd."

"I thought you liked that."

"In its time and place. I don't want to waste these minutes on anyone else."

"Only me?"

"They're not wasted on you."

Every word seemed sincere and meaningful. Like Jeffrey only … different. She ran her gaze over the freshly mown lawn. "Doesn't grass like this make you want to turn cartwheels?"

"I want to see you turn cartwheels. Show me a floor routine." Bo took the food and sprawled out.

"Um … I mentioned an issue, two to be exact."

"Not an issue for me." He formed his wolfish grin.

Since she was a woman, not a kid, it mattered less than it had when she quit. Plus there was no one else in this portion of the park.

"Come on. You've seen me perform. Strut your stuff." He propped back on his elbows, one knee up, the other leg outstretched.

"Okay. You asked for it." She gave him a routine, complete with aerial walkovers, back flips, and shimmy dance sections. As strong and limber as ever, she felt her lack of practice in endurance. She did a slow descent from a one-handed handstand into her final pose, held it, then flopped to her back, breathing hard. "It's more fun with music."

Bo went to one knee beside her. "You are music."

She canted him a look. He bent and kissed her, his mouth a symphony with a heavy metal overlay. Her chest throbbed with the percussive power while her mouth tasted sweet violins. She reached around his head and kept him there, a duet of cello and oboe, soaring over the surging currents of electric guitar and drumbeat so fast and complicated it took her breath.

"I'm in love with you." His words formed a new theme, rich and enticing.

Arms around his neck, she rose up against him, then jolted when two men came through the trees straight at them. One grabbed Bo and jerked him to his feet while the other hooked an arm around her ribs and yanked her all the way off hers. She kicked and squirmed but couldn't scream with his smelly hand crushing her mouth. Her heart beat so hard the rushing blood deafened.

Peripherally, she saw the other man punching Bo in the stomach until he fell to his knees. The scum kicked his back and sides and chest with a steel-toed boot. Then he pulled out a blade so wicked she shrieked through the hand stifling her. The thug grabbed Bo's hair and brought the blade to his cheek.

Before he could cut, a muscular man in charcoal emerged from the shadows. He grabbed the assailant's hand, twisted and drove the blade into that man's side all the way to the hilt. Exi's head filled with cotton. Her assailant let go. She fell to the ground, striking her knees and palms on grass and dirt as he ran off.

The man in charcoal pulled her and Bo to their feet. He snatched their lunch bag and said, "Walk," in a tone that made her spongy legs move. Bo wasn't breathing right, but he moved too.

When they got past the trees, the guy said, "Look natural." Shifting his own demeanor, he dumped their deli lunch into a trash can and nonchalantly used a handkerchief to wipe a smear of blood from his hand as if it were ketchup. He threw that into a different trash can.

Bo winced with every step.

Coming to her senses Exi said, "We're going the wrong way. My car's on Flatbush."

"Keep walking."

She slid her arm around Bo. "He needs a doctor."

"Don't draw attention."

"Look, who are you and why should we listen to you?"

His stare reminded her he'd probably killed the man attacking Bo. She'd witnessed a homicide. The shaking increased. "We need to call the police. We can't leave the scene."

They reached the street, and he moved them toward an idling black SUV with another man at the wheel. She froze. "No way. I'm not getting in there." If she ran, would they take Bo and go? Or chase her down and knife her too?

"Exi," Bo rasped.

She shot him a terrified glare. "What's going on?"

"Eileen's brother." His voice was so tight with pain, she hardly recognized it. She couldn't leave him. Not like this.

The scary man opened the door and she got into the second-row seat. Bo moved in beside her, his face a mask of pain. The driver pulled out. Neither front man talked.

"Bo's hurt. He needs a hospital."

Scary charcoal man said, "He'll get help."

"Who are you?"

"John."

"Right."

"John Helm." He glanced over his shoulder at Bo. "Are you cut? Stabbed?"

Bo shook his head.

But his body had taken blows, vicious ones. Her stomach lurched, remembering. "You can't see what's happening inside. He needs a CT scan, X-rays."

Bo closed his hand over hers. It shook worse than she did.

"Who were they? Why did they hurt you? It wasn't random or these guys wouldn't be here."

"Let it go," he rasped.

"What did you mean Eileen's brother? Why would he do this?"

He caught her face with his other hand and occupied her mouth until she stopped questioning, but this kiss had no song. He drew back, wheezing as if his lung collapsed.

"That's it. I'm calling 9-1-1." She took out her phone. Before her thumb touched a key, John snatched it from her from the front seat. "Hey!" She glared. "Give me my phone."

"When we get there."

"Where?"

John didn't answer. Bo looked gray.

"If he's bleeding inside, every minute counts."

John assessed Bo, then made a call. She'd gotten through, but it didn't change the driver's course. They left Brooklyn and continued north to Gramercy Park. An ambulance waited silently outside Eileen's townhouse. They got Bo on the gurney but didn't load him for transport. Instead, they wheeled him inside her foyer. A man from the ambulance moved with authority behind the gurney bearers.

When she tried to engage that one, John caught her elbow. "He's a combat surgeon. Don't interfere." He put her phone into her hand with an icy stare. "And don't call the police, or we might not be there next time."

Next time? Fear spiraled in as he drove off in the SUV. When had she left real life for this nightmare?

11

Bo felt every breath like hot needles. His back and kidneys and belly formed a continuous throb, but his side felt jagged as they wheeled him into the house and closed the door. The crew-cut doc said, "Shirt," and the female EMT cut the T-shirt off him with shears. That cried for comment—or not, with Exi right here.

She smelled sweaty from the physical strain and anxiety. He liked her scent, but not her weepy eyes. He'd broken the rules. "I wasn't supposed … to touch." If he'd been watching, he might have done something. Yeah, right. The kicks and punches were so swift and debilitating he hadn't even fought back. "I messed up."

Exi shook her head. "This is on them, not you."

He winced. If the doc's probing were interrogation, Bo felt pretty sure he'd spill his guts.

She said, "He's not breathing right."

"Keep back."

Pain didn't stop him appreciating the trouble she kept causing. She moved from his side but only as far as his head. May as well enjoy the view. But crew-cut spoiled his reverie with pressure on a spot that tore a shout from him.

The doc said, "Splenic hematoma," to the EMT and fingered one damaged rib and another, until the jagged one shot searing pain. Bo bit back this cry, mostly because he could hardly suck in breath. The doc directed the EMT to inject local anesthetic, then jammed something through the semi-numbed flesh.

Bo fought for air. Pain became panic.

"… push the rib out of the lung, and now we'll just …"

Air rushed in. Bo sucked a breath and shuddered. He felt light-headed. Exi stroked his hair, her touch exquisite. He'd take a daily beating for the joy of her fingers.

The doctor shot her a look. "Now, can you trust me to examine the rest of his injuries without interference?"

"That was slick, but he needs a hospital."

Who could tell? He'd never been seriously injured, no more than strained muscles until this agony.

The door opened and Eileen came in with the bigger, more robust version of herself that was Liam O'Hare. She introduced him to Exi, then motioned her toward the kitchen. "Come have some tea while these people tend to Bo."

Exi clearly didn't want to, but she lowered her head and followed. He hadn't intended this. He only wanted time with her. Was that so much?

Breath smelling like Altoids, Liam leaned in with a security camera photo. "Is this the man?"

Bo nodded. The bony-faced man he'd noticed outside the park with Eileen had done the beating.

"What can you tell me about the other?"

"Nothing."

"Think."

Bo closed his eyes. "Darker. Stocky. None of the … tattoos."

"What nationality?"

"Come on." Bo screwed up his face.

"Guess."

"Mexican? Middle Eastern?" He swallowed. "Middle Eastern."

"Beard?"

"I think so."

"All right." Liam straightened. With a titanium will and eyes like glacial ice, he was formidable at eighty. What a force he must have been at forty.

"Did they hurt the girl?"

Bo fought off a wave of pain. "I don't think so."

To the doctor, Liam said, "Did you check her?"

"She's fine."

"I doubt she's that." Liam's eyes flared. "Y'might have checked her." Anger thickened his brogue, though he'd lived his whole life in New York.

"Helm assessed her."

Liam relented. "Finish with him upstairs."

As the EMTs folded the gurney wheels to carry him, Bo watched Liam head for the kitchen, then closed his eyes and succumbed to the throbbing pain of bruised tissue and fractured bone.

Exi perched on a bar stool as if it were a cactus bed while Eileen turned off the flame under a stainless-steel kettle. She wanted to be with Bo, not here having tea.

"After breakfast Sondra has Sundays off. She stays with a friend on Long Island." Eileen poured water over a tea bag to steep.

Were they really making small talk as if nothing had happened between breakfast and now? "I'm not really thirsty."

"Yes. But it'll do you good."

Good? When she'd seen—she pressed her hands to her face.

Eileen stirred in sugar and placed the teacup and saucer onto the counter in front of her. "I made it sweet. That helps with shock."

Exi took a sip, then rattled the cup back onto the saucer. "You know what happened?"

"Liam informed me of the attack."

"Your brother had someone beat on Bo?"

The woman's brow furrowed. "It was Liam's man who got you out of there."

Shock must be making her dense. "Bo said …"

Eileen silenced her with a hand. "You'll get it all, but first, drink."

"Not before you tell me what's going on."

Eileen sighed. "Some time ago, Bo got over his head gambling. He owed a very dangerous person a great deal of money. At my request, Liam bought his debt. But shortly after their deal, that man—Sergei Karkov—died in a boating accident. His people believe Liam caused it, but since he's out of their league, they'll retaliate on Bo. Russians bear grudges almost as deeply as the Irish."

Exi stared at her. "What Russians? Like a gang?"

"Gang, Mafia, whatever they're called now. That's why Liam's kept an eye on our young man."

"Guarding him?" She pictured John Helm coming out of the shadows.

"Not directly until recently. Liam learned that one of those fighting for control of the Russian mob thinks he'll solidify his power with a hit on Bo."

A hit? Breath left her lungs in a rush. "Why is Liam involved with Russian hitmen?"

"His business is multifaceted."

"Illegal?"

"Stop thinking in black and white. It's naïve."

Exi pushed her cup away. "I have to go."

"Please wait. Liam's learning what he can from Bo. Then he'll want to talk to you."

"John said I have to keep quiet, if that's even his name."

"John Helm," Eileen said. "Former Special Forces."

Trained to kill. "He—"

"Don't talk to me. Wait for Liam."

Exi clenched her hands. Her nerves felt electrified in a not-good way. She'd had no lunch—thanks to John throwing it out—but it was all she could do to keep the tea down. Just as she climbed off the stool, Liam strode in. He looked older than Eileen, but hardened like heartwood.

"Alexis Murphy?" His voice had an Irish lilt she hadn't noticed in Eileen's, but she had an ear for blarney and didn't fall for Irish charm like her brother Sully's girlfriends.

She cut to the chase. "Did you order that man's boating accident? That Russian whose people are after Bo?"

He raised his brows and looked down at her from a stately height. "You've the Murphy fire, I see."

Exi crossed her arms.

He pursed his lips and considered her. "No. It wasn't my doing."

"Can't you say so and get them off Bo's case?"

"It's not that simple."

Exi swallowed a lump. "If you didn't do it, who did?"

"More of their kind, I assume. Croatians. Chinese. Mexican Cartel. I don't know."

"There must be something you can do."

He leveled a look at her. "What can be done's been done."

"Until someone else tries to kill him?"

"They might have merely meant to cut him. Murder's not always the order of things."

"Oh, if that's all." She huffed.

His brow furrowed. "I have John on him. He's the best."

"What if the police arrest John? They have the murder weapon."

" 'Twasn't murder, and he used the man's own hand."

At that memory, the fight left her. Tears washed into her eyes.

"Aw now. All you need do is stay quiet, so John can be about his work."

"What if people saw us?"

"Of course they saw you. Helm made a point of walking by folks. That makes you forgettable."

"What about the dead guy?"

"That's for the authorities."

"You called them?"

"He's been found. A Russian national on criminal watch lists."

Exi pictured him falling—no—John Helm dropping him. Right before he walked them forgettably away. "I want to see Bo."

"He's medicated. Out cold by now."

"He needs a hospital."

"Broken ribs and bruises don't need a hospital, now the air's back in his lungs. I've had worse in boxing matches."

"He's not built like a brick house."

Again Liam studied her. "The doctor dosed him with pain relief and antibiotics, and the housekeeper's a nurse. He's not assured better care in any facility I know."

Exi propped her hands on her hips. "Sondra's not here."

"We'll get her. Come see Bo tomorrow if you want to. Until then, we'll take care of your lad, Miss Murphy."

The shakes returned. "We left my dad's car at the park."

"Transportation is waiting."

If he said *lass*, she'd have stomped his foot. Well, not actually, but the thought chased some of the sick feeling away. Exi made herself move. Was she really doing flips two hours ago? Things had changed and she didn't know how to make them go back.

She chewed the skin under her lip raw in the town car that took her to her dad's Ford. She reached her parents' home in a daze and found Jeffrey on the porch steps. He raised a yellow rose bouquet and stood, arms outstretched, when she ran to him.

Jeffrey stood solid and sure as she pressed into his chest. He was bigger than Bo and so … sturdy. When she held on longer than he expected, he laughed and said, "Okay, Alexis. Want to talk about it?"

Yes! But she shook her head. "I'm just glad to see you." She'd forgotten they had plans. He'd have arrived with roses to find her out with Bo if the attack hadn't happened. Sunday was the only night Bo didn't perform, so she'd have to make other arrangements with Jeffrey if—it all slammed into her again. "Can we see Mom before going out?"

"Of course. We'll visit, go have dinner, then watch some shows while you cook for your dad."

So normal. "Thanks, Jeffrey."

"You're welcome." His brow furrowed. "Whatever it is, you can talk to me. Every cloud has a silver lining, and I'm pretty good at finding them."

What silver lining would he find in seeing someone killed? That it wasn't her? That John Helm saved Bo's life … or at least his face? And the lining for Jeffrey: Bo Corrigan's rather risky, isn't he? Better stick with me.

She should have been delirious with relief. There was relief. But no delirium. Delirium, thy name is Bo. Ugh. Was she thinking in poetry now?

"Alexis?"

"Yes." All she hoped for in love was a happy marriage like her parents'. Why did she keep falling for impossible cases? For damaged dreamers? For flash points?

"Ready to go?" Jeffrey motioned her to his hybrid.

"Yeah, I guess." She still wore her church clothes, navy capris and a fitted tan and navy top. Great for worship, back handsprings, knifings, and casual dinner out. Could he smell the horror on her? She groaned.

Jeffrey looked concerned. "Is there something I should know?"

I'm in love with you. She swallowed. Just as she wouldn't talk to Bo about Jeffrey, the same held true here—even without John Helm's threats. "It's been a rough day." A horrifying, life-changing day.

"I'm sorry to hear that." He unlocked the car. "Mine's been relaxing. Maybe some of that can rub off on you."

She slid into her seat and thought of Bo wincing in pain. Stop it! She needed to divide her brain. No more gymnastics in the park. That girl was as gone as the wannabe rock star. This woman was an artist who could paint dead people in bathtubs. That thought brought a fresh sort of horror.

Jeffrey got in beside her. "I drove by the museum today. Have you spoken with them about going back sometime?"

"They've replaced me. But now that I'm at Mom's store, I actually feel freer to explore my art." She hoped her voice sounded normal, because inside her head a voice kept screaming, *Someone died today!* And Bo might have. Even she could have been killed. They didn't leave witnesses, did they?

"Didn't your years of study give you that?"

"What? Oh. Yes, in a way. I certainly learned things."

"Your work is good." He started the engine.

"I have technique, just no … passion." That word was starting to haunt her.

He pulled out. "You can find passion in our home studio. Supposing, of course, we have one."

There, finally, a crack in his assurance. "What if I'm just lost?"

"You're not lost, Alexis. You're on a journey leading somewhere. I only hope it's with me."

Another day she would experience the tranquility he conveyed. "If you gave up PR, you'd be one heck of a guru. Or motivational speaker. Or shrink."

He laughed. "I have no intention of changing careers. One of us needs to hold the steady course."

"Does it bother you that I'm not steady?"

"Nothing about you bothers me."

"That's nice of you."

"I mean it, Alexis. Lots of people thought I'd found a perfect match in Kendyl. But when I saw you, I just knew."

"Thanks for your patience."

"There's no room for doubt in marriage. If you need to rule someone else out, so be it."

What if she couldn't rule Bo out?

"Just be honest." His voice thickened. "I know that goes without saying."

Did it? How honest was it to keep something so big from him? If unburdening kept John Helm from doing his job, Bo might not survive another attack. Shock threatened to overwhelm her again. What would Jeffrey tell her to do? *Don't even wonder.* She chewed her nails as she hadn't in years.

At the rehab facility, Exi hugged her mom a long time, careful of her collarbone. More than with Jeffrey, she longed to pour out the day's horror. But, even if she hadn't been ordered to keep silent, she would never terrify her mother that way. Not in her fragile state. Maybe not in any state.

Sensing her distress, or by some miracle, Rhonda said, "It's all right."

"Mom!"

When the words locked up again, Rhonda rolled her eyes with frustration.

"It's coming." Exi beamed at Jeffrey. "Did you hear?"

"I'm right beside you." His dimples deepened.

It was sincere, but she couldn't help wondering how Bo would have reacted if he'd been here instead of home with beaten flesh and broken bones. "Jeffrey, would you mind giving me a few minutes with her?"

"Not at all. I'll confirm our reservation."

As soon as he left, Exi took her mother's hand. "I have to tell you something, but please don't get upset."

Rhonda searched her face.

"We've put the engagement on hold." Before the dismay overtook her mom, Exi rushed on. "I'm seeing someone else, but Jeffrey's not that worried. He believes I'll come to my senses."

Worry became puzzlement.

"His name is Bo Corrigan. He's the star of *Windows and Doors.*"

Her mom mimicked a cell phone, then tapped her hand.

"Oh. Good idea." Exi took out her phone and searched for Bo. She showed the images to her mother. "Grace said he accepted the role for much less than he could have, because he doesn't want to be cast for his looks alone. It's a complicated, meaningful play. Have you seen it?"

Nodding, her mom enlarged Bo's face. She stared a long time, then slow blinked and handed back the phone.

"He's the one who gave me the Albuca spiralis."

Rhonda laughed and tapped her temple, then cleared her throat at the sound of Jeffrey's footsteps approaching. The rest of their visit included him. Then they had dinner at Peter Luger Steak House. Jeffrey told her about the new client he'd signed.

"I thought we'd splurge tonight since I'll be out of town the next three days working this."

"I'm happy for you, happier for Mr. Jenks. He couldn't be in better hands."

Jeffrey's excitement was contagious, their conversation as effortless as always. She had so compartmentalized the two halves of her day that when Jeffrey dropped her at her place and drove off, she almost screamed at the black SUV zooming up to the curb. She crossed her arms and glared at John Helm when he got out. "What are you doing here? Go away."

With one big muscular arm he turned her toward her building entrance and said, "Unlock it."

"Excuse me? My house. You answer."

"I need to secure you while you pack and come with me."

"What?" she half shrieked.

"We have not found the assailant who held you in the park. Liam's afraid they'll use you to get to Bo."

Her heart thumped. "How would they know to do that? Just because he grabbed me doesn't mean he knows me."

"Not because he grabbed you. Because he isn't Russian."

"What?"

"Just do what I'm asking."

"Prove it."

Now he fixed her with questioning eyes.

"Prove they know who I am and where I live."

John took out his phone. He pressed a number and, when it connected, said, "Ms. Murphy would like confirmation that she's in danger." He held the phone out.

She took it. "Who is this?"

"Miss Murphy." No mistaking Liam's voice. "Please do what Johnny says. For all our sakes."

The shaking was back. She glared at John as she slapped the

phone back in his palm. "Where are we going?"

"Eileen's. It's under surveillance."

"Wonderful. I'm spending the night?"

"You'll need to stay until we find him."

Her mouth fell open. "First: I'm running my mother's store and can't just go AWOL. Second: What about my roommates?"

"We'll watch the store. Your roommates are fine. This is a specific threat."

"Lucky me." She flounced up the stairs but stopped outside her door. "What do I tell people?"

"You're going away with Bo?"

"That'll go over great with Jeffrey."

His brow furrowed.

"Never mind. I'll figure it out myself." When he moved to follow her inside, she said, "You can't come in looking like that."

"Like what?"

"All hard commando. Make your face soft like normal people."

He had marginal success, so she opened the door. Suz and Treya were splitting a Ben and Jerry's ice cream carton and paused their spoons. "Hi, guys. Suz, Treya, this is John. Bo got injured and I need to go, um, over there for a while."

"Injured?" Suz said.

"Yeah, so I'm staying at Eileen's. Tonight and, you know, maybe longer." With that terrible attempt at evasion, she made her way to the bedroom. Of course Treya squeezed in and closed the door. They could hear John and Suz conversing, which was kind of surprising since Suz was typically tongue-tied and John a Neanderthal.

Treya braced her hips. "What is going on?"

"Just what I said. John is Bo's bodyguard. He came to get me."

"Just cuz that sexy pants is hurt doesn't mean you go live with him."

Exi pulled her rolling suitcase off the shelf. "Eileen can't manage Bo alone."

"She's got that housekeeper, the Dodo."

Exi swung it onto the bed. "All I know is Bo's asking me to come."

"You said Jeffrey gets a fair chance. How is it fair if you're sleeping with the other guy?"

Exi pulled the zipper noisily. "I'm not sleeping with Bo. Eileen has a four story townhouse full of rooms."

"Really?" Treya tucked her chin back. "Maybe I should come keep you out of trouble. Might get my own ice cream that way too."

"Everything's fine except Bo's broken ribs, so cut him some slack." She loaded the suitcase with nice, comfortable things to work in, nice things to sleep in.

"Uh-huh." Treya said.

"What if there's a fire alarm? Like at Grace and Devin's. Want me traipsing out in my Mickey Mouse T-shirt?"

"You still have that?"

"No. Well, maybe in a corner of a drawer somewhere."

"You crack me up."

She tossed in underwear and jewelry, grabbed her makeup bag and electric toothbrush. Eileen's guest bathroom had fine-quality shampoos and body wash, lotions, and everything else she might need. Last she stuffed in her down pillow.

"You don't think she's got pillows?"

"She doesn't have my pillow." And she'd be squeezing it with all her might when the nightmares hit.

Treya leaned back against the door and folded her arms. "You're not telling me something."

Exi straightened and looked at her, eyes brimming. "I will, okay? When I can."

"You tell me right now if that man out there is trouble."

"He's not. He's Bo's bodyguard."

"Corrigan's that famous?"

"I guess."

"How'd he break his ribs?"

Exi opened her mouth and closed it, furious that she was expected to lie to her friends. "Something happened today, and Bo got hurt."

"Were you with him?"

"Yes."

"Some bodyguard."

"Trust me, without John, you might be seeing us on the news." In body bags. Exi shoved the case shut and zipped it.

"Is it some terrorist thing?

Exi stopped and stared. "Good grief. Does he look like a terrorist?"

"He looks like G.I. Joe."

"He's ex-military."

"But I didn't mean him."

"This isn't terrorists. Not the way you mean." Please God don't let it be. "Now stop asking. I'll tell you when I can. Maybe in a day or two."

"Uh-huh."

"Please don't tell Suz. She can't keep a secret, and it will worry her sick to think of Bo in da—" She gulped it back too late.

"Danger?"

Exi tipped her head back, eyes closed.

"Okay." Treya relented. "But you call me every day. You don't call, I tell Jeffrey. Or the police. I tell your cop brother, Sully, who you should be telling already."

"No. I'll call you. But if I forget, call me before anyone else." Exi dragged the suitcase to the door.

Treya squeezed her in a fierce hug. "You be safe."

Her throat constricted at the thought her friends were safer without her. She pulled her suitcase into the main room, gave Suz a quick hug, then went with John into the hall.

He said, "You'll have to carry your bag. I need my hands free."

Exi sighed. "What's one more piece of baggage?"

He scanned the street, then motioned her into the SUV. The same driver glanced her way and nodded, then pulled into traffic. A thousand questions swirled, but she doubted either man would give her straight answers. The respite Jeffrey provided was gone, and all the fear and misgivings churned again.

Where had things gone wrong? What was the turning point, the one thing she could have avoided? She refused to say Bo. Her hands kneaded each other as they moved through the sinister city. "Is this vehicle bulletproof?"

"It's made with bullet-resistant materials," John said. "And you're not in view back there."

Since he was in the answer mode, she said, "What did you mean, he's not Russian?"

One tick, two tick, three. "It means groups are joining forces, historical enemies banding together." He swallowed. "That's bad for Liam, bad for New York. Hell, it's bad for the world."

She started to shake. At Eileen's, John remained vigilant, but once inside he took her suitcase, which was good, since she was dead on her feet and they climbed all the way to the fourth floor. "Why up here?"

"We have surveillance in this apartment."

"Oh no. I'm not doing that."

"We've turned off your bedroom and bath."

"And Bo's?"

"Uh … for privacy, use your room."

She clenched her fists. "I'm not sleeping with Bo."

John led her to a wine-red room bearing black-and-white photos of interesting New Yorkers in recognizable locations. He swung her case onto the bed as if it held nothing but her pillow, then started to leave.

"Wait. Sound or video?"

"No sound."

She sank onto the bed.

He studied her. "The doctor left some Valium with Bo. Take it if you need to."

She blinked at him.

"I'm sorry you saw what you did today."

Surely that wasn't today. She covered her face with her hands and nodded. When she took them down, he was gone. She unzipped her suitcase and pulled out her pillow, then she curled up in a ball and prayed to get through this without losing her mind … or soul. What did that road paved with good intentions look like if not the driveway through Eileen's gate?

Grace said it was dangerous to think Bo needed her. Clearly it was worse that he did. And yet …

12

The next morning, Grace prepared to leave town with greater reluctance than ever before. She looked at Devin holding a sleep-tousled Mattie as if they couldn't believe she would board a plane and fly away from them. Her heart lurched. "You're not helping."

"We'll be fine once you've gone, but we're pouting until then."

"Very mature."

He looked at Mattie with a distended lower lip his daughter mimicked.

"Devin, I swear." But she couldn't help laughing. "Skype me every morning, and if she starts talking without me, I want it on video." She kissed her baby's head. "Even better is to wait until Mommy's home, sweetie. We can't let Daddy have all the fun."

Mattie climbed into her arms and tucked her head over her mother's shoulder. She didn't need words to express this. "I know, baby girl. But Daddy's bringing you to Atlanta, so I'm going to see you in just three days." She frowned at her husband. "You sure about that?"

"It's what, an hour from Madison?"

"Yes. But every mile will feel like ten."

"They're not coming to see us, Grace. If we can make peace with your family, you'll have that weight off."

"I'm at peace with them."

"You know what I mean. I'm going to stand up and take whatever your dad dishes out, and we'll introduce their granddaughter. If anyone can melt a heart it's Mattie."

"I don't know, conceived in S-I-N as she was."

"Well, at least we'll know."

She sighed. "I know you're right."

"We won't meet at the house if I can help it."

"Good luck with that."

Her parents didn't know what she experienced there as a young teen one horrible afternoon, but Devin did.

He caressed Mattie's head. "We have a good-luck charm."

"The best." She kissed her daughter's fingers. "Do me a favor and check in with Exi, will you? I tried to call yesterday but couldn't reach her."

"I will. Maybe I'll go by the store and see how she's doing."

"She'd like that. So would Mattie."

He circled them both in his arms and whispered, "Can't I take you to the airport?"

She whispered back, "My team will be here any minute. It's better for Mattie not to think of me flying away. Please don't let her be sad."

"We'll be just fine." He kissed her mouth and Mattie did too.

"Thank you." That meant so much. "If I didn't owe them for being so gracious during the crisis …"

"I know. I'm just giving you a hard time. Go dazzle your fans. And you never know"—he raised his eyebrows—"you might come home to a jungle, Jane."

"I'll hold that thought." She kissed him. "Don't forget Exi."

"I'm on it."

She braced herself to walk out the door, making sure nothing in her manner upset her baby girl. Between Devin, Eddie, and Alison, along with Eileen, Sondra, Cate, and Mia, Mattie might hardly miss her mama. She'd tell herself that every minute.

Thank God Devin could get away and join her for part of the tour. With gratitude, she went out to meet her publicity team. She could do this. Truly she could.

Exi groaned when horror woke her up again. At least this time there was daylight in the windows. She pressed her palms to her eyes but still saw the blade sinking in. She grabbed her phone and did a news search. There it was. "Knifing at Prospect Park."

Knifing. The word slashed in with *Psycho* music. She could not imagine going back there, even though it was where she also had her first kiss with Bo—right before they were attacked. Her wonderful day with him, shattered. His beautiful body pummeled. She shuddered.

"Police are investigating. Anyone with information ..." She couldn't read more. She knew exactly what happened. *Stay quiet so John can be about his work.*

And then John's heart-stopping, *It's bad for Liam, bad for New York*—and yeah, for the heck of it, let's throw in the world. Bad people joining forces. Liam and Bo in the middle of it. Now she was too.

Still, why not tell the cops that? Generations of Murphys were police officers, including Sully on mounted patrol. She could call her brother right now, tell him confidentially, if not for Liam's deceptively reasonable request. Why couldn't John Helm go to them himself?

A thought occurred, and she did another search. He was probably scrubbed off every database—but then he came up. John Helm Security Services, Inc. A dynamic website. And apparently legit, by the high-level testimonials. Her panic lessened. Liam wasn't using rogue soldiers to go after the threat.

She could have guessed that by the way John handled her misbehavior. A thug might have clubbed her like the ex-boyfriend who stole her instruments. But, hey, she'd never been in this position before. She climbed out of bed, washed up and dressed, taking John at his word that no cameras recorded her.

She went to the next room and knocked. No answer. She opened it just to see if Bo slept inside. It wasn't a bedroom. It had no furniture, only freestanding frames arranged throughout like a gallery. She walked in and came face-to-face with Bo, no, a life-size image of him. Scratch that. These were bigger than life, though not as humongous as spectaculars. And they weren't ads. They were stills of him acting. The two she recognized were from *Windows and Doors* and *A Gentlemen's Guide to Love and Murder.* She moved to that one and heard his high clear *My Sibella …*

A shiver ran down her back. If he was this obsessed with himself, how would he be with her? Alarm bells joined the singing in her head, yet his voice continued. *I love her just that way.* And yesterday in the park. *I'm in love with you.* People joked that way, like I'm in love with chocolate or New York or some celebrity. But he hadn't joked. She heard a noise and spun.

"Exi?" Rumpled and wrung out, Bo looked exceptionally hot. "I'm ecstatic to see you but … what are you doing here?"

"John goose-stepped me out of my place last night and stashed me in your spare room."

"Why?" He limped closer.

"The other guy is still out there. Liam thinks they might use me to get you."

He made a harsh noise. "Why all this now?"

"Vengeance for Karkov."

"I had nothing to do with that accident."

"They think Liam did. You're an easier target." She started to tell him about John's other concern.

But Bo slumped. "First Grace, now you."

"What about Grace?"

He thrust his fingers into his hair. "The first time they came after me, they found her instead. The trauma triggered premature labor."

So that was the dirty laundry Grace wouldn't air. "I didn't know you were part of all that."

"They constructed the news release to create the least fallout."

"Leaving you out?"

"My crashing on Grace's futon would have looked worse for her."

"They'd have thought Mattie was yours?"

"Lots of ways to twist things."

She lowered her fists. "Were you and Grace …"

"Never."

She saw the truth in his eyes. More relieved than she let on, Exi looked back into the gallery, her heart rate increasing again.

Before she could ask, Bo said, "I know how this looks." He took it in with her. "Vanity of vanities."

"You think?"

He smelled musky when he came up next to her with a hint of mint that suggested he'd brushed or gargled. "This studio is where I remember the roles, play them again in my head, what I learned from each, and how I could have done it better."

Oh. Like her own portfolio, the early works developing into better ones. "Why are they so big?"

"So I feel small."

She slid a look and saw he was serious.

"That's what I've done, but can I do more? Do better? It's motivation."

It sounded more like torment. She wandered through to a younger section. These shots made her smile. Bo had it even then.

"Barb was part of these." He stood so long he seemed to disappear into the images, then rasped, "Sometimes I think she'll walk in, laughing at all the leads they keep throwing at me." His eyes filled with tears. "You know what I thought yesterday? When he held that blade to my cheek?"

She quivered inside.

"Do it. I want to be more than this face."

"Oh, Bo." She wrapped her arms around him before remembering his ribs. "Sorry." She tried to pull back, but he kept her there.

He rested his chin on her head. "I keep waiting for the loss to ease up, but all time does is make everyone else forget." He looked at the images again. "I won't. I frame each one for her to examine. How'd I do, Barb? What would you have brought to it?"

Exi's eyes swam.

He stroked her back. "I come in here to remember and to make myself go on. I'm twenty-eight, and I don't know how to be without my sister."

And she'd thought him self-absorbed? Exi stepped back and said, "Just a sec." She went into her room, got her pillow, and rejoined him. "When I was little I had a sleepover with a friend whose parents got into a fight, the kind with fists and slapping. I was standing in the hallway hugging my pillow when her older brother snuck us out the back door. Now I equate it with safety even though, at twenty-six, I'm *pretty* sure it has no magical powers."

Bo lowered his gaze to the pillow snuggled against her, then looked into her eyes. "How do you know it doesn't?"

Her heart soared. "I guess I don't. Want to hold it and see?"

He drew her in with the flimsy pillow between them and kissed her mouth. This time it was jazz, thick and smoky and herself on sax. "Why do I hear music when we do this?"

"What do you hear?"

"Now? Gato Barbieri. 'The Woman I Remember.'"

He slid his hands around her head and kissed her so slow and deep and long they sank to their knees as electric guitar and high-hat cymbal added the rhythm of her heartbeat. One sliver of sanity slipped in. "Bo?"

He tangled his hands in her hair and took her lips again.

"They can see."

"What?" He pressed his forehead to hers.

"The surveillance."

He searched her, confused.

"John said there are cameras on this floor. They turned off my room, but the rest …"

He jerked his head back. "What? When did that happen?"

"If you don't know, I'm guessing yesterday. After those guys attacked us."

He looked around the room with murder in his eyes. "Turn it

off."

"There's no sound."

He got painfully to his feet and raised a meaningful finger. She stood up, fighting a laugh that might not go over in his current mood. He gripped her wrist and hobbled out of that room and into hers, pacing with growing agitation. "What exactly did he say?"

"Sit down, Bo. You're going to aggravate something."

He lowered himself to the foot of the bed. "Tell me what he said." His voice was tight with pain or anger.

She clutched the pillow to her stomach that was starting to ache. "He wanted me all the way up here because this floor has surveillance."

"Liam's guys are out there watching what goes on in here?"

"Except my room." She tucked hair behind her ear. "It's a professional security service. I'm sure they're—you know—discreet." She brought up the website and showed him.

He handed her phone back. "I want to see Eileen." He tried to stand, then pressed his hand to his side with a grimace. When he took his hand away, blood had seeped through his T-shirt.

She bent toward him. "Let me see."

He groaned. "Please don't do that."

She lifted his shirt, too worried to care if he saw her cleavage. His torso looked like angry storm clouds, purple, black, with hints of yellow. The bandage was soaked in blood. "Wait here. I'll get Sondra."

"And Eileen. I want answers."

She rushed down, found Sondra in the kitchen and sent her up to Bo, then searched for Eileen's room. Peeking through the cracked door, she saw her sleeping. As she turned to leave, the woman said, "What is it?"

"Bo's not doing well. He wanted to see you."

She looked annoyed. "Thinks he can summon me, hmm?"

"He just heard about the cameras."

"Cameras?"

"You don't know?"

"It's too early for riddles." She pushed up to her elbows.

"Don't worry. I'll take care of it." Exi practically ran up the stairs. In Bo's living area she raised and pointed to her phone, certain they'd have her number.

Seconds later it rang. John said, "What's up?"

"You better get here and explain your surveillance before Bo goes ballistic. Eileen's not happy either."

"I'll send someone."

"Sure. Any underling will do."

Silence.

"You invaded their privacy without saying so. Maybe in your world that's okay, but not in ours."

"I'm not working for Bo. Or Eileen."

"Liam ordered it?"

Silence.

"Did he tell you to keep it secret?"

"It's hardly that with you informed."

She sighed. "I have to go. Just … handle it, okay?"

"That's what I do." He ended the call.

Exi released a long breath. Sondra had moved Bo back to his room. As they passed in the doorway the woman said, "I changed the bandage but I don't like what I see. He took some nasty hits."

"The guy had steel-toe boots and maybe brass knuckles."

Sondra softened with concern. "I suspected something. Fists don't leave such sharp bruises."

Exi went into the room, modernly furnished within the stately architecture. It worked well to her artist's eye with the ebony furniture and yellow upholstered sling chairs. Then the fact it was a bedroom—Bo's bedroom—slipped in. It's a sickroom, she told herself before any of the nuns could start yacking in her ear.

And it was. Bo sat semiprone and gray, swallowing pills with a glass of water. He set that on the side table and sighed. "This isn't how I start a relationship."

"You have relationships?"

His gaze canted up. "Don't I?"

"My source says serial seductions."

"Grace?"

Exi sat down in a sling chair. "She said you're highly skilled. Practically irresistible." Why was she poking at him?

"This is different."

"Is it?"

"It's supposed to be." He reached back and rubbed his neck. "But I keep breaking the rules."

"I think I started it."

"Oh, you definitely started it. Just being here."

"I had no choice. John Helm's an autocrat. At least he's coming to explain himself."

"Really?"

"I told him he had no business spying without telling you. Or Eileen."

His mouth quirked up. "Does Jeffrey know you have this side?"

"I haven't had much need of it with Jeffrey."

"Except at the hospital."

"True. It did kind of slip out there. But only because I got frustrated."

"How is your mom?"

"Oh. Wow. You don't know." Exi clasped her hands. "She talked. Three whole words together. She said, 'It's all right.' Just like that." His eyes shone, so she rushed on. "Then I told her about you and that I'm seeing both of you."

His brow furrowed. "Did it worry her?"

How sweet that it worried him. "Not when I showed her your picture."

He groaned.

"Not just how you look. She brought it up big and looked inside. I know she gets it."

"Gets what?"

"That you're not only your face."

"How did she get that from the picture?"

"The same way she instantly knew other guys were bad for me."

"Am I bad for you?"

"She'll wait and see. That's a point in your favor."

"How many does Jeffrey have?"

"A lot. He's very helpful. And generous and thoughtful."

He growled, "I'd have a better chance of that if I were Barb."

"Your mom did a number telling you what she chose your dads for."

"It didn't need saying. I've always been a brat. My mother was told more than once to do something with my reckless creativity. A PC way of saying get your holy terror under control."

"It doesn't sound like you had many rules."

"No. There's a school of thought that no discipline is good discipline. She played the psychologist card and told them where to stick it." He canted her a look. "Thankfully my mischief was not the malicious sort."

Exi made a little space between her finger and thumb. "I might be a tiny bit mischievous myself."

"The nuns didn't cure you?"

"Oh, well, they kind of loved me after my brothers."

Amusement filled Bo's eyes, replaced by heat. "You need to stop being so adorable. I can't keep my hands off when you're cute. And I vowed to do that or die."

"Die?" Her voice rose.

"Figure of speech." He looked grim again. "It isn't easy. It might be the hardest thing I've done."

Why did that mean more than Jeffrey's boundaries? Because Bo struggled and Jeffrey didn't? They were different kinds of men. She could appreciate both. But she responded harder to Bo. That couldn't drive her decision or she'd be right back where she'd been too many times before.

"Where'd you go?" His voice was low and soft.

"Sorry. I . . ."

"Come here."

She didn't dare. He was too magnetic. He drew the iron in her blood.

"Come on." Wincing, he shifted over on the bed. "I can't leave this until Commando Doc gives the word, but Nurse Dodo never said you couldn't join me."

"Cameras?"

"A pox on them. We'll be Tristan and Iseult and lay a sword between us."

"Aren't they the ones who drank a love potion and died of broken hearts?"

"How do you know that and not *Romeo and Juliet*?"

"I saw the movie."

"Then you know their resistance was futile and they sacrificed all for love." He reached over and selected a song, Ryan Adams's "Stay with Me." Bo sang along, love sending him into the flame.

So not fair. "Stop." She turned when Sondra came sideways through the door with a bed tray holding breakfast for two.

"I'm not climbing four flights three times, so you'll have to share a tray."

With a Cheshire grin, Bo patted the bed again.

"I'll hold my plate." Exi eyed the crepes with a creamy sauce and caramel drizzle. Moan-worthy, she was sure.

"There's coffee, juice, and fruit to share."

With a sigh, Exi joined Bo. She had to get right up close for the tray to fit over them, and a sneaking suspicion crept in. When the door closed, she said, "Did you enlist her?"

"I told her I'd like to eat with you before you had to leave. Since I'm confined here, she improvised."

"You have everyone enthralled, don't you?"

"I know I'm enthralled." He pressed his fork into the crepe and brought the bite to her mouth.

She imagined feeding from his fork and shook her head.

"One bite." He nudged it closer.

"I have my own."

"It's no more than you've allowed Jeffrey, I'm sure."

Jeffrey had never attempted to feed her. He would consider it unnecessary, maybe even demeaning. He was all about respecting what people could do. But this wasn't about ability. She looked at the bite, looked at Bo, called on the archangels and took the offering. The sweet, cheesy crepe sent everything else from her mind until Bo leaned in and kissed her.

The music playing became a jungle drum. Or was it her heart? "Bo."

"What if there's only today?"

Her mind flashed to yesterday's attack. "I don't want to think that way."

"What's the guarantee? One day you're healthy, the next cancer's hijacked your cells. Or someone pulls a knife." His voice rasped.

She'd envisioned that all night. They could have had their throats cut.

His slid his fingers into the hair behind her ear. "Stay with me. It doesn't have to be physical."

"But it would. I have no self-control."

He closed his eyes as if that pained him. "I want time with you. Just … time."

He was reeling too. Maybe worse. Probably way worse. He'd had the knife to his face. He got the broken bones and bruises. "I'd be letting Mom down if I don't open the store. There are orders to fill, plants that need care. She's never missed a day, except for planned vacations."

His brow furrowed. His jaw rippled.

"Bo?"

"I want to ask you to make this a vacation, this one day." His gaze bored into her. "I want to say don't leave my side. Let me show you how I feel. Let me make you feel it too." He swallowed. "But I won't say any of that. You have a family that loves you, and you're right to put them first."

She stroked his forearm. "It's just I promised to be there when she couldn't."

"And you're a promise keeper."

"Kind of fanatically."

He brushed her lips with his thumb as melancholy darkened his eyes. She felt it like a fog descending. She wished she could fix his sorrows, but she couldn't bring his sister back or make his mother love him. Or get him out of trouble. "Nothing we do here will take away what's wrong."

"You're not speaking from experience."

"From my own."

"Not with me." He closed his hand around the nape of her neck, his mouth so close she breathed his breath.

"None of your experience has made it go away."

"None of that has been with you."

"I'm just a girl from Flatbush, Bo. There's nothing special here."

"You're so wrong."

"I know what people think. To friends and family I'm sweet and helpless. To guys I'm a body."

"Your body is spectacular. I'm not going to pretend I don't see that. But I can have any *body*. You've lit something inside me. And it's you, not your assets."

"You don't know me. We've hardly scratched the surface."

"That's why I need time. I want to know your story, your dreams, your longings. Every part I see makes me want more."

He was speaking her own desire to understand him, because his real self called to her more strongly than anyone she'd known, even people she'd known for years. "Devin says you get whatever you want because you're Bo Corrigan. It might be interesting to prove him wrong."

"It might, if I cared what Devin thought."

He must care more than he said, because she sensed him letting up. They ate in silence. Every time she thought of something to say, it seemed trivial. Given the extremity of their interaction so far, normalcy was trivial.

Finally he said, "What time do you open shop?"

"Ten."

"Will you come back here after?" Bo tried to lift the tray and grimaced.

Exi slid it to the lower corner of the bed and repositioned herself cross-legged facing him. "Depends how well John does his job. If he catches this dude, I'm safe at my place."

"I don't know if I want success or failure."

She frowned. "Why won't he work with the police?"

"What makes you think he doesn't?"

"If he did, there would have been—oh, you know—sirens and police officers."

"Liam works directly with law enforcement. John is known to them."

"Dirty cops?"

Bo cocked his head. "Why would you think that?"

"Because my brother's an officer and I'm pretty sure that's not how it works."

"It's how it works when your enterprise overlaps law enforcement and the underworld."

"I don't understand."

"It's kind of the devil you know versus actual evil."

She studied Bo's face. "So NYPD lets Liam operate because he keeps worse scum away?"

"Something like that. But not only NYPD. It's federal."

That would take some digesting. As Bo eased back into the pillows, she saw his fresh T-shirt had a stain blooming. "You're bleeding again."

He craned around to see, then fell back. "Sondra's worried about my spleen. No one else seems to be. Liam says he's been thumped worse boxing."

"Isn't he a joy."

"He's old school."

She huffed. "Plenty of young guys are just the same. I'm glad you're not."

"You're making assumptions."

"Am I wrong?"

He closed his eyes. "At least half the youth camps were team building. Peace and harmony."

"Could be worse."

"Weren't many fistfights." He sounded groggy. "No knives. Lots to be said for that." His hand slid to the bed. "Lie down with me."

"No."

"Be my magic pillow. I promise I won't touch."

Because he hadn't mocked her pillow, she stretched out on her side and rested a hand on his chest. "How bad does it hurt?"

"Less with your hand there."

He seemed overly warm. "I'm serious."

"Major league. If I could stop breathing, I would."

"Don't say that." She pushed up on her elbow.

"I don't mean that way." He pulled her back down.

"I think you should see a real doctor."

"If Liam sent that one, he was the best for the situation."

She scowled. "You think your best interests are his highest priority?"

"Are you crazy? I'm a very small fish. A minnow."

"Then why are you going along?"

He spread a hand. "I started it."

"By gambling?"

He roused and looked at her. "When you gamble dangerously, there's a high motivation to continue until you get your buns out of the fire. Not a good strategy, it appears."

"That's a revelation. But why gamble dangerously?" It was truly a concept she'd never understand. Risk as pleasure? Please.

"You won't understand if I tell you."

"You can say it anyway."

He closed his eyes. "Everything's too easy."

"You want things hard?"

The shrug made him wince. "Wasn't easy for Barb."

He clearly meant it, as if whatever pain he caused himself he deserved. "It would be good to stop punishing yourself for what happened to her. You didn't cause her cancer."

Bo said nothing. The blood was spreading in the bandage. His breathing sounded shallow.

She sat up. "I'll tell Sondra you're bleeding again."

No response. Maybe he slept. She studied his beautiful face. No one would believe it if she told them what his looks cost him. Except Grace. She'd bet anything Grace knew all about it.

13

Exi's words went round in Bo's head. He wasn't punishing himself. He just didn't deserve better than Barb got. She'd been passed over for the lead in her own life. Not even a callback. Her genuine talent snuffed out, while his flourished. Mindless favoritism from fate and humanity alike—including the lovely Faye Corrigan.

It had been so subtle their mother might not have realized it herself. Dr. Corrigan could not be so shallow, could she? The crusader for body-image-challenged individuals? And yet her imperfectly shaped daughter missed the cut. He knew it hurt because Barb never mentioned the way their mother's eyes lit for him, even when he acted up. What was a good girl to do?

He hated himself for not seeing it sooner. He could have been a better brother.

Faye had a complete genetic profile for both her offspring. The only thing not included were names. He and Barb had imagined their dads in countless incarnations. Hers would be the one who accepted contact, they decided, being a man of character. But if his genetics contributed to Barb's early death, he might no longer walk this world either.

Bo ground his teeth. His own dad surely thrived, indestructible. Had the guy seen ads and commercials, even those early movies, and said, "That's my son. Has to be." Was he proud? Disdainful? Indifferent.

Out of the blue, he thought of Devin, who'd found his mother a year and a half ago. A strange parallel, except Devin grew up with a man who'd been there for him in every way. At the Bressards' televised wedding, Bo saw a bond between father and son that more than made up for their missing biological connection.

Eddie had been a compass for Devin to steer by while Bo Corrigan's rudderless ship floundered into rocks and shoals. In the years since Barb died, he'd been pushing every limit, breaking every rule. With Grace he'd found some small serenity, her friendship a calm bay with a solid pier. Until he ruined it.

Now there was Exi. What he felt for her consumed him like the potion drunk by the doomed lovers Tristan and Iseult. One look sealed his fate—contrived as that may be. Clichés existed because they happened. He had drunk the draft, and there was no return. "If I have drunk love and death, well then, come death."

He stopped fighting and slipped into the painkiller's embrace. That combat doc might have no bedside manner, but his drugs behaved just fine.

Optimistically, Exi brought her luggage downstairs. She'd take it to the flower shop … and haul it back here if John didn't settle things today. But a dose of positivity was better than a spoonful of sugar to make this medicine go down.

She tiptoed to the kitchen, found Sondra at the stove, and told her about Bo's wound. Then she said, "Could you please ask Eileen to call me when she wakes up? I'll leave my number here." She started to write on a notepad near a potted red miniature rose.

"You can see her now." Sondra delicately removed a crepe from the pan. "She's in the breakfast room."

"Oh. Okay."

Eileen sat at the table, dressed and alert, but no less prickly by her expression.

"I'm sorry for bothering you. Again. I just wanted to say one thing before I go. Maybe we shouldn't make a big deal of the cameras. If it keeps someone from sneaking in and killing Bo, that's good, right?" The mood he was in, he might not even defend himself.

"Don't be overdramatic." Eileen sipped her tea.

"Yeah." Exi crossed her arms. "That wasn't us in the park with homicidal hitmen and a dark-ops-assassin bodyguard. What reason could I have for drama?" She was no less surprised by her outburst than Eileen.

Instead of snapping back, Eileen seemed invigorated. "You have had a time."

Exi tried with everything in her to block the memory of that knife sinking into a man's side, even a bad man.

Eileen's hand trembled when she set the cup in the saucer. "I've seen a lot of things, but that doesn't diminish what you've been through. I'm afraid you won't ever be the same, not entirely."

Tears welled, the crepe aroma cloying. "I need to go. Thank you for letting me stay the night."

"You're welcome here. With or without Bo. Or John Helm's heavy hand."

"Nothing personal, but this isn't my happy place. I'm going back to my normal life whether I'm the same or not."

With that inelegant parting, Exi pulled her suitcase out the door. She saw no guards or SUVs that stood out from the traffic and pedestrians. Good or bad, that was hard to say. She headed for the subway, which she took to Flatbush. She let herself into Every Bloomin' Thing with a sense of relief. No scary dudes in sight. She managed a laugh at that.

She put her purse and suitcase in the office. Then she watered, clipped, and fed the plants, before taking delivery of an order. She hadn't seen that anything new was expected but made room for the interesting additions. Having two smiling friends of her mother's waiting when she unlocked the doors raised her spirits more than they could know.

"Come see what just came in."

They wended to the potted-plant rack near the back wall. The women laughed at the oddities.

"I need to find the invoice to know how to price them."

"Hmm," Ann Mabry said. "Rhonda isn't usually so adventurous."

"That's true," Exi bit her lip. "I'll have to ask about it because—guess what—she might answer. She talked last night." Their joyous exclamations warmed her heart like a big, fuzzy hug. "It was only three words, but that means it's coming, right?"

"Oh, yes indeed. We'll pass the good news down the prayer chain."

"Thanks."

After they left, Jeffrey called to tell her how it was going with the new client. He sounded so buoyant it cheered her even more. She might have been rude to Eileen but what she said was true. Here was her life as she knew it. "Seems like a great fit, Jeffrey."

"Yes, I think so," he agreed, then, "Sorry, Alexis, Simon's coming back in. I have to go now."

For the rest of the morning she arranged flowers and waited on customers. She shared her mom's improvement with everyone who asked, and each time her assurance grew that it *would* be all right—for both of them. When the store emptied for a while, she went into the office and checked the computer. No order for the plants that had arrived first thing this morning. Could they be like the Albuca spiralis?

She texted Bo: *More crazy fun plants?*

He replied: *My mission: to find every odd plant you've never seen.*

They're so great. Thank you.

I wish you were here.

I do too.

Come either way.

She thought for just a minute. *Okay. I'll see you soon.*

Can't be soon enough.

She sent him a heart. He sent a gritted teeth emoji. She laughed, then pressed the phone to her chest with grateful tears that his mood had lifted. If the rest of it wasn't so horrifying, she'd be ecstatic.

When the bell at the door jingled, she left the office to find Devin in the store. "Hi there. Flowers for Grace?"

"No, she left on tour this morning. I came to see you. I was going to bring Mattie over, but Cate and Mia kidnapped her yet again for catalog photos, or so they claim."

Exi laughed. "They'll sell a million dresses."

"No doubt." He looked around. "How are things going?"

Oh, the things she could say. She spread her arms. The front window exploded. Something stung her right before Devin pulled her down with him. Three loud bangs and shattering pottery kept them on the floor.

"Counter." Devin pushed. "Get behind the counter."

She had barely started crawling when the door flew open. Over Devin's shoulder, she saw John Helm.

"Are you hit?" His voice was low and hard.

She shook her head.

He looked at Devin. "Jeffrey?"

Pushing up, he said, "I'm her cousin. Devin Bressard."

"Get her into the office."

Devin pulled her up and started moving. Just like that? He didn't wonder who John was to be bossing them around? He closed the door and rasped, "You're bleeding."

"I am?" She looked where he pointed and gripped her arm.

"What the hell is this? Since when does East Flatbush have drive-by shootings?"

"That was a shooting?"

"What did you think?"

She slumped. "I didn't have time to think."

"Let me see that arm." She parted her grip for him to study the gash. "I think a bullet did this."

Her legs gave out and he sat her on the desk as a fist pounded the locked door. "It's John."

Devin shot her a look.

"Yes, open it."

John's expression could not be sharper if he'd used a whetstone. "Let's go." He hustled them out of the store and into the SUV. It took off. This was starting to feel like déjà vu.

The bodyguard reached past his shoulder toward Devin. "John Helm."

Devin shook his hand. "You're police?"

"Private security."

"For Exi? What's going on?"

"I work for Liam O'Hare."

Devin sat back, a picture of puzzlement. "What does Eileen's brother have to do with my cousin? And why is someone shooting at her?"

Blood was streaming down her arm in spite of her hand clamped there. And now the pain hit. She bit her lip. John handed her a handkerchief like the one he'd used yesterday to wipe the dead man's blood. She pressed it to the wound. Clearing the tightness in her throat she managed, "Did you get him?"

"He took a body shot. He won't get far."

"Who?" Devin barked.

Exi's voice shook. "The people after Bo."

For three whole seconds, her cousin digested that. Then his face went stone cold. He said nothing, and that scared her more than if he'd yelled.

"Devin?"

He put a hand on her knee and told the driver. "The hospital's on Clarkson."

"I have other instructions."

Oh yeah, déjà vu.

"Where are we going?" he asked John.

"Eileen O'Hare's townhouse."

"Naturally." His scowl etched his brow.

She sank against the seat and fought off waves of pain. She had broken her heel dismounting uneven parallel bars, pulled ligaments and strained muscles. But nothing felt quite like a bullet slicing through a biceps. Her breathing got ragged. She started to shiver.

Putting his arm around her, Devin leaned close to her ear. "As soon as we're out of this car, I'm getting you to a hospital. And calling the police. They need to secure Rhonda's shop. And get to the bottom of this."

She nodded, thankful for his sanity. Twice leaving the scene of a crime was two times too many. She moaned, "Mom's store."

John said, "Officers are at the scene. They're securing the business."

"How do you know?" Devin bit out.

"We have someone on site. No one came in or out after we left."

She slumped against her cousin, relief softening the edge of pain. He wore a nice cologne. She'd bet anything Grace picked it out. Breathing it diminished the scent of her blood and the bitter taste in her mouth. Her arm stung like fire but she was nowhere near as bad off as Bo yesterday. Angels on duty today. Well … yesterday too she supposed.

A bubble of laughter boiled up at the thought of John Helm in that role. No wings. Uh-uh. No way. Devin, sure. Not John. Unless they were batwings like the Dark Knight's.

"Exi." Devin's voice.

"Huh?"

"What's going on? Why are you mixed up in Bo's stuff?"

"Because I'm seeing him. Also."

"You're seeing Bo and Jeffrey."

She nodded.

"Your fiancé—"

"That's on hold."

His jaw rippled as he looked straight ahead. Foreboding filled her belly.

Once more the ambulance waited at Eileen's, no lights or sirens drawing attention. "I'm not riding a gurney," she told John.

"Okay." They parked and John got out, surveyed the area, then opened her door.

Devin helped her out and supported her by the uninjured arm into the house. She felt shakier than she should with such a minor wound. The arrogant doctor hadn't come, only a squatty paramedic. He had mad skills with sutures, he assured her in Eileen's foyer.

"Not plastic surgery, but I'll get you looking good."

She hadn't even thought about that.

"Let's go all the way up so I can check on Mr. Corrigan too."

"What's wrong with Bo?" Devin demanded.

Eileen came out of her parlor. "Devin, why don't you join me?"

"I'm sticking with Exi."

"You'll make me climb four flights of stairs?"

"You are capable of that and more."

Exi winced when the paramedic, whose name badge read Kent Smith, took hold of her. She felt Devin's seething like dragon breath on the back of her neck as he followed her up the stairs. She glanced back to see John giving Eileen a hand. This was not going to be pretty.

Exi sat at Bo's bistro table while the paramedic opened his kit. She rested her arm as instructed, though Kent's flushing the gouge with an astringent solution nearly launched her.

"That's the worst part."

She was too busy sucking hard breaths to answer.

"I'll place a few sutures in the muscle, then carefully close the outer derma." He injected her with lidocaine while Devin and Eileen had a stare-down.

"Is this your doing?" He drilled the question in a tone Exi had never heard from him.

"*This* is very broad."

"I'm in no mood for games, Eileen."

"Leave her alone." Bo came out of his room, one arm tight to his side. "The person to blame is me."

"No it's not," Exi twisted to see him, and the paramedic told her to hold still.

Devin's glare withered Bo. "Not enough to nearly kill Grace and

Mattie? Shooting for a hat trick?"

Bo flinched.

"It's not his fault." Exi tried to pull away, but Kent held onto her arm. "There's an underworld power struggle and he's a target too."

"Why would that be?" Devin's tone could etch glass. "Gambling debts to criminals who attack innocent women? Could that be it, Bo?"

"There's no one here who hasn't made poor choices," Eileen spoke through the choking tension. "Though I can't speak for the medic."

"Poor choices R us," Kent said.

"If we all calm down—"

"Calm down?" Devin spun on Eileen. "Eight inches to the right and that bullet would have been through Exi's heart."

Head swimming, she turned to see Bo. His face had blanched. The tendons in his neck were ropes.

Devin might have been shot too, but it was fear for her—and thoughts of Grace—that hollowed her cousin's eyes.

"Just one last suture right here," Kent murmured. "A bandage, and now we'll get it in a sling." He produced one from his kit and strapped it on her, adjusting the Velcro closures.

She looked at Bo, but Devin put himself between them, his back to her a solid wall.

"You leave Exi alone. You leave my cousin out of your disaster of a life. Are we clear?"

Bo said nothing.

Kent handed her antibiotics and midrange pain relief. She went to put the bottles in her purse and realized she'd left her things at the store. "I don't have my purse. Or my suitcase." Or her pillow.

"We'll get them," John said from the doorway. He took out his phone and texted.

"I should have grabbed them from the office."

"You were holding your bleeding arm," Devin said. "The arm someone *shot*."

Eileen cleared her throat. "She's safe here."

Did she really believe that? John was right there at the store and someone still almost killed her.

Devin shook his head. "She's coming home with me."

"Liam's men are watching my house, Devin. Can you say the same?"

"I don't need my home guarded from violent criminals. I lead a sane, legitimate life. And so does Alexis when she isn't influenced by some who should know better."

John spoke from the doorway. "The threat is neutralized."

Exi swallowed. "Were they the only ones?"

John swallowed. "Liam is assessing the situation."

"She's coming with me." Devin sounded fiercer than she'd ever heard. He gave John his address to deliver her belongings, then said, "Let's go." He put a determined hand on her back.

Exi looked over her shoulder. Bo's face had shadows she could only guess at. "I'll call you."

No answer. She tried to sense him as she had earlier, but the fog enshrouded him. Devin moved her out and down the stairs. Once again a storm brewed. Now Devin was caught in it too. Best to take shelter and call Bo when this bad wind stopped blowing.

Bo went into his studio and closed the door. He moved between the frames to the place where he'd kissed Exi and lowered himself to the hardwood. His heart pounded like a fist on his ribs.

Not enough to nearly kill Grace and Mattie? Shooting for a hat trick?

Never. And yet … here it was. Again. He must be charmed, charmed and toxic for others to keep paying the price for his screw-ups. *Eight inches and the bullet would have gone through Exi's heart.*

Devin's rage was justified. His edict unnecessary. Bo pressed his hands to his face. He would keep her as far from this, as far from him, as humanly possible. The ache moved from his injuries to his mind. He looked up at the mocking, taunting images. His face everywhere, all these pictures of him pretending to be something else, anything else.

His teeth ground. His hands clenched. He sprang up and slammed into the nearest frame, grabbed it with both hands and smashed it into the next one. He used the shards to demolish the one behind that, image after image shredding as he went berserk. One refused to come apart, and he threw it so hard against the wall it smashed the window. He heard falling glass shattering on the ground below.

He threw himself into the next and the next, raised his arms to shove one huge frame over, but someone grabbed him from behind. Thrashing sent agony through his side.

"Stop."

John's order did no more than the pain already had, freezing him in gasping spasms. He couldn't get his breath. The grip loosened. Bo dropped to his knees, barking like a seal on air that left his lungs but would not return. He collapsed into a ball.

John rushed out and came back. He pushed Bo to his back, ripped the bandage off, and jammed something into the wound. Once more air rushed in as blood poured out. Bo writhed. A whimpering whine came from his vocal chords. John raised him up against his chest, their size difference and John's sheer mass making it useless to resist.

"Breathe."

It hurt, but his body fought for oxygen. He hollered when John shifted, a sign that air had refilled the lung, yet still he felt boggy.

"That was remarkably stupid."

"F—" Bo started. Blood clogged his throat. He coughed, amplifying the pain until stars floated in his eyes. His head spun.

"Come on. Stay with me."

Bo sagged. The stars blackened until the spots took over his vision. Before everything went black, he felt John hoisting him.

14

Safe inside the condo, Exi watched Devin pace and scowl. He wanted to call the police.

"For what? I didn't see anything, did you?" She could tell he hadn't. "They're already investigating the shooting at Mom's shop. John's guy gave them a statement."

"What about your statement?"

"I didn't see anything."

"But you know something." Devin glared. "You know who's involved."

"Bo was not involved. He was laid up at Eileen's, because someone attacked him too. I know you're not slow, so I can't see why you don't get that."

"I get it." He bit the words. "He's never around when other people take the heat. That doesn't negate the crux. Bo's responsible for you being in danger."

Negate the crux. Wow. "This is Liam's mess. He and John Helm are dealing with it. I'll do whatever it takes, just ... wait until they come to us."

Devin's countenance could hardly be darker, but he stopped pressing it.

Moving to the wall of windows, Exi called her dad to explain about the store. Police had already informed him. They had tried her mom first, since she had the business license, but of course she couldn't answer.

"Where have you been?" he said. "I'm worried sick."

"I'm with Devin. He was in the store with me when the … drive-by happened. I got medical attention. Now he wants me to stay here tonight. I'll get into the store tomorrow to clean it up, so don't let Mom worry."

"We don't want you anywhere near there. I hired a service to clean it up. Insurance will pay. And someone's coming to water for a week or so. After that we'll see."

"I can do it, Dad. I'm fine."

"No, you're not. The police said you were grazed by a bullet. Almost put your mom in the grave. So stop arguing."

"What am I going to do? I can't just sit around."

"It's called recovering."

"Dad, seriously, I'm not badly injured. A few stitches."

Devin made a noise that she ignored.

She would not get anywhere with this. "Fine. A few days. Then we'll talk."

"You take care of yourself."

"I am." She disconnected.

Cate and Mia had brought Mattie home while she talked. With his daughter snuggled into his shoulder, Devin used a calmer tone. "You're not fine. You don't even know how this might mess with you. Cops who take a shot—any shot—see a counselor before returning to duty."

"Maybe I will. But right now I don't want to think about it. According to John the shooter's dead, so it's not as if I have to help them catch him."

"Stop pretending it's nothing."

"I'm not. But sitting around won't help."

"So do something. Paint."

"My supplies are at the studio. If you drive me there—"

"Get online and buy what you need on my credit card. Have it delivered."

"Devin …"

"I mean it. I'll clear my work stuff from the library—"

"Library?"

"Office. Grace and I don't call it that since our work is art, not business. But that's not the point. You can make yourself at home in there."

"It's not necessary."

"Yeah? Well, I need someone to house-sit when Mattie and I go to Atlanta."

"When is that?"

"In three days. We'll be gone two weeks."

She looked around. Not a terrible prospect. Except for being alone. In a fishbowl.

"This building has security. The condo's alarmed. You have none of that at your place."

"John said the threat is neutralized."

"I don't know who he is or how he thinks he knows—"

"Here." With her free hand, she brought his website up. "He's legit. Big-time."

Devin looked at the site. "So he does security. Didn't help at the store."

She shuddered to think if John hadn't been there. Both attacks. "His guys stopped the shooter while we were on the floor. Neither one of us could have."

"Fine. But I'm not connected to this madness. He won't need to clean up a near miss here. You're as good as hidden."

She wished she had his certainty. "You really don't mind?"

"I absolutely don't mind. I can't leave town if you're not safe."

He and Mattie and Grace would be out of danger. And no one could guess she'd be living like this. Two weeks to paint and recover her sanity? She swallowed. "Okay."

He pulled out his wallet and turned over his Visa card. "Hold on to that while I'm gone. Get anything you need. There's cold storage downstairs that Grace keeps stocked with FreshDirect. You'll do us a favor eating what's there and the next standing order."

"I won't have income to pay you back for a while."

"I'm hiring you to house-sit."

"Oh."

"Until I go, when you're not resting and recovering, you can occupy Mattie. I have a lot on my plate before we take off."

She released a slow breath. "I can do that." Knowing someone tried to shoot her did mess with her head. And her arm was awfully sore. In the morning she'd call Bo and let him know she was okay. That gave her tonight to make it so.

Voices brought him back, but Bo wasn't in his apartment. This time he'd scored a hospital with blinking LED screens, intoning monitors, and a bed like a robotic crib. John and another man were speaking, but seeing his eyes open, John leaned in. "Hey, buddy. I don't know your name, but there's an officer here who needs to hear about your mugging."

Even fuzzy, he got John's point.

"I told him I saw two guys attack you near the Vineyard Theatre in Union Square."

Bo glanced past John to the cop. "Only two? Felt like twenty."

The cop's amber buzz stood up like waves of grain after the thresher. "Officer Dent. What can you tell me?"

He stuck with knowing nothing. "They hit me from behind. Never saw faces." Except his own. Over and over.

"What about build?" Dent came forward.

"Bigger than me." Those images that made him feel small. "Did they get my wallet?" Talking was easier than it had been after the combat doc's ministrations. This team must not have found his injuries negligible. Which didn't mean there wasn't pain.

"They got your wallet," the officer said, "but you clearly fought back."

Bo raised a hand and found it bandaged. Injured smashing the frames, he guessed, but no need to say so. This was all make-believe.

"Might be less damaging to give it up without the fight."

Bo swallowed. "Don't recall a choice." He was feeling the role now, flowing with it. Remembering the real attack put him right there, more clearly than he wanted. Except it wasn't only him that time. The other guy had Exi, kicking and thrashing.

"Lucky this guy saw it go down and scared them off. He drained your bleeding lung with a ball point. It's evidence right now, but you can have the souvenir when we wrap the case."

Bo glanced at John to make sure that was the narrative.

The cop continued. "Someone with your notoriety should hire protection."

"Notoriety?"

"Might not be the word." Dent scratched his thatch. "Notability. I recognize you from commercials. Bo Corrigan right?"

"Uh, yeah."

"My wife buys me Giorgio. She says it could smell like tuna and she'd buy whatever you're hawking." He laughed. "With that racket and your face plastered everywhere, you should watch your back going out."

He looked from the cop to John, who'd set this in motion, as if for a cue to move the scene along.

"It could be random," John said. "Two bigger guys seeing someone they can take."

"Sure." The cop nodded. "But my instinct says whoever did it knew this guy."

Did he ever.

"Could be." John turned. "I'm in security. I'll leave you a card."

"Hire this guy if you need protection. But if you think of anything, call me." Officer Dent set a card on the table, then took out another. "Would you mind signing the back of this one for the wife? She'll get a kick out of it. Make it to Kim."

Bo made it to Kim with love and scrawled his name.

Moments after the officer left, Eileen came in with a bag of his clothes—which was good since they'd confiscated his bloody ones. She stuck it in the narrow cabinet and turned, sharp-faced and crotchety. "You're lucky John was still on hand."

Lucky?

"He saved your life, kept your lung from filling with blood and drowning you in it."

Bo canted John a look. "With a ball point? How'd you know that trick?"

"Combat. We're trained to find a resource and use it."

"Thankfully, the ambulance hadn't gone far." Eileen gripped the bedrail. "But John's quick action kept you alive."

He said, "Your spleen wasn't salvageable after you beat it up a second time, but I did what I could for the rest."

Bo sank back. "I owe you." Chalk up another debt he could never repay.

"I grabbed this." John handed him the supposedly stolen wallet. "Stick it somewhere."

Bo pulled it under the sheet. He dragged his eyes to Eileen. "Sorry about the window."

"Original to the house. Not to mention walls and moldings."

Nothing he could say but, "I lost it."

"You let Devin get to you."

That wasn't it. But not even Eileen would understand. "I'll clear out."

She made a disgruntled noise. "Glass can be replaced. I'm not sure you can."

"You'd be surprised." Weren't demons driven out? Cancer excised? Had his presence in Barb's life tipped some scale against her? Gunmen shooting at Grace and Exi? And from the corner of his eye he saw Eileen's head tremor. She'd been hale when he moved in. Now look at her. He swallowed a lump in his throat. His course was clear.

Scented steam wafted from the bathroom where Grace had turned off the shower to take the call. Wrapped in the hotel robe, she listened with dismay as Devin described what happened in the flower shop. His focus was on Exi, but she quaked at what could have happened to him. "But you're all right? Both of you?"

"I am. Who knows how Exi is."

"And Mattie wasn't with you?" What if he'd taken her as she'd suggested? Could he have hit the floor with their daughter in his arms? What if Exi was holding her? What—

"I told you she wasn't."

"Thank God." She slid down the wall in her hotel room, feeling so far away.

"I'm keeping Alexis with me until I come to Atlanta. Then she's staying on at our place."

"That's good. Oh, Devin, that was too close." Her heart raced.

"Now you know how I felt, how I feel."

Tears welled up. She already knew, but this was visceral.

He said, "Bo shouldn't be impacting our lives like this again."

"I know." This time she couldn't argue. Her husband had been in the line of fire. And it did go right back to Bo. "How's Exi taking it?"

"Way too lightly."

"Your cousin has more gumption than she gets credit for."

"That's not a good thing."

"Yes, it is."

"I'm not going to argue. I just need to know we're on the same side, Grace."

"I love you with my whole heart."

He was silent a long moment. "That's the best I'm going to get, isn't it?"

"We don't always agree, but this time you're right. Bo's trouble caught Exi in the crossfire, as it did Mattie and me. I imagine that's breaking his heart."

"Seriously, Grace?" His voice graveled. "That's your response?"

"What would you like it to be?"

"How about we're through with him?"

"He's my friend, Devin. I think he needs at least one."

"I'm getting off now."

"Don't be angry." Her phone bleeped. Well, that was clear enough. She pressed a palm to her forehead. "Still working on that heart, Lord?"

She wrapped herself in her arms and trembled. "Could you spare a little for mine?"

She understood Devin's feelings and blamed Bo herself. But that didn't mean she would betray a friendship. And maybe Exi's words haunted. What if Bo needed real help, and there was no one for him—as there'd been no one for her?

Grace shuddered, thinking of herself at thirteen with nowhere to turn. Her whole life had shifted. Bo was a grown man but in many ways as lost and confused as she'd been. She'd had faith to fall on, even if it stopped looking like everyone else's. What did Bo have?

Her mind tripped back to Devin and Exi and Mattie. Now she was shaking in earnest. They're all right, she told herself. They're … all … right. Her phone rang. She touched to answer.

"I love you too," Devin said, and the warmth of it flooded in and chased the shakes away.

The surgeon showed up after John and Eileen finally left him in peace. Here was the one who completed John's and the hack surgeon's efforts. The cleanup hitter. He informed Bo that losing a spleen was no small thing. "The spleen fights infection and filters bad cells from the bloodstream. Without it, you will have a weakened immune system from this point on."

Right. Like anything could do that.

"As serious as that is, the life-threatening issue happened here." He touched the bandage just below and to the side of his right pectoral. "One of the fractured ribs ruptured a blood vessel that flooded your lung. Mr. Helm's immediate action is all that stemmed the flow."

Yes, he'd gotten that.

"Even so, you lost a substantial amount of blood. It is imperative you limit motion and strenuous activity until all of that heals."

Well, sure. Why not?

"I anticipate five to ten days of recovery before discharge. Some of that depends on how well your immune system modifies its response. The nurse will give you instructions, and I'll answer any questions you have at rounds in the morning."

Bo watched how the guy walked out, a squirrel-like man with tufts of hair atop his ears. He internalized it until he could imitate exactly what he saw, then realized that was senseless. He was done with all that. Finished acting, finished pretending. Finished trying to be something worthwhile.

The nurse brought sleep meds, which he left in the pleated paper cup. The floor grew dim and quiet, though they'd be in at intervals to check vitals and make sure no one really slept. The agony of multiple injuries ganged up on him. He fought the urge to give in and address it. Midway through the night, he rose, removed the IV, and gingerly dressed in the clothes Eileen had hung in the room's closet.

Even the slightest movements caused screaming pain, but he could score something for that in the social circles where anything goes and everything flows. They'd happily provide to have him back among them, the decadent elite. With the hope of Exi lost, what did it matter? What did anything matter?

He shapeshifted, as Barb had called it, left the room, and got to the street. The lights of the city made smears and halos through the taxi window. The city that never slept. He could feel its energy. He let it embrace him.

The first bash throbbed with sound, hellish in force and fever. Then came the resonating tones of Disturbed covering "The Sound of Silence." *Hello darkness.* The mugging and surgery explained his condition and garnered sympathy. *Fool, you do not know.* Oh, but he did.

"Bo, you poor baby," Callie thrust her silicone assets into him. "Let me make it better."

"Don't touch the ribs."

"Oh, sexy, it's not ribs that interest me."

He downed a martini on top of whatever he'd popped and sank into the morass.

15

Exi didn't try to reach Bo until Devin took Mattie to her grandpa Eddie's the next morning. Her wound hurt, but the sling immobilized the biceps. She had some use of her left hand as long as it didn't activate her muscle, and her dominant arm was strong as ever. Could be worse, eight-inches-to-the-right worse.

Exi brought Bo up on her phone. He didn't answer, so she left a voice mail. "Bo, it's me. I told you I'd call, but maybe you're sleeping. Please call back when you get this."

Her supplies arrived while Devin was out, so she talked the energetic delivery guy into opening the packages and assembling her easel.

"Sure. What happened to your arm?"

"Got, um, stitches."

"Ow."

"Yeah." She had paid for the order with Devin's credit card, but she tipped this guy her last twenty since it was all she had in her wallet. Worth it as he even unboxed the paints and loosened all the caps. "Thank you so much."

He grinned. "You could really thank me with your phone number."

"Oh. Sorry." She cocked her head. "I'm in a relationship." Which one, she didn't know, but neither left room for another. She stifled a groan at the thought.

"My bad luck." He gave her a salute and left. She closed the door, armed the alarm, and kept herself from checking it again. And again. John said they weren't coming after her just now, and Devin said they wouldn't find her. But her head shouted, *They tried to kill me!*

Unless the drive-by was a warning. Maybe it was just to scare Bo or Liam. Maybe the shooter meant to miss, aimed to send a message. Had she stretched her arm into the line of fire? Liam said murder wasn't always the intention. They might stop at disfiguring. Dang. The shakes were back. She tried Bo again. This had to be messing with him too. Pick up, pick up.

But he didn't. She looked at the canvas on the easel in the room Devin called his library. She should prepare a palette, but the hues depended on her subject.

There was the cityscape outside the windows. She could abstract a still life of things in the house. She walked around and considered potential combinations, but nothing inspired her. If she could just reach Bo. She sent a text. *Bo, please call. I really want to talk to you.*

She arrowed back and studied his picture in her contacts. Something stirred, more than stirred. She felt that buzz of creativity. She'd painted Jeffrey …

She rushed into the library, sent Bo's Internet picture to the printer, then drew it out and absorbed him. She chose her hues. She'd painted Jeffrey in colors so bright they were almost neon. For Bo, she prepared a Zorn palette: ivory black, cadmium red, yellow ocher, and titanium white. Anders Zorn had developed this palette for his work at the turn of the twentieth century. It seemed right for capturing Bo's complicated nature.

The geometric normalcy of Jeffrey's face had invited an abstract rendering. His eyes were perfectly aligned in his face, directly above his dimples. Bo's were a little closer set, but so alarmingly sensual that placement only added to their impact. "Bo," she breathed.

Neither the city outside the windows or anything in the room distracted. They might not even exist. Nothing existed but this. The light in the room showed the passage of time, but nothing penetrated until she heard the condo door opening. Her brush jerked off the canvas. Her heart struck like a clock chime until Mattie's crying broke through.

Exi swished her brush in mineral spirits and wiped it off with paper towels. She was never shy about people seeing her art in progress, but painting Bo was not something Devin would get or approve. She didn't want another lecture. Or maybe she wanted to keep this to herself. She went out and closed the door behind her.

Mattie was having the first meltdown she'd seen outside of the fire-alarm episode. Devin said, "She didn't want to leave Eddie. And I couldn't give her M-O-M-M-Y."

Exi wasn't sure why he spelled when Mattie wasn't talking yet. She did seem to understand things though. He carried the crying child to her room and rocked her until the sobs subsided. It was sinking in how consuming having a child was. Jeffrey was ready. Was she?

Devin came back out of Mattie's room, looking a little ragged. "You doing okay?"

"It was only a graze."

"I meant—"

"I'm fine. You don't have to worry. If you're going to worry I should go somewhere else. I'm not fourteen, looking out through starry eyes anymore."

"You're not fourteen." Clearly that was all he'd give her.

"You think Bo's conning me but he's not."

"You think anything he's shown you is real?"

"I know it is."

"Exi …"

"What? I'm not a good judge? I get taken in? It's true in the past I haven't seen things I wish I had. But guess what? I learned from that. I grew up, Devin. And I do see Bo. His life is messed up, but it isn't his fault."

"Of course not. Nothing is ever Bo's fault. What is it with you women? Why can't you see he's faking everything?"

"He is not." But she remembered how smoothly Bo transformed

into a junkie. One second he was one person, the next someone else. Even he said the line was porous, his acting more real than living.

Devin braced his hips. "You can tell me to back off, but hear me first. I'm not even sure there's a real man in there."

She pictured his gallery filled with imaginary Bo Corrigans. Bo yet not Bo, only roles, one after another. Then she remembered him in her shop and at Eileen's, talking about Barb. "He's in there. He's just afraid to come out."

"Bo's not afraid of anything. He gallivants through life as if it's all his playground, taking whatever he wants and leaving the pieces behind. Ask Louisa."

Exi frowned. "His costar?"

"Before *Windows and Doors* she was as confident in life as on the stage. Then Bo happened."

"Happened?"

"He thinks women can take him or leave him as easily as he does them. Now she's seeing a shrink about it."

"Maybe it's your script, putting her through that angst night after night for, what, almost two years?"

"Maybe it's sleeping with Bo, oh, whenever he feels like it."

Exi blinked. "Still?"

His throat worked. "Not for some months. That's why she's in therapy. She thought they had something. Even she couldn't tell it was smoke and mirrors." Concern etched his face.

Was Bo really that callous? "He isn't mean. I know mean."

"Carelessness is just as bad."

"No it's not. It's worse when someone intends to hurt."

"The result's the same."

"I don't agree and there's no point arguing. I hear you. I really do. I'm not blind or stupid. I'll be careful. But I won't turn my back when he's done nothing to deserve it."

Devin cocked his jaw. "We have different definitions of *deserve*."

Exi shrugged. "Okay."

"Okay." His was halfhearted at best.

"I appreciate everything."

"I know."

She lowered her chin and raised her eyes. "So … friends?"

He pulled her into a hug. "Family."

She hugged back with her good arm.

After a moment he let go. "Do I smell paint?"

"I've started a piece. Nothing much."

"When Mattie and I leave you can move your operation out here. Have a little elbow room."

"Thanks. I will."

He chucked her under the chin, then tipped his head. "I probably shouldn't do that, since you're old and wise now."

"As long as you don't ruffle my hair or pinch my cheeks."

"I've never pinched your cheeks. Do people even do that?"

"I hope not." Exi laughed and it almost sounded natural. They were going through the motions and she'd bet they both knew it.

She hated conflict, but neither would she back down when it mattered. She wished every word he'd said about Bo wasn't jangling in her head. Especially the part about Louisa. Exi sighed. She was the one dating two people. What right did she have to get bothered? When Bo called, she could make sure it was over with his colleague—or not—and at least she would know.

She felt bad for Louisa. She'd had enough hard endings to know the pain of it. She didn't plan to sleep with Bo. She only wanted to hear his voice. How pathetic would she look if she called him again? Um, pathetic. She left her phone in her pocket and went back to painting with the door closed while Devin did whatever he did.

Somehow they managed to keep the peace for the next three days. She drew illustrations for Mattie, eager to see what attracted her and what she found uninteresting. Since Mattie didn't talk, Exi read her expressions. That scrutiny brought something new to her process, and she started sketching Mattie in a series of life studies.

As with Bo, Mattie's face cried out for the realism Exi had denied herself for years. She hated to think the time, money, and effort she had put toward her degree were wasted—and they weren't. Dabbling in abstraction had broadened her skills. She couldn't help it if it hadn't changed her mind.

Now Devin and Mattie were leaving. She would have this place to herself, free to create without tension or exposure. The only thing holding her back from fully enjoying this opportunity was that Bo still wouldn't answer his phone.

While Devin packed their bags, she considered her options, then braved the lion in his den. "Could you give me Eileen's number?"

He straightened. "Is something wrong?"

"I want to ask her how Bo's doing. He's not answering his phone." She tried not to let the satisfaction that passed over Devin's face annoy her. Two sides of the same coin Eileen had said. But Bo wasn't the dark twin this time.

He took out his phone and read off the numbers.

"Thanks." Maybe she should wait until he left, but his gaze dared her to go ahead and call, so she did. She wasn't prepared for the answer.

"I couldn't tell you how he's doing. He walked out of the hospital without discharge."

"Hospital?" Her heart plummeted at the scene Eileen described of Bo destroying his studio, then nearly drowning in his blood. If she'd known he would react that way, she would not have gone with Devin. Her mind replayed every word of that awful scene. *Not enough to nearly kill Grace and Mattie? Shooting for a hat trick?* Why hadn't she realized how that would hurt? On top of his survivor's guilt? It was brutal.

Eileen said, "I haven't heard from him and neither have his directors."

Not working? Exi pictured him tearing down the framed images, destroying the thing that connected him to Barb.

"Have Liam or John?"

"I'm afraid not."

Heart aching, she disconnected.

Devin frowned. "What's up?"

"He's missing."

Devin folded his arms. "He's not missing. He's on a bender somewhere."

"You don't know that."

"Yes, I do. I'll tell you what I told Grace. More than one production has gone over budget because Bo took off partying. He's irresponsible. Eileen will tell you the same thing."

"She doesn't know about his sister."

Devin pressed his tongue to his eye tooth. "What sister?"

"Grace didn't tell you?"

"Uh, no. And I don't know why it matters."

"She died."

Devin blinked. "Okay."

"Okay?"

"Did he kill her in a car accident? Shoot her up with drugs?"

Exi looked at him with horror. "She died of cancer. He's not handling it well."

Devin swallowed. "I'm sorry for him."

"Are you?"

"I know that's hard to go through."

"Because you did it with your uncle Robert? I'm not making light of that, but it isn't the same."

Mattie got up from the toy farm she was playing with, and Devin hoisted her into his arms. "It's still a choice, Exi. One decision or another. Wherever he is, Bo is choosing to be there, doing whatever he's doing. You are better off without him."

Her eyes burned. "And he's better off without me?"

"Probably not. But I don't care. He's trouble you don't need."

"You really don't care."

He sighed. "I care about Bo, but not about you trying to fix him. It won't work—Eileen's schemes notwithstanding."

"He doesn't need *fixing*. He needs healing."

"He has to take the steps. Maybe he was for a while. Now he's not. And you're the one with a bullet wound."

She shook her head. "I should have stayed there. I betrayed him leaving with you."

"That's wrong thinking. Even Bo said he's to blame for the danger you're in."

"What about his danger?"

Devin shrugged. "He knows where the safe house is. Eileen's been more than generous in every way."

Exi left the room and texted Bo again. *Please answer, Bo. If you're wearing your Apple Watch, I'm over your pulse. If I had that kind of watch, you'd be over mine too. Please text me back.*

She got no answer, but he was still on her mind when Devin and Mattie left for Atlanta, and when she dressed for her date with Jeffrey. She took her arm out of the sling and borrowed a three-quarter-sleeve blouse from Grace that covered the bandage. When he asked why he was picking her up at Devin's, she told him she was house-sitting and left it at that.

In a fog, Bo saw Exi's face come up on his wrist. Beautiful, though he missed her throwback photo. Better it was gone since it would remind him of their picnic in the park and the motion of her body that seemed as playful as a kitten's, as alluring as a siren. His Sibella. Gone.

Gorged on booze and drugs, on sex he barely remembered, he felt emptier than he'd ever been. He dragged himself up from the floor, paused on his knees, and held his head. All around, the party continued. He wasn't sure where he was or who half the people were.

He got to his feet, still doped enough he hardly felt his injuries or even the surgical incisions. People called his name, but he kept walking … or something close to that. He made it to a hall and clung to the wall until he found an elevator and took it down. Out on the street, under the night sky, headlights sent pain through his eyeballs to his brain. He covered the offending orbs with his hands, staggering until he felt a thump and fell back.

"Get outta the street, you effing junkie!"

Junkie. He wasn't even acting. He kept moving until he found a street bench, but it was occupied. He moved on until he found a culvert. It stank, but no worse than he did. He crawled in and curled up. The pipe's corrugation seemed to spin, but his eyes closed, and he passed out.

When sunlight brightened one end of the culvert, a scrawny dog moseyed in. It eyed him warily, then moved on.

Bo slept. When he woke, his Apple Watch, wallet, and phone were gone.

16

Inside the Atlanta hotel lobby, Grace saw them coming through the revolving door. Mattie looked fascinated while Devin explained the mechanism in little-girl terms. "A merry-go-round door."

Grace could hardly contain her joy and relief at having them here, safe. "Mattie, baby girl!"

Mattie's head swung from the door. Her excited cry contained a homing device straight to the heart. Grace threw her arms around both.

Devin laughed. "Mind if we get inside?"

They were inside, but she let him proceed into the lobby. Mattie nearly leaped from his arms to hers. "Oh, precious girl, let me see you." Devin had dressed her in a sailor dress by Mia. "You are the cutest, cutest, cutest."

"You've only been gone four days." Devin kissed her cheek. "And do I get any of this?"

She turned and kissed his mouth, then wiped a little gloss from his lower lip. When he gave it another swipe just to make sure, she laughed. "Careful what you ask for."

His eyes smiled. "Let's get these bags upstairs so we can hit the road."

"Mattie needs a rest from traveling don't you think?"

"We'll give her a bite and she can nap on the drive."

Grace wanted to object. Her nerves crawled like ants. "All right." She hoped Mattie didn't sense her anxiety. If one word or cross look upset her baby, they were out of there. "Did you like the airplane?" she asked her daughter in the elevator.

Mattie raised her arms over her head as if reaching for the sky.

"Yes, it went very high. Then came back down and brought you here. Just for Mommy to love, love, love on." Mattie squeezed her neck, clearly understanding every word. Talking was overrated when hugs sufficed.

They buckled her into the rental car seat and headed for Madison, Georgia, the town Grace Evangeline Pratt left behind through no fault of its own, but very much because of events that happened there. Blocking those memories, she experienced the drive through Devin's eyes.

"I've never been down south."

"That will be obvious."

"Oh yeah?"

"Yes indeed."

"Even if I don't talk like a New Yorker?"

"Well, you don't speak Southern."

"I suppose not."

"It's the least of our concerns."

He peeked back to make sure Mattie slept. "How do you want to do this?"

"I don't."

He reached over and took her hand.

Grace squeezed back. "I know. I encouraged your reconciliation."

"Forced."

She slid a look. "And it was good for you and your mother."

"Life changing."

"This isn't like that. They turned their backs on us. Intentionally."

"Maybe they can't turn back."

She blinked at him. "You're being very generous."

"*Generous* doesn't require an intensifier."

She giggled. "You're a pain, you know that?"

He grinned. "I think we should choose our spot in town—there is a restaurant, right?"

"At least one. Madison recently made the top sixteen most picturesque villages in the world. It's the town Sherman refused to burn."

"Really?"

"Would I lie?"

"Not straight out for no reason."

He was making this so much better, she might even bear her family's rejection. She only hoped it didn't wound him.

"So I say we stake out our spot and give them a call. Doesn't have to be a restaurant as long as we grab something to eat. Flying makes me hungry."

"Does the opposite to me. I have to force food down on these book tours."

"Mattie had her snack, so she's okay. We could use a park where she can run around."

"Madison Park has a fountain and a wall we could all sit on."

"Sure. If we can take the heat. Mattie's a New Yorker."

"She has Georgian blood too."

"But she hasn't had to use it."

Grace smiled. "You're silly."

"You bring it out. I was never silly before you."

"I believe Eddie said something to that effect. The perfect little man."

"I don't know about perfect."

"You? You think you're perfect in every way."

"Only where it matters, Grace."

"In your work?"

"Exactly."

"Hmm."

"I've never heard anyone put so much meaning in a nonword."

"Except Mattie."

"Maybe that's where she gets it."

"Could be." She sent an adoring glance at her sleeping angel.

"Useful talent."

"Isn't it."

"At some point I'd like to hear words."

"So would I." Her throat constricted. "If they refuse to see us, don't say anything Mattie will catch on to. She's very aware, even if she doesn't say so."

"I know she is. I'll say 'I hate boiled peanuts' in place of invectives."

Grace laughed. "Do you hate boiled peanuts?"

"The very thought disgusts me. They're supposed to be roasted in the shell and eaten at the ballpark."

"That might be a Yankee thing you keep to yourself."

"You like them?"

"No. But I discreetly avoid them and don't blab it around."

They talked about North-South differences, especially things that would give him away and earn him the Deep South version of a cold shoulder. "They'll bless your heart so many times you'll glow."

Coming into Madison, she could see Devin's appreciation as he found a parking space and got out. "It's like going back to a kinder, gentler time."

"It is, isn't it." Wishing that applied to family dynamics, she reached in and helped Mattie climb out of her car seat. "Are you making the call or shall I?"

"Your choice." He locked the car.

They started into the park with Mattie dancing on her toes in excitement. The fountain trickled. Insects hummed. The verdant aromas of grass and trees and blooms soaked her in sweet honeyed nostalgia. This place would always be a part of her. It had good memories. Plenty of them. She drew a steadying breath and phoned home. "Hi, Mama. I'm calling from Madison Town Park, hoping you'd like to see us."

Her mother's voice sounded whispery. "You mean … all of

you?"

"Devin and Mattie joined me in Atlanta where I'm signing tomorrow. He'd like to meet you and Daddy, and I thought you might like to see Mattie Angelica."

"Oh, Grace. It's so sudden."

"I'd hardly call twenty-two months sudden. But we're here and if y'all want to join us in the park, we'd love to see you." She watched Devin playing tag with his toddler and smiled.

"Your daddy won't sit out in the park." *With you* she meant, because he'd sat in this park his whole life. "Y'all should come for dinner. I'll see if Marvalee and her bunch can join us."

"I don't want to put you out."

"She can potluck. She always has something great to bring along."

"I'm sure. But Daddy might not want a big to-do."

"I think in this case the more the merrier."

"If it's going to get ugly, I'd just as soon not have a crowd."

"Grace Evangeline, why would you say such a thing? As if your daddy could get ugly."

Grace bit her tongue. "We'll bring ice cream."

"Oh, I have dessert. Just bring yourselves."

Apparently only Marvalee's donations qualified. Grace sighed. "That sounds lovely, Mama. What time would you like us?"

"You know we always eat at six."

"We'll see you about then."

Devin joined her, concerned by what he saw in her face. "They said no?"

"We're coming to dinner."

He swallowed. "Is that what you want?"

"It's what Mama thinks is best."

He nodded. "Okay. But I reserve the right to pull the plug." He held her eyes. "Even if we don't step foot inside. I'll take my licks, but you and Mattie are off-limits."

"Mattie for sure. But they'll have words for me."

He scratched the back of his neck. "This heat is daunting. Did you say ice cream?"

She smiled. "Want dessert before dinner?"

"Only if it spoils my appetite."

She laughed. "Have I said how much I love you?"

"A time or two."

"Too many?"

He merely smiled.

She turned to watch Mattie spiraling with her little arms in the air. Who wouldn't take one look and love her with their whole heart? "Ice cream, Mattie?"

Her baby squealed and charged into her arms. Grace waited just a breath hoping for a word, any word, then started for the ice cream shop, Devin strolling tall and sure beside her.

"That was a great idea," she said as they left the shop with sweet teeth sated.

They browsed the numerous antique stores, Devin intrigued by the Civil War artifacts and even more by the shopkeepers' versions of events. He listened politely, taking it all in like the voracious academic he was. Lord, how did she get such an amazing man?

Mattie picked out a faceless ragdoll for an outrageous sum. Devin dickered it down, then handed over his card for still more than it was worth. The shopkeeper knew they wouldn't deny her. Not this day anyway. Grace picked up pressed-flower note cards for her mother and an antique pincushion for Marvalee.

"What about your dad?" Devin said. "A book maybe?"

"He only reads theological works. I don't think we'll find that here."

"What about a tie tack?"

"That'd be nice. You pick it." And he did, as if it really mattered to him. She was in danger of saying she loved him all over again.

She found an odd mechanical bird for Tommy, a silk pocket square for Charlie, and slingshots with bags of marshmallow ammunition for all of Marvalee's kids except her youngest twins, who got embroidered bibs.

"How much delight are you taking in the thought of your sister-in-law picking up all those marshmallows?" Devin wanted to know.

"Way more than I should."

He rubbed her back approvingly as they returned to the car. The relatively short, scenic drive still gave her stomach time to knot. She owed this to Devin and Mattie, but at the same time, they were the ones she wanted to protect. That sounded wrong. Why would they need protection from righteous people who lived the golden rule?

Her mouth went dry when Devin parked in front of the house where she grew up. It wasn't her family she dreaded, but the memories crowding in. *You know you want it, brat.*

He cocked her a glance. "Okay?"

She smiled. "Sure." By the time she'd unbuckled Mattie, her mother had the door open. Was that a look of eagerness in her eyes? They walked up together, and Grace said, "Devin, this is my mother, Phyllis Pratt. Mom, this is Devin Bressard, the playwright/producer I mentioned on our last visit. He's clearly not gay since we produced this beautiful child"—whose face was buried in Grace's neck.

Devin held their collection of gifts but extended his other hand and said, "I'm pleased to meet you."

Her mother seemed surprised by his decorum … or something. She said, "I can see why Grace fell for you." Then she remembered her manners. "It's nice meeting you too. Why don't y'all come on in." She tried to get a look at Mattie when they passed, but their little girl's stranger anxiety had arrived full force. Good instincts.

"Is Daddy home?"

"He's out with Tommy fixing the Sprawls' lawn mower."

"Mr. Sprawl's arthritis still giving him fits?"

"Yes, bless his heart. I suppose it excuses his bad temper. Lord knows, pain's a trial." Phyllis led them to the kitchen. "Sweet tea?"

"You'd arm her?" Devin's remark puzzled Phyllis as she reached for the pitcher.

"We had a little incident," Grace told her with a glare at her husband. "Before we learned to get along."

"Oh, Grace, you didn't."

"Oh, but she did." Devin received his glass. "And may I say she has very good aim."

"Since that's not something we're talking about"—Grace thanked her for her own glass—"why don't we step out to your lovely veranda, Mama."

"Oh." Her mother blushed. "The blooms are coming in pretty, aren't they? I'm fixing to fertilize but haven't yet, so that's all their own glory."

When Grace gave Mattie a sip of her tea, Phyllis glimpsed her granddaughter. "She sure looks like her daddy." Her voice quavered.

"Except when she's naughty," he said. "Then she's all Grace."

"Devin." Grace huffed, but her mother found it funny.

Then Phyllis sobered as if realizing they were talking about an illegitimate child. "Even raised up right, they don't always go the way they should."

"Good thing life's a journey," he said, "even if you have to backtrack to find your way."

Phyllis blinked at him.

"Grace was definitely grace to me."

Her mother's eyes welled. "That's a nice thing to say."

Throat swelling with emotion, Grace carried Mattie to the porch, where sweet scented nasturtiums embarrassed the stinky geraniums. She stood Mattie on the rail to look out at the well-tended yard. Who'd have thought Devin—master of biting wit—would have all the right words?

Mattie pointed. "Swimming pool, Mommy. Go swimming?"

Her breath hitched. She caught Devin's eye. He winked, so she kept it cool, as if it were the most natural thing that Mattie talked. Of course Mattie talked. In sentences. "We left your swimming suit at the hotel, honey."

"Oh, we have children's swimsuits," Phyllis said. "Have to with all the pool parties. And you could use mine, Grace. It's modest."

How could she refuse when her little one talked? Talked!

"Sorry we don't have men's trunks."

Nothing spoke quite so eloquently to her daddy's dismissal of the pool she had provided her family several years ago.

Devin said, "I'll just stay here and visit."

Phyllis blushed again. "Suits are in the laundry room's cupboards, Grace."

Grace glanced at her husband, who seemingly endorsed this, and went to change with Mattie. She went out the back door and got into the pool. A water bug, Mattie giggled as the level deepened with each step.

"Like that water, Mattie?"

"Like a water."

Tears stung. It wasn't a one-time thing. She was talking. Maybe she'd needed the Southern voices from the other half of her heritage to flip the switch. Grace glanced at Devin, also talking, though she didn't hear his conversation. He'd tell her whatever she needed to know. With Mattie attached to her back, Grace did a modified breast stroke. When she stopped, Mattie said, "More." Exactly. More words, my baby girl. You just keep them coming. Whatever happened tonight would be nothing to this joy.

As she and Mattie got dry and dressed, her father and Tommy came home. She could hear their voices coming in the door, then her mother's, and—oh, Lord—Devin's. With Mattie in her arms, she left the laundry room to face the judge and wish for a jury.

"As for me and my house," Gilbert Pratt pronounced, "we serve the Lord. What kind of faith do you bring to a union with my daughter?"

"A tried and tested one," Devin said and stopped her dad in his tracks.

"I see." He cleared his throat.

A quick knock and the door sprang open. Marvalee and her offspring whirlwind pressed in. "Grace! Auntie Grace." The onslaught was wonderful, and Mattie returned their hugs.

"Charlie's not off work yet but he'll be along." Marvalee enclosed her and whispered, "So happy for you. I'd have attended your wedding if I could. Don't think for a minute anything kept me away but the twins making me a beluga."

"Thank you. Now let me look at these cherubs. Have you ever seen such cheeks?" Mattie had been such a little elf compared to these.

"Phyllis says Charlie's were just that way."

"Well, I never saw that, but I believe it. He's the one with dimples." They laughed together.

Then, scooping Mattie up, Grace turned to her father. Before she could speak, she felt Devin's hand on her back. He must have filled the space Marvalee vacated. "Hi, Daddy. Devin thought you might like to meet your granddaughter, so here we are. If it's all right with you, Mama's asked us to dinner. If not, y'all can have a wonderful potluck and we'll be on our way."

Devin increased the pressure of his hand, but she'd be okay either way. She'd never seen her father at a loss for words, but his mouth moved several times before he managed, "That's a beautiful little girl."

"We think so. She had a rough start, but she's making up for it in every way."

His eyes moistened. "No point standing in the doorway when good food's waiting."

"No point at all."

Charlie arrived and Grace introduced that brother. Tommy must have snuck off when he realized they were here, but he came down as they all moved toward the kitchen.

He might have kept to the edges, but Devin said, "You must be Tommy. Grace tells me you're a talented cartoonist. Graphic novels are really coming on. Have you tried it?"

Tommy said, "Hadn't thought of it."

"I'm Devin, by the way." He extended his hand. "Guess we're brothers-in-law."

"Yeah." Tommy shook it. "I do more models than cartoons now. I'm making a new world."

"We can use one."

Tommy laughed, actually laughed. "You can see it after dinner."

"I'd like that. Thanks."

So many times throughout the evening, Grace glanced at Devin with gratitude. But never so much as that moment with her poor awkward brother.

As they were leaving, her mother pressed a small packet into her hand. "I'd saved this for your wedding day. I hope you'll take it now. They're granny's pearls. I wore them for mine and put them aside for you. Maybe you'll do more than keep them in a drawer. And when the time comes, pass them on to Mattie."

Grace hugged her hard. "Thank you, Mama." Could it be they weren't such worlds apart as she'd imagined? "I admire you, Mama. You and Daddy, Charlie and Marvalee, even Tommy with his issues. I admire your quiet, heroic lives, being salt and light."

Her mother looked startled. "Well, I don't know about heroic."

"I do. And guess what? My baby said her first words here with you, so you haven't missed all that much after all."

"Imagine that." Phyllis pressed her fingers to her cheek. Then her eyes filled. "I'm sorry I wasn't there for you." She cleared her throat. "At thirteen in your time of need. I didn't know. I don't know how I didn't, but that's the truth."

"I believe you, Mama. And I think it had to be that way. In going through it alone, God gave me stories. And my stories help others be strong and face trials."

Her mother blinked back the tears. "I'd like to read them."

"I don't know about that. I never want to cause trouble between you and Daddy."

"Might not hurt him to read one either."

Grace scoffed. "That'll be the day."

"Oh, you never know." Phyllis tipped her head. "God parted the Red Sea."

Grace squeezed her mother's arm in this rare moment of womanly solidarity. There might still be a little Pratt in Grace Evangeline Bressard after all.

17

After nine days with no response from Bo, Exi knew she should take the hint. She'd always been a slow learner when it came to giving up on people. Had Bo dumped her like the exquisite Louisa, whom he loved while acting on the stage—and off it apparently? Before delivering champagne the night they met, he'd kissed his costar. Then what? Electricity like nothing she'd experienced had blurred everything else.

Maybe now he'd found a new attraction. If it was only that, she'd get over it. But she couldn't stop seeing his face when she left, hollowed like a husk. And destroying his studio? That wasn't someone who went off for a good time. He was lost and she had to reach him. But how?

As much as she hated to, she tried Eileen again. The woman's brusque answer scared her even more. "No, he isn't back. No one's seen him since he left the hospital."

"How do you know he left? Maybe they took him. Maybe they're holding him for ransom."

"John saw the security tape. Bo walked out. And no one's asked for ransom. Neither John nor Liam have located him, but it's not for lack of trying."

"Was he okay to leave?"

"He would not have been discharged so soon after surgery. Not with the risk of infection. And he hasn't filled a prescription for antibiotics or other relief."

"How do you know?"

"John's monitoring his financials. Bo might have cash, but he hasn't used a card."

"Devin thinks he's out partying."

"It's the likeliest scenario."

"Doesn't that take money?"

"In his circles he can go indeterminate lengths of time without paying for a thing. He's quite popular to have around."

Her heart sank. "So you think that's it?"

"I hope it is. Liam would prefer to protect him, but if Bo refuses, it might be safer if he doesn't surface for a while."

Ending the call, Exi jumped at a knock on the door. As worried as she'd been about Bo, she'd almost forgotten her own potential danger. She crept over to peek through the peephole and saw Jeffrey. Huh. She opened the door and gave him a quizzical smile. "This is a surprise."

"May I come in?"

She smelled the cologne he wore for work, not their romantic evenings out. That confirmed she hadn't forgotten a date. "Is something wrong?" She closed the door behind him and set the alarm.

He walked into the condo and looked out the windows, then spoke without turning. "I went by your dad's to see if he needed anything."

"That's nice." It should have pleased her. Instead a bad feeling started in her tummy.

Jeffrey faced her. "He told me you were shot."

"Grazed." She closed her hand over the wound under her painting smock. She wasn't using the sling anymore unless the muscle started throbbing.

The look on his face was uncomprehending. "We've been out together twice since then and you didn't feel that was worth telling me?"

"I didn't want to worry you. I'm fine. It's healing." Better than her nightmares.

"You were shot in your mother's store."

"Stuff happens, Jeffrey. You were out of town, and when you got back I wanted to move on. There will hardly be a scar."

He came over and clasped her elbows. "My fi—significant other gets shot and thinks I don't deserve to know. Does that seem right to you? Because I'm not sure I feel that way."

"Would you like to sit down?" She pointed to the café stools at the counter.

He took a seat.

Reading his face, she said, "I'm sorry you're upset."

"Oh, it might have been interesting when we've been married ten years or so to suddenly learn my wife is a gunshot victim. You know how I feel about firearms."

"Which is one reason I didn't bring it up." The other being Bo. Good thing her dad didn't know that part.

"Alexis, I must not be expressing the depth of my disappointment."

"No. You are." She bit her lip. "It's just … I'm trying to get past it."

"Without me."

She sighed. "No. Yes. I don't know."

He frowned. "Have they caught the shooter?"

"Yes."

"How do you know? Your dad didn't."

"Joe's not …" in John Helm's confidence. "It's my understanding that the shooter was wounded in the altercation and found dead some time later."

"You were caught in crossfire?"

It would be easy to take that and run but she had promised not to lie. "A bullet shattered Mom's window. Devin and I took cover. I got the wound treated, and he brought me here."

"So you're not house-sitting."

"I am. I don't lie to you, Jeffrey."

"You withhold. Is that different?"

She swallowed and said, "Who decided my portfolio wasn't good enough?"

He frowned. "What?"

"Did you turn it down because you wanted to date me?"

His Adam's apple rose and dropped. "I expressed an opinion and the sales team made the decision."

"And your opinion?"

"Can you blame me, Alexis? I was infatuated."

"I don't blame you. But you've withheld that from me."

"You're right." He seemed relieved to have it out. "Though I might say your secret has more weight."

"Does it? Our relationship was based on that interview, Jeffrey. All this time I've thought I wasn't good enough."

"I never meant that, Alexis."

"I know. But I didn't mean to hurt you either. I meant to save you from distress."

He nodded. "All right. I see that." He rose. "Would you like to go out tonight? It's a business dinner, but we could do something more afterward."

"Suz and Treya might come over." If she called and asked they really might.

"Next time?" He gave her the dimples.

"Okay." She rose to her toes and kissed him. Then she saw him out, locked the door, and set the alarm, thankful he was neither broody nor prone to rage … or even outrage. Calm waters, her Jeffrey. Calm, calm waters.

He would never self-destruct like Bo seemed to. *Bo.* She pressed a hand to her heart, holding him there for God to see. That was something her dad had taught her when she worried over things too big for her.

It's hell, she remembered Bo's words and added, "to want to change something that only God can."

She went to the library and pulled her pillow off the couch. *How do you know it isn't magic?*

"Because you're lost. And I don't know how to find you." She pressed the pillow to her heart and murmured, "Abba." Of all God's names, that was the one for desperate causes. God didn't think her babyish for calling him Daddy. He brought her into his heart and held her there as she wanted to hold Bo.

If partying involved the "bad things" he did to himself, that still reflected the shattered man inside. She wished her pillow was under his head right now, wherever he was.

Bo cupped his hands to catch rainwater dripping from the rusty culvert rim but shook so hard it all ran off. He licked his filthy palms. It tasted foul, but he got what he could, then huddled back down. The dog slunk back in and lay down against his legs. Bo shifted to give him room. Fleas, lice, ticks. Share and share alike. He drifted back out, then woke with a jolt.

"Barb?" That couldn't be right. What was she doing here in this pipe? "It's too cold for you." His teeth chattered. "No, that's you. You're cold, so cold and still." His throat stuck when he swallowed. "I wish I could warm you. But you're so thin."

How had she gotten thin when she'd always carried those extra pounds? "Remember how sorry we felt for Faye's clients? How you wanted to feed them?" He made a low laugh. "I gotta tell you, you better feed yourself. I can see your bones." He rubbed his eyes, wishing the skin was back on her skeleton, because this was really freaking him out.

Disturbed resonated in his head. Had this vision crept in, planting seeds in his brain? He reached a trembling hand. "Barb?" He rasped, but she was gone.

He was alone. Not even the dog remained. Longing for his sister hollowed his chest. If she came back, he'd trade places. Here. Take my skin. Have my face. You can be the lead now. I won't do as well in your parts, but have a shot at stardom. What do you say? "Barb?"

He pressed a hand to his swollen torso. It felt like coals burned him from the inside out. How long had it been since he'd eaten or drunk anything but gutter water? "Should take my own advice," he muttered. Maybe tomorrow. He closed his eyes.

Since it was a travel day and her team had it all under control—even Devin and Mattie—Grace took a minute to call Exi. "How are you doing?"

"I'm good."

"That's nice, but how are you doing? I was shot at too, remember." She hugged the place Mattie had filled during that awful incident. The bullet hadn't touched them, but Exi was grazed. People said it like that was no big deal, just a graze. But she knew how the mind conjured a different trajectory.

"The dreams are kind of brutal." Exi admitted. "I keep seeing the knife at Bo's face, or sometimes his throat or—you get it."

"No, I—what are you talking about? Was Bo at the shooting?"

"Oh. No. The day before. Didn't Devin tell you?"

A finger of annoyance became an angry fist. "He hasn't told me anything except what happened at the shop."

Her publicist, Raine Davenport, touched her watch. It was almost time to catch their flight for the next tour event. Grace indicated that she needed a minute.

Exi said, "Devin might not have noticed Bo's injuries while he was getting all masked avenger. A whacked guy beat on Bo and would have knifed him, but the bodyguard Liam hired—" her voice broke. "I'm not supposed to tell what happened." She started crying.

The events team was beginning to squirm, but Grace couldn't care about flights or book promotion at the moment. "Devin said it was someone after Bo who shot you. I had no idea his trouble was ongoing."

"The Russians want revenge, and others are involved somehow. Now that he's missing—"

"Missing?" Her chest went cold.

"Eileen said he went ballistic after Devin laid into him. He destroyed all his acting stills. Do you know about those?"

"Yes." She went colder still. If Bo did that …

"I shouldn't have gone with Devin. I should have stayed with Bo. I know he feels responsible for everything, even his sister's death. He's not thinking straight."

A ticket agent opened the boarding-gate door, but Grace didn't care about boarding first. Devin could get Mattie aboard.

"How long has Bo been gone?"

"Ten days, no, eleven. He left the hospital right after surgery."

Her head reeled, and she felt a familiar tightening in her stomach when someone she cared about could be in danger. "He might be with friends."

"He's missing performances."

She bit her lip. "I don't think it's the first time for that."

"That's what everyone says. But something's wrong inside him and I'm scared he might—" She sniffed. "Devin told him to stay away from me, and Bo hasn't answered my calls or texted me back even once."

"I'm sorry, Exi. He was different with you, but …"

"Now he's dumped me, so get over it?"

"I would never say that."

"I'm probably a fool, but I think you're wrong. We haven't had long, but he matters to me and I believe I matter to him."

"I believe you do too. But that doesn't mean he won't find solace somewhere else."

Exi drew a ragged breath. "I hope there is solace for his sorrow. Some cure for his guilt. Being with me gave him hope. But now that's gone. He was already hanging by a thread."

Grace quaked. "I hope you're wrong." Because that was on Devin.

"Anyway." Exi sniffed again. "If no one hears from him soon, I'm going to the police."

"Better check with Liam on that one."

"He's not in charge of me. I did what he wanted for Bo's sake."

"Getting the police involved might turn up the heat."

Exi was quiet for a while. "Do you really think that, or are you trying to keep me out of trouble like Devin does?"

"Exi, if this is still going on there must be layers to it that we can't imagine. If you let people know he's missing, more than the police might go looking. That can't be good for Bo and it might make you a target again." She understood Devin's concern enough to balance a little of her anger. He'd had a chance to do something this time and did. It just wasn't the right thing. "I understand you're frustrated with your cousin, but please be careful. This isn't something to mess with."

"Yeah? Devin should have thought of that before he interfered."

"Maybe. But he was terrified for you."

"I wish he could have been terrified for Bo too."

"So do I." Her voice broke. Signing off, Grace shouldered her carry-on and boarded the plane. This was not the time to accost her husband with Mattie and the publicity team in earshot, but the moment they were alone …

A soft whining woke him. The dog was back. This time at his head in the drainpipe. Bo could smell its breath. Rotten teeth probably. It licked his forehead. He had no strength to respond, to even look at the animal. The day was hot, but he shivered so hard it seemed his bones would come apart.

Barb leaned in and shook his shoulder. "Hey. Get up."

She knew he couldn't. All the other times she had lain still beside him. She had looked at him with mocking or sorrowful eyes. Or skeletal hollows. He shuddered. But she hadn't shaken …

"Come on. Come out of there."

The dog licked furiously, but it was Barb's nagging he wanted to stop. "Don't."

"You gotta come out. I can't get you."

Kind of hard when you're dead right? He slitted his eyes open. The voice wasn't Barb's. It was a kid's. A weird looking youth. Had he seen him before? "Whad'you want?" He slurred. Not drunk or drugged. He just had no energy to enunciate. E-nun-ci-ate. His drama coach had drilled that in. No need now. No need for anything. Just stop the shakes.

The kid let go of his shoulder. Bo couldn't see him anymore. The dog left. Good. Right. He swallowed with a ravaged throat.

Barb was back. "Stupid, Bo. Very stupid doing this."

"Stop talking and let me die in peace."

She shook her head. which seemed to shimmer. "I had no choice. What's your excuse?"

"No excuse. No excuse for anything." As Devin said before he took Sibella. *My Sibella.*

Why do I hear music when we do this? Not Sibella, Exi.

You are music. Music and dreams and hope.

As with all great tragedies, the need was intense, as intense as the loss. He had seen Exi and known. He'd felt the immediacy but couldn't turn the tide. Now their moment was gone.

"You need to fight."

"Not a fighter, Barb. You know. It's all been too easy."

"Dying's not easy."

"No? Then at least I'll be like you. It's all I've wanted."

"You want Exi."

He frowned. "How do you know her name?"

"I know because you know."

"Oh." He settled back.

"If you give up you lose her."

"Can't be helped. I'm bad luck. I bring harm to people."

"That's stupid."

But it wasn't. Devin knew. *Leave my cousin out of your disaster of a life.*

And Grace. And Eileen. They didn't say, but they knew.

"Wake up, Bo. You have to wake up."

"It's no use." His teeth hurt from chattering even though the heat in the corrugated pipe rippled the air. "You were the better of us, Barb. You didn't deserve it."

"Yeah, well, life's not fair. But guess what? Death isn't either."

"I wish you could be here. I miss you."

She started to reply, but the dog darted back in, its wiry fur flying when it assaulted his face again.

"See? What did I say?" The kid's voice.

"Yes. I see." Aged voice. Man, woman? "But it's not a kid."

"He's sick."

"By the stink I agree."

Go away and it won't bother you.

"Wake up, Bo," Barb said in his ear. "You have to go this time."

Tears burned, but he was too dehydrated to shed them. "Don't make me. I have nowhere else. No one else."

"You do. People love you. They always have."

Hands reached in, one pair grabbing one arm at the shoulder, the second pair grabbing the other. Hands of fate? He couldn't wait to see the twist.

18

The place he was in smelled of unwashed bodies, but for a change Bo didn't think it was his. The cot barely held him but was better than the culvert he supposed. An IV seemed competently inserted and secured. He guessed his veins no longer withered inside him. He felt them like tributaries running under his skin. Best of all he had stopped shaking his bones apart. Barb was right telling him to come—not that he'd had any resistance left—but she wasn't here. This time the tears moistened his lashes.

He didn't call for her. The fog had cleared. The hollow remained. When he pushed to one elbow, his ribs didn't scream. That was something. Someone had washed his hands. Maybe more than that. The T-shirt and drawstring pants were none he'd seen before. He sat up on the cot and realized they had set him up as a continuous drain, fluid in the vein, fluid out a tube. He shielded himself from the ragged females conked out on the other two cots and put an end to that.

"Do not remove the IV," someone said from the doorway.

Holding the spillable end of the catheter, he turned to find a wizened, battle-ready woman.

"It's providing you necessary antibiotics and hydration."

"Okay."

From a cart by the door, she took a clipboard. "Name?"

"Bo." From the number of letters she scratched, he guessed she spelled it Beau. When she glanced over for him to go on, he shrugged. "Just Bo."

"You apparently had surgery a short time ago."

He nodded.

"And some kind of altercation."

That much was evident.

"Are you a regular user of street drugs?"

"I wouldn't say regular. More like premium … when I do it. Which isn't that often actually."

"Are you an addict? That will impact our treatment."

"I keep trying, but I must be missing that gene."

That pulled her brows together. "Are you jonesing for something now?"

Jonesing sounded funny from the old woman, but he didn't grin. "No. I can take it or leave it."

Her face said *I've heard that before.*

He shrugged. Believe him or not. He didn't care.

"Why were you lying in a drainpipe?"

"Seemed as good a place as any."

"In delirium perhaps. How do you feel about it now?"

"Nostalgic."

She eyed him sharply. "You'd like to be back?"

His shoulders slumped. "One place is the same as another."

"I don't believe you're homeless, or you haven't been for long."

"Is it my teeth?"

"Teeth, skin, fingernails. You're healthy … or will be with another course or two of strong antibiotics. So I surmise the drainpipe experience is new to you."

Astute.

"You live in the city?"

Now that was a question. Going back to Eileen's wasn't an option.

"My concern is your mental state."

Because he spent the last days talking to his dead sister? An involuntary wince. "Can I do something with this?" He held up the catheter tube and bag.

"Empty it into the toilet since you started the process without us. You'll have to take the IV along."

Urine bag in one hand, lifesaving fluid in the other, he went into the single john, disposed of his waste, and left the apparatus on a metal shelf. He washed his hands and blinked at himself in the off-kilter mirror. She was waiting when he came back.

"How long have I been here?"

"Three days."

"How long do I stay connected?" He waved at the IV, disinclined to abort treatment this time.

"If I had some indication you would finish the antibiotics by mouth, it could be until that bag is finished."

"Do I just say so?"

"Are you taken at your word?"

"Depends. Grace and Eileen do. Devin … not so much. Exi—" No, he couldn't think of her. "Most people don't really care what I say unless I'm perf—" He closed his mouth. "I will take the medicine as directed. But my wallet's gone. I can't …" He'd never been unable to pay before.

"I will provide what you need. What can you do for me in return? Do you have skills?"

"Acting," he said before thinking. "It's really all, though I did assemble a crib once." And made a lousy bouquet. That thought hurt.

She studied him. "If I let you stay awhile, would you teach the kids?"

"Kids."

"Ours is a ministry to homeless children, runaways and castoffs. Street kids. An acting workshop might be a welcome change of pace."

He shook his head. "No."

"Why not?"

"It's worthless. Why would I give kids with nothing something worthless?"

She studied him. “Well, then. Can you drive?”

“Is that a trick question?” He flashed on Eileen’s vintage Rolls.

“It is not.”

“I don’t have my wallet.”

“How are you at handing out sandwiches?”

He didn’t know how to answer that one.

“I’m down a staff member. If you want to help, there’s room in the dormitory.”

“You don’t know me. Why do you think I’m safe?”

“I don’t know you, but someone I trust does.”

“Must have crossed wires. I’m hazardous.”

Again the shrewd appraisal. “In my experience, hazardous people keep it secret.”

“Not when they’re a target. And others get hurt in the process.”

Understanding filled her eyes. “You got in the pipe to hide.”

“I got in the pipe because I was too messed up to see straight.” She stayed quiet long enough, he said, “Do you have a name?”

“Are you staying with us?”

“I shouldn’t.”

“I’m Sister Ann.”

Sister. If the old bat meant nun, she didn’t dress like one. Work shirt and khakis. And that would be too ironic after Exi—stop. Maybe she was that missionary, arm-swaying kind like *Brother Bo, can you lend a hand? Amen hallelujah.*

“These kids have had very little fun in their lives. Some don’t know how to play, much less act. You might bring something bright to their existence, something more than street survival.”

“Oh, acting’s survival, believe me. Except not in the way you mean.” He felt bad for saying it. What did he know about survival? “But I still won’t do it. Kick me out if you want.” He sat back down on the cot, feeling woozy.

“Let’s do another day of intravenous medication. You can use the bathroom. In the morning I’ll tell you about our outreach program.”

"Outreach? I don't do God."

"Yes, well he can still do you."

Bo looked at the other cots. "What's with these two?" The girls had clearly been living rough. Neither had stirred through all of this.

"They're coming down. I doubt either will stay once the craving starts again, but they know they can when they're ready to follow the rules."

"One of those places, huh?"

"We're a family, usually the only family who's ever shown them love. All we ask is respect for one another and themselves. They show that by living clean and applying themselves to work and study. For most, even that is too much. But we don't give up, and they know we'll do whatever they need to help them heal and become productive human beings."

"Not members of society?"

"Most will never be that in the way you are. They're too damaged."

He frowned. "What's this outreach?"

"It can wait until tomorrow."

"No, tell me now."

"Our vans drive the streets at night and hand out sandwiches, blankets, something to drink, an ear, and an invitation."

"To be saved?"

"Yes. From the hell they're living."

Her straight words chastened him. "Sorry."

That got him the first faint smile. "There. My source was correct."

Maybe this was the right move. Hard to think of a less likely place to search for Bo Corrigan. Less likely place and activity. He lay back down. "I'll be good to go tomorrow."

"I think you will."

"I'm not calling you sister."

She hardly blinked. "Ann will do."

As he drifted off, he heard Barb laughing. "Finally got the tough role, Bo. Let's see if you're up to it."

Since she had started painting Bo, Exi couldn't stop. She had two canvas boards drying in Devin's main room and one on the easel in the library she was still touching up. It turned out that room lent itself to creativity, maybe charged by Devin and Grace working there. The image she had chosen for this one showed Bo in a dark mood—as she imagined he might be right now. She liked finding shots of him that weren't advertising, pictures that were closer to the man she knew.

Her phone rang and she snatched it so fast from the desk that she dropped it on the floor. *Please, please, please.* But it was her brother, Sully. She answered with, "What's up?"

"Hi, Mitten. I'm downstairs and the doorman says you have to give permission for me to come up."

"Didn't you flash your badge?"

"I'm off duty."

Right. Like Sully ever stopped acting and thinking like a cop. She told Vince it was okay to send him up but wasn't entirely sure it was. Keeping Jeffrey in the dark was one thing, her family another.

She let Sully in and he watched her reset the alarm. Jeffrey had hardly noticed, but she bet Sully now knew the code.

"Dad made me wait awhile for you to rest and recover."

"Uh-huh."

"Then sent me over to find out what the heck is going on with you."

"It was just a graze. It's almost healed." At his hard look, she added, "Crime happens, duh."

"Don't duh me, Mitten."

"Stop calling me that. It's been like twenty-two years since that small period of time when I tended to lose things."

"What did you end up with, a dozen mittens without a mate? And what's this about another guy?"

"You know?"

"Jeffrey told Dad."

"Oh."

"Did it upset him on top of everything else?"

"He likes Jeffrey."

"Do you?"

"On a scale of zero to ten of me getting you out of an abusive situation, Jeffrey's a zero."

She was sure he didn't mean that the way it sounded.

He leaned in. "Are you telling me or not?"

"I'm dating two guys." Or was she? "Jeffrey's fine with it."

"Not as fine as you might wish." He fingered the dark locks off his forehead.

She shrugged. "He wants me to be sure."

"Who's the guy?"

"Bo Corrigan."

"The Giorgio dude?"

"How do you know that?"

"He got mugged in Union Square, beat to a pulp. Lost his spleen."

She felt the blood leaving her head. Mugged in Union Square? Her heart hammered. "When?"

"I don't know, a couple weeks ago. He left the hospital against doctor's orders and before the officer could build a case. That raises a flag."

She released her breath. That must be the story they came up with for the hospital. "Oh. Yeah."

Sully's eyes narrowed. Dang it. Exi opened and closed her hands.

"Let's have it."

"I can't tell you." She bit her lip. "Not if you're a cop. I maybe, maybe could if you're my brother. And only then if you won't tell anyone else."

His whole body slumped. "Not again. What are you into now?"

"I'm not going to say until you promise."

"Okay. Start talking."

"That's not a promise."

"I swear on Sister M's toe." Every word was clipped between his teeth. "What's up with this guy?"

She told him.

His face when she finished wasn't as grim as it could have been. He took out his phone, logged into something and searched. He closed out and looked at her. "You can stop worrying about the first incident. The case is closed. Your protection specialist must have good contacts."

So she'd been told.

"I wish I could tell the department to drop the mugging-that-wasn't but I imagine that will be swept away also."

"What about Bo? Grace said if I tell the police he's missing the Russians will know it too. They'll guess John isn't protecting him."

He studied her. "How attached are you?"

He knew enough to say attached instead of interested. "I really care."

He studied the two paintings on the table. "So I see. How do I get hold of this bodyguard?"

"He's in my history since he called me at Eileen's." She located that number and handed it over. "Call from mine. He'll think it's me." She liked the thought of confusing and annoying John.

"I want some space to talk alone, and I'm supposed to check out your situation for Dad and make sure you're safe here. Vigilance at the entrance was a good start."

Vince gets a star.

He headed for the master bedroom. Exi walked to the table and studied her paintings. Did they reveal her feelings for the subject?

She hoped Sully didn't notice how many calls and texts she'd sent to Bo but didn't really care. Not if her brother could bring him back. A pipe dream, she knew. Or a prayer. She itched to get back to her canvas and paints, as if forming him there kept him real, kept him vital.

She jumped at a soft knock on the door and frowned because Vince had not informed her of a new visitor. Peeking out, she understood why. She pulled open the door to Cate and Mia carrying a baking dish and sides that looked and smelled Mexican.

"Full disclosure." Mia held up the bag of tortilla chips and a wine bottle. "Grace asked us to come upstairs and see how you're doing."

"She didn't tell us to feed you," Cate said. "But we thought if we're visiting, we may as well make it a party, ri—" She froze when Sully came out of the bedroom. "Oops. You must be Jeffrey."

"This is my brother, Sully. Cate. Mia." Exi got them all introduced and resigned herself since she could hardly feel less like partying if she had pneumonia.

Cate's color heightened. "Brother. Right. Want some enchiladas?" She held the pan up.

While he lived on pizza, Sully hated Mexican food. He'd made an art of refusals.

He said, "Smells good."

Exi looked at him.

"Join us." Mia passed him on her way to the kitchen.

Sully moved like he was caught in dual tractor beams. Guess he wasn't worried anymore, Exi thought as she followed him. The sisters knew their way around the kitchen, since they had one just like it. Exi took a stool by her brother but there were two on his other side.

She wondered which would get up close and wasn't surprised when Mia set out four plates and left the nearer stool for Cate. She must have noticed her sister's reaction too. Sully was good looking. In his faded jeans and T-shirt, it was clear he worked out and not clear he wrote tickets and arrested people.

Mia poured the wine she must have uncorked before coming upstairs. "How freaked are you that your sister got shot?"

"Pretty freaked."

Exi stifled a groan. "I'm fine. It's almost healed. Let's eat."

Cate reached for the spatula and served the enchiladas while Mia opened the chips and salsa.

The most religious of her brothers, Sully crossed himself and blessed his food. Cate's eyes widened, but if anything this notched up her enthusiasm. And Sully hadn't even turned on the charm—which saved gagging on his sister's part. As it was, she had to keep from snorting when he took the first bite.

As they ate, a kind of hysterical laughter vied with irritation that nothing was being done about Bo. This was not what she envisioned when she spilled her guts to Sully. But that frustration didn't compare to what she felt when her phone rang again and she saw the caller.

"Tell the doorman to let me up." John Helm did not sound happy.

Did he ever? Maybe happy wasn't something he did. Fine. She wasn't happy with him either. She told Vince to let him pass go and not collect two hundred dollars. Vince laughed. At least someone had a sense of humor. After a couple minutes of elevator travel, John arrived, scanned the group, and resigned himself to passing time. She introduced Cate and Mia.

He said, "I'm John."

Sully rose from the stool and shook his hand. "I'm Officer Sullivan Murphy. Thanks for coming."

Cate's mouth opened with surprise, but Exi now understood why he'd stayed for Mexican food. He'd planned this rendezvous.

John said, "I saw detective in the report."

Sully hesitated. "I just passed. Haven't been assigned. And I hadn't told my family yet." He looked at her.

"Congratulations." Exi squeezed his arm. And then she realized what *report* meant. John ran a check on her brother. Before she could call him on it, Mia rose and got a fifth plate and wine glass.

"Just water," John said when she reached for the bottle.

No drinking on duty, Exi thought. Mia looked wary serving him. Who could blame her? John hadn't softened his commando face.

"You're a cop?" Cate said to Sully as John accepted the plate of enchiladas and remained standing to eat.

Sully met her eyes. "NYPD, mounted police."

"On the horses?" Any second she would rise in the air like a helium balloon.

"It's a glorified photo op." Exi elbowed her brother since his head was too big already.

Mia eyed John. "Are you a cop?"

"I'm in security. Protection specialist." A little of the steel left the muscles of his face.

Huh. Must not be immune to breathtaking beauty. He'd make an interesting sketch, Exi thought, then wondered if her irritation would show in the outcome as her feelings did for Bo. Sensing her scrutiny, his return glance conveyed something. Probably *keep your mouth shut.* She didn't know why Sully asked him here or why he acted so deferential when the man lost Bo. Some protection specialist.

Wickedly, she offered the last third of her enchilada to Sully.

His eyes hooded. "I'm good."

Not even teasing could lift her mood. She circled the counter and John standing at the end of it, scraped her plate into the sink, then rinsed and loaded it.

"You don't seem cop-ish," Cate said, "I mean cop-like. You don't seem like a cop." She handed her empty plate to Exi.

"Yeah?" Sully pulled a crooked smile.

"You do," Mia told John. "No, not police. Military."

You think? Exi pulled the baking dish into the sink and started to scrub.

"You don't have to do that." Mia loaded her plate and Sully's. "We can wash up."

"You brought dinner. Dishes are on me." As much time alone as she'd had this past week, she should have enjoyed company. But she was sick with worry and missing Bo. She wanted to paint and block out everything but his face forming under her brush.

Mia came closer. "You shouldn't strain your injury."

"I'm not." Though it was throbbing.

Mia took the heavy pan and held it under rinse water. "Grace is really concerned. She wants a report."

"Tell her … tell her painting helps."

"Is that your work on Devin's table?"

Interesting how she referred to everything as Devin's. But she had known him before Grace moved in. "Yes. They're drying."

"Bo Corrigan?"

Exi's throat tightened. "You know him?"

"We hung out at some photo shoots and agency parties. Before I left the biz."

Struck again by Mia's stark beauty, Exi couldn't help wondering what "hung out" meant.

Mia looked over her shoulder at John talking to Cate. "What's his story?"

"What do you mean?"

"You're not happy with him. I'm wondering why."

Tears blurred her vision. Before she could say anything, Sully was there with an arm around her shoulders. "It's all good. Exi's just been through a lot."

Mia sensed the shuffle, but nodded sympathetically.

"If we're done here"—Sully flashed the charm—"why don't I walk you and Cate to the elevator?" Short odds he'd have a phone number when he came back.

Exi appreciated his clearing out the party until she realized it left her alone with John Helm—whom she had not invited. But her brother brought John here for a reason, so she might as well get it over with. When the door closed behind the other three, she said, "What?"

"I need to know who else you told."

"That you lost Bo?"

"I didn't—" His jaw rippled.

"Grace and Devin know he's missing. Only Sully knows the

rest." And she wasn't apologizing. If they'd gone to the police at the start, Bo might not be in trouble now.

He braced his hips. "Your brother won't be a problem."

"Gee, glad you think so."

"Are you always this belligerent?"

"Almost never."

He blew a slow breath. "It's a complicated situation when a Russian and a Syrian act together."

"That was a Syrian in the park—who then shot at me?"

"According to the CIA file. And that's not all. Whoever killed Karkov is making a move. There might be other factions or cells involved. A leadership void is an invitation, and any significant power shift impacts Liam and by extension, Bo. Your best plan is to marry your fiancé and leave Bo Corrigan to us."

"Oh, that's worked charmingly. And Jeffrey's not my fiancé."

At the knock, Exi stalked past John and let Sully back in. She didn't set the alarm because the rotating door was driving her crazy and if Special Forces and NYPD couldn't keep her safe, she'd give up right now. She chewed her lip while they talked some more. She wished they'd leave already so she could paint.

When her phone rang they both looked at her expectantly. She checked the screen, choked back her disappointment, and went into the library to talk to Jeffrey. He was recording a new show for them to watch and wondered when she could make it over. When she came out only Sully remained. Exi went into his arms.

He held her tight. "This time it might not be your lack of judgment."

"It's not Bo's fault either. He's done everything he can to make things right."

"Sounds that way. At least you're in good hands."

"John Helm's?"

Sully held her at arm's length. "Are you surprised?"

"I don't know. Why are you so impressed?"

"Exi, he has a Distinguished Service Cross."

"That's good?"

"A level below Medal of Honor."

She digested that. "He told you?"

"I pulled his records."

"Oh." That evened the field.

He released her shoulders and fought a grin. "I get the idea you're a thorn in his side."

"If he's so great, why did he lose Bo?"

"Your guy almost bled to death en route to the hospital."

She ached hearing it.

"He had major surgery that removed a vital organ. How could they anticipate him getting up and leaving?"

"Um, by watching?"

"His men were switching the guard when Bo walked out. Neither noticed."

She drew a ragged breath. "He probably changed his look." Her shoulders slumped.

"Who was it on the phone?"

"Not Bo, if that's what you're thinking."

"I wasn't. He hasn't responded to—"

"You checked my history? Did you read my texts too?"

Sully rubbed his face. "I only scrolled enough to see he hasn't answered."

"It was Jeffrey calling. He has a new show for us to watch."

"And?"

She swallowed. "I'm not that person anymore."

"Because you're falling for Bo?"

"Even if I wasn't."

"Okay."

"You're not disappointed?"

"It's your business, Exi. Mine is working this end of things for John."

"What do you mean? You have your own job."

"I passed for a detective position but haven't been assigned. I have a week's vacation I can use."

"For this? Don't you want to hit a beach with some leggy blonde?" When his expression shifted, she added, "Like Cate?"

"You're my priority."

"This is ridiculous. I don't know where Bo is. I wish more than anything I did." Her voice broke.

"With John's resources, he'll find him."

Maybe. But would it be alive?

19

Bo woke with difficulty when the street lamps came on and twilight filled the city sky. Rain speckled the high row of reinforced windows but no longer fell. No scent of it penetrated the clinic walls. He groped his way to the john with the IV pole for support. The shakes were back. His teeth chattered. His back and abdomen throbbed. Had the part where he didn't hurt been a dream? He stumbled and caught himself on the bathroom door, took care of business, and staggered back. He barely registered that the other cots were empty before falling into his with a curse.

The soaked sheet had cooled in his absence and hit him like an insult, until minutes later he was burning with fresh internal fire. He half expected Barb to take up residence on the neighboring cot, but she must prefer the culvert. Or maybe her parting shot was all she had left to say. What would he do with this role now that he got the hard life he wanted?

Might not matter if he didn't live to play it. He only half cared whether he did. And when he thought of Exi, he cared even less. Ridiculous how she'd invaded him. Light and joy and laughter. Desire. Was she Juliet? Or Sibella. No, Iseult. Tragedy enfleshed. He drew his knees up, curling around himself.

He wished he had his watch or phone to see her again. Just to look. Was she still calling, texting? He knew she was. She kept her promises. And he kept his. He would not entangle her in his disaster of a life. Whatever was left of it.

A hand came down on his head. He peeled his eyes open to Ann.

"Why didn't you press the button? You should have summoned someone hours ago."

Go away would be rude, but those were the words moving through his mind. He hadn't asked to come here, to be part of her mission to misfits. She went to a locked cabinet and replaced the IV fluid, then injected something into the line. "I thought we were past the high-spectrum antibiotic. You must not be fighting the infection as well as you should."

He could tell her about—

"Did they remove your spleen?"

What was it with old women reading his mind?

"I'll take that as yes. It explains your morbid condition when we found you. You had almost shut down."

So close to slipping away.

"That might seem desirable now, but this morning you had some small initiative. Let's see if we can't find that again."

He rasped, "Give up while you're ahead."

She sat on the cot beside his. "I'll tell you what I say to the kids who come through our doors, kids who have never known love that doesn't fail. Patient and kind love that isn't angered and keeps no record of wrongs."

He wanted to close his eyes and shut his ears. But his gaze stayed fixed on her face and her words kept coming.

"We form a covenant that never quits. We believe in their future. We trust and commit to them, asking only that they let us love them, that they try to believe in themselves and find ways to make their lives better."

The words sank in and stunned him. He could hardly fathom it.

"I think you could be a valuable part of this. And I think perhaps you could use that promise yourself. Have you known unconditional love?"

That didn't exist. Not even from Barb, who left him here with no purpose. Nor Exi, who walked out the door with Devin. Everyone wanted something.

"Beau."

He met the old woman's penetrating eyes.

"I want you to be part of this. I want you here. And I won't let you fail. Can you agree to trust a little, try a little?"

The fire in his body shifted back to chills, clacking his teeth together.

She put a hand on his head and closed her eyes. Like a mother. Maybe the warmth was merely that. But it seemed to spread from her hand down his body, easing the shudders and unclenching the muscles. "To heal you have to want it just a little. Let go of despair."

His stomach jerked. How could she know?

"Believe that you can make a difference."

In the time he had left? Maybe …

Exi paced the next morning, waiting for Jeffrey to stop by before work. The French toast she made for breakfast sat like a lump in her stomach. She wished she hadn't eaten. Instead of fortifying, it threatened to revolt.

This was typical tardy Jeffrey, but waiting chafed now that his arrival would not brighten her day. Or his. She had thought she could divide herself, could be fair to both, but why? She'd never been that person. She loved with single-mindedness that had sometimes blinded her, sometimes left her reeling, bruised and broken. But always she sprang back, ready to trust again.

Jeffrey deserved trust. And loyalty. He was strong and honest and meant well. He wanted the best for them, for her. He deserved the best himself. Her throat constricted. She'd wanted to be that, but now she wasn't. Or maybe she'd been fooling herself all along. He was the kind of man she should want. Bo was the man she wanted.

Not because of his fame and recognition, his stunning good looks, or even his talent. It was that part inside him that wanted love. He might call it sex, but he meant more than lust. Something in him called to something in her, and it went deeper than anything she'd felt with Jeffrey—as great a guy as he was.

She looked at the drying paintings. Bo was beautiful. But it wasn't perfection in his features. It was the impact of them. And that came from inside. She loved the part of him that caught the irony in things. And the part that saw good where others found fault. She remembered him holding her with the silly pillow between them, only he hadn't thought it silly.

He understood how seeing violence between her friend's parents had messed with her innocence. Didn't mommies and daddies love each other? He had entered the scene she described and accepted the pillow's comforting power. She loved him for that.

Tears burned. If she had spent the day with him as he asked, she would not have been shot. Devin would not have confronted Bo, and Bo would not be lost. And here she was waiting for Jeffrey but invaded by thoughts of Bo.

She tapped her fisted palms together and walked the wall of windows. She found no peace in motion but was unable to stop. Finally, the knock came on the door. When she opened it, Jeffrey greeted her with daisies, lilies, and button carnations. Her stomach knotted. She hadn't expected this on his way to work. He bent to kiss her, and she kissed him back, thankful things had not been more physical between them than that.

He cocked his head, dimples hinting at a smile. "So what is it that couldn't wait, Alexis?"

She had asked him here instead of some public place, because she couldn't bear to have one person see his disappointment—if he was disappointed. Maybe he'd be relieved, glad even. She would tell him right here and he could go.

"Thank you for the flowers. You're always so thoughtful." The paper crackled in her hands as the fragrances drifted up.

"You're welcome." He studied her, catching something off in her response. Before she spoke, he moved past her into the condo, where three paintings were drying on the table. They lay flat so maybe he wouldn't notice. She set the flowers on the counter and followed him toward the view.

"What are you wanting to say, Alexis? More time again? I've put no pressure on you, so there's no need to feel bad about that."

He'd been incredibly patient. If only it were that simple.

He almost reached the windows, then noticed the canvases and paused. "You're painting. I'm glad to see it."

"You are?"

"I just watched something about art as therapy after trauma. I doubt the shooting has left such a light impression as you want me to believe, so yes, I'm very glad for it." He lowered his head to study her art. Did he not recognize the subject?

"The thing is, Jeffrey, I'm not the person I was. I'm not even sure I was that person."

He shifted his gaze from the paintings to her. "What person?"

"The one I wanted to be for you." She watched comprehension reach his eyes.

"That sounds ominous." He looked at the paintings again. "Are these …" He cleared his throat. "Bo Corrigan?"

It was on her tongue to say he was missing and she was trying to find him through art, but she held it in. "Yes."

"They're a lot clearer than my portrait."

"It's a different method. Representational realism. Not at all what I learned in grad school, the way I painted you."

"You're good at both methods."

"These are just studies. I haven't mastered the technique by any stretch."

"This one's rather somber." He pointed to Bo's moody portrait, not so much somber as troubled, even tormented.

"Jeffrey … I don't think it's fair to see you anymore. I can't see it happening for us."

"Because of him."

"No. I'm not seeing him right now either." Bo might have left her so far in the dust he hardly remembered her name.

"Really." He turned to her.

"I have to get my own head straight. I keep going from person to person and trying to be what they see in me. It's not working."

"I would think not. Maybe we could—"

"Please don't make a suggestion. You're always so helpful, but I have to do this myself."

He moistened his lips. "You don't want me to wait."

"I would never ask that. I know you want to start a family. And … I'm not there."

He nodded a few times, letting her words in. "I'm not entirely surprised. You haven't been yourself, or the self you tried to be." He gave her a faint smile. "I'm grateful for your honesty. At the same time, I want to throw these paintings."

"You do?" The words rushed out on a breath. Her mind filled with Bo tearing apart his studio.

"I wouldn't, of course."

"No, of course not." Her eyes filled. "You're a great person, Jeffrey, and I wish … I really wish you all the best."

"I wish that for you too." He looked her up and down for long moments, then drew himself up. "If you find yourself sooner than you think and want to talk, it wouldn't hurt to try me."

She sniffled. "That's really nice and way too generous."

"It's not generous. I love you."

Words clogged her throat.

He leaned toward her cheek, then stopped himself and went out. Tears ran down her cheeks and smeared the city outside the windows. How would she feel if Jeffrey acted on his urge to throw the paintings? Did it mean he cared less if he never lost control?

It didn't matter. She had done the right thing, the fair thing. Now she was alone, but she wouldn't fill the void. Bo had asked her who she saw in the mirror. It was time to find out.

Except … she had a promise to keep. She took out her phone and texted. It might not matter to him at all, but what if her breaking with Jeffrey could bring Bo home?

This time when Bo opened his eyes, someone else was checking his chart. The man had the most delicate bones he'd ever seen, grayish brown skin and huge eyes, like a clever grasshopper.

He said, "I'm Dr. Patel. I help with the children."

"I'm not—"

"I know. I guess you are twenty-seven, twenty-eight."

Bo said nothing. The less specific anything got the better.

"Sister said you are new staff and she would rather you not die before your first shift."

"Nice of her."

"Workers of the right temperament are not easy to come by."

"Right temperament, huh? She just met me."

"She has a sense for these things."

"I thought she had a source."

"It is one and the same."

Hocus pocus.

"Without a spleen, your immune system is compromised. It must learn a new way to function. I think, maybe, more than your body must learn this."

"Call it good enough if you can keep the shakes away."

"I have adjusted the medication. Sister is very knowledgeable. She has worked in hospitals and camps all over the world."

Somehow he doubted that meant youth camps for privileged brats like himself.

"Here we have a few more options." He motioned to the IV.

"Whatever you put in this bag seems to be working. Pretty quick too."

"It has been two days."

Sure enough, the drain was back in place. And a new pair of ragamuffins flanked him, one black, one enormous, both male. By the jerking legs and moaning neither enjoyed a peaceful sleep, but better than they'd get on the street.

"You are so much stronger than what she usually sees, she miscalculated your wellness."

If what she pulled out of the culvert was better than normal, this was a sorry operation indeed.

"When I see you again I trust you will be closer to recovery."

"Someone lifted my wallet. I can't pay for this."

"We have donors who keep us operating. You are a member of the team."

"Like charity donors?"

"Does that offend you?"

"Of course not. It's just …"

"You would rather be on the other side?"

"Wouldn't you?"

"Often it is easier to give than to receive."

He thought of all the things he'd thrown money at. Had it ever been a worthy cause? Here were people throwing money at his useless self.

He didn't need a wallet to change that. He could replace his credit cards and driver's license. But that was easy. This was hard. So he kept his mouth shut. He was playing the role of a lifetime, the last he'd ever play. He meant to give it everything he had left.

The dream woke Grace with unusual force, and Devin's arm came around her at once. Since Mattie slept in a portable crib in the suite portion of their hotel room, he put his mouth to her ear and murmured over the air conditioner, "It's all right. You're safe. Mattie's safe. We're all together." He kissed her temple. "You're all right, Grace."

She stilled her heaving chest but felt his quaking against her back. Even though he meant to soothe her, his anguish renewed every time they did this. Exi's experience seemed to have reactivated her own. Devin wasn't happy she'd been calling to check in, and he'd noticed the renewed intensity and frequency of the nightmares. No one could go through her level of trauma without impact, but surely at some point it would diminish.

No matter how she prayed, the memory just kept pushing past her defenses. Devin wrestled his own demons. She could imagine what he'd say if she told him this one involved Bo. She really wished Exi hadn't told her about the knife to his face. She truly hated knives, a weapon that always seemed particularly vicious, even though the one she grabbed from her block had been her only recourse to protect herself before she knew her assailant packed heat. She gulped at her mind's feeble attempt at humor.

"Okay?" Devin murmured.

"I'm all right." She turned into him. "I think it's that you're leaving today."

"I wish I could stay for the rest, but …"

"I know. You have commitments as important as mine. I can't tell you how much these two weeks have meant to me."

He stroked her cheek. "You know I love seeing you in action. Queen of all the honeybees."

"Stop."

"The way they swarm in, drawn by your sweetness. Only a few get to feel your sting."

"Like you I suppose."

"You deny it?"

"You stung first."

"Can't argue that. Want to make up again?"

She bit her lip on a laugh. "You know what phase of my cycle it is. It's amazing I didn't jump you the minute my eyes opened." Except she'd been in the nightmare throes.

He touched her cheek. "I've been thinking about what you said."

"Which amazing thing are you referring to?'

He gigged her ribs and made her jump. "The baby-making one."

"What?" She half rose on her elbow. "You mean Mattie not being an only child?"

"That's the one."

Her heart raced. "If you say baby-making one more time, I'm not responsible for my actions."

"Let's buy a house and pop them out as fast as your books."

She punched his shoulders, but the look in his eyes did her in.

He took charge of her mouth, pausing only for his graveled voice to say, "Baby-making time."

Exi turned from her fifth painting when Devin and Mattie came in. Had he told her he'd be back this afternoon? Time had lost relevance when she had nowhere to be and art happening. She had moved her operation to the main room as he'd recommended, so the different versions of Bo were right there for him to see in order of dryness. By his expression, he more than saw.

He carried his sleeping daughter to her toddler bed and came back out, looking weary. "What's all this?"

"You told me to paint. I'm trying a new style."

"Bo's your style?"

"Bo is my subject. Representational realism is my method … or will be, when I get good at it."

"You're plenty good." He took in the canvas boards propped up around the room.

She tapped the handle of her brush against her chin. "I learn a little more with each study, but I'm nowhere near proficient."

A crease formed between his brows. "He's been here, posing for you?"

Her throat swelled. "I haven't seen or heard from him since you drove him off. No one has."

"He hasn't surfaced?" He looked surprised but not overly concerned. "How long has it been?

"Almost three weeks. No calls or texts, no credit cards, nothing."

"How do you know that?"

"John Helm."

Devin nodded. "Bo's a grown man, Exi. Not a lost pup." He turned from the last of her paintings. "Isn't this a little obsessive? When I said paint I meant—"

"What?"

"I don't know, just … have you thought of anything else?"

"Oh, I don't know." She plunged her brush into the mineral spirits and wiped the paint off. "If Grace were missing, you probably wouldn't think of her at all."

"Grace is my wife."

"I didn't realize caring required a license."

"Alexis …"

"I should never have left Bo and come with you. I thought you needed me—"

"What?" He cocked a brow.

"You were so upset. I thought you needed to know I was okay so you could stop stressing about me and Grace and Mattie. But you're not upset. You're mad. And that needs a target, a target named Bo."

He stared at her. "What do you see in that self-absorbed miscreant? I don't get it. I just … don't … get it."

That couldn't be clearer. "I'm leaving."

He braced his hips. "Why?"

"Because you don't care about Bo. And that makes me unhappy with you. And you're my cousin so—"

"I care about Bo. I just don't want him with you."

She held up a hand. "You're only making it worse." She stacked the finished and mostly finished paintings and slid them into the giant tote with her supplies. "I'll be back for that last one when it's dry enough to move."

He blinked. "Where are you going?"

"You don't need to know. I'm not a lost puppy either." She strode into the library and started packing.

He came and leaned in the doorway. "I'd like to know. After everything I think I have a right to."

She pulled his credit card from her wallet with all the receipts. "I'll pay you back when I can."

"I told you I hired you." He slipped the card into his wallet and left the receipts. "Please tell me where you'll be."

"Probably home."

"That's not safe. At least go back to Eileen's."

She spun. "Oh, that's okay now that Bo's gone?"

He opened and closed his mouth, then said, "I hoped this would be resolved by now."

"I did too. You have no idea how much." She tugged her suitcase off the bed and shouldered the giant tote.

Devin held the door for her. "I can't leave Mattie to help you."

"I don't need help."

"Will you talk to Grace when she's back next week?"

She sighed. "Okay."

"Okay." He swallowed. "Be careful."

She took the elevator down in a turmoil of emotions. Anger, hurt, longing. The only thing she accomplished by leaving was not strangling her cousin. In the lobby, Vince helped her out the door. "You need a cab?"

"I don't have money for one. I'll take the subway."

"You sure?"

"Yeah. Thanks for all your help."

"You take care now."

"I will." But how? She really did have a decision to make. If the Russian gang and whoever else knew where she lived, that would endanger her roommates. She could go home to her dad, but what if they knew that address too? They had found the store.

Sully lived with two other cops, one who'd been hitting on her since his academy days. So not doing that. There might have been Jeffrey, but even if she hadn't ended it that wouldn't be fair. She had to keep painting. By the time she descended the subway stairs, she'd accepted the inevitable and took the train to Gramercy Park. Her suitcase and tote boxed her in like a big, fat warning to keep away. Whoever looked over probably thought she'd been kicked to curb. She had. In more ways than one.

Sondra opened the door when Exi tugged her baggage up the steps. Eileen stood with her as if she'd been waiting there all along.

"Please don't tell Devin I'm here."

Eileen looked past her. "Thank you, John. I've got her now."

Exi almost jumped out of her skin when she turned and saw him on the street behind her. "What are you doing? Why aren't you out finding Bo?"

"You're my best chance of doing that."

What did he think, Bo would rush out of hiding if he saw her? Tears filled her eyes.

"Come in, Exi." Eileen soothed. "You made the right choice coming here."

"I made the only one." She dragged her luggage up four flights and entered Bo's apartment. Memories flooded in and washed away her anger. She laid her suitcase on the bed she'd slept in and carried her tote to his studio. It was there her heart finally broke for the man who lay in shreds across the floor.

20

When it vibrated, Grace checked her phone and saw Devin's text. *Home safe. Miss you.*

She replied. *Thanks for letting me know. I miss you back. But I'm not happy with you.*

Instead of asking why, he wrote: *Get in line.*

Oh?

Exi gave me an earful.

Good. *Why didn't you tell me about Bo?* Instead of confronting him on the tour, she had waited to see if he would bring it up. The whole time he accompanied her, he never told her Bo was missing.

Her phone rang. When she answered, Devin said, "I think he's somewhere partying, but … I'm sorry I didn't mention it. Things went so well with your family, and I was having such a great time in your professional aura—and privately—it didn't register as necessary."

Well, that was hard to stay mad at. "I loved having you and Mattie with me, and I'm so grateful you mended things with my family. But I'm awfully worried about Bo."

Devin sighed. "Is there anything I can do?"

"Find him?"

"His security guy's looking."

"He might not know the theater people you know. Can you call around?"

"Yes."

She pressed a hand to her heart. "Thank you. How's Exi? Can I talk to her?"

"She's not here."

"When she gets back, have her call me, okay? If I can't pick up I'll call her back."

"She's staying somewhere else now that we're back. I don't know where."

Grace tapped her mouth. "She really is unhappy with you."

His sigh resonated.

She felt for him. "How badly are you kicking yourself?"

"How much do you think?"

"If it weren't about Bo, I'd say a lot."

"I think I reacted appropriately under the circumstances. But I might have worded things better at Eileen's."

"Hmm."

"I won't apologize for holding Bo accountable. I'm the only one who does."

With her blood pressure rising, silence was best.

"I could have been less … insulting."

Again she waited.

"I apologized to Exi."

"Hmm."

"Okay, I know. I'll straighten things with Bo. Apologize for my words, not my message."

She really wished she was there, doing whatever she could for the situation. Hanging up, she told Raine, her wonderful publicist, "I'm not sure I'm cut out for this touring anymore. Life is too complicated."

"I hear you. But don't tell Corbin."

"I suppose not." The publisher had been steadfast through the scandal. Of course, it helped that her sales recovered. Readers who repudiated her were replaced by ones who either hadn't heard of her before that or found her contrition sufficient. She'd made no excuses for failing to live what she wrote. The message remained. And her new stories reflected the maturity she gained from walking through that fire. She hated to think how much better they'd be if she ever faced something like that again.

That brought her back to Bo. Three weeks with no word? That couldn't be right. Her friendship with him was complicated by his choices. But he mattered to her. There was something vulnerable inside his devil-may-care facade. A searching heart, maybe.

Raine signaled they were ready for her, so she'd have to call Exi later—and maybe even try Bo.

Exi stared through tears at the wrecked studio. Devin's words were harsh, but to cause this destruction? There must be so much more wrong in Bo's head than she knew. Maybe more than losing his sister. This was a repudiation of his life.

She brought her fingers to her lips and felt his kiss. If not for the cameras they might never have stopped. She wished she hadn't told him, wished she hadn't cared who saw anything, that she'd thrown caution to the wind and stayed with him. What premonition told him that day was all they'd have? And why hadn't she listened? Why had she left him so vulnerable?

Her ringing phone jarred her. Treya's ringtone. Exi dredged up the brightest greeting she could manage. "Hi."

"Hey, girlfriend. We told your cousin we're coming to steal you, but he said you're not staying there anymore."

She swallowed. "I'm at Eileen's."

"That townhouse with ice cream?"

Exi bit her lip. "I don't know if there's ice cream, but yes that townhouse."

"You're hanging with Bo?"

"He's not staying here right now."

"Then why aren't you home with us?"

"I'm painting. Eileen has a room I can use for a studio. So it's easier to be here."

"Well, you're coming out with us tonight."

She didn't want to, but, overwhelmed with grief and worry, she might actually lose her mind if she didn't … like the recluse in Grace and Devin's play. "Where do you want to meet?"

"Oh no, we are coming to get you. Give me that address."

"I don't know it. Let me see if I can find some mail or something." She went into Bo's kitchen and found three unopened letters. Return label Louisa Bourne. Exi gave Treya the address, trying not to wonder what was written inside.

After ending the call, she ran her fingertips over the envelopes. Handwritten letters seemed like something a therapist would suggest. Did Bo's leaving them unopened make him as heartless as Devin claimed? Or was Louisa forcing something he never intended? Not. Her. Business.

She made herself look good and planned to be on the curb when her friends arrived. But the closer the time came to meeting them, the less she wanted to leave Bo's apartment. What if he returned when she was out, came in for something and left again? It might be only minutes to see and speak to him, to convince him to stay. Her heart raced.

This was crazy. She pressed a fist to her mouth. How could he have such a hold on her? It was more than attraction. It approached obsession. Except it wasn't about her. The thing speeding her heart was fear for Bo, fear and the need—yes need—to help him hold on.

Maybe her fears were groundless. He'd never said anything suicidal. Only that he didn't know how to go on, and he had a pattern of reckless behaviors. That and the harrowing loss that filled his eyes when he couldn't hide it. Grief was killing him, and Devin made her an accomplice. No, she made herself by walking out. She could have stood with him and didn't.

The timer on her phone chimed. She had to go if she didn't want them coming in here, violating Bo's privacy. She hustled down the stairs and out the door. Her friends looked disappointed when she jumped into Treya's ancient Fiat, but she didn't care.

"We were going to park and come in," Suz said.

"Better just get going." She looked out the back window where cars had waited for her to get in.

Treya let up on the brake. "Okay, but we're coming in after."

"I don't feel right bringing people in without permission."

Her friends looked at each other, then her. "You know that's weird, right?"

In the side mirror, Exi saw a black SUV pull into traffic. John Helm or his guys following their best lead? Too bad it would get them nowhere.

"I don't think it's weird at all. It's not my house. But I'll ask Eileen," then think of an answer that closed the subject. She loved Suz and Treya. She just couldn't stomach them ogling Bo's place. Her protective streak seemed to have no limits. Too bad it was too late. Stop. She had to stop the fatalistic thinking.

She must be a better actor than she thought, because the whole time they shopped Union Square, her friends never guessed how close she was to breaking down. And neither asked about her watchfulness. She didn't see John's security personnel in the crowds as they went shop to shop, though she wouldn't necessarily recognize whoever it might be. Nor did she see crazed shooters.

"Let's eat," Suz said.

Exi started to decline, but Treya said, "Our treat, don't even argue."

As they grabbed a bite at The Pavilion, Suz brought up the flower shop. "Are you going to work there again?"

"I might if Dad would let me. I need a job."

"Yeah," Treya said in sympathy. "But I sort of get him not wanting you back there."

"I couldn't do it." Suz clasped her chin, bulging her freckled skin around her fingers and thumb. "I couldn't set foot in any place I'd been shot."

Exi restrained a shudder. "I guess I won't know until I try. But it's my mom's store, and I have more great memories than one bad one." Including Bo's courtship proposal and flower arranging. That brought the ache that didn't leave the whole rest of their time together.

When Sondra let her back in, Liam was in the foyer. "Did you enjoy yourself, Miss Murphy?"

None of his business, but she said, "Yes."

"They look like nice young women."

She folded her arms. "How do you know?"

"The surveillance camera at Eileen's door."

"They are nice, thanks." She started past.

"Alexis."

She stopped.

"Johnny says your brother knows our business. It would be better if your friends did not."

"They don't." She met and held his eyes.

"Good. That's good, then." His face softened. "How is your arm?"

"It's healed."

"If you need to talk to a professional—"

"I don't. But thanks."

"Do you know where Bo is?"

He'd caught her off guard. "No." Her eyes pooled. "Do you?"

"Sadly no."

Did he think she'd snuck out to meet with Bo? Used her friends as cover?

"I understand you doubt our commitment. I assure you I'm taking this seriously."

She sniffed. "Thank you."

"Now is there anything I can do for you?"

Her last paycheck from the store had hit her account and evaporated. "I need to go back to work. If not my mom's store then I need a different job."

"What if I covered your bills for a while?"

"Like you did Bo's?"

"His was debt to be repaid."

"What then, a loan?"

"I'm asking a lot of you. The least I can do is make the favor feasible."

"By paying my bills."

"In the Renaissance, patrons supported artists so they could create their masterpieces without financial concerns."

She slacked a hip. "Are you making fun of me?"

Humor found his eyes. "No, lass. I'm saying there's precedent for my offer."

For some reason his using *lass* didn't make her want to stomp him after all.

"Eileen mentioned you came with art supplies. If I'm preventing you from seeking employment, you can think of me as a patron."

Her heart jumped in her chest. This was better than Devin's house-sitting offer. Except she'd never been a moocher.

He must have seen her hesitance and said, "It makes Johnny's job easier and might bring Bo back if he learns you're here. If we can bring him out of the cold, wouldn't that be worth accepting my offer?"

"Yes." That answer was obvious.

"Good. Give your bills to Eileen and I'll have them paid. You have a credit card?"

She nodded.

"Then we're set."

"I want the cameras off upstairs."

"That's already been done."

Exi drew a slow breath. "Then … thank you."

"It's my pleasure," Liam said. "And if I might add I'm finding Johnny's reports quite entertaining."

"I'm not trying to be funny."

"No, Miss Murphy. I'm certain you're not." He put on his hat and walked out the door as Eileen came in and took hers off like a changing of the guard.

"Everything all right?"

"I guess so." Exi studied her. "Is it really all right for me to be here? I haven't been that nice."

"You've been honest. And devoted to Bo. We may be all he has."

"Grace cares too."

"Yes, but Devin won't allow her to practice it."

Exi spread her hands. "I keep praying."

"In this house? That might be a first."

"It works a little better when two or more agree."

"My dear, if I uttered a prayer, the forces of darkness would rise from the deep and drag me away."

"That's not how it works."

"I'd better not risk it."

"You sound like Bo."

She smiled. "Yes. Rather."

Exi cleared the tears from her throat. "I'll pray for you both."

"God help us all."

Exi headed up, thinking that was probably the most powerful prayer Eileen could have uttered.

"You're not telling the truth," Bo said with more heat than he should on this morning tour of the facility. Ann's expression caused instant remorse. "I don't mean you're a liar, just ..." He looked at the fifteen-year-old girl with the misshapen head, staring at the wall while a rotund woman read a story aloud. He'd asked what happened and wished he didn't.

"You don't want it to be true."

Struck regularly in the head with a skillet? Burned by the grease when her father pulled it directly from the stove?

"Thankfully it wasn't the meth operation she interrupted. Or they might have all blown up."

This brain-damaged girl had found her way to their door. But ... thankfully? Did Ann really think that word applied?

"Hurts the heart, I know. That's why what we do is so vital."

"You said they hadn't been loved, not—not that. How can you

do anything about that?"

"How can we not? They're ours now. We can't undo the past, but we can try to heal the present and give hope for the future."

"Look, Ann. I'm out of my depth. I can't imagine one thing I've got that would help."

"Tanaya's needs may be more than we're equipped to handle. She'll be assessed to determine the level of care she requires. If she is able to benefit from our instruction with some hope of success, we'll do what we can."

This was his first day out of the clinic, and he wanted to crawl back there. He'd take that discomfort over this.

Ann moved him on in their tour. "At this time during the week, most of our kids are studying for GEDs in the classroom or being tutored individually at whatever level they require. Some quite basic."

"They didn't go to school?"

"Often their behaviors, disabilities, or home situations made that inconsistent."

"What's different now?"

"We work with the individual. We believe in them. We don't give up. As long as they try, we try."

Okay, he could see that.

"They'll all be taught life skills of budgeting, hygiene, interviewing, anger management, and good work ethics. Our counselors are available all the time. Our pastoral ministers provide the spiritual undergirding of our unconditional love. It's optional, but most gravitate there for the big questions, like why has this happened to me?"

"What's the answer?"

"There are many. The biggest is no matter the reason, love, trust, forgiveness, and faith can fill the shadows with light and hope."

Bo looked back to the damaged girl, forever etched into his brain. "That's just words."

"Not when they're steeped in action, every moment every day.

You asked what could possibly help Tanaya. That's what. A place where she isn't tortured. A gentle hand. A story to engage her mind. Food and shelter. No, it may not be enough, but where would she be without it?"

His throat constricted, not with anger now but pain, as if this kindness burned through a barrier that had protected him. Ann seemed determined to break him down.

"If they pass the equivalency and demonstrate the necessary responsibility, they may move into transitional housing. In subsidized apartments they learn to be good neighbors, to use their life skills, hold a job, pay their rent to our accountants. When they graduate from this, we give them the rent we saved in their accounts, and they go on to college, to work a trade, or find other employment. It's a joyous time for them and us."

"How many go to college?"

"However many want it enough. We don't create or qualify their dreams. Any direction is a good one that leads to a fruitful life. Even yours, Beau."

Still working him for that acting workshop. She didn't understand Barb was the teacher. He would be a lousy substitute.

They came to a nursery area. "Our mother-and-child program helps teenage mothers learn healthy parenting."

Was there such a thing?

"Often these pregnancies occur on the street, sometimes from rape, sometimes within the home situations they've fled or been thrown out of—a stepfather or Mom's new boyfriend. The girl's only crime is catching his eye."

Bo clenched his teeth.

"Many times when the pregnant daughter reveals the violation, she's blamed."

"Brilliant."

"We address emotional and physical needs. Our free daycare allows them to finish school and hold a job. We give their babies a strong, healthy start in life."

"I know nothing about babies or parenting. Don't plug me in there."

Ann looked at him quizzically, then turned when a scrawny youth sauntered down the hall toward them. His brown skin was mottled with pale patches like clouds.

"I heard my project was up and roaming."

"Beau, this is DeShawn. He found you."

"I remember." Vaguely. "There was a dog."

His eyes brightened. "Sheriff. I call that dog Sheriff for the star on his chest. And cuz he patrol the hood."

"That's clever."

"That's me, clever. Sister don't let our dogs come in, but he's around." The kid eyed him. "You gonna die?"

"Not yet. You?"

DeShawn gave him a big grin and parroted, "Not yet."

"What are you, fourteen, fifteen?"

"I'm seventeen, man. Getting my GED."

"That's good."

"Back to class," Ann said. "The others need your example."

DeShawn hooked his thumbs in his pants. "That's right. I'm an example to others." He walked back the direction he came, angling one hip and the other with his thumbs still hooked.

"He's an example?"

"We believe they can all be examples to each other. Often we're the only ones to tell them they're worth something, that they can be someone others could emulate."

The only place he felt that was onstage. "He doesn't look seventeen."

"On the street they strive for that. Younger gets more sympathy. Especially the girls."

"He doesn't seem to be trying too hard."

"Chronic malnutrition. A crack-addicted mother."

At some point he would learn to stop asking if he didn't want the answers. Somewhere nearby, a female started screaming. He jolted.

"That's Imogene. She doesn't know a better way to express her frustration when she can't understand something."

"How old is she?"

"Twenty. She aged out of the foster program without being educated."

"That screaming might be why they didn't keep her in school."

"There's a high percentage of mental illness among the homeless. People assume that for war-torn veterans and lifelong alcoholics, not kids. Yet it's a factor at all ages."

"Are there meds or something?"

"There are, though we find patience often works as well."

He scratched the back of his neck. "So … I'm not a good candidate for screamers either."

"I wonder."

"Don't." He shook his head. "Put me where I'll do the least damage."

DeShawn came back out like a yo-yo on the rewind. "I could show him around, Sister. He's my project."

"Later, DeShawn. There's plenty of time for that."

Bo watched him slump down and walk back. "Short-term memory deficit?"

"He's on the upward arc of his cycle. Finding you gives him status and something to look forward to. All too soon he'll begin the descent." She fixed him with a penetrating stare. "Do you experience mood shifts?"

"I'm not bipolar. I'm not anything. I mean nothing's wrong with me. Not like these."

"We stay away from comparisons."

"Yeah, I know the jargon. But everything is relative, like it or not."

A ghost of a smile. "I'm going to enjoy knowing you, Beau whatever-your-last-name-is."

She might think so, but it would be a mistake. Look what happened to the grande dame. Eileen had backed the wrong horse. These people better watch themselves.

21

The second Bo sat up and rubbed his face, DeShawn was in it. "Hey, man. Want to come feed Sheriff?"

When Ann said dormitory, Bo hadn't realized she meant for him to sleep with the kids. Except for the times he'd chosen to share his bed, he'd never shared a room. Even the camps had individual cabins or tents. All around were other eyes like alley cats, watching to see how he would answer.

"Can I hit the john?"

"Yeah." DeShawn laughed. "I gotta take care of business too."

Oh good, a buddy system.

Bo had raided the donations for jeans and a button-up shirt. After "taking care of business" beside DeShawn and a kid named Sticks—whose bone-thin arms and legs were a physiological marvel—Bo rolled his sleeves and washed up.

DeShawn found this funny. "You wash like a white boy."

"Imagine." He rubbed water over his face.

Sticks said, "You got money?"

Bo dried off. "Someone pinched my wallet."

"Yeah." The kid's sallow face fell. "Out there someone always gets your stuff."

"What about here?"

"Nah. You take stuff here, you're gone."

"Well," DeShawn countered, "staff gives you a chance to make it right. You don't fess up and restitute, then you're gone."

"Restitute, huh?"

"Yeah, you know, give it back."

"Except if it's gone," said Sticks. "Then your nads are in the wringer."

"Don't say nads to him."

"I do actually know the word," Bo said.

DeShawn howled and Sticks sniggered. They headed out and sure enough the wiry-furred dog prowled outside the door, hair falling like needles from a dying tree. One cloudy eye suggested age while his nervous energy gave a different impression.

"What do you feed him?" Bo followed when they started walking.

"Whatever we find. See, he can't get in the trash bins. So I got to reach it for him."

"A lot of you have dogs?"

"Out here, yeah. Cops run them off, but they come back. Can't run off the sheriff."

"He has a good thing going. You're like a big brother."

"Yeah, I like that." DeShawn studied him. "You got a brother?"

"No. I had a sister."

"She die?"

"Yeah."

"Sorry man. My grandma die and her no-good landlord throw me out. He say no crack baby livin' in his domain. Get that? Domain, like he some king. And the place falling down."

"When was that?"

"Four years about."

He'd have been thirteen. "Where did you go?"

"I been travelin'. I come up from Baltimore. You been to Baltimore?"

Bo shook his head. "No. Just LA."

"Like Hollywood?"

"Like."

"You look like Hollywood," said Sticks.

Bo hunched a little. "Where are these dumpsters? Shorty's hungry."

"He's not Shorty." DeShawn looked aggrieved. "He's Sheriff."

"Sheriff Shorty, law dog."

The boys laughed full out, repeating the name. "Yeah man. He's the law." DeShawn rubbed more hair off the mongrel's head.

They stopped at a big metal trash bin whose stink preceded it. Besides the rank garbage inside, nostril-stinging urine suggested this corner served double duty. The kids went right in and lifted the lid. Trying not to gag, Bo held it open while Sticks and DeShawn searched inside. Apparently they weren't just looking to feed the dog. Sticks pulled out a lace-up boot with no ties, then rummaged for the other.

"Aren't shoes donated to the mission?"

"These're not for me."

DeShawn found part of a sub sandwich and Sheriff devoured it. Yeah, that dog knew the score. So why had he climbed into the culvert with someone who had nothing to offer, then brought help? Hey, maybe he was the sheriff patrolling the hood.

Bo walked with the kids beneath a train trestle on a street that crunched and glittered with broken glass. The piles of rags wrapped in blankets or newspaper were life forms, he realized, when Sticks set the boots next to one of them. A skeletal hand with gray hairs pulled the footwear into the mound. Stench like a fetid swamp arose, as if those rags were kept from lying flat on the street by a heap of decay.

No words passed. Sticks nodded once and again. Then the kids turned and walked back the other way.

"You know him?" Bo looked back over his shoulder.

Sticks shrugged. "Elmo."

"You're friends?"

"We're all travelers," DeShawn answered for him.

Bo watched to see if Sticks had a different answer, but he just kept walking. Sheriff found what looked like a flyblown rat intestine and gnawed it. Bo kept his gorge down, but that dog would not be licking him again.

Back inside, the boys took him to the cafeteria for breakfast. The buffet held day-old bagels and breakfast burritos donated by local eateries and driven over by volunteers. What little appetite he had died on the street, so he poured some juice and called it good enough. A woman of indeterminate race came down from the girls' dormitory. While Louisa's mixed heritage created a dramatic beauty, this counselor's slab-like face, overhanging lids, and broad mouth seemed all wrong together. To top it off, his fellow staffer looked at him with disdain approaching disgust.

He didn't think they'd been introduced, so it had to be first impressions on both their parts. He took a drink and let the orange juice fill his mouth with flavor before swallowing. Because of Barb, he had a soft spot for beauty-challenged women. This one had no fondness for freakin' beautiful men.

"Hey, Hollywood," Sticks called. "Try the burritos." He waved one around.

Bo cocked an eyebrow. He'd have to nip that nickname before it gave him away. Helga the Horrible looked put out. He hoped she was nicer to the young people and guessed she was or she wouldn't be here. He was the one who didn't belong.

Ann came in and blessed the food. Some stopped eating to pray, others kept on. No one scolded or demanded piety. When she joined him he said, "Are you the director?"

"Of this location."

"How many are there?"

She told him and named the cities. As they talked, three young women came in and kissed or snuggled Helga. The transformation of her face was supernatural. What had been ugly now radiated compassion. She spoke to each of the girls, then listened as if every word they said mattered.

"Georgia Warren," Ann said.

"What?"

"One of our operation specialists, counselor, teacher, mother, friend, resource. Whatever our young people need, she's there for them twenty-four hours a day, by phone if not in person."

"What does she have against me?"

"Some Hollywood types sashay in, wanting applause for good deeds. Some have good intentions but no staying power, like seeds in shallow soil. The weeds overcome them."

"The kids are weeds?"

"Their problems are. Every homeless youth is a bloom to her. She thinks you might be a thorn. And she'll protect them with her lifeblood."

"She should."

"There you go again. But I saw you with Jason and DeShawn."

"Jason?"

"Street name Sticks."

"We had to feed the dog. And he took boots from a Dumpster to someone named Elmo."

"He likes to give things."

"To him?"

"He matches his finds to those he thinks they suit best."

Bo looked over at the kid who'd said *out there your stuff gets taken.* Had losing things triggered a Santa complex? His mother would explore what makes a kid a pathological gifter.

"Being able to give is a rare privilege for someone with little or nothing."

There she was in his head again. "What do you want me to do today?"

"I thought you might go in the van tonight. If so, you should rest this afternoon."

"I'm okay. I don't sleep much."

"Why not?"

He shrugged. "I used to. Took a foreign invasion to roust me from REM."

"Then something happened."

He didn't explain. She could read his mind if she had to know.

Talking with Suz and Treya made Exi wonder what effect the shooting would have if she went by the store, but her dad quashed that idea when she called to ask.

"You're not going anywhere near there. Mother's orders."

"Did she say so?"

"Clear as a bell … with her eyes. And you know what I mean."

"Aw, Dad."

"You scared eight years off her life."

"All right. I get it." She really did.

"You want to go somewhere? Go visit her, let her see you're okay."

Hmm. Maybe John could take her instead of following like a hulky shadow. "I'll see what I can do. Talk to you later, Dad. Big hugs."

She was still getting her head around all this. Nothing clarified her situation like Liam paying her to paint—code for *hide out.* But the monsters were winning if it stopped her from living her life. She made the call and John agreed, but it would be a little while. So that left time for the thing she'd been avoiding. Bo's studio.

She went in and made herself see it as a mess like any other. She reached for one fallen image that was almost intact, but the poster stuck to the floor. She tried to peel it without tearing, then yanked it up and jumped back, gasping.

Blood. Bo's blood coated the floor like burgundy paint performing a tragedy. She grabbed her stomach with a sob. Bo had almost bled to death. Right here! She pressed a hand to her mouth. He'd been so weak, so damaged that John—who thought of everything—hadn't considered his leaving the hospital.

Yet he had.

She took out her phone. *Bo, you don't have to talk to me. Just do one thing. An emoji … something, anything to let me know you're okay. That's all I ask. Please. Please.*

She held the phone to her heart but it didn't vibrate. She sank to her knees and stared at the stain. Her mind formed Bo writhing over the spill. "God," she moaned. She wanted assurance that Bo would survive, that he'd come home and they would have the chance that violence and their own reactions stole.

The Lord didn't work that way, not with her anyway. No voice said, "You got it, babe. Your wish is my command." She had only what she knew. God heard, cared, and answered. Somehow.

She pushed up from the floor. Surgery repaired the damage. Bo was fit, young, and strong. He might be partying with friends. Selfish bad judgment sure beat a body bag.

Okay. She would do this. Down four flights she found Sondra sorting mail. "Would you have something I could use on the blood upstairs?"

Sondra paused. "Ms. O'Hare said to leave it for Mr. Corrigan."

"I'm not doing that."

"She meant for him to see how close he'd come. It scared her badly."

"Oh." That was different, but she still couldn't leave it.

Sondra's voice softened. "She loves that young man. She's sick with worry."

Exi wiped the teardrop that slid from her eye. "I'm trying so hard to believe he's okay."

"We all are." Sondra measured her. "It's good for Ms. O'Hare that you're here."

"Me?"

"You don't think your little temper can put her off, do you?"

"I guess I did."

Sondra shook her head. "Not when her own daughter's a nightmare. She kidnapped Eileen and tried to extort money."

"No way."

"Besides that, Eileen knows what you mean to Mr. Corrigan. She said he may not come back for a foolish old woman but might very well for you."

"She's not foolish, and he thinks the world of her. Everyone does."

"It seems there are fewer true friends in her life as time goes by."

Devin had been harsh. "What should I do?"

"Maybe if you have meals together, it would encourage her to eat."

So the untouched waffle wasn't a fluke. "Is she sick?"

"I haven't been told."

"But you're a nurse."

"It could be stress. I think she's aching for Bo." Sondra shook her head. "She thinks she drove him away."

"How?"

"Being cross at the hospital."

"It can't be that. I know it."

"Maybe you can convey it."

"Is she here?"

"She's at her theater, interviewing directors for a new play. She'd hoped Mr. Bressard would participate, but …" Sondra sighed.

"That's my fault."

"No. You're caught in the middle right now, but as long as I've known them, it's been complicated."

"It's not complicated between Devin and Bo. That's just ugly."

Sondra sighed. "There might be more involved there also."

Grace had suggested that too. Exi checked a text that came in. "John's taking me to see my mom. He'll be here in a minute, so I'll tackle the studio when I'm back. If you could have the supplies ready?"

"Of course."

The guy who came wasn't John. It was the driver from the park incident, the shooting incident, and the time John marched her out of her apartment. "Are you like the designated driver?"

He looked over his shoulder. "I'm behind the wheel a lot. But I'm also a protection specialist. You're safe with me."

He looked so ordinary, he could blend in anywhere—unlike John. "I'm Alexis Murphy."

"Brett Gross." He verified the address of her mother's rehab facility. "Brooklyn?"

"Yes."

He proceeded to drive.

"Are you former military too?"

"Yes, ma'am."

"How come you're not all commando looking?"

His mouth twitched. "Not everyone is built like John Helm."

"I don't mean build. I mean your face. You look normal."

The smile flashed and vanished.

"My artist's eye analyzes things like this."

"You'd make a good witness."

"Huh. I never thought of that."

He kept driving.

"Did you serve with John?"

"Yes, ma'am."

"You know why he got the Distinguished Service Cross?"

"Yes."

She caught closure in his tone. "Just yes?"

He switched lanes. "Civilians don't have context."

"Not even someone grazed by a bullet who saw a Mafia gang dude try to slice Bo's face?"

"Not even."

She nodded. "However bad it seems, things can always be worse."

He let that line stand.

"Are you and John friends?"

"I would die for him."

"Okay then." She tapped her knees. "He really is looking for Bo?"

He swung his head her way and back. Yeah, okay. But still, if someone of his caliber couldn't find Bo … Her throat ached. "I just … don't want to lose him."

Brett Gross said nothing, but maybe they all agreed on that. He parked at the nursing home's rehab wing. He walked her in, scanning as John had. Exi greeted the woman at the reception desk, moved down the hall, and paused outside her mom's room.

He said, "I'll wait here."

"Thanks." She went in, ecstatic to see her mother up and walking with a safety cane. Her left wrist had been repaired with a surgical pin and bone glue and was still in the sling, but she was getting around. "Mom." She went over and hugged her. "Look at you!"

"Look at you."

"Hah!" She clapped hands to her mouth. "You're talking?"

Rhonda shook her head and pointed.

"Only to me?"

Her mother shrugged.

"Rocking the mother-daughter bond." Exi did a little shimmy.

Rhonda lowered herself to the bed with a searching expression that spoke volumes.

"I'm fine." Exi sat diagonally. "Stop worrying about me, okay?" Nightmares or not.

Her mother shook her head, solemn and a little fierce.

"Okay, I get it. No worrying but you can pray. And could you pray for Bo? I don't know where he is. No one does. He had surgery and left the hospital and no one's seen him since." She couldn't keep her voice steady, but even as Rhonda nodded prayers were rising.

When her mom tapped the naked ring finger, Exi rubbed it. "I let Jeffrey go. It wasn't fair to keep him hanging on."

Rhonda pressed a hand to her heart.

"I'm okay. I didn't like hurting him but it was right."

Her mother frowned and pressed her hand to her heart again.

"Oh. Yeah. Bo." She swallowed back tears. "I can't help it. Even though he's gone, the feeling keeps getting stronger. I just …"

Rhonda squeezed her hand.

"Thank you for understanding. You're the best mom ever." A voice outside the door sent a wash of concern. "I have to go, Mom. Be watchful, okay?" Slipping into the hall, she looked from Brett to John, whose voice had alerted her.

"Let's go out the back."

"You're kidding, right?"

John gave her a narrow-eyed look.

"This is just wrong."

He tried to move her with a hand to her spine.

"I want a guard for my mother."

John nodded to Brett, who placed a call as he headed toward the front.

"We can't leave until someone gets here."

Brett called, "Your brother's almost on site."

"Yeah but—"

John got her feet in motion. "They're discharging her. He'll take her home."

"Great. Now I'm costing her care."

"Her physician approved it."

A supervisor let them out the back exit without sounding the alarm. As John got her into the middle seat of a silver SUV, she guessed Brett was taking off in the black. "Won't they go inside if I'm not with Brett?"

"We brought a decoy."

"Of me?"

John closed her door and got in the passenger seat. The tattooed, African American linebacker behind the wheel started the engine.

"If you stopped the Russian and the Syrian hitmen, who is it now?"

"It's still the Russians after Bo. Or the Russian-Syrian alliance."

She clapped a hand to her forehead. "This has to stop."

"It will."

"When Bo's dead?"

"He's only a piece of it."

"A puzzle's not much good if it's missing a piece."

He exhaled. "You've had no communication?"

"Aren't you monitoring my phone calls?"

His head swiveled like the Terminator's. "May I?"

"No. If I hear from him I'll tell you." She looked out. "Where are you taking me?"

"Back to Eileen's."

By the roundabout, roundabout route.

He said, "Liam thinks it's coming to a head. We need to find Bo or hope he stays hidden just a little longer. But…if you're our best lead, you're theirs too. I guessed they might be staking out the house and would make a play for you in a less secure location."

"So you set up the bait and switch?"

"And they took it. Brett and Laura will draw them away. HSI agents will intercept."

Exi thought longingly of her peaceful time with Jeffrey. That might be the only oasis in her entire turbulent life. Why hadn't she been content? Did she need drama? Danger? Damage? No. She cared for Bo, even if that made her vulnerable.

When she reached the house and dragged herself upstairs, she saw that Sondra had thoroughly cleaned the studio. All the posters and frames were gone. A discoloration marked the walnut floor, but it no longer looked as if something had been butchered.

Deeply grateful, she set up her easel with a fresh canvas and prepared for the long haul. If her activities put others at risk, it was time to stop pretending she could wish this away. She would not see her family or her friends unless they entered this fortress. Like Angel in Grace and Devin's play, this would be her world until the crisis resolved.

She set up a table to hold her supplies and prepared a palette. After blending three different hues, she raised her brush to the canvas and began to paint. This time she copied no image. In this space she visualized him so clearly, she needed nothing but her own aching memory.

22

Back home in New York, after a week apart, Grace spent three hours soaking up her husband and daughter before mentioning Exi. When she broached the subject, Devin dashed any hopes that he had resolved or even mellowed on the subject.

At the counter where Mattie perched, he handed his daughter a wooden square to fit through the corresponding hole in the shape tower and said, "Talk to Exi if you want, but you shouldn't see her."

"Why not?"

"Did you miss the part about her being shot?"

"No, I didn't. But you must not be that concerned if you let her leave."

"Let her? Since when does anyone listen to me?" His voice rose with frustration. "I could be talking to walls for all the good it does."

"That isn't true."

"Try it from my side."

Grace rubbed his arm. "Does Eileen think there's an end in sight?"

"I haven't talked to her."

"Since when?"

"Since I took Exi out of there."

That didn't sound good. "Why not?"

"Because Eileen started it all with that scheming dinner party."

"No. We started it by inviting Exi to the play."

Devin gave Mattie a circle. "She fanned the flames. Exi had a plan. Now she's left Jeffrey—

"She has? How do you know?"

"I talked to Sully." At her puzzled look, he added, "her brother."

"Another cousin I've never met."

"The point is, Eileen's at the epicenter of this mess. She doesn't care who she twists into her spider web."

Grace pressed a thumbnail to her lips. "You called me a spider once."

"To my great regret."

"You may regret this attitude toward Eileen."

He sighed.

Grace twined his fingers with hers. "Why don't we go see her together?"

"Because I suspect Exi is there, and I don't want her running off if I show up."

"You suspect?"

"Sully would neither confirm nor deny. He inflected."

She smiled. "I like a man who can inflect."

"If Exi's safe there, I want her to stay that way."

"Maybe I could—

"No. I mean it, Grace. Don't push me on this." Their hands parted.

Grace slid a lock of hair behind her ear. "Well, I intend to talk to her. But I won't go wherever she is."

"You can't meet her somewhere either. She comes with armed guards and assassins."

"Assassins?"

"Sully inflected."

"I'm starting to suspect these inflections."

"After what happened to you?"

"I see your point."

He dragged his hand down his face to hug his jaw. "I wish we could go back to deciding whether we liked Jeffrey. I keep thinking if I'd been more positive, more encouraging …" He let his hand fall.

"Did Exi say why she broke it off?"

"If she did, Sully didn't tell me."

"There could be lots of reasons."

"You know the reason."

"I know she was having doubts." Grace handed Mattie a wooden star, then helped her turn it to fit the hole on the tower. "I'm not sure she really loved Jeffrey. She thought she should because he was right for her."

"What a concept. But wait. Let's choose door number two for Mr. Wrong."

Mattie reached for a diamond and said, "Mr. Wrong."

Grace rolled her eyes. "You don't know that, Devin. Bo could be the one she's meant for. It's just a shame this business isn't over."

"A shame? A shame, Grace, is cleaning sweet tea off a sport coat. Bo isn't a shame, he's a disaster."

"Since we're not talking about that first part, I'll address the second. Bo is not a disaster."

"Yeah?" Devin pressed both hands to the counter. "Where is he?"

"I don't know, and you have no idea how much that upsets me."

His jaw rippled. "I think I do have an idea. I just don't understand why."

"I can't make you understand, and I'm not sure I should have to. It should matter to you because it matters to me that my friend could be in trouble. If you want us on the same side, I'm waiting."

He pinched the bridge of his nose. "I can't change how I feel because you want me to. All I can say is I'll try to understand." He took her hand and kissed it. "I'm glad you're home."

"I am too." She kissed his mouth. "But I have some calls to make."

"Calls plural?"

"Exi. And Bo."

"Knock yourself out. If you reach him, tell him to get his butt back onstage."

"I'll use those exact words."

He turned her hand and kissed her palm. "I don't want to fight."

"There's a lot to be said for that."

Grace took out her phone. Bo didn't answer, but Exi broke her heart with what she told her. Almost certainly both their dreams tonight would include Bo's studio floor.

Bo listened to the instructions as if riding shotgun in an outreach van required higher education. In a way it did.

Ann eyed him as if guessing his unspoken questions. "The kids have a solidarity as junkies. It identifies and binds them. It gives them a sort of power. They're smarter, wilier, braver than you'd guess by their circumstances."

"Then why not change their circumstances?"

"Logic is ineffective with addicts when every part of their routine revolves around the drugs. It is their god, even if worship wounds and kills them."

His brow furrowed as it did almost every time this woman spoke.

"They'll share their longing for a home, for things, for people who love them. And you think they'll jump at this chance to get all that. But stronger than all is addiction. Out there nothing is required but meeting their bodies' demands." Her gaze penetrated. "Do you understand that, Beau?"

"No." If she still thought his demons included addiction, that he might reveal himself through this opportunity, she was mistaken. Maybe she saw, because her face softened.

He kept the rest of what he felt from showing. Fear that he would fail in this simplest service. Pain in the parts of his body he'd thought were healing. Suspicious chills crawling his spine. Worse by far, the pain of what he might see. Who was he to talk to even one of them?

"Go feed the sparrows," Ann said.

She had paired him with Luke, a seasoned driver at thirty-one. Having graduated from their program, Luke might have something to say. His face bore acne scars, track marks on his arms. Bo thought of his own childish drug use—some snorts of cocaine, some pills popped. No addiction driving every action. No overdoses. More evidence of his luck that was a Death Star to others.

Could he stomach what he saw out here, when the ones Ann's bunch were rehabilitating already challenged everything in him? "How accurate was that?"

Luke glanced over at his question. "What Sister said? A hundred percent. To the power of ten."

"Then what's the point?"

Luke shrugged. "Relationship. Mercy. Hope. Sister's big on all three. The whole organization is pretty much about that."

"Even if it does no good?"

"Who says it doesn't? Failure outweighs success. But I'm here."

Bo nodded. "Not about numbers, I guess."

"It's never about numbers. It's about hearts. And souls."

Two more things he knew nothing about. "Not sure how much good I'll be."

"Don't quit before you try."

"Right."

Luke pointed out kids by name along the streets, in empty lots and alleys, and at the Trans-Bridge bus station on their first pass. Some, he claimed he'd spoken to hundreds of times, in the life and after. "I was copping like them."

"Coping?"

"Copping. You run between the consumer and the dealer. Customers don't go where the dealers hang. Too dangerous for the provider. Too scary for the buyer."

"But the kids go."

"Once they're known, if they're trusted. Dealer's gotta know they'll deliver the goods and bring back the payment. Not shoot it themselves."

"Right." Like any kid wouldn't rather shoot poison in a vein.

"You get a rep on the street just like anywhere else."

"What happens if they don't deliver?"

"Then they're running from the dealer's gang and the cops. Running, hiding until it blows over. Sometimes they leave town."

"How?"

"Jump a train."

"Really?"

"Or hitch. Train's safer."

Bo considered that. "Then what?"

"Most come back."

"Or what?"

"Die somewhere else."

Bo shot him a look. Dead serious.

"Sometimes dealers get back at them with bad junk. Make them guinea pigs for some crap they're trying out."

This time around the bus station, Luke went at a crawl. The kids had seen the van, knew they could have a meal. Some were too stoned to care, others out cold. Bo wondered if any of those would never wake. Die somewhere else, or right here.

"Put your window down. Let them see you. They got to know you're no cop."

"Don't they know the van?"

"They know me. They know the van. They don't know you."

"Then how will they know I'm not?"

"You're an actor right? Don't act like a cop."

When Bo put his window down, two young females looked over. He saw the instant their interest kindled. He recognized the look from thousands of others, yet never quite like this. Luke parked the van and waited. They rose from the bench and sauntered over.

"Hey," Bo said.

"Hey."

They might be younger than Exi, but their eyes were infinitely older. Freshness had withered in these until they looked like youthful husks. And still they reacted to his face.

The one with lavender hair and pale blue eyes almost entirely overtaken by pupils leaned her elbow into the van and walked her broken fingernails along the rubber window channel. "You got money? I'll give you sugar." How many party girls had said the same? Except the money part. He felt nothing physical. He'd felt nothing sexual since he climbed into the culvert. Maybe that had burned away in the fever. It would make this role he played easier.

Luke stirred. "You tricking now, Vi?"

"Nuh-uh. Just, I mean, look at him."

The petite black-haired one with silky skin and a cupid mouth started rubbing his arm. "Are you real?"

What put them here? Rebellion? Abuse? Drugs clearly. Mental illness? He ticked off issues Ann described, trying not to picture other things she'd said. "You guys want a sandwich?"

Vi leaned in. "What you got?"

"Turkey. Ham. We have Gatorade too."

"Can we come in, Luke?"

He activated the sliding door. The women crawled in among the coolers. Luke kept the van parked with the door open. The husks gobbled sandwiches but their hunger remained. Bo absorbed it, though he tried not to. Why had Barb trained him to see? He wanted a blind eye.

You have to get inside the skin. Look out through the characters' eyes. Feel the beat of the heart until every breath you take is theirs also.

He had imitated the outward mannerisms of junkies without comprehending. Luke and the girls talked as they guzzled Gatorade and watched him warily. He showed them his surface and as always it was enough. He could count on two fingers the women, since Barb, who got underneath. Both were lost to him, and he wouldn't repeat that mistake.

When Vi asked Luke for money, he said, "You know we don't carry it. You want to come back with us?"

"Are you there?" the one who'd petted him asked.

"For a while."

She looked wistful, but Vi said, "No, Misty. Spider would kill you."

"I don't care what Spider says."

But she must because they got out. Bo watched them flop back down where they'd been and Luke closed the door.

"What happened to her arm?"

"You're observant."

He'd caught a glimpse when Misty's blouse slipped down to her wrist. It might not have stood out so starkly if the rest of her wasn't so silky soft.

"Someone missed her vein and shot H under her skin. Cellulitis did the rest. Lucky she didn't lose the arm."

Lucky meth didn't blow that damaged girl up, lucky this one had her ruined arm. The people he'd partied with whined and complained about unfair auditions and demanding directors. He'd agonized over losing his extravagant apartment, afraid the paparazzi would learn he'd been evicted. Oh, poor Bo. His stomach turned.

"She gets donations with it."

He jolted back. "What?"

"People pay her to see the scar."

"Tell me that isn't true. Just … say it." He didn't know why it bothered him except it was such needless cruelty.

Luke shook his head. "To some they're freaks, not kids. They can put money in the jar, or they can lord it over them in some power trip. They need their fix bad enough, the kids do anything no matter how stupid or degrading."

Bo's jaw ached from clenching. "Who's Spider?"

"Dealer. He would kill her if she tries to go straight again."

Once more Bo looked for the lie or exaggeration. "Why?"

"Because she's his. About three years ago, she came with us and cleaned up but couldn't maintain it. She went to him for a fix, and he mixed a cocktail that almost ended it. If he hadn't shot her with crack, she would never have breathed again. Now she owes him her life because he loved her enough to save her."

"That's messed up."

"It's the life." Luke drove on.

They gave out food and drink. They laughed at exaggerated exploits. They heard grumbles and complaints and excuses. As Ann had said, some kids shared hopes and wishes. One or two were homesick. More than one missed something or someone. Most were angry, disillusioned and suspicious. Too many were ill or disengaged with reality. Bo had thought this the easy job. He didn't know pieces of himself would break off and stay with these castaways crawling the night streets.

When they got back to the dorm in the early morning hours, he crashed. He dreamed the Russian stabbed him again and again in the side. He woke to masked faces, Ann and Dr. Patel. In the clinic. He closed his eyes with a groan.

"You must listen to your body," said the doctor. "Learn to hear pain."

He heard pain all right. All their stories had seeped inside, and the poison pumped through his organs.

"Beau." Ann this time. "You can't ignore this. Stop trying to tough it out. Let yourself heal."

Tough it out? Like there was anything tough about him.

She leaned in. "I'm not giving up, and I won't let you."

He wasn't giving up on the only role left. Barb was watching. He'd heard her. *Play it, Bo, as only you can.* And then, *I especially liked, "Are you real?" Best laugh in a long time. Long, long time …*

He pressed a hand to his eyes when tears burned. Only Barb could find humor amid the horror. While he was overcome by despair, she'd walked her own demise with levity. *Gotta laugh, Bo. What else is there?*

What else? How about tears that bore down inside and created an inky pit of never-ending sorrow? He recognized Ann's hand on his head but it was only flesh. He slept.

When he woke, DeShawn sat in a slump on the next cot over. He dragged his eyes up and mumbled, "Not supposed to be here."

Bo cleared the tatters from his throat. "You … or me?"

"Me, man, but you either."

"Not my preference." He studied the IV pole once again performing its service.

"I can't find Sheriff."

Bo rolled a little to his side and regretted it but kept his eyes on the kid. "How long?"

"Whole three days you been down here."

Three days. He had to stop checking out like this. What way was that to play a role?

"You still burning up?"

"Don't know." He pushed up to mirror DeShawn's slump. "Where'd you see him last?"

"Outside. I slept late, had class. When I got there, he was gone."

"Probably went to find his own meal."

"I think they shot him."

"Who?"

"The Blue."

"Why?"

"If I don't feed him he prowls. Looks scary."

"Shorty scary?"

A hint of smile found his mouth, then vanished. "Three days gone. I can't eat or sleep or concentrate. I can't be an example."

Bo eyed the kid. He glanced at the almost empty IV bag. After studying the mechanism, he closed a clamp and disconnected the line from the catheter, leaving the needle in his hand. He removed the other catheter and took care of it in the bathroom. He washed. Not as comprehensively as a shower, but that would come later. "Let's go."

DeShawn glowed, and not just the cloud patches on his skin. Bo rested an arm around his shoulders, and not just to comfort DeShawn. His legs might be string cheese. His side felt like fire. Learn to hear pain? Feeling it was bad enough.

The city teemed around them, purposefully striding suits on cell phones, sidewalk-congesting visitors. The smart, the beautiful, the useful, and—intermingled—Bo saw those who'd been invisible. Kids copping for dealers, begging on corners, thieves and cons and shoplifters, the hopeful, the needy, the battered, misused, and rejected. Every step he took hurt in so many ways.

He was almost at the end of his strength after searching street after street, the noise and stink of traffic, the chaos of pedestrians. Even the leaden air molecules pressed on him. No sign of the dog living or dead. If law enforcement had dealt with the problem, they wouldn't leave a carcass. DeShawn was almost too despondent to put one foot in front of the other. Bo hurt almost too much to do the same.

"Come on. I have an idea."

They made their way to the culvert. Bo caught a whiff of the pipe that wasn't much better without him in it. He couldn't make his body crouch, but he told DeShawn to look in. The kid grabbed the edge of the pipe and went onto his knees.

"Hey. I think I see him."

Bo's hands clenched. Please, not a corpse.

DeShawn crawled in and whooped. "It's him. It's Sheriff!"

His chest heaved with relief and tears. "Can you get him?"

"He's hurt."

"Take off your shirt and drag him on it."

A minute later, shirtless DeShawn emerged with a battered Sheriff, whose wiry fur had grease stains.

"Looks like he got hit by a truck. Can you carry him?"

"No. I'm shaking too bad."

He was. "Lift him up to me."

Bo took the dog and pulled the shirt around it. He caught his breath a moment, then made his legs move.

"Is he okay? Is he okay, you think?"

"We'll have the doctor look."

"Doc Patel?"

"Why not?"

"Yeah, why not?"

When they reached the door to the clinic, Bo pressed his shoulder to the wall, stars flashing in his eyes. "Ring for someone to open it."

DeShawn rang. The slab-faced operation specialist, Georgia Warren, opened. "What on earth?"

Bo held her eyes. "He needs help."

Her mouth opened and closed. She looked from the dog to DeShawn to the dog. "Bring him in."

Bo put the dog in DeShawn's arms. DeShawn followed Georgia. Bo crumpled and his lights went out again.

23

Finishing breakfast with Eileen, Exi said, "My brother's bringing some stuff over for me. Is it okay if I hang around down here to let him in?"

"You can be anywhere you like, Alexis. No need to stay hidden away upstairs. Bo didn't."

"He had a right to be here. I'm just … I don't know what I am."

"A friend I hope." Eileen looked sincere.

Exi smiled. "Thank you. That means a lot."

"What is your brother bringing?"

"My old art supplies. He'll just drop them off and—"

"Oh, that reminds me. There's a box in the coat room off the foyer for you."

"There is?"

"Sorry I've forgotten it until now. I don't know where my mind is these days."

Exi rose. "Want to see what's inside?"

"Of course."

She dragged the box from the oversize closet and frowned. "This is addressed to Bo, not me."

"He ordered it sent here, but it's for you. He said so."

Her heart jumped. "When?"

"Before he disappeared. I'm sorry."

She slumped. "That's okay."

The coat room also served as a package receiving area, and a drawer held scissors and stuff. Exi cut open the box and removed the top Styrofoam. She pulled out a rectangular case, puzzled until she opened it and stared.

"He said he wants to hear you play."

Exi brought a hand to her throat, amazed and overwhelmed. There was no part of her life Bo wanted lost. What that abusive jerk had stolen, Bo restored. But he wasn't here to listen. She clutched her chest where the ache could be a heart attack, was a heart attack.

"I don't think he meant to make you cry."

"I want him back so much."

"As do I." Eileen rested a hand on her shoulder. "But come on. Take it out. Let's have a look."

Exi lifted the immaculate saxophone. She reverently ran her hand over the neck. "I can't believe he did this."

"He was really tickled that you play so well."

"He's misguided in that opinion."

The bell ringing brought her up. "That must be Sully." Since Sondra was off on Sundays, Exi started for the door.

"Check first." Eileen indicated the camera monitor.

That brought everything home with a thud. "It is." She admitted her brother, who had her art supplies in a big duffle over his shoulder. No sense duplicating what she already owned, Liam's dime or not. "Sully, this is Eileen O'Hare. Eileen, Sullivan Murphy, my brother."

"A right charming Irishman." Eileen laid it on.

"Don't swell his head. It's big enough."

Sully enclosed Eileen's hand with his free one. "Charm begins and ends with you."

Exi groaned, but Eileen ate it up.

"What's this?" He pointed to the sax.

"Bo ordered it. Since mine was removed from my possession."

"It's a beaut."

"Yeah." She closed the case.

Sully returned to Eileen. "Thank you for giving my sister a safe place."

"It's entirely my pleasure."

Upstairs, her brother asked how she was doing.

"I don't know." She laid the sax on the table. "I feel like I'm holding my breath under water, waiting for the nightmare to pass."

"It's not going to. It has to be dealt with." Sully looked around. "It's situation critical for the Irish, Liam in particular."

"You sound like John."

He shrugged. "We've talked."

"Is Liam a criminal?"

Sully rocked his hand. "Like the Kennedys', his business started out shady at best. Smuggling, bootlegging, protection rackets, and graft. With his brother, former congressman Brian O'Hare, there's been a fair amount of political maneuvering, but nothing overtly illegal. Let's just say the feds and the force prefer the devil they know to the ones he keeps in check."

That was almost exactly what Bo had said.

"We don't want the Russian mob or ISIS terrorists using Liam's channels for weapon and human trafficking."

"Please tell me Liam isn't into that."

"If he were, we'd take him down with the others. Liam operates within the law, but he's well informed in darker circles."

"Like a secret agent."

"Yeah, Mitten. Like a secret agent." Sully pinched her nose, which made her slap his hand. He sobered. "If these others infiltrate, it'll be chaos and bloodshed. That's why there's now a task force. I'm the liaison between that and Helm's organization."

"Are you okay with that?"

"Special assignment goes in my jacket." He carried her materials into the studio and set them on the floor by her work space. Straightening, his eye caught the discoloration. "Is that—"

"Please don't make me look at it."

He pulled her in for a hug.

Her throat swelled. "Do you think he's dead?"

"I don't know. The surgeon who removed Bo's spleen is concerned."

"You talked to him?"

"John did."

It tripped her mind to have Sully talk about John Helm like they were friends. If John's men had stopped Bo from leaving—disguised or not—he might be here now, healing and safe.

"I just can't—" A knock stopped her. Could it be? She rushed for the door and yanked it open to find Cate and Mia. Of course Bo wouldn't knock. He lived here.

"Hi, Exi. We brought you something." Cate held up a pastry box.

"For me?" She wiped the tears as unobtrusively as possible.

Mia said, "Baklava."

Her mouth fell open. "How did you know?"

"We're not supposed to say."

Exi searched her memory but couldn't guess how they knew her secret passion, unless … She groaned. "Devin?"

Cate shrugged a shoulder. "We went upstairs to visit, and Grace told us you'd left."

"Not happy with your cousin?" Mia probed.

"I just can't be around him."

Cate nodded. "Grace said to tell you she sent the baklava. Devin merely suggested it."

Exi frowned. Should she stand on principle?

Mia stage whispered, "He doesn't have to know."

"Well. Thank you. And Grace."

Sully came out of the studio and leaned a shoulder to the doorjamb. "Do you always come as a pair?"

Both heads jerked toward him. Mia shot back, "Are you always lurking around?"

"Not lurking." He came forward. "I brought my sister art supplies." He bent. "Is there a piece for me?"

Cate opened the box and Sully broke one diamond slice off from the others. He caught the loose, honeyed pastry flakes with his other hand and licked them off. Both sisters watched.

"Mmm. Thanks. Now I have to go." Sully shot her a warning glance, as if she needed the reminder to keep quiet. "Nice seeing you, Cate, Mia."

"Later." Mia smirked at her sister when the door closed. "Here's what Cate wants to know. Is he available, and is he as yummy as he looks?"

"Yuck."

All three burst into laughter. It felt like a rusty gear turning, her old friends and these new ones reminding her to laugh. "He's working lots of hours on"—she caught herself—"becoming a detective. I don't think he's seeing anyone."

"So this is Bo's place." Cate breathlessly changed the subject as she handed off the baklava. "Have you seen it, Mi?"

"Only his last apartment."

What exactly did that mean?

"It was super mod, everything controlled by a computer center with this palm reader to unlock the door." She looked around. "This is old. I don't see Bo doing old."

Exi set the baklava on the counter, far from laughter now. She'd never seen a place Bo chose. He lived here because of the trouble. Who was he without that?

Cate wandered into the studio through the door Sully left open. "Oh what? Are you kidding me?"

Exi followed reluctantly when Mia joined her sister and stared, slack-jawed. "Devin said you painted. He never said … this."

"Bo's a good subject."

Mia hooked a hand on her hip. "Are you two …"

"I'm just hanging here awhile, since he's … away."

"House-sitting like for Devin?"

"I'm using the studio until he's back."

"I heard he's not performing," Cate said. "What's that about?"

"I guess he needs a break."

Mia walked over to one canvas and scrutinized her work. "You are freaking good. Why don't you have an exhibit? 'The Many Faces of Bo Corrigan.'"

That would be a dream come true. But what would Bo think? "I wouldn't know where to start. I don't have those kinds of connections."

"Eileen does." Mia looked over her shoulder.

Exi chewed her lip. "I'm just ... painting."

"You're crazy if you don't get these out there. You'd make a killing."

Sell them? Her heart raced so hard she thought she'd faint. Profit from Bo's beauty? That would be such a betrayal. She didn't know what to say. What came out was, "Thank you for the baklava."

"But don't let the door hit us on the way out?" Mia arched a brow.

"You are such an artist." Cate cracked up.

"I don't know how long I'll have the studio." In this *old* place where Bo didn't belong.

"We have to run anyway. But call us sometime," Cate handed her a card. "Let's hang out."

Then they were gone. Exi opened the duffle and unpacked the supplies. Best of all was a huge roll of linen she could cut into pieces larger than her canvases to capture more of Bo than his face alone. Before she started, she sent a text. *So I'm painting and it's going okay. Cate and Mia said I should have an exhibit: The Many Faces of Bo Corrigan. What do you think? I wish I knew. My heart aches with everything I want to ask you.*

Like did you sleep with Mia? How much did she mean to you? Instead of painting, she walked back to the kitchen and shuffled the letters from Louisa that numbered four, since another arrived yesterday. Exi raised the sax to her lips and began the intro to "Harden My Heart."

At least it was minutes not days later when Bo came to. Ann was there. Georgia and DeShawn were not. "They took the dog to the vet," she said. "Georgia will cover the bill herself so it doesn't violate our bylaws."

Bo raised his head from the pillow to find himself reattached to the IV line. "The kid was worried."

"Yes."

He held her eyes defiantly. "Go ahead and scold, Ann. I know you want to."

Instead her gaze grew pensive in a way that tightened his wary gut. "What do you have against sisters?"

He hadn't braced properly and the question penetrated. "Nothing, why?"

"You're averse to the word."

"I'm not averse." Even if he wouldn't call her that, Ann didn't have to know his reason. He had chosen to tell Exi, given her that part of himself. She had cradled his grief in gentle hands. Except for telling Grace—since she didn't understand the singularity of his confession—she had guarded it. Now she was lost to him and he didn't want that cavity opened again.

Ann waited. Sweat broke out on his skin. "I'm sorry," she said.

He stayed mute.

"I was coming to speak with you this morning when I found you gone."

Slowly the bands loosened around his chest.

"Dr. Patel is quite concerned with your infection."

"Thus the masks." He cleared his throat. "You're not wearing yours."

"The test results came in and it's not staph. It's your surgical wound getting septic again."

He felt the burn as if mentioning it turned up the heat. "I'm not sure it ever stopped."

"That would have been good information to convey."

Amazing how much she reminded him of Eileen, except in every surface way possible. Faith—irreverence. Austerity—wealth. Reserved—raucous. Yet there was something in the way both dealt with him. "I've never been injured or even sick to speak of. I don't think that way."

"That can be excused. But not intentionally ignoring symptoms." Her wizened face sharpened.

"Now I know."

"Strenuous activity such as today's can pump the infection through your body. Rest is critical."

He spread his hands. "Now I know."

"Luke wanted you to go out with him again. He said you have a nice way. But you can't be any real use until it doesn't take a toll on your recovery."

Or his sanity? "I didn't do this on purpose. You can believe me or not."

"I believe you. Infirmity can confound a healthy person." She lowered her hand and squeezed his knee. "Won't you tell me what else ails you?"

He slid his gaze to the pale green cinderblock wall. "DeShawn says he's not sleeping or eating. Can't concentrate. I hope finding the dog helps."

"That was kind and foolish. I can't help loving you for it."

He cocked an eyebrow at her. "Ever tried saying no to DeShawn?" He captured the tone just right.

"I tell him no all the time. Don't pretend you were coerced."

He swallowed. "Well, Sheriff Shorty rescued me. Least I can do is repay the favor."

Ann smiled. "Your wit makes people laugh. That's a gift around here."

He rubbed his temple. "I know you're busy. You don't have to babysit." Leave before I spill my guts and hate you for it.

"Please don't scare us again."

He shrugged.

"Until you're cleared for activity, send all wandering miscreants back to me. I barred everyone from coming here until we had the test results. DeShawn knew that."

"He didn't think you'd help the dog."

"He's right. I wouldn't have scoured the streets and drains for that dog. Now I see the error."

Bo pulled a crooked grin. "Well, Sister, that's a start." The word was out before he realized, spearing them both he presumed. He didn't take it back, but it wouldn't happen again.

"I'll see you later."

"A promise and a threat."

She tongued her cheek as she walked out.

Bo settled back, too weary to keep his head up. Something in the IV seemed to be helping the pain. He slept, then pushed up to sit that evening when Georgia brought his meal of toasted cheese and pudding.

"I thought you might want an update on Sheriff."

Those were the first words he'd heard from her. "He made it?"

She set the grayish-pink cafeteria tray on his thighs. "There's more wrong with that dog than right."

No surprise.

"And Sister won't let it inside or we'll be overrun with every stray on the street and all their fleas, ticks, and lice."

"A motley crew. But?"

"He was probably rolled underneath the carriage of a vehicle, banged and bruised and maybe knocked senseless, but the wheels didn't roll over him. Nothing crushed or broken."

Bo closed his eyes, each word weightier than she knew. They were foxhole buddies, that dog and he. "DeShawn okay?"

Once more the features transformed. "He's sleeping. First rest in days."

Again, too much emotion rose from that.

"Want something to read after you eat?"

"Sure." He wasn't convinced he would stay awake, but the offer was nice.

"What do you like?"

He shrugged. "You choose."

"Plato?" she quipped.

"Could probably use a refresher."

She narrowed her eyes, but with humor. "You're not as flimsy as I thought."

"Tell that to my legs."

She chuckled, then sobered. "I should ask your forgiveness."

"Please don't."

"I won't then." But they both knew she meant it. He'd passed some test. Helping a kid while getting his butt kicked by infection. Oscar-worthy so far, Barb. Just this once, the thought didn't hurt.

24

Grace had called a meeting with Cate and Mia. They did have merchandising to discuss, but mostly she wanted a firsthand account of Exi's state of mind. They sipped iced chai lattes at a street table while people walked by, window shopping or checking out their reflections in the glass.

"She scooted us out in a hurry like she couldn't wait to paint, but seemed kind of emotional," Cate said.

"I saw her dabbing tears." Mia ran a finger down her moisture-pearled cup. "Is it because she's not getting along with Devin?"

"It's a lot of things." But that reinforced her desire to visit Exi herself. Devin could make his peace with Eileen, and if the rest was true, they'd be safer visiting there than other places. She might leave Mattie with someone though. No sense tempting fate.

Mia feathered her hair back. "Have you seen her paintings?"

"I saw some illustrations. I'm thinking of adding toddler books and having her draw them."

"That's a great idea, but I mean paintings." Mia leaned in.

Grace looked from one to the other. "I haven't. She said she was rethinking her style, maybe shifting from abstract to realism."

"Ultra realism." Mia said.

"Lifelike," Cate added. "But sort of impressionistic around the edges. Like a blur that gets clearer and clearer until the eyes are alive."

"Sounds fascinating."

"What's fascinating is they're all Bo." Mia crossed her leg.

"What's Bo?"

"Every painting." Cate shifted her chair so someone in a motorized wheelchair could get by. "Every painting is Bo Corrigan."

"Oh." Grace considered that. "Every one? No landscapes or anything?"

"Every painting I saw was Bo to the max." Mia reiterated. "Can you imagine an exhibit of just that? I told her she should call it 'The Many Faces of Bo Corrigan.'"

Was Exi recreating the acting stills he had destroyed? And if she was painting Bo and nothing else, was it healthy?

"Grace," Mia leaned in.

"Yes?"

"Don't you think she should exhibit her paintings?"

"I guess that depends on her reason for painting them. Maybe it's practice to learn the new style."

"Practice." Mia sat back with a knowing look. "You have to see for yourself."

"I will then. I need to see Eileen too. Is there a time you could keep Mattie if we ran over?"

"You can't take Devin," they said simultaneously.

"Well, I know they had a tiff."

Cate shook her head. "She is not over it. She almost wouldn't accept the baklava."

"Well, that's just silly. They need to forgive and forget."

"Grace," Cate said. "People aren't always sunshine."

"I know. But I saw what Devin did with my family, and I think he can do that with Exi."

The sisters shrugged and left it at that. They discussed business and Grace signed an author photo for someone who approached from the street, then headed home while the others went shopping.

She wasn't as naïve as Cate and Mia thought. There were more than personal reasons for reconciling, given the dangerous situation. When she pictured what happened in the flower store plus her own experience it took an effort to stay calm.

If she closed her eyes she could see the thug charging up her stairs. She could feel the terror as she curled around the baby in her womb on the kitchen floor. The warning shot that scattered paint and drywall rang in her ears. It was meant to bring Bo out of hiding, except he wasn't there. Or he would never have hidden. She knew that.

So what was he doing now? Staying away from people who could get hurt? Devin told him to keep away from Exi. Had Bo taken that to the extreme? She hoped he wasn't gambling or indulging in other vices that could get him in more trouble.

Maybe he had checked into a treatment center. He might be sitting by an infinity pool overlooking an ocean with a power smoothie and someone massaging his temples, oblivious to everyone's concern. Nice fantasy, but did she believe it?

She entered her building and greeted Vince.

"Hey, Grace. I want to show you something."

She leaned over his phone as he brought up a picture of a shy-looking Asian woman showing off a glittery ring. "You're engaged?"

"Nori said she'd have me."

"Well, of course she did. Vince, I'm so happy."

"I knew you would be."

"When do I get to meet her?"

"You mean that?"

"Do I look like I'm lying?"

He grinned. "I'll phone up next time she comes by."

"You do that. And keep trying if you don't get me the first time. My schedule's just crazy."

On the elevator, she tried to fathom people whose lives followed an ordinary course with no drama or danger. Or maybe that was an illusion.

When she entered her place, she found Devin coming down with a flu that sounded scarily similar to the one they suffered while writing the play. All thoughts of taking him to see Exi or Eileen fled. But that didn't mean she wouldn't go. Grace prepared to do battle, but Devin was either too sick or saw the sense of it. Maybe he worried about Exi too.

He said, "She left one of the paintings here to dry."

"She did?"

"It's on top of my scripts shelf." Where no one could see it, least of all him.

In it she saw a little of what Cate and Mia described. It wasn't show worthy, but Exi had captured Bo. Especially his eyes. "Are you up to keeping Mattie?"

"We'll manage. But stay alert. If anything looks wrong, get out of there."

"I will." She kissed his head. "I'll stop at the store on the way back."

"Wedding soup?"

She smiled. "It's amazingly curative."

"Grace," he said when she reached the door. "Just don't *think* anything, okay? Turn off your imagination."

"I'll be a blank slate."

"No, honey. You like nothing better than filling a blank."

"I'll be careful." She blew him a kiss. "I love you."

"But you're still going."

"I'm worried about Exi."

He held her eyes. "Could you try to clear the waters?"

"You know I will." Her heart swelled for him, such a good man, doing his best. Once again she thanked God for all the things that brought them together in this beautiful life. That was her focus, not the rest. Things happened. It's what you did with it that mattered.

Exi gripped her hair when she heard another knock at her door. The only person she wanted there wouldn't be, and if he was, her questions would burn a hole in him. She kept painting.

"Exi, it's Grace. I'll leave if you don't want to talk to me, but I'm hoping you do."

She laid her brush down and went to the door. She hadn't showered. It hurt too much to use Bo's bathroom, his products and towels, to stand at his mirror. She just couldn't face it today. The second bathroom had a sculpted glass basin and toilet with a heated seat, but no shower or bath. So her only choice was Bo's jetted tub or multifunction steam shower. Either one tormented her imagination as Bo became more and more a part of her.

Her hair was wild, wilder from being gripped. She opened the door anyway. "Hi, Grace."

In answer, Grace set down the left-behind painting and pulled her into a hug. "I am so happy to see you."

The tension gave way to tears.

"Oh, honey, I know. I miss him too. And I'm so scared."

"Have you heard anything?"

"No. I've tried, but he doesn't respond. I wondered today if he might be in a treatment program."

"Treatment for what?"

"Drugs, drinking, gambling, grief… I don't know. Some of those places take away all contact with the outside world."

Exi swallowed. "Maybe." She closed her eyes.

"What is it?"

"There's a hollow so deep." Her voice broke. "Why do I only want the one who's bad for me?"

"How is he bad, besides these circumstances outside his control?"

Words tangled.

"I know his morals have not been stellar in God's eyes, but—"

"He has no concept of that. His mother had Bo and his sister with men who agreed to take no part in their lives. Then she took off all over the world and sent them to camps or left them with nannies who gave in to every whim but never really cared, you know?"

"That's heartbreaking."

"When I imagine how many people he had to figure out, it's no wonder he became a chameleon."

"Good point."

"People act like they're his best friends, but I've never known anyone as alone as Bo. He's hungry for love and goodness and things the rest of us take for granted, yet I wonder if he'll know any of it when he sees it."

"Oh, Exi."

Her face twisted. "If he's gone, he might never have the chance."

"Let's not think that."

"I try and try not to. It's like if I can paint him, he's not. So I paint and paint and paint."

"If this is an example—" Grace picked up the canvas board.

"That's only a study. I was still learning."

"From what I heard, you've got it. Can I see?"

With a twinge of protectiveness, not of her work but of Bo revealed in it, she led the way.

Grace entered with her and stopped with a gasp. "I thought you might be recreating his acting gallery. But this … Exi, I'm speechless."

"It's just coming out. At your place, I worked from pictures. But now I just think of him, remember an expression, a moment we had, and it comes through my brush."

"I can't even tell you what a gift I see."

"It's really Bo. I mean, look what I have to work with."

Grace smiled. "There is that."

"At night I fall to my knees and beg God to please not make these a memorial. The more time goes by the harder it is to see him out there somewhere. If he left the hospital and did something … irreversible …"

Tears filled Grace's eyes. "I can't bear that thought. So let's not go there." She reached out and they clasped hands. "I am believing Bo is alive somewhere. Want to pray for him?"

"Okay."

After their earnest supplication, Grace said, "When you listen to your heart, to that discerning spirit, what are they telling you?"

"That he's worth fighting for."

Grace hugged her. "You are brave and resilient. A daughter of the king and a warrior."

"Wow. Okay."

"I mean it. Now I'm going to ask something."

"What?"

Grace held her at arm's length. "Forgive Devin?"

Exi drew a breath. "I do. I know he's afraid and he cares about me. I just can't stand him saying he doesn't care about Bo."

"I understand. But he's really sad things fell out between you."

Exi looked around at the faces of Bo watching her. "Tell him I'm not mad. But until Bo's back, I can't see him."

Grace nodded. "I'll tell him. I hope that will change, but I'll tell him."

Alone again, she took out her phone to text: *Grace and I prayed for you. Be okay, Bo. Be alive and come back. I'm fighting for you whether you want me or not. You're worth it. You are.*

"DeShawn wants you to know Sheriff is back to begging at the door." Georgia wafted in on a cloud of Jimmy Dean from the microwaved biscuit sandwich on the breakfast tray. "He also said the dog is clearly superior, since you've been hobbled up three days while a dog that was hit by a truck is back in action."

"I'm not hobbled up." He was walking around every day. They just wouldn't let him join the general population where germs might overload his immune system before he'd fully kicked this infection.

"I'm passing the message as I got it." And enjoying it by the grin that drilled the corners of her mouth.

"Tell him that's good news about Sheriff."

Georgia handed him the tray. "Luke wants to know when we'll stop coddling you so you can pull your weight. Sister told him not to lead you astray. Are you easily led astray?"

"What do you think?"

"By your looks, I imagine you feed the bad wolf more than the good."

"Wolf?"

"I'm sure you've heard about the fighting wolves."

Bo sipped the cup of tepid coffee, probably due to all the people who stopped her on the way with comments on his deficiency. "I can't say I have."

"One wolf inside represents virtues. The other vices. They're in constant conflict. The one that wins is the one you feed."

Bo blinked. "Interesting concept." He hated to admit it was. He didn't want Georgia having something over him. Especially when she could tell. Must be some voodoo priestess.

"Think about the people in your life. Do they make you better or urge you on in wrong directions?"

Ah. That was the difference between Ann and Eileen. He'd been trying to nail it down. Both had a maniacal desire to play him like a pawn. Both succeeded. Only their ends differed. Eileen liked him wicked, while Ann imagined a knight inside.

"Even better," Georgia said, "think about why you listen where you do and not where you should."

"You don't know that," he said to her departing back. She didn't know, even if it was true, which it wasn't … necessarily. He took a bite of the breakfast biscuit and licked grease from his lip. Which wolf would that bite feed?

25

In the ten days since she talked to Grace, Exi's hope had revived a little. Her compositions grew in size and depth. She had started including Bo's upper body and couldn't help thinking he'd be glad to have the entire focus off his face. His playful, conversational, or clenched and fretting hands added to the emotion of these pieces, sometimes only a hint of thumb and fingers emerging from the shadowy background, other times a prominent element.

Occasionally to clarify a particular detail, she checked online photos, but none of those really showed what she'd seen. Those were Bo the star. These were Bo the man.

When she needed a break, she picked up the sax and played, as if the music he'd given back could bring him through the door. The woman in Grace and Devin's play had a fantasy life of people who mattered, but in this production she lived and breathed Bo Corrigan.

Now her phone brought her out of her reverie. She answered because it was Grace, taking time from her busy life once more for her husband's cousin. "Hi, Grace."

"Exi, if you could break away, Mia and I would like you to come to an art exhibit that's something like what she imagines for your paintings."

Her instant reaction was *no way*, but was that about the exhibit or Mia? Exi tapped her chin with the saxophone mouthpiece. "I guess I could ask my security detail."

"Eileen's already arranged it, if you give the go ahead."

"She has?"

"Eileen put out feelers and got back to Mia on it. There's an agent who specializes in unknown talent. He said he'd speak to you."

"Oh. Wow."

"You ought to come. Eileen thinks you're too lively to be locked up in a tower."

"She thinks I'm lively, Liam thinks I'm fiery, and John says I'm belligerent. Do any of those sound like me?"

"Only in the best ways."

Exi smiled. Time with Grace would be nice. She put away the instrument, got herself ready, and went downstairs. To her delight, Sully was the one who came inside for her. She asked him to wait in the foyer and found Eileen in the all-white room where she worked on her own theatrical projects. "Thank you for arranging this." And then as an afterthought, "Would you like to come?"

"I appreciate the invitation, but no. I'm working."

There was a hint of something off, but it didn't feel right to push. "I won't bother you then."

"Stop in when you get back."

Her mind made that *if* she got back.

Seeing her unease Sully said, "We've got it." He snuck her from the garage into the SUV backed in to minimize visibility from the street. They pulled out through the coded gate. Even knowing she wasn't visible through the side windows, Exi shrank in toward her brother.

Behind the wheel, Brett said, "We allotted extra time for an indirect route. We won't be followed this time."

She knew better than to count on anything.

Seated beside her, Sully squeezed her knee. "I'm watching for a tail."

She nodded. "I guess all this isn't weird to you."

"It's weird. Especially having you in it. Though, not really, with your penchant for trouble."

She glared. "How's the case going?"

His expression said it was bigger than a case but she didn't know what else to call it. "I can't tell you particulars, even though you're involved. But it's a strong task force."

She looked out the window as they drove. Brett played no music, obviously, so she was tempted to put on earbuds and crank something up on her phone. Instead she asked Sully for updates on the family.

Not surprisingly, he knew less than she. "I'm working around the clock on this."

She would have apologized if his eyes didn't glow with excitement. His mind wasn't on Bo. It was on the operation. "Just tell me if there's been any word on Bo."

"I would tell you that immediately."

Sully never said things he didn't mean. "Thanks."

Her mind wandered to the exhibit. She hadn't thought to ask who the artist or artists were. Or what subject or media. Did she even care? It had sounded fun, but once again her heart was back in the studio with Bo.

Maybe she should see a counselor. Not about being shot, but about him. That made her think of Louisa. How would his costar feel about her living in his apartment and painting in his studio? A sad thought, but then another struck like a bullet to the chest.

Was he hiding at Louisa's? He'd lain low with Grace—platonically—when all this started. Would that be the case this time? Chest tight, Exi replayed Bo kissing Louisa at the cast party, casual yet full of history. Her heart raced so hard she got dizzy. Breathing felt like sucking air through a coffee stirrer. Her vision tunneled.

"Exi." Sully nudged her.

"What?" She forced the word out.

"What's up?"

"I need to go back."

"Why?"

She had no good reason. Sweat dampened her forehead. She wrung her sweaty hands.

"Hey, Mitten. I think you're having a panic attack." He pushed her head down to her knees and rubbed the back of her neck. "It's okay. Just breathe."

Easy for him to say.

"I think you should go to this exhibit. It's not healthy holing up and obsessing. Don't worry. We'll keep you safe."

It wasn't that, but she didn't argue because in substance he was right. It wasn't healthy. After a while she straightened.

"There you go." Sully gave her hands a squeeze and resumed his surveillance.

She leaned against the window where the air conditioning blew past the front seat headrest with a faintly musty scent. The cool air relieved her burning face. She had not had an attack like that since Sully helped her escape fist-swinging, musical-instrument-stealing Drake Bowman.

Instead of violence, this trigger had been the thought of losing Bo to someone else. That needed scrutiny. Ugh. She was circling the drain. Snap out of it.

Finally Sully said, "Brett's going to take a pass around and we'll get a look at things. Then I'll take you inside."

She nodded. When they were satisfied, Brett paused in traffic for them to get out. She and her brother passed between parked cars to the sidewalk and started toward the door of a cleverly designed building. She recognized the place because it was only a door down from Jeffrey's office building. The moment that realization hit her, she saw him emerging with several other professionally dressed people. It was as if someone hit rewind when their gazes collided. His stride stalled, then resumed.

Sully recognized him and played it cool, watchful without appearing to guard her. Brett had pulled into a loading zone, climbed out, and stood at the opened driver's door. Exi noticed all this peripherally, without taking her eyes from Jeffrey.

If she had ignored him and gone straight in, their vigilance would not be tested now, but she couldn't cut Jeffrey that way. She smiled. "Hi."

"Hello, Alexis." He seemed uncomfortable. "How are you? You've lost weight."

"I have?" She'd sort of noticed the dress she put on floated more than usual.

"Not in a bad way. I—what are you doing here?"

"There's an exhibit in that gallery." She pointed. "Sully and I are checking it out."

Only then did Jeffrey seem to notice her brother. As he greeted him, a serious-faced brunette slipped her arm through his. The ring on her finger sent a familiar flash. Exi's jaw slackened before she caught it and put the smile back.

Jeffrey collected himself. "Alexis, this is Kendyl. Kendyl, Alexis and her bother, Sullivan."

As the guys exchanged small talk, Kendyl released Jeffrey. She leaned in and hissed, "The fact that you never slept with him allows me to ignore his ludicrous detour, but don't even think of interfering again."

Exi swallowed. "I'm happy for you." And she was, well for Jeffrey.

"We should get in," Sully said as if there was nothing involved but an art exhibit.

"So nice seeing you, Jeffrey." Exi held his eyes to show her sincerity. "And congratulations."

"Oh. Thank you."

One teeny snarky part wanted to say good luck having a Grace Evangeline wedding, but Sully took her arm.

When they'd gone a short way, he leaned in. "Was that your engagement ring?"

"It was recyclable."

"Already?"

"Jeffrey was with Kendyl before we met. For all I know, the ring was hers first, or intended for her anyway. It's not as if we shopped for it together."

"Jeffrey has now entered the scumbag ranks."

"He's not, Sully. I broke up with him."

"Little sister, you're an airhead when it comes to men. A loveable, intractable airhead."

Her track record gave her no room to argue. How she wished she could break that cycle with Bo, but he might prove her worst judgment ever. Sully pulled open the gallery door and they entered. Through the tinted doors, she watched Brett get back into his vehicle and drive off. He must think Sully sufficient.

Inside the gallery, she caught sight of Grace and Mia. Behind them, looking as inconspicuous as a missile launcher, stood John Helm. Aha. The slight shake of his head warned her not to draw attention with her typical reaction.

She smiled at her friends and returned their hugs, then introduced Grace to Sully—another cousin Devin *kept* from her. Exi looked over while they chatted. John was nowhere in sight. But an almond-shaped man with tiny head and tiny feet, coal-black hair, and aquiline nose approached and said, "Alexis Murphy?"

"Yes." His cologne had heavy tones of musk and his voice matched it.

"Jared Weiss. Eileen O'Hare asked me to keep an eye out for you."

"Oh."

He treated her to his impressive credentials, then asked if she had brought photos of her work.

"Only on my phone. This trip to Midtown was spur of the moment."

He shrugged. "Phone is fine for starters. I'll know right away if it's nothing I can push."

She opened her photos and handed the phone to him.

Beside her, Sully jutted his chin at Mia. "No Cate?"

"See, we're not always a pair. But she's going to wish we were."

Jared Weiss studied the pictures, stretching them on the screen to see detail, then looked up. "All the same subject?"

Before she could answer, Mia said, "Entirely Bo Corrigan. And if his looks aren't enough, there's the whole mystery of his disappearance."

"Disappearance?"

Exi stiffened. Mia had no idea how dangerous the situation was, but—

Sully's grip on her arm kept her from lashing out. He said, "Bo Corrigan just isn't performing right now. Everyone needs a break."

Grace touched the phone in Jared's hand. "What do you think of those paintings?"

"Well, I'd have to see the real things. Let's schedule an appointment."

Exi was shaking so hard she almost couldn't answer. "I'm pretty sure I'm not ready to exhibit."

He raised his eyebrows. "That's not the hard sell I usually get."

"I'd love to talk when I am."

"Why don't you let me judge?" He pulled out a card. "You're at Ms. O'Hare's, right?"

The panic in the car was nothing to what brewed inside at the thought of this man—or anyone with commercial intent—viewing Bo in his studio. Here was her lucky break, her chance to make it in the art world, and she wanted none of it. Not at Bo's expense. "Thanks. I'll let you know."

Irritation arched the man's neck so that his gaze slid down his nose. "Have you any idea how many hopefuls are dying for a chance to show me their art?"

"I truly appreciate the offer of your time and interest."

"But you don't intend to call."

"I … I'm not sure this is the time."

He studied her with combined arrogance and curiosity. "Don't lose my card. We may still talk if you wise up."

She didn't suppose he meant that as a pun, but then again … "Thank you, Mr. Weiss."

He walked away, shaking his head. Grace and Mia stared at her. Sully lightly rubbed her back, knowing more than anyone the dream she just surrendered.

"Well," Grace said. "Let's tour the exhibit."

Now that the threat to Bo had passed, Exi relaxed. The paintings in the first room were portraits of young women with a dramatic use of color in a contemporary style of heavy dots and dabs. The energy popped. "I like these."

"l like yours better," Mia said. "And not just because it's Bo."

Exi bit her lip. What she felt whenever Mia said his name might indicate a slide to the dark side.

"I agree." Grace adjusted her purse strap. "These all look alike even though they're different people. Yours are the same person but each unique."

"Bo comes out that way. Complex I guess." When Sully and Mia moved ahead a little, Exi held back. "Grace, could I talk to you for a second?"

"What's up?"

She meant to ask about Louisa but whispered, "Did Bo sleep with Mia?"

Grace blinked. "I don't know."

"Really?"

"Bo never boasts."

"What about her? She hasn't said?"

"Not exactly." Grace sighed. "Exi, in the wilds of Alaska, there might be someone Bo hasn't slept with. But you knew this going in. You have to decide if his past rules out a future."

"Okay. Right." She gathered herself. "So … could he be with Louisa?"

Grace's forehead wrinkled. "With her how?"

"Hiding there, like he did with you."

"Why would he be with Louisa?"

Would Grace pretend, to spare her feelings? "I know about them. Devin told me."

"I guess he never told me unless you mean their hooking up sometimes. I hate how casually the world treats all that. But it's no secret."

"She's not over him."

"Oh." She shook her head. "If that's the case it's even less likely. Bo would never take advantage." She hesitated a moment, then shook her head again. "No, I don't think he would."

Exi sighed. She'd hated the thought, but at least he'd be safe.

"Besides, Devin called around the theater crowd. He'd have heard."

"He did? When?"

"After you left our place. He wanted to help, but no one has seen Bo since he left one party in pretty bad shape. They thought he was messed up, but he was right out of the hospital, so who can say how accurate that perception was."

Exi gaped. "Why didn't you tell me?"

Grace frowned. "It wasn't new information."

"That he went to a party? Devin accused him of that, but this confirms it. Did he tell the task force?"

"I beg your pardon?"

Exi caught her mistake. "Grace, where was the party?"

"I'd have to find out."

"Do it. Please. Ask Devin."

Grace glanced over her shoulder. "I'll text him but I need the ladies' room."

"Okay, but hurry." Exi pressed a hand to her revving heart. She had to find John.

As if her body language cued him, he shifted from behind a panel. Fighting the urge to run, she passed calmly through the exhibit. A great use of color, but so many bright hues in one place were starting to feel like too much sugar.

Over her shoulder John sent Sully an optical message like *keep the blonde busy while we talk*, then Exi stifled a squeak when his mammoth arms came around in a hug that shocked her speechless. "Don't say anything that can be overheard." He released her.

She gulped before managing, "Um. Wow. We need to catch up."

"Let's go have a drink." A dryer more laconic invitation she'd never heard.

"My friend's in the ladies' room, uh, getting something for me." That sounded so bad, even John's commando eyes lit. "I mean—"

"I'll wait here." Then he murmured, "The exit stairs are right behind me."

Exi turned on her heel and hurried to find Grace. Mia started to follow, but Sully asked her something and she turned back to him. In the ladies' room, Exi said, "Did you get it?"

Grace held up her phone. "First tell me what you meant by task force."

Exi blew out a breath. "It's the whole Liam O'Hare thing. The police and the feds are involved. Sully's on it and John Helm—"

"Who?"

"The scary looking guy you're going to see me with. He was ... is Bo's bodyguard. Actually he's more than that. He's Liam's protection specialist. It's complicated. But if he knows where Bo was last seen, that's a lead right?"

"I hope. Devin said it's a nonstop party with these people. I'll forward you the info Devin sent. But my head's spinning. Eileen's brother?"

"Liam's like ... undercover, kind of. There are lots of factions and very nasty people involved."

"No wonder you're afraid to leave Eileen's."

"No wonder Bo's afraid to come back."

Grace pressed a hand to her face. "It's hard to believe any of us are mixed up in something like this. I admit my heart's racing."

"I'm surprised mine still works. But I have to go. Thanks for getting that information."

"Devin said you came with bodyguards and assassins, but he exaggerates, so I had no idea it was true."

Exi swallowed. "Grace, we shouldn't be out together. I appreciate all of this, but you have Mattie."

The bathroom door opened, and Mia came in. "Exi, what is that alpha stud doing here? And don't pretend you just ran into him. You looked like a rabbit being mugged by King Kong."

Grace hadn't seen it, but she and Mia burst out laughing.

"Have you seen his arms?" Exi demanded. "And his chest's an armored truck." He did it to keep her from blabbing, but seriously? She joined the laughter.

Then Mia sideswiped her, saying, "Is this about Bo?"

Her breath caught.

"Is he in witness protection or something? Nothing less would stop him performing. And that guy looks official."

Witness protection? She'd never considered that. By her expression neither had Grace. "If he witnessed something, I don't know what. Now I have to go."

Moving through the doorway, she heard Mia say, "There's more between them than she admitted, isn't there?"

The door closed on Grace's answer. Exi found Sully to explain, but John had already informed him.

He said, "You go with John. Brett and I will follow Grace and Mia home."

"Okay." Trying not to look like a rabbit, she pushed through the stair door to where John Helm waited.

He fixed her in a stare. "What do you have for me?"

She raised her eyebrows. "No drink?"

He folded his arms.

"Is Bo in witness protection?"

John blinked. "Not to my knowledge. It's a dead end if he is. So what do you have for me?"

Man, one track mind. She brought up Grace's text and copied it to him. "Bo was seen at this party after he left the hospital. He left there messed up and by himself. The apartment's leased to the names on the text. My cousin talked to at least one of them. He told Grace it's a revolving party scene, but Bo was there." She searched John's face. "It's a location, right?"

He nodded. "We'll talk to them and anyone else we can find,

then work our way out from there."

Exi gripped his steely arm, her chest heaving. "Thank you."

"Let's get you home."

Home. Yes. It was as much home as anyplace had been since she left for college.

Before opening the exit door, John turned. "Is the man you met outside going to be a problem?"

She had to think a minute. "Jeffrey?"

"Brett said he looked like he wanted to devour you."

"Oh my gosh no. He's engaged to that other woman now."

John looked as if he wanted to comment but pushed the door open, did his surveillance thing, then motioned her to come. He let her into the silver SUV, took the passenger position, and said, "Go."

"You don't drive," she said from the back.

"I drive."

"No, Brett and this cool tattoo guy drive. You bark orders."

The driver's mouth twitched. John said, "This is Max."

"You're also a deadly Ninja assassin?"

The men shared a look. Max said, "Nice to meet you."

"You too." She sank into the seat, chewing her lip as they crawled through traffic. She couldn't block the disappointment anymore. Bo out partying? Then he didn't leave the hospital in despair, he …

No. How could she guess what was in his mind? Maybe he had nowhere else to go. Maybe he knew they'd let him in at that hour in the middle of the night, no questions asked. Maybe that was hiding in plain sight. All of that made more sense than Bo out for a good time. Didn't it? Or had everything she'd based these last weeks on been as foolish as believing Jeffrey would miss her?

That relationship seemed like another life. She'd been dealing with other things. Jeffrey apparently had only one thing. Interesting to put a face to the name. Kendyl. Exi found a smile inside. She truly wanted Jeffrey's happiness. Whatever Brett saw, it wasn't what he thought.

Jeffrey probably felt awkward—if he ever could—about running into her with Kendyl. But to think Jeffrey could be dangerous? That almost made her laugh. She leaned her head against the seat and caught John's sidelong glance. She reassured him with a shrug. "Just a weird head trip."

He nodded. "Yeah. Done that."

She felt a friendly flicker almost as surprising as his monster hug. She bit back the smile, but he might have caught a glimpse since his jaw got a teensy bit less commando.

26

This time out in the van couldn't have the crushing effect of the other trips, Bo thought, as he had every time he and Luke left the lot for their usual shift. The element of surprise had diminished. If he saw the blows coming, he could fend them off—or not. The fact that Ann and company had developed no discernible armor did not bode well.

The mission built relationship through consistency. They fed the hungry sparrows, as Ann called the street urchins too hard and wounded to leave the life. They listened and cared. Even so, trust found no foothold in most of those who entered the van or accepted food through the window. Bo put blankets in hands that sported homemade ink and sores, provided bottled water for cracked and bleeding lips, fed youths who smelled like rancid garbage with rotten teeth, scarred and pimpled skin, and damaged psyches.

He said there was a program to help them live differently, a mission that could change all this. Beds, showers, food, training, safety, hope. He spoke into blank eyes, stoned eyes, shifty, angry, wounded eyes—and watched them turn away. He needed a victory. One step from one lost soul. Was that asking so much?

At the Trans-Bridge station, Luke admitted Vi and Misty for pastrami and juice. Tired of treading on eggshells, Bo leaned toward Misty. "Hey."

Her eyelids dragged upward until he came into view.

"Listen. Coming with us isn't unsafe, only going back to Spider."

She looked pretty stoned and he wasn't sure the words sank in. Vi's face darkened, and he wondered whether she or Spider held Misty's leash. "Nothing stopping either of you," he told Vi, in case it was jealousy that he'd reached out to Misty first.

"Except we don't want what you're selling. You know why we're junkies? Because it's fan-effing-tastic. Think your best sex ever on and on and on." She leaned in so close the smell of her cat-urine breath wafted into his nostrils. "Doesn't touch it." She leaned back with a smug smile.

"Then what?" he said.

"Then what, what?"

"How does too much feel? How does not breathing feel? How does Spider stopping your heart and kick-starting it feel?" He said it to Vi but hoped Misty heard.

Vi's face got volcanic, each eye mini eruptions. She grabbed Misty's wrist and jerked her toward the open door. Misty crawled out sideways like a crab and went down on one knee. Vi hauled her up.

"You want to talk to us, Luke, leave him behind." She stalked off down the street, dragging Misty, stumbling, after her.

Watching them disappear, Bo exhaled. "Guess I blew that." He turned back to see Luke grinning.

"I didn't know you had fire."

"Stupid fire."

"Never know. After my girlfriend OD'd, it was those questions that got me clean."

"Yeah?"

"Even then I almost didn't. Unless you've been there, you don't realize how tight the community is, how encompassing the identity."

"It's like that in theater. And there is a fair amount of substance abuse. I'm no angel."

"Yeah, I guessed as much. That's why I agreed to drive with you. I don't need some pantywaist alongside."

Bo grinned. "They use that word on the street?"

Luke chuckled. "My dad. I put him through hell. At least he lived to see me clean before the heart attack took him."

"Sorry."

"Wish I had the lost years back."

Bo felt the ache in his own gut. But it wasn't his lost years he wanted back.

In their building's exercise facility, Grace hung the towel on her neck and studied Devin. He'd gotten well enough for a strong workout and had no more excuses, so she nudged. "We need to talk to Eileen."

"Why?" He guzzled fortified water from his carafe.

"For one thing she has a project she wants me to look at with her. But mostly, I have a bad feeling. I'm afraid you'll regret holding this grudge."

"It's not a grudge, Grace." He spread his long-fingered hand. "I just don't know what part is real friendship, and how much is scheming."

"I know. But that's not what matters." They left the exercise room. "You're well now, and I never caught that bug, so I think we should go visit." She pushed through the door to extract Mattie from the contemplation garden and paid the college student and fan who'd kept an eye on her.

Taren said, "You know I'd do anything for you guys free of charge, Grace. You've done so much for me and my writing."

"I also know you're in college and making ends meet. To be able to work out with my husband sometimes and know Mattie's in good hands is worth every dollar."

"Thank you, but playing with Mattie is like being inside a Grace Evangeline novel. You and Devin married with a little girl living happily ever after …" She made a swooning sound.

"She really enjoys her time with you. And I appreciate it." She pressed the bills into their young friend's hand, then gave her a hug as Mattie ran to Devin. He scooped her up and got the octopus-around-the-neck hug.

Taren swooned again. "I'm dying of cuteness."

Grace laughed. "I know what you mean."

"I knew you'd get together. You and Devin."

"Or die in the process."

More laughing. "Well, call me next time you need someone."

"I surely will. Get after that writing assignment. You're doing great."

Taren waved and left.

Devin said, "Let's go clean up, then I'll call Eileen and see if she has time for us."

"Sounds like a plan."

"See Nana Eileen?" Mattie squeezed Devin's face between her hands.

"I see how it is. If I didn't give in to Mommy, you'd start on me, hmm?"

"She's only asking because you mentioned her." They moved through the lobby.

"Where did that 'Nana Eileen' come from anyway?"

"She was standing in for grandparents at the NICU, so we had to tell the hospital something. I like it, and so does Eileen."

"I like it." Mattie hugged his neck.

"Female unanimity. Why am I always outnumbered?"

"You didn't produce a son. That time."

He slid a look. "Are you telling me something?"

"It's simple mathematics." She pressed a hand to her abdomen. "If this baby's a boy, we're even."

He stopped in his tracks, searching her face like a scholar on the Rosetta Stone. "Already?"

"I told you those were magic words." At his look of confusion, she mouthed *baby-making.*

He tossed back his head and laughed. "I think it has more to do with chemistry. Ours obviously jives."

Mattie said, "Jives."

Grace giggled. "You better watch yourself, Daddy."

His eyes heated. "We should have naptime before seeing Eileen." He pressed the elevator button.

"It has been a busy morning." They rode the elevator up, locked in a gaze that would have steamed the interior if Mattie wasn't with them.

After tucking his daughter in, Devin came into the bathroom where she'd started the shower. He took her hands, serious and intense.

"What?"

"I never got to see you pregnant." He moved closer. "Bo did."

She wrapped her arms around his neck. "Bo never saw me like this."

"That's why he's still alive," he growled. "This time I want it all. Every centimeter you grow taking its place in my memory."

"Mmm. I think I'll like this."

"Don't ever leave me out again."

An ache filled her throat. "I won't."

Though the plea was sincere, his kiss had more of the conqueror than the postulant.

"Maybe we can start a litter."

"Don't you dare." She couldn't help laughing.

By the time they left to see Eileen, Grace could only hope she didn't still carry the glow. That woman was too shrewd by half. They were meeting at the shabby chic theater that had launched *Windows and Doors.* Except for that shining success, if she believed they deserved a voice, Eileen produced projects hardly anyone cared to see—one more way she carved her place in the annals of society.

Thankfully, their "naptime" had mellowed Devin, and Grace entered the theater with high hopes of reconciliation. Mattie walked between them, gripping a finger of each until she saw Nana Eileen on the compact stage and took off at a run. Seeing her, Eileen moved toward the ramp at one side. She reached it and paused, one hand to the wall. “There never is enough light without the production lamps,” she said.

Grace hurried over, not sure she bought the act. It looked more like Eileen had zoned out or lost her balance.

Mattie tugged Eileen’s pant legs. “Uppy me.”

It was all Grace could do to let the woman lift her child without offering assistance. But Eileen managed and Mattie squeezed her neck.

When she could speak, Eileen said, “To what do I owe this visit?”

Grace touched her arm. “Let’s sit down, why don’t we? Mattie, show Nana Eileen how you can run down the ramp.”

Eileen lowered Mattie and cocked her head. “Our usual seats?”

They sat in the center front row as they had for the premier. Oh, what joy and angst that night had held. Sort of how she felt now.

Devin said, “I want to apologize for my rudeness the last time we were together.”

“Those good manners again.” Eileen chuckled. “Eddie Bressard showing though.”

“I wish they didn’t disappear so easily.”

“Well, we’ll let bygones be …” She frowned at the stage searching for the word even though it was the one she’d just used.

Grace reached out and squeezed her arm. “What’s going on?”

“You’re always too perceptive,” Eileen griped, then sighed. “If you must know, it’s a brain tumor.”

It hit like a hammer to the chest. Color drained from Devin’s face.

“Grade II precancerous, but invasive. The good news is that it’s slow growing. Less good is that I’m shaky, woozy, and forgetful. I haven’t much appetite.” She turned to Devin. “But I can still climb four flights of stairs and more.”

He closed his eyes, crestfallen.

Eileen guffawed. “Oh, I couldn’t help myself.” She took his hand. “You keep me young and entertained.”

"Entertained?"

"Oh heavens, yes. Your indignation. Your biting wit. Sometimes I replay our battles for the sheer pleasure." She turned. "Bringing Grace into the mix was my masterstroke." She squeezed Mattie. "And look what came of it."

"On that note," Grace spoke through the lump in her throat, "you can be the first to know. We have another on the way."

Eileen lit. "The first? With all those blood relatives?"

"I only found out a couple hours ago." Devin raised her hand and kissed it. "So yes, our honorary grandparent is first to know."

"Well . . ." She settled back and stroked Mattie's hair. "This one's a hard act to follow."

Devin nodded. "Grace doesn't think we've exhausted the assets we each bring to the table, but I'll have to see it to believe it."

"I'm so happy for you." Eileen's gaze drifted. "Now if we can just get Bo home safe."

With tears in his eyes, Devin pulled her to him and kissed her head.

Driving together, Bo and Luke found a groove. Luke claimed they drew twice as many females with him aboard. "I'd say ten times but that would hurt my pride."

Bo couldn't argue since he hadn't seen the percentages before. He would guess guys might be less inclined to accept handouts, until he remembered—male or female—they were feeding addiction. If food came free, that left the cash they begged or stole to satisfy their deepest need. Nothing was beneath them, not even shoplifting items and selling them to shady retailers, who would give the kids a pittance and resell the goods. They were all in fear of getting caught, of doing time, but nothing conquered the need.

Two females they didn't attract this entire week were Vi and Misty. He should have kept quiet or talked to Misty alone—if she ever was alone. He could have been less confrontational, less righteous, could have kept taking Vi's lip and playing her game. He could have ignored thoughts of Misty showing her damage to frat boys for a few bucks in her jar. But he didn't. He'd done more harm than good.

Ann said that wasn't true. She said it didn't hurt to show he cared, whatever words expressed it. She said it devastated everyone when Misty left the fold and almost paid with her life. They all wanted her back. And he'd blown whatever chance they had.

"Dude, you're brooding."

"I keep thinking about Misty."

"I hear you. But no story's over until it's over. Hey." Luke hit his arm.

Bo followed his gaze to the bus station and saw Misty all alone. His breath hitched. She sat slumped over on the ground against a pillar, by herself for the first time in his experience. Bo scoured surrounding faces for Vi or someone who might be Spider. It wasn't impossible they'd use Misty as bait, then strike whoever went to her. But no one paid attention, at least that he could tell.

Luke slowed to a crawl. "You want to check it out?"

"Yeah." When Luke double parked, Bo climbed out. He strode over and crouched. Misty smelled stale and ripe at once. Her breathing sounded labored. Her hair, haphazardly cut, hung over her face like crow's wings. Even so he could tell things weren't right. He touched her shoulder and she jolted, but instead of looking up seemed to curl in more.

"Misty?" He spoke softly and refrained from touching her again.

This time her face came up. If she looked into a fractured mirror, she'd see what he saw. And it wasn't only her face. Bruises covered her neck and shoulder where the blouse hung loose again. Her thin legs in the short shorts were scraped bloody and bruised. She was Sheriff times ten, and no truck had done this.

Wordless, he slipped an arm under her knees and another behind her back. He lifted her like a bird who had flown into a window and carried her to the van. Luke opened the passenger door and Bo buckled her into his seat. No need to discuss their destination. Bo climbed in with the coolers and rode there.

At the clinic he once again carried Misty while Luke rang for admission. Ann and Georgia were ready since Luke had voice texted their ETA. Bo settled Misty upright on a cot and Georgia drew the girl in against her broad hip. Misty's half open eye met his. He couldn't imagine the other opening again.

Before either could speak, Ann said, "You two go on. We'll take it from here."

Dr. Patel said Ann had treated people all over the world. She could handle this or she'd call for reinforcements. Even so …

"Come on." Luke took his arm.

Bo released a slow breath. So much for thinking every night would not destroy him. "Okay."

"You tired?"

"No." Something like speed ran through his veins, inciting the hemoglobin. He climbed into the seat that smelled like Misty and said, "I don't know how you go on. Any of you. How it stops hurting."

"If it stops, you got no business here."

"I'll let you know when that happens," Bo rasped.

They moved through the alternate universe of the city he knew. This one crawled with shades. *Walking Dead* wasn't far off. Luke asked each person they talked to what happened to Misty. No one knew. No one admitted they knew. They feigned ignorance like bad actors. None convincing.

Bo thought for a minute the old man Sticks called Elmo would speak, but when he tried, his booze-addled brain had no answers. It made it worse that those who could say wouldn't.

"Why won't they tell us?"

"Why do you think?"

"Spider."

"Give the man a Cheerio."

Bo slid him a look. "Your dad again?"

Luke's smile spread, then sagged. "Let's call it a night."

They entered the dormitory building with the key code. Bo shifted foot to foot. "Should we check on her?"

Luke shook his head. "Leave her to Sister for now." He stretched. "Go get some sleep."

Good luck with that. Bo sat on his bed and hung his head, then remembered Misty in that position and had his first homicidal thoughts. Huh. Might be in everyone no matter how conditioned toward peace and harmony.

He stretched out and pictured Exi on the sofa with him that night at Eileen's. He played back their conversation, what he told her about growing up, about his deficient mother and the invisible dads. He remembered how bad she felt about his family, how eagerly she wanted to hear about Barb yet hesitated to ask in case it hurt him.

He would have told her. He would have brought Barb to life with lots more stories than they had time for. He wished he'd had a chance for Exi to know his sister that way, wished the two could have met in real life. But what right did he have to wishes when he'd drawn the long straw in a fistful of short ones?

He closed his eyes and drifted. "I don't like this role, Barb. You didn't tell me it hurt."

Apparently, she had nothing to say about that.

27

Staring at her bedroom ceiling, Exi felt the enormity of the opportunity she had rejected. Doubt and self-recrimination grew claws. Breaking into New York's art scene took exactly the influence Mr. Weiss offered. She was certifiable, turning him down, especially when Bo might care nothing for her at all—except he starred in every piece. If she wanted success, she had to stop painting him. Tell that to her brush.

She rose to shower as she had every day since Grace saw her in crazy mode, forcing normalcy until it came naturally to eat, sleep, exercise, and wash in this apartment. Jeffrey was right that she'd lost weight, and some of that was muscle. She'd get it back. Her sanity, not so much.

Treya was bringing more clothes over. Since she hardly went out, it didn't matter as much as it might, but living out of one suitcase's worth of wardrobe was getting old. She hurried downstairs when Treya texted that she had parked. Sondra beat her to the door and admitted her friend.

"Yowza." Treya's eyes bugged as she pulled the luggage inside and got her first look.

"Want to hang out down here?" Exi said. "I can return the luggage to you later."

"No way. I want to see your place."

"It's four flights up with heavy bags."

"You take one, I'll take one."

Exi glared. "You can really be a pain."

"My middle name, girlfriend. Now haul."

She caught Sondra hiding a grin.

Halfway up, Treya said, "Don't know what all you're keeping to yourself, but I came without Suz to get some truth."

At the third-floor landing, Exi paused. "I can't tell you what I'm not allowed to. That's just the way it is."

Treya got in her face. "Well there's a bunch of stuff you can say and I intend to hear it."

On the top floor, Exi let her in and rolled one suitcase to her bedroom while Treya rolled the other. They shoved both onto the bed.

"He decorate this apartment?"

"I don't know." By Mia's account probably not. Only the studio had been definably his—including DNA.

Treya walked out to inspect the kitchen and living area. "You can start talking."

Exi pressed hands to her lower back and glared. "I don't know why you're in my business all of a sudden. You weren't a tyrant when we went shopping."

"Yeah, but I saw how twitchy you were, and you wouldn't let us come in so I'm guessing you don't want Suz to know you're living with Bo. Are you with him, girlfriend?"

Saying yes would end speculation, but it wasn't true and devalued Bo's restraint. Plus she loved Treya and hated lying. And no one believed her lies so she shouldn't bother. "No. He's not here."

Treya headed in the direction of Bo's closed door.

"That's his room. I don't go in there." Not since she refused to stay when she might have made a difference. She could have given him one day and changed everything that came next. Thankfully the bathroom was also accessed from the main area.

Treya sent a look over her shoulder and adjusted her trajectory toward the home gym in what might otherwise be a dining room. Then she headed to the only other door. "What's in here?"

"Right now my studio." Exi braced herself as Treya let herself in.

"Get outta here." She circled open-mouthed.

Exi held her breath fighting the emotion of more eyes on Bo, even though Treya was someone she had cared about since her formative years.

"You said you weren't in love with him."

"I said we're not together."

Treya folded her arms. "This is very confusing. Start talking. Begin with G.I. Joe."

Exi sighed. "He's Bo's bodyguard. I told you." She was not going into Liam and all that jazz.

"Uh-huh." Treya moved in close to study the smaller paintings of Bo's face. "You told me something bad went down. If you don't tell me what, I'll wait here for Sexy Pants to do it himself."

"He's not coming. I wish he was. That's all I can say."

"If he's not here, how are you painting him? He's jumping off these walls like he's alive."

Her heartfelt prayer. "I started with photos, now I'm just painting from memory."

"You've always had talent but this is ridiculous. People will buy these like crazy."

"They're not for sale."

Treya braced her hips. "You're crazy, then. When did you go crazy?"

"Bo didn't give me permission to paint him."

"Yeah, neither did Elvis and he's on velvet all over the world."

"What a great comparison. I'm so proud."

"Maybe you have a point, though. These are personal, even I can see that." Treya came toward her. "But why aren't you painting things you can sell? Or did you get rich living here?"

"I didn't get rich. This is temporary. And I'm painting Bo because I want to." Needed to, but Treya would not get it without the backstory.

"Huh. You have any food? I had to skip lunch."

They went to the kitchen, and Exi sliced apples, sharp white cheddar, and hard salami. With any luck Treya's short attention span would save further examination. As she opened the refrigerator for sodas a clatter rose downstairs—something shattering, and shouts. Exi hit the floor so hard she split open her chin.

Treya hunched down like the ceiling was falling, though of course it wasn't. Slowly Exi registered voices: Sondra, Eileen, Grace, and Devin channeling up the open staircase. She heard concern, but no gunshots, no invasion. She peeled her hands off her head and raised her face.

"You're bleeding."

She felt the split on her chin, the slippery spill that tripped her mind onto Bo bleeding on this same wood floor. She pushed up to her knees, then her feet. Treya thrust a napkin at her, and she pressed it to her chin, feeling woozy. How did fighters do it? One uppercut and she'd be out for the count. Her mind flashed to Bo being beaten in the park. Tears stung.

Treya pulled the napkin away. "You need something on that."

She pressed the napkin back. "I need to know what happened." Even if it involved her cousin. What was he doing here anyway?

"Dripping blood all over?"

Fine. "First-aid kit in the bathroom." She headed there.

Treya followed, swooning over the fixtures. "Good thing Suz isn't imagining Bo Corrigan in here."

"He's not a thing," she snapped, then said, "Sorry. Just do this. I have to get downstairs."

After a stinging alcohol wipe to disinfect, Treya applied a butterfly bandage. "You have that PTSD, don't you? From the shooting."

"I guess." If breaking glass put her on the floor.

Treya braced her hips. "You don't think Jeffrey might have been a safer choice than all this?"

"I know he would."

"But?"

"I don't love him." She stalked out of the bathroom.

"You made a good show of it."

"That's what it was. He deserves better. He's back with Kendyl, by the way. I'm happy for them."

Treya snorted. "You are one weird chick."

"I'm catching a theme here." As she opened the door, she heard an incoming siren. Oh no. She hustled.

From the second-floor balcony landing, she watched Grace, not Sondra, admit the emergency responders. Was the housekeeper-nurse-companion occupied? Or had something happened to Sondra? Exi hustled double-time. Reaching the foyer, she said, "Treya, this is—"

"Like I don't know Grace Evangeline? You're crazier than I thought. And that's saying something."

She hardly heard her. "What happened, Grace?"

"Eileen had a seizure and fell into a curio cabinet."

"Is she okay?"

"A little cut up. And there's more to it, but that's her story to tell."

"She's in the parlor?"

"Yes." They all looked that way.

"Why are you and Devin here?"

"Eileen has a project she wants me to work on with her. Devin's helping her choose a director for another."

"Isn't he mad at her?"

"They're past that."

"Oh. Good." So why did it not feel good? Unfair to Bo? Or herself? How petty was that?

As the ambulance pulled up, Treya squeezed her arm. "I'm going back up to unpack. You go ahead."

While this was diplomatic, Treya had always been squeamish, especially with old people. Almost a phobia. Suz teased but Treya didn't find it funny. Exi wished she knew why, but in all their years together, her friend had never said.

Chin throbbing, Exi went with Grace to the parlor. On one knee, her cousin cradled Eileen's hand between his with a wounded expression. The ambulance crew flattened the gurney to get her aboard. As they wheeled her out, Exi pressed a hand to her heart, tears filling her eyes. Then Eileen was gone and Devin was there, pulling her into a hug.

"Are you okay?" He eased her away to look. "What happened to your chin?"

"I banged it. What's wrong with Eileen?"

His throat worked, the Adam's apple rising and falling, then he said, "Brain tumor."

From her knees on the carpet, Sondra sucked a breath. Exi felt rooted in cement. She hadn't known Eileen long and most of their acquaintance prickled. What hurt was how much Bo and these who loved her would suffer.

Devin looked at each of them. "She's kept it to herself long enough. Eileen's going to need everyone she has."

"What stage?" Sondra half whispered.

"Precancerous. They were holding off on surgery and trying other things, but that may no longer be an option."

Exi knelt beside Sondra, picking up the shards of broken glass and china. "You're her caregiver. Go with Devin and Grace. I'll do this." Sondra's agreement showed the measure of friendship they'd developed.

With everyone out of there, Treya came back down. She rolled the empty suitcases to the door, then peeked into the parlor. "This place is a museum."

Exi dumped shards into a trash can. "This is where we played *Alice in Wonderland* that night I told you about. Even has a looking glass, except it's over the mantel." What a magical night, enjoying her family and falling for Bo, and Eileen, the puppet master, pulling all their strings. She fought a sob that Treya didn't notice.

"I ate that food you got out, so let's have a quick tour before I leave."

She showed Treya various rooms and the posh nursery Eileen created for Grace and Mattie.

"And your hot cousin didn't know?"

"He was producing a play in Australia."

"That whole time she was pregnant?"

"No. But Grace didn't tell him before he went. She was trying to keep it quiet. Bo helped her avoid the media, but then that bottom-feeder attacked her."

"I forgot she was shot at like you. Wonder if she still hits the floor."

"It affects her."

They finished the tour, then Treya took the suitcases and left. Exi looked up and around the foyer. The great house held its tales—including this newest.

Brain tumor. If Bo knew, would he come back? Maybe, but she couldn't bear to text something so painful. So she wrote: *You should come see Eileen,* and added: *You should come see me.* Her emotions were too raw to say more without begging.

In a film of sunlight warming flower-scented earth, Exi came to him, a nymph with her self-deprecatingly droll expression. He took in her tear-sparkled lashes, her softly parted lips. He reached to clasp her outstretched hands and found his were skeleton bones, rotting flesh hanging in shreds. She kept coming, her smile rich and warm. Didn't she see the decay?

"I've missed you, Bo."

"I miss you too." His voice was dry as the grave. No resonating tones to fill a theater, to move the hearts and spirits of hundreds at a time. No inflection so perfect he brought tears or laughter. No timing so right his fellow cast members rose to new heights, feeling the thrill of excellence, riding the wave like surfers on his sea.

"Please come home," Exi pleaded.

He wanted to, but a force like a howling wind tunnel tugged his ragged bones. Reaching for her, he wailed as it sucked him into darkness so consuming it crumbled him to dust.

He clenched the sheets and sat up. Fear clutched his chest with vise fingers. Where was he? Dormitory. Rescue mission. Ann, Luke. *Misty*. His head ached. He rubbed the temples.

Exi had no part in this, no connection to him here and now. She was safe. Safe and alive. No shooters. No knife-wielding madmen. No corpse lovers spreading a swathe of death that struck the innocent.

Slowly his heaving breath stilled. The dark fog cleared, but what remained in the light of day had its own misery. He rose, showered, and went downstairs. Ann was not in her office. The alternatives were many, but he headed for the clinic. From inside the main building, the door required no code or buzzed entry. Often it stood open. Today it was closed. He knocked.

Seeing him through the glass, Ann said something to the doctor, then came out to him. "Let's take a walk."

They went outside, but not in the direction he usually headed with Sticks and DeShawn for Dumpster diving. This was more residential. Lower-income apartments, bodegas, corner stores. He pulled his shirt collar up and hunched, changing his stride just enough to suggest a limp. Ann didn't comment. He said, "So what's the deal?"

Her hesitation warned him to prepare himself, but it almost never helped. "Misty's friend Vi told Spider she was hot for a guy who wanted her out of the life."

He swallowed that bitter pill. "They're friends. Why would she do that?"

"To take Misty's position with Spider. Better drugs, higher status. Friendship is ephemeral on the streets."

"So Misty lost his protection and someone beat on her?" They paused at an intersection with no one else waiting to cross.

"Spider ordered his captains to beat and rape her."

Bo felt the street fall away as the darkness he'd dreamed swept in.

"Even so, she would have stayed, hoping to be restored, if she didn't fear for her baby."

He closed his eyes and tipped his head back. "Did she lose it?"

"Amazingly no. At least so far. The womb can be remarkably protective."

His voice rasped. "Is that good? That she has a kid by this monster or … whoever? With all the crap in her system?"

"That's never good, Beau. But it's a life to be protected. Misty had already quit everything but heroin."

"So we cheer?" He didn't try to cross when the light changed.

"We celebrate the steps she's taken, steps you helped her take. You did what we've been unable to these last years. You brought her home. I can't tell you what that means to me."

"Like this?"

"Alive. Fighting. Trying. So yes, like this."

By her fierce expression she meant it. "Okay. What now?"

"Now it might get complicated. You are her shining knight. She's deeply wounded and hungry for love. Do you get where I'm going with this?"

He cleared his throat. "You want me to leave."

Her face slackened. "No. Nothing like that. You are valuable. We treasure you." She clasped his forearm. "I want you to be careful. Avoid physical contact with Misty … if you can. The last time she attached to Luke and, well, you get the idea."

"What am I supposed to do, push her away?"

"Of course not. Just keep it friendly. You're a young, virile man—"

"That won't be a problem."

She searched his face. "You prefer—"

"I'm not gay. Just not interested." They crossed the street.

"There may also be jealousy."

"From Luke?"

"From the kids. You're popular. If Misty tries to appropriate you, try to dispel that without wounding her. We don't allow special relationships between staff and clients. That doesn't mean they don't try."

Back on the sidewalk, he said, “I’m sick over what they did to her.”

She released a breath. “It’s not a new story, Beau. Women and even young girls suffer like that all over the world. Even without force, people live licentiously. We’ve lost the sense of sex as sacred.”

“Sacred?”

“Who do you think created it?”

He thought of all the women he’d been with, the pleasure, the fun, but nothing sacred. “You think sex is holy. Sorry, Ann, but have you ever had it?”

Her laugh caught him by surprise. He’d thought she might get offended, but laugh? “I wasn’t trying to be funny. I don’t see the connection. When I’m with a woman it’s flesh and fire and I promise you there’s no prayer involved except, ‘Oh God, that was good.’”

Her eyes lit. “You’re like Solomon with his thousand wives and concubines, taking pleasure in what God made pleasurable. In the end, that did him in.”

“Not a bad way to go.”

Her gaze intensified. “It cost him everything. He lost his soul.”

Bo rubbed his face. “I’ve never forced anyone. I’ve beaten some off—only not like—I don’t mean beaten.”

“That goes without saying. You’re a gentle soul.”

He shook his head. “You think you know me.”

“I know the one who does. He calls you son and longs for your return.”

His throat constricted. “No man’s ever called me son.”

“But God does.”

“I haven’t signed up.”

“And yet you’re his hands and feet and voice in this world.” She took his arm and turned around.

He didn’t know how to respond. So he didn’t.

28

Eileen was still at the hospital, so Exi wasn't sure why Grace and Devin wanted to come back over. "Obviously you can come," she told Grace on the phone, "but it's not necessary. Sondra filled me in—unless you have something new?" That naïve part of her hoped Grace would say the brain tumor was a mistake, a misdiagnosis, that the seizure meant a different thing.

"No, I'm sorry."

She had dreamed about Bo getting the news, hearing it too late. Her throat constricted. If something unthinkable happened while he was gone, what would that do to his spirit?

Too worked up to paint, she went from portrait to portrait asking him to come back, reminding him where he belonged. He should be here for Eileen. She pressed her hands to her face, then dragged them down and texted: *Bo, come home. Just do it!*

Out in the living area, Exi brought the sax to her mouth and poured everything she felt into Kenny G's "Love Song," then just improvised until she heard knocking. She set the instrument in its case and opened the door.

"Wow, that sounded wonderful." Grace and Mattie wore matching grins.

"Thanks." Bo wasn't only restoring things she'd lost, but her very sense of self. He'd reminded her who she was before the worst boyfriend punched and stole, others lied and cheated, and the last replaced her without a blink.

As Grace started by, Mattie reached out. "Hug Mattie."

Exi took the child, shooting Grace a look of surprise. Grace air-clapped her happiness at this development. With Mattie propped on her hip, Exi looked at Devin standing apart. She quaked a little when their eyes met. They'd come about Eileen, but how could this not be about Bo?

He stretched his hand out, palm up. "Friends?"

No, but she rested her free hand on his. "Family." She couldn't help if it sounded strangled. Family meant you had to love, no matter how hard it was.

"That was you playing?"

She glanced over at the sax. "Bo got it for me."

"Grace is right. You sound good."

"He thinks my various skills and interests are a wealth of talent, not a lack of focus." She gave them a crooked smile.

"He's right." Grace agreed. "And insightful."

"How's Eileen?"

Devin said, "She's having surgery. As early as tomorrow or within the week."

Though she'd wished, Exi wasn't surprised.

Grace said, "She'd love a phone call."

"Okay."

Mattie squeezed her face with tiny, soft hands. "Draw? Exi draw pictures?"

She really was talking. "Maybe in a minute, honey." How cute the child remembered her from those few days before the chasm opened up.

Devin slipped a bag off his shoulder. "Why don't you color, Punkin, while the grown-ups talk." He put four thick colored pencils and a pad of paper on the table. Exi stood Mattie on a bistro chair where she settled to her knees to scribble.

"I'll stay here with her if you want to show Devin your work," Grace said.

Exi stiffened. She had closed the studio door to prevent him from seeing her work. Grace had to know it would set him off. "I don't think he—"

"I'd like to see. I've heard the rave reviews."

She lolled her head to the side. "You won't want to see. They're Bo."

"I know."

She folded her arms. "I'm not sure it's fair."

"Exi." Grace touched her elbow. "Let Devin see."

She blew out a breath and opened the door. Devin came in with her. Perfectly silent, he moved around the room, studying one likeness after another. There was no help for it. He was seeing Bo through her eyes. She braced herself as the minutes passed.

Mattie's little voice and Grace's murmurings came through the doorway, but Devin's silence and her own made this room a tomb. Finally he crossed to her with something she might call anguish pulling his brows in and bending his mouth. "I'm sorry," he breathed.

Her eyes filled and tears spilled down her cheeks. A sob rose from her throat. He pulled her in and held her while she cried. She almost thought he cried too, but that wasn't possible, was it? Unless he thought … "Did you hear something? Is he dead?"

Devin's eyes were red-rimmed. "I haven't heard anything. But I admit this is longer than he's ever gone. Days, a week, two weeks maybe. But not like this, not completely out of contact. I'm so sorry, Exi. I don't know what else to say."

But he cared. Finally. It was too late, but he cared.

It took a full ten minutes to compose herself enough that her distress wouldn't upset Mattie. Devin waited with her, a silent witness to her struggle. Finally they left the studio. She drew pictures for Mattie while Grace told Devin about the agent interested in her art.

He said, "It's really personal work. I understand the reluctance. It's how I felt with my first novel. You remember, Grace?"

"Yes, but every creation is an outworking of something inside. Exi shouldn't hide her gift. It's magnificent."

"It isn't about me. It's about Bo. He doesn't show everyone what I've painted in there. If he's gone, no one has a right to see it."

Grace reached over the table and clasped her hand. "I'm believing he's not gone."

"Then it's less fair to make them public."

"You don't have to make these public. But you could let the agent see, so he knows the quality of your art. Think of the time and effort you put into your graduate degree. When we met you were longing to do what you love and make a living with it. This is a top-level agent."

"It is?"

"Do you really think Eileen would set you up with anything less?"

Exi gulped. "I thought he repped nobodies."

"He discovers unknown talent. That's not the same thing. There are only so many chances that come in one life."

Her pulse raced at the truth in that. "Won't he want me to sell these?"

"You're clearly prolific without sacrificing quality—like me, I might say." She elbowed her husband, whose mouth twitched. "That shows you're productive, even if it's a little ways down the road. And maybe you could create a few alternatives."

"Like what?"

"Would you consider painting Mattie?"

"Paint Mattie," the little one echoed.

Exi stroked the toddler's head. "I'd love to. But it feels like turning my back, like giving up to stop painting Bo now."

Grace shrugged a shoulder. "He and Eileen were the first to see my little girl. I was still mad at him, so he didn't stay long, but that smile he got when he saw her, I'll never forget it." Her voice thickened with emotion. "Maybe you can paint things he cares about. Things he'd like to see when he comes back."

Exi studied her. "What besides Mattie?"

Devin answered, "Eileen's Rolls."

Grace giggled. "In which he gives that poor woman heart failure."

"I could paint Eileen."

"She would be thrilled." Grace emphasized every word.

"And Sondra. Bo kisses her hand when she serves him waffles."

"Of course he does," Devin growled without heat.

"And you guys."

Grace said, "He'd especially like it if you painted yourself."

Exi tried to picture that. Paint how she felt in the moments they had together? Paint how she felt about him every day? She would still have him in mind, but he might prefer a crowd to himself alone. Why hadn't she thought of that?

Grace said, "Let's let the agent have a look while the iron's hot and tell him you're branching out. Think that could work?"

Exi raised and lowered one shoulder. "I guess." Maybe she could crawl a little bit away from obsession back to life and her love of art for its own sake.

"Grace is very savvy," Devin said.

"Savvy doesn't require an intensifier." Grace dodged his pinch.

He continued. "She's built an empire on talent and good timing."

"All that to say, don't miss a chance if you can help it." Grace slid her hand into her husband's.

"Okay." Exi nodded. "I'll give him a call. And start broadening my portfolio. I have sketches I did of Mattie while you were away, or do you have a picture you want me to use?"

"I have a few thousand I could send." Grace laughed. "But I'll bet your sketches are special."

Exi looked toward the studio, itching to start.

"Your creative juice is flowing, I can see." Devin jutted his chin. "We know how that is, but call Eileen before you immerse yourself. She wants to talk before the surgery."

"I will. Thanks for coming over." Her throat constricted. "Thanks for caring." He knew what she meant.

"Hang in there, okay?"

She nodded. After they left, Exi walked to the window that overlooked Gramercy Park. Rain spilled in silver shafts as light passed unevenly through the clouds. Watching the storm, she called Eileen.

The woman sounded insubstantial. "I may be like your mother soon, no words to express so much."

Exi didn't waste Eileen's time pretending that couldn't happen.

"Bo needs to know he has a home if I'm not there or able to say so. Can I count on you?"

"He knows you care about him."

"It's not enough to care. He needs to know he belongs. There's a difference."

There really was. "I'll tell him."

Outside the window, a young couple in soaked clothes shook their dripping hair, laughing as they came through the black iron gate that separated the park from all who had no coveted access.

Eileen said, "He might not be himself when he comes back."

"I'm praying he'll be fine." An opalescent rainbow formed in the moist air, then faded almost as soon as it appeared. "I'm praying for you too."

Eileen's voice softened. "Maybe it's time."

"Jesus calls everyone who's weary and burdened."

Eileen didn't answer, but neither did she scoff.

"And welcomes the wandering."

"I've wandered all right."

"Then there's even more rejoicing."

"You and Grace." Eileen laughed weakly. "The problem is living up to it if I survive."

"A little repentance goes a long way."

"I imagine it might." Eileen's sigh was almost a song. "I'm happy to know you, Alexis Murphy. And happy Bo has you on his side. Don't give up."

"Never."

"If there is a God, I imagine he or she is a lot like you."

Not even close, Exi thought but didn't say. Because maybe it was Christ Eileen was seeing in her.

Grace didn't expect Devin to talk about it, but as they drove in the rain to Eddie's from Eileen's, he glanced over. "I'm not an expert in fine art, but Exi's pretty good, right?"

"I think so. Once she stopped trying to force a style others thought relevant and found her passion."

"Wherever it's coming from, there's a wellspring of talent in my little cousin."

"You should start thinking of her as a grown-up."

"I know." He drove quietly for a while, the wipers swipe-thunking. "I didn't know that about Bo. What you told Exi about him seeing Mattie."

She hoped this was not going to open old wounds. "He told Eileen my secret so I wouldn't be alone in it all, then brought her over and bowed out. He's far more intuitive than one might think."

"One being me."

"One being anyone who takes him at face value. It's a front, his self-absorption."

"He plays it so well." Devin maneuvered around a delivery van, shifting lanes like a Big Apple native. "My opinion begins with fact. I just haven't looked past the surface."

"He snowed you."

"Why?"

"I'd guess your opinion matters."

"So he shows me the worst?"

"Where does Mattie misbehave?"

He looked back at his daughter in the car seat playing with her shoes.

"She needs to know over and over again that we're on her side no matter what. We're the center of her world."

"I'm the center of Bo's?"

"Professionally. I think you've filled a space his sister left. You're his guiding hand creatively, maybe even personally. He had you on such a high pedestal it never entered his mind you'd messed around with me. He never guessed until you went street thug and pushed him up against Eileen's Phantom with all those cell phones and one brazen reporter recording it all."

He slid her a look.

"I think at first his interest in Exi had as much to do with you as her."

Devin took that in without comment.

"He baited you at Eileen's and you swallowed it whole. Then I think he really fell for her. I know she loves him."

"That's obvious in her work. Shockingly real." His brow creased. "So why did he take off?"

Smears spread and evaporated on the windshield. "You voiced his worst fear, that he causes bad things to happen to people he loves."

Devin didn't defend himself. He listened.

"Exi tried to tell him he's not responsible for his sister's cancer."

"That's crazy thinking."

"You thought you ruined Eddie's life by existing."

The wipers squeaked as the rain dissipated. Devin turned them off. "I see your point."

"I don't know how he's completely disappeared." Grace dabbed a tear. "But I pray Exi's wrong about him taking himself out of the picture."

Devin's face twisted. "She thinks that?"

"When is it just too much?"

"I hope to God you're wrong."

When they reached Eddie's, Mattie played with her grandpa in the dripping curtain of leaves trailing from the weeping willow that nearly filled the backyard. Devin said, "I'm glad he didn't listen to me and cut that down, even though it's ancient and ready to split open."

"Some things are stronger than they seem." Grace slid her hand into his. "Look how well Eddie's doing. And Alison. I think their renewed contact has invigorated them both."

"Did I tell you he's looking at the house next door for her?" He pointed.

"No." Grace looked at the single-level brick-and-white house with a tiny yard like Eddie's. "When did that come up?"

"You were on the last stretch of your tour when we started kicking it around. His neighbor hasn't completely decided to sell, but if she does, she'll come to Eddie first."

"That would be wonderful for Alison."

"She'd have to learn a new environment. Her little shotgun has served well for a blind person to know every inch."

"But she'd have a yard and garden."

"And Eddie to mow it."

"Alison loves flowers." Grace leaned into her husband, smiling.

"It's probably a perfect arrangement for both of them, close enough to keep an eye on each other. Less worry all around." His voice held tones of his own worries.

"You want some time with Eddie while we're here?"

"Yeah." He stroked her back. "I think I need it."

From the first time she'd seen them together, the depth of love and respect between father and son had shimmered like sunlight after rain. They would talk through this as they did so many other things, Devin more open here than he could ever be with her. Eddie's mentoring never failed to challenge and restore this man she loved. How she wished Bo had someone so solid, wise, and good.

29

"First my dog, now that girl shows you up." DeShawn grinned all over his face.

Bo looked across the classroom at Misty, still scabbed and bruised, clearly sore but taking her place in the class, trying to make her way back into this system. These people had nurtured her once and stood ready to do it again. Doc Patel had her on a medication regime to ease her craving without harming the life she carried.

"She hurt bad, but not staying in bed for weeks like waa-waa baby you."

Bo let him razz. He'd explained the infection situation, and DeShawn just wanted a rise. Plus he was proud of Misty. She had nothing hard on the outside, but resilience inside. Like Exi. His heart flared, but he pressed thoughts of her down where he kept things that hurt. Separation kept her safe. Her safety kept him sane.

"Man, you too serious." DeShawn left the table where they'd been trying to compose an essay.

He'd rebound. Bo gave Misty an encouraging smile. She might never have made the break without Vi's betrayal and Spider's brutality. But she was braving it now.

DeShawn returned and flopped into his chair. "You'd rather help her write these stupid things."

"Sure, Sparky. That's why I'm sitting here with you."

The kid spun the spiral notebook with one finger on the table. "So what I gotta say now?"

"You decide what to say, I help you write it. The content has to come from your head, not mine." His scant patience for teaching was running out. But Ann wanted him here for a while, and he'd ruled out babies and screamers. He was about to rule out DeShawn if the kid didn't make some effort. "Listen. You want the GED? You need to write this essay. It's that easy."

"It's not easy."

"The concept is. You work for what you want."

"Hey. I like that. I'll make that my *theme.*"

"Good. Start writing."

"Okay, I will." DeShawn scribbled a title and strung some words while bouncing his knee so hard the table shook.

The energy had to come out some way, as had his own back in the day. They actually made some headway. Bo felt as happy with himself as DeShawn for surviving a full hour. Dining at the staff table, he told Ann, "I can grab a nap and go out in the van tonight."

"It's best to let things cool down." Ann sipped her tea.

"You mean with Spider?" His spaghetti and meat sauce curdled in his stomach. He'd acquired another enemy, made himself a fresh target. How could these things still surprise him?

Bo looked over to Georgia sitting with Misty, so determined to pour out all her love and care on their recovered street sparrow. Nothing would pry Misty loose if Georgia Warren had any say in it. Yet the girl's eyes came to him as if she couldn't keep them off. Ann had not exaggerated, and Georgia missed none of it.

When the kids and staff dispersed for evening activities, she made a beeline. "I don't suppose you can dial down the sex appeal, Plato?"

At least she hadn't jumped on Hollywood. "What did you have in mind?"

"A pillow case?"

"That's a little clannish for my taste."

She sniggered. "A paper sack might do just fine."

"Can I cut eye holes?"

"No. It's the eyes that do it."

Bo shook his head. "Just fill her up. She won't need me."

Georgia plopped down at the table the others had vacated. "She's highly sexualized, as I imagine you to be."

"Past life, Georgia. Past life."

"She wants to tell you what happened. She thinks it'll turn you on."

He looked at her in horror. Georgia wouldn't be that crass, so it must be true. "Why?"

"In her experience, that's what men like. To hurt and watch her be hurt."

He dragged a hand down his face. "I was upset they made her show off her scar."

Georgia melted. "You really are a softie."

"That's not a compliment."

"Yes. It is." She squeezed his hand and let go. "Right now she hurts. But when she gets stronger, it's going to be physical. If you respond sexually, she'll go with it."

Bo cleared his throat. "I think I can control myself."

"Mmhmm. So did Luke."

He frowned. "Look, I just want to be some use here. If you have a better plan, let's hear it."

"No plan. Just warning you."

"Thanks." Between the street stories and Ann's sacred sex, he doubted he would ever think of having it again. Unless Exi—he slammed that thought down so hard it hurt.

Luke sidled in and took Georgia's spot. "How you doing?"

"Not great. Why are you okay to go out there? If I'm a target, aren't you?"

"Nah. I'm known out there. Not the mysterious new guy."

"Even though Misty hit on you?"

"Old news. Old, old news. And she never told Spider."

"Misty didn't tell about me. That was Vi."

"Point is, now he knows. He'll be gunning for you."

Get in line. Bo stretched his back. "I need to work out."

"Use the gym. It's small but there's weights in the closet."

He didn't know whether weights were in Doc Patel's plan yet, but it sounded good. "Where is this gym?"

"Basement. Kind of creepy if you don't like tight spaces. Want me to show you before I go?"

"Yeah." Bo rose and cleared his tray. As the stairway door closed, he thought he caught a glimpse of Misty peeking back into the cafeteria. Good time to disappear.

Descending with Luke, Bo gripped the back of his neck, rubbing out the stress. They followed a low-ceilinged, narrow passage with heavy pipes and ductwork into an open area that could pass for a gym in the sense the floor was concrete and there was a standing basketball hoop at one end where any but a perfect shot would hit the ceiling before it sank in.

"Should probably take it slow." Luke opened a musty-smelling closet where a dilapidated bench and mismatched weights held little appeal. "Don't lift anything that needs spotting."

He couldn't help thinking of his top-of-the-line home equipment. "I might just unroll that mat, do some squats and stretches."

Luke squeezed his shoulder and headed back across the gym. "Oh. Don't let that closet door close, or it might lock you in. Could be days before we miss you."

Bo cocked his head, fairly sure Luke was messing with his mind, but he'd be careful just in case. He dragged out the mat made in the day when they weighed pounds not ounces and let it slowly uncurl. The light was dim, and the place smelled dank. If his muscles didn't cry for action, he would bag the whole idea.

He got down on the mat and began to stretch. Of course that reminded him of Exi showing up on his Apple Watch. He closed his eyes and pictured her flipping on the lawn. What a perfect day that could have been. The ache settled like an old unwelcome friend. He covered his eyes, then jumped when an icy cold hand chilled his neck.

"Barb?" He yanked his hands down to see Misty crouching.

Gulping back the jolt to his system, he said, "What are you doing here?"

"What are you? And who's Barb?"

He looked into her hollow eyes and considered saying none of her business, then answered, "My sister. She died."

"You thought I was a ghost?"

"Feel your hand." He clasped her wrist and moved her hand toward her face.

She touched it to her discolored cheek and laughed.

"Yeah. Very funny."

She sank onto her butt and laughed harder. Had to admit it sounded as good as it seemed to feel. After a while she petered out. "DeShawn said you were funny. But you seem so serious."

"I am serious. And maybe a little funny." Exi and her friends had laughed hard at his performance. "You can't be down here."

"I don't want to play games. Or watch TV. I want to watch you."

"Nothing to see here."

"Then you could watch me." Clearly not the direction this should go. Before he could explain, she said, "Do you like blood?"

"Is that a trick question?"

"No." Crooked into her palm was a triangular piece of plastic packaging. She sliced the point over her scarred forearm. The pink welt beaded.

"Stop." Didn't she have enough wounds?

"It doesn't hurt. That's the funny thing about scars. They're the parts that don't hurt." She touched the tip of her tongue to the blood, then she stretched her arm. "Taste?"

He gripped her wrist and eased her arm down. "No thanks."

Her eyes filled with hurt, oceans of it, galaxies. "What do you want? Anything you say."

Nothing. No stirring. No hint of desire.

Her voice got thick with wanting. "I can make you feel good."

"And break Ann's trust?"

Her brow wrinkled. "You mean Sister?"

"She's been longing for your return." He unconsciously used Ann's words. "You don't want to blow that."

"No one has to know."

"That's not how it works."

"It can be." She pressed in. "There's no one but you and me."

How could she want another hand on her after what they did?

"Please? Make it better."

Ann didn't say whether Luke succumbed, but who could blame him if he did? To be the hero, the healer, the knight—that was heady stuff. He felt nothing but sick in the pit of his stomach.

"I can't make it better, Misty."

"But look what they did." She started unbuttoning her blouse.

He closed her hand in his, stopping its action. "Don't show me your body. Ann says it's sacred. I want to believe that."

The words seemed to strike her dumb. Unfortunately, she recovered. "I want to touch you."

"Trust me, you don't." He leaned away. "People who get close to me have bad things happen."

"Like your sister?"

His throat constricted. "Keep that to yourself, okay?"

"A secret?" Her face lit.

"Just keep it to yourself." He rose and moved her toward the passage leading out.

"How did she die?"

"I'm not going into it." He pulled her into the passage and stopped short, thankfully, or he'd have bowled Ann over.

"Ah, you found our wanderer."

"She found me with an ice-cold hand to the neck that almost put me through the roof." That had its intended effect of making Misty laugh again.

Ann gave him warm eyes, then wrapped an arm around the girl and started back through the maze. Bo returned to the gym, wondering how much Ann overheard and whether she'd been standing there to catch him getting it on, or if she'd just arrived.

The thought of touching Misty that way disgusted him. And not because of her, because of him. He'd never used force, never wanted to, never had to. But how different was it to get what he wanted, when he wanted, with whomever he wanted? Life was one jolly roll in the hay for someone like him—and his progenitor? Wasn't life a freakin' party.

Mr. Weiss perused her paintings for almost an hour in Bo's studio while Exi tried not to throw up. Opinions like Devin's meant more emotionally, but this one mattered professionally. For some reason, she wondered if Jeffrey would be proud of her taking this step. A ridiculous thought, but she imagined texting: *Guess what?*

She could almost hear his reply. *Of course he likes them. You're a talented artist.* She hadn't been told yet whether the agent did like them, but Jeffrey would be positive.

Thinking of Jeffrey helped to block the excessive emotion flooding her from letting this stranger see Bo in this place. The music playing on his sound system changed to Anna Nalick's "Breathe," which was appropriate. Not that this would make or break her. Other things hung heavier in her mind and heart. This was only her career, and no one knew better than she how likely it was she'd have to find a job doing something else once the situation with Liam normalized.

Finally Mr. Weiss stood before her. "Ms. Murphy, I'm intrigued by the nuanced portrayal of your subject and impressed by your brushwork. There are galleries I could call as we stand here."

Even taking the song's advice to breathe, she could hardly manage more than a whisper. "That wasn't the agreement."

He sighed heavily. "How likely is it you'll bring that sensitivity to other subjects?"

"I can't really say. I've only done one other."

He looked bored at the thought. "Let me see it."

She had intended to start with Mattie, but when she brought brush to canvas, it was Eileen who emerged. And while the mouth bore a hint of a smile, the eyes were steeped in regret. It stood on an easel in the kitchen where natural light brought out the gossamer skin and silvery hair. A single hand emerged from the background, held pensively as Eileen so often did in thought or conversation. Light sparkled off her rings.

Jared Weiss examined it with his eyes, then with magnifying binoculars. He took them off and stepped back. His shoulders relaxed. His face looked self-satisfied, and she had no idea what that meant. "Apparently, you're not a one-theme wonder. Let me know when you have stock you're willing to part with. I'll present you to galleries where you'll have tough competition as a talented newbie."

She hugged herself and smiled. "Okay. I will."

At the door, he said, "I like what you've done with Eileen. What does she think?"

"She hasn't seen it." Since she had yet to wake up from yesterday's surgery.

Watching from the stairs, Exi squeezed her fists together in excitement as Sondra closed the door behind the agent.

Sondra said, "He liked your work?"

"He did." She steepled her hands against her smile. "He really did. I wish I could call and tell Eileen."

Sondra arched her penciled brows. "We could sneak over to the hospital in my Saab, using your brother's method."

Exi lit up at the thought of going sans bodyguards and all that hoopla. Even if Eileen hadn't awakened, she could tell her the good news and thank her profusely. "Okay." She ran up for her purse, then met Sondra in the garage. Sondra's car wasn't the shield John's SUV's had been, but she squatted down and crept around to the door while Sondra got into the front.

It was an awkward duck walk, but she managed, then lay across the seat under a shawl. John might object, but they were only going to the hospital where he lost Bo. The whole drive, Exi craned to hear anything out of the ordinary, but nothing happened. When Sondra parked, Exi arranged the shawl around her head and shoulders and prayed for half of Bo's mojo. They reached the ICU without drawing any attention.

Sondra told the attending nurse, "This is my sister's granddaughter."

Her sister? Granddaughter? She fought a giggle at Sondra's chutzpah.

"Ms. O'Hare hasn't wakened yet."

"That's okay." Exi clenched and flexed her fingers. "I just want to tell her something." The nurse smiled so kindly she felt bad about the deception, then decided she could call Eileen Granny in real life. It was almost true. She lived with her after all.

"Ten minutes." The nurse showed them in and left them alone.

Exi swallowed hard. The shaved hair and bandage on Eileen's delicate head screamed damage. Beside Sondra, her legs started to shake. She sank into a chair beside the bed where a respirator breathed for the unconscious manikin that could hardly be Eileen. Thank God Bo wasn't seeing this. But please let this woman wake up and come home.

She reached out for the frail arm. "It's Alexis, Eileen. Sondra snuck me here to tell you the agent wants to represent me." Nothing. Not a flicker. "Grace says he's a top agent, not just any old guy. And I really want to thank you. For that. And for everything. I don't know where I'd be if you hadn't let me live with you. When you come home, Sondra and I will get you so strong. We all love you. So, the sooner you wake up, the better."

Exi stood up. "Oh, and I painted you. Mr. Weiss likes that too. He wants to hear your opinion so, um, there's another reason." Her shoulders rose with a long breath and dropped back down. She turned to Sondra. "I guess that's all."

They thanked the nurse and stepped out of the ICU to John Helm's folded arms and frowning face.

Exi blinked up at him. "Drat."

Sondra put a hand over her mouth and looked away.

Exi scratched her neck. "How did you know?"

His voice flattened. "A member of my staff saw you sneak into the car on the surveillance camera. She followed."

"She?"

"Justine Marr."

"Then why are you here?"

"Eileen."

"Oh." Of course they wouldn't leave Liam's helpless sister unprotected.

"Your ride is outside."

"I can't go with Sondra?"

John moved his head side to side.

"Guess I don't need this." Handing Sondra the shawl, she expected that would be all.

But John said, "Just so you know, we had a hit from Bo's cell phone. It was powered on and data accessed at a McDonald's."

Her breath caught.

"No sign of him on their surveillance."

"He's in disguise?"

"That's possible. Or he's not the one with his phone."

She wouldn't think that. Not for a minute.

"We've increased surveillance of that general area. There's also been chatter about his disappearance. The task force thinks it'll be news before long."

She pressed a hand to her chest. "That's bad, isn't it?"

"A situation I was hoping to avoid. But with social media the way it is, I'm amazed it's gone this long."

"Please find him before anyone else." If this lead meant Bo was alive, they had to keep him that way.

Bo dug his hand into his hair, about to lose his mind from working with DeShawn for the fifth agonizing day. He liked the kid—who wouldn't? But DeShawn had the attention span of a gnat. Bo almost cheered when Georgia called him away from the doorway. His relief faded the instant he read her expression. "What's up?"

"Jacinta just informed me she saw Misty leave. Apparently Vi sent a message saying she had to tell her something important."

"No way. She wouldn't fall for that."

"She said it was about you."

"Me? What would Vi know about me?"

"Probably nothing. But it was the right carrot to dangle."

Bo swore.

"Sister Ann's away in meetings all day, and Luke's sleeping so deeply I can't wake him. Must have used a sleep aid. Today's volunteers are new, and I'm not sure they'll have any sway with Misty or even know where to look." Her voice trembled.

"It's okay. I'll go."

"Sister doesn't want you out. But I'm in charge here until she gets back."

"Don't worry." He squeezed her shoulder.

"I'm afraid she drove the van. It's our only insured transportation."

"I'll hoof it. Probably better, if Misty's on foot too. How much of a lead does she have?"

"Half hour, maybe. Jacinta was conflicted about reporting it."

"Did she say where they were meeting?"

Georgia shook her head.

"Okay." It wasn't much to go on, but the sooner he left, the better his chances.

Bo pushed through the door. Heat radiated off the pavement as he strode along the sidewalk to search out the haunts he'd become familiar with. He'd barely covered three blocks when Sticks and DeShawn came running after. "Hey, what are you guys doing?"

"Coming with you." Sticks spoke softly, his pale coloring heightened by the sunlight as if he'd been hung out on a line and bleached.

"Yeah, we're your backup." DeShawn thumbed his chest.

"Georgia know you're here?"

"Yeah, she knows." The kid shifted foot to foot.

Bo raised a brow.

"She saw us going," he amended. "Three are better than one. Sticks got good eyes. I got instincts." From who knew where, the dog appeared. DeShawn bent over laughing. "Now we got a posse."

Since time mattered, and they might search better as a group, Bo started on. "Any guesses where she'd meet Vi?"

Both kids had ideas, so they started checking those possibilities. Street and sidewalk traffic increased the closer they got to Times Square. Every block or so, Bo shifted something about himself to diminish the chance of recognition. Neither boy noticed or commented.

They asked vagrants they met if they'd seen Misty. A few had but didn't know where she was now. How stupid was she, coming out after what Spider did to her? But logic had no place in Misty's reality.

And then, like a miracle, she came around a corner. She saw them and called, "Hey, Bo!"

He didn't holler back. If none of Spider's gang had seen her, he didn't want to shout her name and alert them. He just closed the gap.

"This is you!" Misty ran up, flapping a newspaper.

He paused while people parted around them.

"You're this famous guy." Misty jabbed the paper.

"Hollywood," Sticks said, leaning to see.

The headline read: "Where in the World Is Bo Corrigan?" Beside the article, bright and bold, his newest head shot.

"Crap," he muttered.

"It's you." Misty pressed in and stroked his arm like he might rub off on her. "You're famous."

He folded the paper under his arm.

"Hey, I want that." She jabbed a hand in for it.

"You're not supposed to be out here. It isn't safe."

"Give me the paper."

DeShawn gripped his arm, quailing. Bo whirled and saw a tattooed devil moving through the street crowd. Dead eyes. A long coat in spite of the heat. Liam's enemy or Spider's man, it didn't matter. The killer reached into his coat … then froze. From the corner of his eye, Bo saw John Helm at the opposite end of the block, police stance with his weapon ready to fire. He never would with all these people, but that guy didn't know it. He spun and sprinted away, shoving people as he went.

Bo pushed Misty and the paper into Sticks and DeShawn. "Get her back to Ann. Don't talk to anyone. Go, go, go."

He took off running the other way, creating distance in case more gang members or hitmen were gunning for him. He heard John shout but kept running, ducking and weaving. His feet pounded the sidewalk, his wound sending twinges like sparks. His chest burned and heaved as he rounded a corner and saw—well, smelled—Elmo. He skidded to a stop and bent to the old guy against the wall with his feeble hand out. "Hey, Elmo. I need to borrow your coat. Can you do that for me? I'll bring it back, I promise. I'll bring you that and more."

Elmo's eyes searched him, his mouth dangling cloudy drool. Slowly, he pulled the coat off, the smelly knit hat as well.

Bo grabbed both, the rancid stench engulfing him. "Thank you, man. Thank you." He rushed to the first garden-level entrance and stumbled down the five steps into the cement alcove surrounding the locked door. Throwing the coat on and pulling the hat low, he slouched into a heap and breathed as if each intake might be his last. It was all he could do to keep from vomiting. He knew the moment John's shadow paused, searching, then moved on.

After a while, he pulled himself up the stairs, lurching as if he might fall down them again. He'd take Elmo a new coat and hat or launder these. But right now, he wended back to the mission by a different street like a wino with DTs. He had to get there. He couldn't go back to that face on the paper.

It was Georgia who pulled him inside when he tried three times to code the door open, Ann who stood behind her, keys in hand with a bleary-eyed Luke as if they were on their way out—to look for him? He raised his head to see all the young adults, including Misty and the boys, crowded into the cafeteria behind them.

"Phew." Georgia yanked the coat off his shoulders and onto the floor.

Bo pulled the hat from his head and dropped it too. "Elmo needs those back and a new shirt or something."

A radiant smile flickered over Stick's face. "I'll do that."

DeShawn gawked like he'd been raised from the dead. It had been close. He doubted the shooter shared John's scruples. Bo's throat constricted. "You guys okay?"

"You are the master." DeShawn bowed from the waist, entangled emotions vying for dominance.

Near him, Misty clutched the newspaper, her adoration magnified. No, not here. But how could he dispel the truth? He saw it in Ann's eyes. They all knew. He gripped the doorframe with one hand, pressed the other to his eyes.

"Are you injured?" It was Ann's calm voice.

"Just out of shape. And whatever toxins I breathed in from Elmo's coat." That got a laugh.

"Nothing a shower won't cure." Ann turned. "Give the man some room."

Heart swelling, he passed through them. He hadn't even realized how completely he'd expected to be kicked out. Standing in the shower, it was as if Bo Corrigan had been washed down the drain. Here he was Beau, no last name. Man, he liked that.

30

Weird how things could be honed down to their simplest parts. What would have annoyed—had annoyed—him days ago became acceptable, even precious. When the janitor got sick Bo took on cleaning the cafeteria, the clinic and bathrooms, mopping the halls. He worked not only with DeShawn, but anyone who needed a boost on the GED or remedial coursework—including Imogene, who was too transfixed to scream, even though it took more than an hour to correctly solve a single long-division problem.

Though starstruck—or maybe because of that—Misty shifted her amorous pursuit back to Luke. Bo gave her friendly encouragement and even let her talk about the baby he still wasn't sure had a place in this world. She had some kind of fog in her head that made her look forward to having it, but at least she saw Spider for the train wreck he was.

When Ann asked him to help DeShawn prepare for job interviews he embraced the chance to help the kid shine. The runt had wormed into his heart, and DeShawn's success in this small thing mattered as much as his own crucial auditions. "In fact," he said, "it is an audition. All you have to do is play the role."

"I don't know what that means."

"Let's break it down. In theater, when you want to play a certain role, you get the audition script. You see what's expected of you, then you imagine it."

"We're talking fast food."

"Okay." Bo pulled the jittery kid back down to the classroom table. "Your job description is the script." He opened the computer and brought up the job site. They went over expectations of employees in the corporation where DeShawn had applied. Bo helped him read it all. "Now see yourself as that kind of person. Clean, respectful, and"—he ad-libbed—"an example to others."

The light went on. "Yeah." But then his face fell. "My daddy told me I'm nothing but dirt. No one will ever want a worthless crack baby working for them."

"I thought you lived with your grandma."

"That was after he beat my mom into a coma and took off."

Bo swallowed the pain. "Is that someone whose opinion should matter?"

"No, but he's right. Look at me. I got more things wrong than Sheriff."

"Yeah, well, who did Sheriff choose from everyone out there?"

"Me." DeShawn puffed his chest.

"And he's one smart dog. I bet Sheriff Shorty law dog knows more about what's good or worthless than your old man."

DeShawn's eyes welled up. "Man, you making me cry."

"Just speaking the truth."

For a solid three days, he prepared DeShawn for his "audition." Now he reminded him, "Get less in your head and more in your body. Feel yourself working there. Feel yourself the best they have."

"Sure." DeShawn grinned. "What greasy burger can I supersize for you and your enormo kids, ma'am?"

Bo gave him the laugh, then said, "It doesn't matter what the job is. You respect it, you respect yourself. That's what counts."

"Man, that's not what counts. It's what others think, what they see when they look at me."

"They'll see what you show, DeShawn. That's all it is. People seeing what you show."

"When I was a little kid, my heart's right out there plain as day. No one saw, or if they did they stomped it flat on the floor."

"Keep the private parts private, just show them the example you know you can be."

"That's Sister-talk."

"Sister knows her stuff." The interview was in a little more than an hour, and Bo understood the jitters, the critical chorus playing in the young man's mind. Bo hadn't experienced it, but he'd gotten inside the heads of actors who did. "Keep your chin up. Don't let them see you sweat."

"Sure. Yeah, sure."

"You can do this."

"Wish I could take Sheriff on the bus."

"Maybe Georgia can drive you in the van, wait outside with Sheriff while you strut your stuff."

"You think?"

He hoped. He'd offer to do it himself but that could make DeShawn a target, so no go. And he had no driver's license to operate the nonprofit's van. He wouldn't get Ann in trouble for anything.

"Either way, DeShawn, you got this. It's all you."

The kid's face was glum at best.

"Let's find Georgia." If she shot it down, he'd think of another motivation.

They found her in the laundry room. Georgia's expression when they asked said this was not how things were done. "How do you know you can even find that dog?"

"He'll find me." DeShawn visibly shook in his shoes. He emitted teenage sweat the dog would scent from miles away. "He always does."

She looked skeptical but resigned. "If he's around when it's time, I'll do it. But you won't be late waiting on him."

DeShawn ran for the door. "I'll get him right now."

When it slammed behind him, Georgia gave Bo the stink eye from the Maori part of her lineage. "Your idea?"

"Only partly."

"Hmph."

"A little extra confidence can't hurt."

"Mmhmm."

Bo pulled a smile. "Come on. You wish you'd thought of it." Before she could reply, Bo winked and left her spluttering.

Exi exulted when Grace, Devin, Mattie, and Sondra brought Eileen home from the hospital. Still weak and unstable, she came with a wheelchair, but confirmation of the tumor's benign nature made everything celebratory. Devin had just wheeled her up the ramp fitted over the steps when a black SUV pulled to the curb. He turned Eileen to face the street as Liam emerged with a light step and eager glint, happy for his sister, Exi could tell. John walked beside the elder O'Hare, looking strangely relaxed.

They gathered in the foyer, expectancy rising like bubbles. With his hands on Eileen's shoulders, Liam looked around the group. "Great news on two accounts today. Eileen's triumph, and they got the bastards." Liam formed a victorious fist.

John said, "It's breaking news right now. Over seventy arrests."

Exi whooped. "Bo can come home. He'll hear, won't he? If it's on the news?"

"Hard to avoid news these days," Liam said. "And since Johnny saw him—"

"What?" Exi wheeled on the man. "You saw Bo? When?"

"Some days ago, in the part of town where we tracked his phone. I tried to talk to him, but … he ran the other way."

She frowned. "He didn't see you?"

"It was a dicey situation. Although I cleared that up, Bo must not have felt safe coming out of hiding."

Devin squeezed her shoulder. "Once he knows the coast is clear, he'll be back. We'll all be back to normal."

Exi looked at them all, lighthearted and celebrating. She felt like a tattered leaf snagged in a stream, while everything else flowed smoothly by. What did *normal* even mean? She smiled at Eileen.

"I'm so happy you're home and doing well. I guess you don't need—"

"If you're thinking you should leave, I'd like you to stay. You're a beacon for our lost boy."

Exi saw her sincerity and appreciated the sentiment, but what use was a beacon if Bo ran the other way?

Bo stared at the TV, every hair rising on his arms and neck. His hand clamped his mouth and jaw.

Major strike against terrorist operatives …

Gang leader arrests …

Extend gratitude to prominent citizen Liam O'Hare …

He watched Liam at the podium shaking the hands of law enforcement and city officials. It was over. He could go back, find Exi—he shook his head. Couldn't he?

Bo pulled his eyes from the TV when DeShawn and Georgia returned from the interview. He expected to see success or failure written all over DeShawn's face. Instead he saw … fear? Had something happened?

An unidentified source revealed a possible connection between this threat and the disappearance of actor Bo Corrigan. A video clip followed of him playing Peter in *Windows and Doors.* It was like an apparition.

A female newscaster said, "Anyone who's watched a performance knows what a skilled talent he is. We certainly hope he'll be entertaining us again very soon."

He swallowed acid rising in his throat. The eyes in the room burned into him. He brushed over them until he met Ann's. She had come silently to his side.

"I spelled your name wrong."

"I like it your way."

"We should talk, once this settles in a little."

"Okay." His voice graveled with uncertainty. He was split in two, like Peter Pan trying to reattach his shadow. He jutted his chin at DeShawn, who came over with a dragging gait. "What happened today? Are you okay?"

"I'm okay."

"How did it go? When will you hear?"

"I got it." DeShawn's eyes grazed over him.

"The job?"

"Yeah, man, I got it. Start training day after tomorrow."

"Way to go." Bo extended his fist, awash with joy.

DeShawn bumped it, then waved at the TV. "We heard all that breaking news driving back."

That might explain his weird behavior.

"You going back now?" DeShawn stood, clicking his fingers.

"I don't know what I'm doing. That's the truth. But even if I do, I'm not finished with you guys."

DeShawn stared at his shoes. "Can I talk to you? Alone?"

"Sure."

"I gotta get something first." DeShawn shuffled off.

Bo joined Georgia. "What's up with the kid? I thought he'd be bouncing off the walls getting this job."

"It's hard to predict DeShawn's reactions."

"The bipolar stuff?"

"Lot's of things." Georgia folded her ample arms. "If these kids were simple, they wouldn't be here."

No, probably not. "Do you know what he wants to see me about?"

She cocked her head. "No idea. But he was quite a chatterbox until the news came on."

"It's messing with my head too."

"How serious was the threat?"

Bo rubbed his face. "Serious. I told Ann when I first came."

"That's how you were injured?"

"Yeah. But it's not that simple."

"Or you wouldn't be here." She smiled.

DeShawn came back with a screwdriver of all things. He said,

"Outside?"

Exhaust fumes infused the humid air as Bo walked out the door with him. Sheriff hadn't gone far and came loping over, always eager. Bo gave him a hand to lick as the kid headed for the building next door. Low down, where the back of the building met a cinderblock wall, DeShawn applied the tool to a vent. He freed one end and pulled it some inches from the brick wall.

Still squatting, DeShawn tipped his head up. "Promise you won't get mad?"

What was there to get mad about? "You know I won't."

DeShawn pulled out three things. Bo's breath hitched.

"I thought you were a dead guy when I took them. But Sheriff kept coming, and then I heard you talking. Sounded weird but not dead. So I got Sister."

Bo remembered in a hazy way.

DeShawn stood up. "I should've given these back. But I thought if you got them, you'd leave."

Would it have changed things? He'd been so sick, but after that? Leave and go where?

"Then I got the idea to charge up the phone. And you got all these messages. I know I shouldn't listen, but I liked the things people said. It was like someone saying it to me, like someone missed me and wanted me." His face screwed up. "You mad I took these?"

Bo shook his head. "I was the loser in the drainpipe. The way I see it, you've had them in safekeeping."

DeShawn blinked. "You mean it?"

"Have I ever lied to you?"

DeShawn shrugged. "I don't think so." He held out the wallet, phone, and watch.

Bo took the phone and wallet. "You keep the watch. I'll get you a charger."

"No man, I don't need it. It's all good. Just wish I had people who love me like those ones in your phone."

"You do. Everybody here."

"Yeah, maybe. It's all good."

"What's good is you getting that job. You rocked it, DeShawn."

"Yeah man. They think I'm something."

"You are. You got the part. Now it's just learning the role. If they send you home with materials, we'll work on it. No sweat."

"Yeah, no sweat." He rubbed his palms down his thighs. "I got to go find Sheriff some chow."

He'd offer to go along, but the end of Liam's turf war didn't extend to Spider. "Don't take too long. It's almost dinnertime here."

"Nah. Real quick."

Bo squeezed his shoulder. "I'm proud of you."

"That's cool." Tears swam in the kid's eyes and darned if they didn't trigger his own.

"Go feed that dog." The cash was gone from the wallet, but he didn't care. Bo slid it into his jeans pocket and put the watch on his wrist. He held the phone a moment, then slid it into the other hip pocket. Later. Maybe.

As everyone gathered for the evening meal, Ann commandeered him. "Will you join me in my office?"

"Sure." He carried both trays and she let him into the space that held a desk with an older model computer, three chairs, and files. The walls were papered floor to ceiling with snapshots of kids' faces, a few fluttering when the air conditioner wheezed to life.

Seated at her desk, Ann lifted a triangle of toasted cheese. "Quite an event in the news. You know that man, Liam O'Hare?"

Bo nodded. When she continued to hold his gaze, he started talking and didn't stop until he'd laid out every ugly detail.

"Where do you see yourself now?"

"I don't know."

"Our mission is to tend the wounded, train the needy, then watch them fly."

"You want me to fly?"

She flattened her hands on the desk. "I want you to confront whatever you're hiding from—besides these killers they've locked up.

What is it you can't face?"

He could tell her about Barb, about their mother and the invisible dads. He could express his emptiness, his confusion. But he lowered his eyes.

"You're stronger than you think. You claimed no skills when you came. Yet you've become an integral part of what we do. I can't think of anyone who assimilated so easily. Is it acting?"

"Maybe. I pick up cues and follow suit."

"I haven't seen you onstage, but I imagine those accolades are true."

"Another life."

"Is it?"

He shrugged. "I don't know. Need to get my head around this."

"You have a place here as long as you want it. But you have to think of others too. All the people missing you and worrying. Please consider what you can do to relieve that."

"Okay."

She smiled. "Let's eat."

He took a spoonful of tomato soup. As they shared the meal, Ann asked about his experiences onstage and in life. She told him hers from around the world, some tragic, others amusing, all more meaningful than any of his success.

"People are people, whatever their conditions, education, opportunities. Every soul has a shine."

Hers certainly did. When they'd finished, he brought their dishes to the kids washing up in the cafeteria kitchen. Others had dispersed to play board games, watch TV, or work on studies. He wanted to get more details from DeShawn about the interview and tell him again there were no hard feelings about taking his stuff. But he couldn't find him.

When Luke came down to go out in the van, Bo said, "Want to walk with me instead? DeShawn went to feed the dog. I don't think he's back."

Luke took a flashlight from the closet. "Don't want to drive?"

"The van will draw attention. Plus it's easier to gauge how far he can get on foot."

"Makes sense."

They set out, searching all the places he knew to look, asking anyone they recognized. They jumped a couple chain-link fences into abandoned lots and searched decrepit buildings on false leads. The night grew stark. With all his senses heightened, Bo stared through shadows cast by street lights, making the dark places that much darker. "I don't like this."

"I hear you," Luke said.

"Would Spider hassle him? His guys?"

"Don't see why. It …"

Luke took so long to go on, Bo said, "It what?"

"Might be the job."

"The one he just got?"

"If it's like the other times."

"What other times? Has DeShawn had jobs he can't keep?"

"He maybe could. But he never gets there. It's some kind of freak-out, I think. As scared as he gets to interview, it's ten times that to show up. Puts him in a tailspin."

"Sounds like performance anxiety, some sort of stage fright."

"Could be. Yeah."

"I can work with that." Bo searched the street, wishing he could find the kid and start the process. "Where could he be?"

Luke shrugged. "They all got spots they favor. But DeShawn's been off the street for a while, so his places are probably claimed."

"Wait a minute." Bo grabbed Luke's arm. "Hear that?"

Luke shook his head. "No, what?"

"I know that whine." He followed the sound into an alley so dark, Luke's flashlight hardly penetrated. But then Sheriff's eyes lit like faintly glowing marbles. "Hey, Sheriff." The dog whined and yelped. "Are you hurt?" Bo tripped on a piece of aluminum flashing.

"Hold on," Luke said. He raised the beam from the pavement to the trash bin at the dead end. "Look there in the corner."

"DeShawn?" Bo maneuvered around putrid trash, broken glass, and rusted metal. Sheriff darted to him and back with a high-pitched whine amplified by the alley walls. "Hey, DeShawn. Is that you?"

The light beam hit his face. DeShawn's face. Eyes half open. Mouth half open. Bo crouched and shook him. "DeShawn, what's wrong? What happened?" Bo gripped his face, stunned to find it cold and rubbery. "DeShawn!"

Luke moved the light beam to the tubing tied around his arm, the needle still in place.

"He's doped? Let's get him to the clinic."

Luke's voice went flat. "It's too late. Look at his eyes. Probably H laced with Mexican fentanyl."

Bo pressed a hand to the brick wall that seemed to be closing in. He couldn't breathe. If the Russian kicked all his broken ribs in, it couldn't hurt like this. He dropped to his knees and touched his fingers to the kid's throat. "Come on." He tried the other side. DeShawn's head flopped, but was that … "I think there's a pulse. Call 9-1-1."

"Never come in time. Not this neighborhood. Not for this."

Bo pulled out his phone and placed a different call. "I need emergency assistance now. Kid with an overdose." He looked at Luke. "What block?"

Luke gave an address. Bo stopped John Helm's questions with, "He's dying. Do something." He hung up. "Let's get him to the street." He reached around to pick him up. DeShawn weighed hardly more than Misty, and adrenaline had kicked in when he felt that sluggish pulse. Luke led the way with the light so he wouldn't trip over trash. Sheriff trotted and whined alongside.

When they got to the street, Bo nestled DeShawn against the building. Sheriff rose with paws to the wall, licking the kid's face. People moved around them in disgust and irritation. "Hold on, kid. Hold on."

Luke's eyes looked as lifeless as DeShawn's. "A few grains of acetyl fentanyl are all it takes. Added to heroin, it's Russian roulette.

A high bad enough to kill. That's the good stuff."

Bo wanted to tell him to shut up, but Luke went on.

"More people die from drug overdose than traffic accidents now." Losing his girlfriend like this must be kicking hard.

"Luke." Bo said it sharply to break through. "Get a grip."

Luke tipped his head up and rasped, "Out of the depths I cry to you, oh Lord."

Lord? Bo shook as badly as he had in the drainpipe. He'd invested in this kid who'd made him his project, who'd saved his life ... who'd orbited the Death Star. At the sound of sirens, Bo rose. A firetruck blasted its horn and came to an exhaust-reeking stop in the street. "You take it from here, Luke." If he got away, got far enough away, DeShawn might make it. He started walking. After a while he waved down a cab. DeShawn had taken his cash, but the credit cards were there.

He told the driver to drop him at the corner of West 179th Street and Cabrini Boulevard in upper Manhattan. He watched the city through the windows, wiping DeShawn from his thoughts, severing even a mental connection. It might be the only chance the kid had.

The cab stopped. Bo ran the card, tipped the cabbie, and got out. The south bike path and pedestrian way closed between midnight and six a.m., but it was patrolled. The north walkway had been closed since 2008 on account of the handicapped-inaccessible stairs he ascended now. At the top of the steps he climbed onto the cement wall with its metal rail, swung around the first gate and dropped down. Back up and around the second gate gave him access to the north George Washington Bridge sidewalk.

The bridge crossed over Henry Hudson Parkway and Fort Washington Point. He walked with the steel railing on his right, the guardrail separating the traffic lanes on his left. Finally his steps took him out over water, the whirlpools and currents of the Hudson flowing beneath the bridge. Above him blue lights adorned the elegant sway of cable between the two steel towers. It was a marvel of beauty and engineering, this hazardous place to hurt.

Around the midpoint between New York and New Jersey, he climbed onto the railing and sat where one of the quad pillars supported the massive dual suspension cables. His legs dangled over nothing but the water far below. Carefully, he took out the phone DeShawn had kindly charged and started listening to everything in his maxed-out voice mail. All the unessential, he deleted. The people who mattered he absorbed. Exi's voice penetrated every cell until listening became torture.

He moved on to texts, deleting entire threads so all that remained were precious. He read and reread every word. DeShawn was right. These people cared. They just didn't know how dangerous that was.

"Always so dramatic," Barb said in his ear.

"You made me that way."

"No. I just made use of it. Something had to be done with your reckless creativity." She laughed. "That was the best of all their desperate descriptions."

"Do you have a point?"

"Not really."

"Then leave me alone."

"You've never been good alone, Bo. You need people."

"To their detriment."

"You are so hung up on that."

"Uh-huh."

"Not surprising, I guess. Always the center of attention. Why wouldn't everything in the world come down to you?"

He said nothing. Shore lights glistened off the river, faintly noisome even from here. The bridge lights reflected up to him. Stars seemed absorbed by the currents and made a poor showing.

Barb kept on. "A body hits the water at eighty miles per hour. Multiple-organ damage and fractures."

"It's over fast," he told her.

"It's a waste." Irritation made her harsh.

The biggest waste was her prolonged and agonizing death. "It's not about me."

"That's bull. I should have told you what matters before it was too late. You wouldn't be so lost if I had."

He blinked back tears. "I know what matters." He clutched the phone. "I just can't have it."

"You're right that people matter, people who love you. But there's more, Bo. That's what you need to find."

He tipped his head back between the pillars. "You mean God? I'm more likely to find that on your side. Here I'm nothing but the devil. I see that now in ways I never did." But even when he tried to change, tried to do good in the world, evil came. Right now it was trying to steal DeShawn. What would it do to those he loved more? "It's not for my sake, Barb. It's for the ones who matter. So stop talking. I can't hear you."

Ann told him to find a way to relieve their concern. He'd start with making amends. From his contacts, he opened a conversation with Louisa.

Hey gorgeous. Just want to say I'm sorry about the way things turned out. I thought we came from the same place, had similar expectations or rather no expectations. I realize now we didn't. I think I hurt you and I never meant to. I hope you can forgive me. Have a beautiful life. Bo.

One down. Not that many more to go.

31

Grace groped for her phone on the night table when incoming texts woke her. She must have forgotten to turn the notifications off, but who would message her in the middle of the night? She sucked a breath when she saw it was Bo.

Hi, Grace. Sorry to communicate like this, but it is what it is. Just needed to say how much your friendship means to me. Even when it cost you. I never meant for my stuff to come back on you, Grace. I hope you know that. You can't imagine my relief that you and Mattie survived. I'm sorry for the nightmares and everything else that came out of that attack. I'm sorry for the stress on your marriage. But what can I say? You always saw the real me. It was nice to be real. Think of me kindly. Bo.

She jolted up in bed. "Devin?"

He jerked awake. "What? What is it?"

"It's Bo." She held out the phone with a shaky hand. "I think this is a suicide note."

Devin read it, his expression darkening. He drew and released harsh breaths.

Her voice rose. "We have to find him."

He scratched his head. "How? I've tried. We've all tried."

She took the phone and texted: *Bo, where are you?* Nothing came back. Her thumbs flew. *Please don't do anything crazy. Tell me where you are. I'll come.* Nothing.

Tears filled her eyes. "There must be something, someone we haven't tried."

Devin rubbed his face, swaying and thinking, then lowered his hands. "There's one person I didn't talk to. I hesitated to upset her more than she already is."

"Louisa?"

"Yes."

"I'm trying her now." Grace grabbed the phone.

"Put it on speaker."

Her heart sank when Louisa's phone went to message. She probably had her volume off.

But then Louisa called back, sounding foggy. "Grace?"

"Oh, Louisa, thank God. I wouldn't bother you but it's really, really important."

Louisa yawned. "What's up?"

"We need to find Bo. Now."

"He's not here." She sounded irritated. "Why would you think—hold on a sec. That's weird."

"What?"

"I have a text from him."

Grace's heart rushed. "Is it—what does he say?"

"It's an apology. And he wishes me a beautiful life."

Meeting Devin's eyes, Grace stifled a sob. "Can you think of anywhere he could be? Anywhere?"

A long silence then, "Have you checked the GWB?"

"The … the bridge?"

"One time when he was totally wrecked, he told me he sits out there and imagines jumping. Like visualizing the role."

Devin swung out of bed and strode to the closet.

Grace said, "That's a long bridge. Do you know where?"

"Um … maybe the side that's not open. Yeah, the sidewalk with the steps."

Grace heard Devin dressing, but they couldn't both go. "Thanks, Louisa." She ended the call. "Devin, someone has to stay with Mattie."

"That's you."

"No, I—"

"Yes, Grace. I drove him off. Let me bring him back." The need in his face convinced her.

"Should I call the police?"

"Not for Bo, the original rebel. That kind of pressure might seal it."

She clutched her throat. "Okay. Go." But please, God, don't let this break them both.

Exi startled. She had fallen asleep with her phone in her hand, never having it more than inches away since she heard Bo could come home. Her chest heaved when she saw the text was from him. Yes, yes, yes. She opened the string of messages.

Hey Exi. I know it's late, or early. Hope this doesn't disturb you if you're sleeping. I just have a few things to say that can't wait. The first is this: you are everything that's right with this world. Don't let anyone dim your light. No one knows who you are inside so don't let them define you. All those gifts of yours are good. Use them. Including the sax. Ask Eileen if you haven't gotten it. You are music, and motion, and beauty.

As she read, more came up. *Our moment was brief but no less incredible. I meant what I said that day in the park. I'm in love with you. If I could take one thing with me, it would be that. I wasn't acting. It's so real it's the thread I'm hanging by. But it's also why I can't be here. I can't risk you. Find joy and be joy. If anyone can it's you, my love. I don't pretend this won't hurt. I know the agony of loss. I can only hope with everything in me, that you will heal and move on. Please find it in your generous heart to forgive me. Forever, Bo.*

Her breath stopped. Her spirit quaked. Everything in her shrank into a single point like light through a magnifying glass. She dialed the phone and got his message. "Bo? Please pick up. I'm begging you." No answer. She texted: *Bo, I love you. Call me, please, please, please.* No call.

Sobbing, she dialed Grace, gave no apology for the hour, just shrieked, "I got a message from Bo."

A sharp inhale. "I did too."

"Oh, Grace. He's leaving us."

"Listen, Exi. We might know where he is. Devin's gone to check it out. He should be almost there."

"Where? Tell me."

Silence, then, "I don't want to. Not yet. Please wait until I hear from Devin."

Again that point of light, searing. "It's bad, isn't it?"

Grace sniffled. "When did your message come?"

"Just now." She sucked a ragged breath. "Am I last?"

"I don't know. Let's get on our knees and pray. Lord, speak to his heart. Open Bo's ears to hear. Give Devin your words. Please save our friend from this darkness. We stand in the gap for him."

On her knees, Exi wept. But she also felt the power. "Please God. Please God. Please Lord, Jesus." Neither said amen. Neither ended the call. Until they heard, this prayer would not end.

Bo had nothing left to say and no strength to say it, but of course it couldn't be that easy. He shifted only slightly when a car came to a stop behind his position, emergency flashers warning traffic behind. Not police, though, or the lights would be a more strident violation of the night. Some do-gooder? He always chose this side of the bridge since its closure conditioned people not to see the walkway.

"What are you doing, Bo?" Not a stranger's voice, it was Devin's. He came over the guardrail onto the sidewalk as traffic streamed past, light but continuous.

"Just … playing the role."

"It's not a role you need to play."

His words had as much effect as the water flowing so far down, passing over and through. The words that mattered were the ones Devin spoke before, words that confirmed what they both knew.

"It's all good, man," he echoed DeShawn right before he put the needle in his arm and pulled the trigger. Russian roulette. Had the kid survived? Or would they meet on the other side? Was there another side? Either way, this had to end.

"Come down from there." Devin was right beside the pillars. He could touch, even grab Bo's arm. But he'd never hold on, never stop the plunge. Not even John Helm's iron strength could do that.

"Thanks for not bringing Grace. Or Exi."

"It won't make any difference. Doing this will break their hearts. They will not recover."

Bo swallowed that bitter lump, but his head swung side to side. He knew the score.

"I can't stop you, not physically. But I have something I want to say."

"You always do," he muttered. He'd thought about texting Devin, had things he could say too, but hadn't.

"I've harbored a lot of anger these last two years. I thought it was your ass I wanted to kick. But it's mine, for not being the man Grace could tell about our baby." He huffed. "Who did she tell? You. And that stuck in my craw. I thought, what does Bo Corrigan have that I don't?"

"The kiss of death."

Devin shook his head. "Look. I said things I didn't mean."

"True things I had to hear."

"Not the whole truth. What almost happened to Grace and Mattie drives me to my knees. But it's my actions, Bo. You were taking care of her when I should have been. As much as yours, my actions put her in that position. That's what I can't forgive."

"You didn't know."

"Why? You know Grace. Why would she keep something like that from me?"

Bo slid him a look.

"She didn't trust me. She couldn't trust me with her secret but she trusted you."

His throat ached. His chest felt hollow. He didn't want to hear, didn't want to feel.

"She trusts you and believes in you. I've been jealous as hell."

Bo cleared the hurt from his voice. "I love Grace." From the corner of his eye he saw Devin's scowl and enjoyed the moment.

"She reminds me of Barb. Her wit, her compassion, her loyalty. It's like having part of my sister back."

Devin released a slow breath. "She loves you too. I can't think of a time she's taken my side over yours."

It felt good. But none of that mattered. He couldn't go on wrecking people's lives.

"And then there's Exi. I was wrong about you guys too. There's something vital in what you have. Anyone can see."

Bo shook his head. "The more I'm around, the more things go wrong."

"You're not responsible for illness or other people's actions."

"You don't know that."

"Well, here's something." Devin's voice graveled. "My mother conceived me with a monster married to another even worse. She escaped and hid me with Eddie. When she wouldn't give up my location, they blinded her with acid, scarred her lovely face, and took visual beauty from her life forever. You could say I caused it all, that I'm directly responsible for her suffering by coming into her life."

That wasn't the same. Was it? *You think you're the center of everything.*

"I spoke harshly to you, thinking I had a high road to travel. But I don't. Things happen, and sometimes it's because of our choices. But this is never the answer. Come on, Bo. Get off that railing and stop this craziness."

He closed his eyes. This was the moment. If he leaned even a little, gravity would pull him over. He was so tired he doubted his body would even struggle.

"Would your sister want you to throw away the life that was taken from her?"

Yeah, Bo, would I?

Devin went on, relentless as the water below. "She never turned thirty or forty or fifty. But you can. You can celebrate the life you have. In her honor."

He couldn't think. If he came down, would DeShawn die? If he took the plunge, would Exi never recover? What was right? What was real?

"Come on. Do this for us. Eileen will never forgive me losing you. You're her stinkin' favorite."

Bo snorted. "There's a reason for that."

"I'm sure there are dozens."

Bo raised his face from the reflected bridge lights wavering in the water. Predawn tinged the sky. His lungs filled and emptied. "Will you give me a hand? I'm … shaky."

Devin gripped his arm and waist. Bo swung his legs over and eased his feet to the walkway. Devin let go of his jeans, but kept hold of his arm. "How long were you up there?"

"Hours, I guess."

"What if you dozed or lost your balance? Anything could have happened."

"It didn't. I think I'm that guy who can't die."

"Let's not test that."

Bo shrugged.

"Do you need a facility?"

"The john?"

Devin fought a smile. "A treatment center. Seventy-two-hour hold, all that."

Bo thrust fingers into his hair. "If that's the plan, I'll jump. I had all the shrinking I could stomach as a kid. More than I ever needed." He wobbled as Devin moved him toward the sedan.

"Your place?" Devin opened the door. "Exi's there."

Bo gripped the doorframe. "No. I can't see her. Not like this, not now." Shame like nothing he'd ever felt washed over him.

"Get in." Devin gave his shoulder a push. "I have another idea."

"Not home with you and Grace."

"You could, but no." He closed the door and went around to the front, checked that traffic was skirting the vehicle, then got behind the wheel. "It's a bit of a drive. Why don't you rest."

Bo closed his eyes. Almost equal to the shame came a bone-deep exhaustion. Deeper than bones. Down into his soul if he had one. What on earth was he supposed to do now?

Exi held the phone tight to her ear, arms folded on the bed, knees throbbing. She had stopped praying aloud. Grace sometimes murmured, but it had become a silent, shared vigil. They could have hung up and kept praying in their own places, but keeping the open line, knowing Grace was just a breath away, knowing the Lord was in their midst took the edge off the agony. She startled when Grace gave a little cry.

"Exi?"

"I'm here."

"Devin just texted. It says: *Got him.*"

"Oh, God." Sobs overtook her again. Why was she such a crier? It didn't matter. Nothing mattered but Bo safe. Bo safe! "When will he get here? Can you call?"

"He might not want to talk with Bo in the car. I'll text."

The wait seemed interminable. Then Grace said, "Right now they're going to Eddie's."

Exi frowned. "Cousin Eddie?"

"That's a good thing, Exi. That man is a powerhouse of grace and wisdom. I'm happy Devin thought of it."

Why was her own heart breaking? "Where was he, Grace? Where was Bo?"

A soft sigh. "The GWB."

The breath she drew felt like knives. Bo was on the suicide bridge. He would have done to her what Barb did to him. Only on purpose. She rolled off her knees to sit on the floor. Her emotions pinged around like pinballs. "Does Eileen know anything?"

"He might have texted her. Probably did."

Exi nodded to herself. Her mouth felt dry, her hands clammy. "It's going to be morning soon. I don't know what to tell her."

"Tell her he's at Eddie's, figuring things out."

"Is that what he's doing?" It killed her that relief and gratitude were souring into resentment and fury. He'd wanted to die.

"I think we should hear it all from him, Exi."

She rose and went into the studio, looking into his face over and over again. How could he? "I guess you're right." Her dispassionate tone reflected the deadening of her heart, the fear and longing that had burned there fading to ash.

Bo dragged his eyes open when Devin shook his arm. They had stopped outside a small brick house in the pale dawning of the day. He got out and walked stiffly, the tense position he'd held for hours taking a toll. The door opened. Bo raised his eyes.

"You remember my dad, Bo. Eddie Bressard?"

Bo bobbed his chin. "We met at the wedding."

"And I watched you perform at the premier where this one learned he had a daughter." Eddie waved a hand toward Devin.

A reminder they were all fallible?

"My son said you need a place to bunk for a while. His old room might do if you're not particular about sharing with my books and workbench."

Bo swallowed. "I'd appreciate a day or two to get my head straight."

"If you can do that in a day or two it's better than most of us. Come on. I'd offer coffee but you look more like sleep's in order."

Devin said, "Thanks, Dad. I'll show him in."

Just inside the door hung a large cross with that same dying Jesus and a picture of Devin as a kid. Bo took them in, then followed him down the hall to a pint-sized room that held reminders of the boy who'd grown up here. It was oddly intimate to be given this glimpse and the opportunity to stay. He hadn't expected it.

"The bed is short and narrow," Devin said.

"I'm used to that, actually." He pictured the dormitory. The need to know about DeShawn speared his guts, but fear kept him from placing the call. He reneged on his deal with the devil. DeShawn might be lying on cold hard steel in the morgue. Bo ran a hand over his eyes.

"Want to talk about it?"

He canted a glance at Devin. No words came.

"I have to know you'll stay put. Grace and Exi are counting on me. If you don't want professional help ..."

"I'm good. Just tired."

"Okay."

He managed to raise his eyes once more. "I owe you."

"It's not that way, Bo."

He lay down and rolled to his side, heard Devin leave, and let sleep steal him like a band of goblins.

32

Exi pushed things into the one bag she'd brought with her and two she borrowed from Sondra. There was no way she could stay. Not shattered like this. True to form, her heart had stayed numb for about three seconds. Now it felt like pulp, flapping in her chest cavity.

Eileen had received her own alarming text from Bo, but a call from Devin relieved her fear. Still, she looked fragile when Exi came into the breakfast room with the painting she'd framed in her arms. "I have something for you." She turned it face out, and Eileen's gasp made her smile. "Not as beautiful as the real thing, but my first attempt."

"Oh. My. Word."

"I hope you'll find a place to hang it. There isn't that much of you personally in this house, just your old relatives."

Eileen snorted. "How I love your honesty."

Exi laid it on the table and knelt on one knee. "So, I have to go now."

"Go …"

"Back to my place."

"Oh, dear."

"This is Bo's home, Eileen. If I'm gone he can come back. I know you want that. And you're right that he needs to belong."

"There are so many other rooms. Just move down a floor. It worked for Grace and Devin."

"I can't force him to see me. And I'm not sure I can see him. It's just cleaner this way."

"Oh, dear." Eileen stroked her fingers. "I understand. But I think it's you he needs."

No. You don't leave people you need, not temporarily with no word, and not permanently by choice. He might have cared once, but that ended the moment he got on that bridge. She kissed this woman who mattered more than she'd realized. "I'll stay in touch if you want."

"You'd better."

They hugged. Then she hugged Sondra, who helped carry the bags to the taxi on the street. "Let me know if there's anything you or Eileen need. I'm happy to do whatever." They hugged again. She took the cab back to Brooklyn. After unloading her stuff into her cracker-box room, she went to see her mom at home.

From her seat in the sunroom, Rhonda greeted her with joy and surprise. "Exi." It was slow and slurred but better every time.

"Mom." She threw herself into the hug, settling onto the cushioned wicker loveseat.

"Tell ... me ... what's wrong."

So she did. Gangs. Terrorists. Liam and Eileen. John Helm and his protection specialists. Sully and the task force that made the news. Grace and Devin and Cate and Mia. The agent and the paintings she left in the studio. And Bo.

Her mom rubbed the tears from her cheek, then her warm hand settled on her shoulder. Exi pressed her ear to it.

"You ... hurt for him."

"Like a thousand times worse than anything. But I'm mad too." Her teeth clenched. Suicide? It's what she'd been afraid of, but now it kicked her hard. "I could almost understand if things hadn't resolved, if the danger was too much or the stress put him over the edge." Tears welled again. "Why would he do it when he could have come home?"

"Ask him."

Exi shook her head. "I can't. I don't even want to hear. Or see or think of him." Or hurt. She'd done nothing but that—for what? "Can I have my job back?"

Her mother drew back, eyes alight. "Yes. With me."

"Work together? Like we used to?" It would get her mom back in the store she loved. Exi whooped. They laughed. They hugged. They cried.

"It's going to be … okay."

Exi sniffled. Right now she'd settle for bearable.

The sun was setting when Bo woke. He used the bathroom. He showered. He went to the kitchen for … something. A voice came through the back screen door.

"Help yourself to anything in there. I'll just be a minute."

Nothing wrong with the guy's hearing. "Okay. Thanks." He could probably stomach whole-wheat toast.

Eddie came through the door as the toast popped up. "There's margarine or cottage cheese for that. I'm not allowed butter with my tricky ticker. But I can pick some up."

"Margarine's fine. Thanks." He spread it on the toast and carried the plate to the table with two chairs. Had they never needed more than the father-son set?

Eddie took the other seat. "I used to keep beer in the fridge, but that's also off the list. Red wine? Tea or coffee?"

"I'll get some water." Bo filled a glass from the sink, then sat back down. This should feel awkward to the max, yet it didn't. Eddie acted like every day some guy who tried to kill himself sat down at his kitchen table.

"Glad you got some sleep. Might throw you off tonight though."

"It's more than I usually get."

"Bad dreams?"

Bo took a bite, chewed, and swallowed. "Since my sister died." And others had populated them these last months.

"The brain's its own worst enemy. When it needs to idle, it kicks into overdrive. What took your sister from you?"

"Cancer."

"Slow and hard?" Eddie's voice was soft, his eyes warm with compassion.

"Slow for her. Way too fast for me. And now … it just never goes away."

"I'm sorry, son."

Bo startled, but it was just a word people used. He took another bite.

"I don't imagine that's all that had you on the bridge."

So Devin had told him. Okay. Accountability. "It's not." He washed the bread down with water and explained about DeShawn. "I don't know if he's made it or not."

Eddie rubbed a spot on the table with his thumb. "Now that your head's cleared, you know it isn't your fault if he didn't."

Bo shrugged. "I know it logically. But inside …" He blew out a breath. "I didn't keep my end of the deal."

"Who'd you deal with?"

"I guess the devil."

"Well, that's your problem right there. No point turning to the useless one when there's an all-powerful God."

Bo frowned. "It was evil at work."

"It was life at work. Plenty of trouble happens without Satan's personal touch. Sounds like this DeShawn has good people in his corner but still went astray. Happens to the best of us."

"And the worst."

"That's just wrong if you're meaning you."

He shook his head and told him about Misty and the things he'd come to realize in his own life. Eddie rose and went to the front room. He came back with what had to be a Bible. Bo stifled a groan.

"There's a story in here." Eddie opened and paged through but not randomly. He knew where he meant to go. "It's not long." He flipped the book around and pushed it over. "Right there where it says The Prodigal Son."

Bo looked from the book to the man across the table. "Save yourself if I go up in flames."

Eddie's eyes shone. "Extinguisher under the sink."

Bo pulled the book closer and read. On the surface it seemed a kid's tale. But fatherless son that he was, it pierced like a spear and lodged there. His actor's mind put him in the scene. He could easily play the one dragging himself from the pigsty in disgust, everything squandered. Booze, drugs, sex. Starving. Stupid. But smart enough to plan a way back. A loser sure. But better off than this.

There he was on the journey, preparing his speech. *Look, I screwed up. I'll take my lashes. Just let me work for food.* His father's house coming into view. His brother working in the field, diligent, righteous. He wore Devin's face, scowling at the miscreant.

But that's where he stalled. He could not see the father running to him, only away without looking back. Bo swallowed.

"That's the picture of God, Bo. Not sitting on his throne in judgment, but running, arms spread to welcome back his profligate son."

That was too big, too painful. Inconceivable. "The brother's more realistic." *Leave my cousin out of your disaster of a life.*

"Sure." Eddie nodded. "He's human. Jealous, self-righteous, indignant. He's lost nothing, while this son has nothing left … except his father's love. All the old man asks is for that one to share his joy."

"So the jerk admits he's worthless and asks to be a slave but gets to be a son again."

"A cherished son."

That struck so many parallels it hurt. "How is that fair? He wastes everything and gets the party?"

Eddie studied him so long he squirmed.

Bo slouched back from the table. "My sister Barb never got the leads she deserved. Everything was heaped on me. Even her love and attention. Then she's just wiped out." His hands fisted. "Where's the open arms in that?"

Eddie let the anger splash over him and ebb into a frothy tide. "I believe they're around her now. In the eternal view, she got there first, while you're still floundering here."

Bo stared. He couldn't help it. Barb the lucky one? And yet …

"It's a picture of God's unquenchable love. If you're sorry, weary, and lost, there is a way."

Bo pressed a hand to his eyes. That old man in the story did not wear the face he'd always imagined matched his own. No. That father just might look like Eddie Bressard.

The next morning during Devin's production meetings, Grace and Mattie headed for Eddie's. She had a bone to pick but really just needed eyes on Bo to know he was okay. She hadn't realized how shaky she was until she stood at Eddie's door.

Mattie clapped her hands. "Papa's house. We seeing Papa, Mommy?"

"That's right, sweetie." She wouldn't mention Uncle Bo until she'd ascertained his stability. Mattie added her little knocks as Grace rapped the screen door, then went on in. Eddie knew they were coming. She lifted Mattie to kiss her daddy's picture on the wall as they did since Mattie learned that boy was seven-year-old Devin.

"That you, Grace?"

Mattie wiggled free and went running for Papa's voice in the kitchen. So much for checking things out. Before she could follow her daughter, Bo stepped out of the room that used to be Devin's. He stood in the hall wearing jeans and T-shirt, hair overgrown, rakish stubble, and eyes awash with emotion. It just about broke her heart.

"I'm not happy with you, Bo Corrigan." She strode over and pulled him in for a hug.

His mouth edged up on one side. "I know."

She stepped back, still holding his shoulders and took him in at close range. Even gaunt and ragged, he was gorgeous. Of course.

"You scared the life out of me."

"That's why you sent Devin?"

"He sent himself. I couldn't keep him back if I tried, but I didn't. He had things to say. I'm so glad you listened. Don't ever do that again." She punched his shoulder, her emotions bouncing like a tennis ball between angry and ecstatic. She expected some glib answer, his trademark smirk.

But he looked away. "Sorry."

There he went again, tying her heart in knots. "What happened?"

"Just stuff I'm working through."

"With Eddie?"

He shrugged.

"Because alone in your head isn't a good place."

"Don't worry."

"Don't—" She expelled a breath.

He ran his hand down her arm, his eyes sorrowful again. "Grace ..."

"There's Mommy." Eddie said, coming into the hall. "She needs the little-girl's room."

"Big-girl's room. Big-girl potty." Mattie ran and grabbed her leg.

Bo crouched. "You can't be old enough for that."

"Uh-huh. Have big-girl panties."

She started lifting her skirt but Bo pressed it down grinning. "I'm sure they're very nice."

"I shouldn't be surprised," Grace huffed. "There's not a female alive who won't show you her panties."

"Is that an offer?" He crooked a brow.

"You're only saying that because you know it's not." She whisked by with Mattie in hand. Before she closed the door, she heard Eddie ask if Bo made a call and left it open a piece.

"I'm working up to it."

She propped Mattie on the toilet and stood by the door.

"It might be a big relief."

"It might make me wish I left the bridge the other way."

She pulled the door a little wider to see.

"You can live with the result. Either way, you're not responsible." Eddie's voice softened. "Make the call, son."

Bo's back tensed. He took his phone from his pocket, hesitated, then did a voice search for something she didn't catch because Mattie started singing. She shushed her little girl with a smile and whispered, "You can sing in a minute, okay?"

"All done."

Grace took care of her and held her up to wash. She could hear Bo's voice, but not the words. She handed Mattie the towel and rushed back to the cracked-open door. Bo leaned his shoulder to the wall as if he'd gone suddenly weak. "Thanks, Ann. Yeah, I know. Okay. You too." He ended the call.

As Mattie ran to her papa, Grace walked out, more steamed than she ought to be when she knew how he was. "New girlfriend?" And Exi painting her heart out. She should sell every one for top dollar.

Bo came off the wall. "I doubt *Sister* Ann would call it that."

"Sister."

"She doesn't dress like a nun, but she acts like one. Couldn't get anywhere with her."

Grace glared. "You're involved with a convent?"

"Now that might be interesting."

Eddie cleared his throat. They shared a sidelong glance. Bo sighed resignedly. "It's a mission I helped with."

A mission. She had never imagined those words in Bo's mouth. She could hardly imagine *helped with.* "And the call?"

"Someone I'm worried about."

Grace cocked a hip. "And?"

"Jury's still out."

"I'm sorry to hear that." Grace considered her next words, then went ahead. "Bo, there's a reason I'm here."

"I sense a scolding coming."

"I should. I should blister you."

He waited.

"But I came to suggest you go home as soon as you're ready. Eileen needs to see you."

"Eileen?"

Clearly not what he'd expected. But she wasn't suggesting anything with Exi. While she hadn't cheered last night when Exi told her she'd moved back to her apartment, she agreed it was the right thing. Having Bo under the same roof would be an unfair advantage for him.

"What's wrong with Eileen?" His voice graveled.

Grace rested a hand on his arm. "They removed a brain tumor."

The breath left his lungs in a rush.

"It's benign, thank God, but still a brain surgery. Worrying about you doesn't help. Can you please go see her at least?" At his hesitation, she added, "Exi's not there. She moved back to her apartment." She couldn't tell if that made things better or worse in his troubled mind. "The coast is clear. Go see Eileen." She started past, but her daughter ran over to Bo, arms up.

"Kiss Mattie."

Grace rolled her eyes when Bo kissed her baby's head. Sure enough, Mattie touched her mouth and demanded a kiss right there. She knew how it worked.

Settling down on his heels, Bo touched her little mouth with his finger. "Save those, Princess. They're not for frogs."

A toss up whether Mattie or she was more surprised. As the child worked out if he could really be a frog, Grace led her to the door.

Bo called, "Thanks for telling me."

"You're welcome. You're welcome at our house too, if you want to talk."

"Okay." Those two syllables held a world of *won't happen.*

Whatever he'd been through had changed him. He could fake the surface, say the ornery things about nuns and panties. But it was all an act. And he wasn't playing it well. Had the prince become a frog?

Walking through Eileen's doors felt like traveling in a time machine, arriving exactly where he'd left as if everything had stood still. But it hadn't. He found Eileen in the breakfast room with a scarf tied around her head. Her skin looked brittle as a winter leaf. Yet the eyes she raised were awash with love, chased by relief.

"There's my lost boy."

"But you've grown up, Wendy." He crouched and kissed her cheek, her neck, and rested his forehead against her temple.

"I grew up before you were born. Now let me see you."

He returned the scrutiny, relieved beyond words that her mind was undamaged. "You're okay? It's"—he cleared his throat—"the tumor's gone?"

"Gone and good riddance. And before you start talking nonsense, it was growing in my head before I knew you. They estimate a decade or more. We just hadn't discovered it."

He searched her face for any hint of a lie.

"No, my dear Bo, you didn't cause it. But if you ever give me a fright like the night before last, I can't say it won't kill me."

He raised her hand and kissed it. "I'm sorry. Really."

"I'm personally more inclined toward homicide, but I've had dark moments. Let's make a pact to face them when they come our way."

He managed a smile. "Okay." Sounded good anyway. He rose and looked toward the stairs. "Exi's gone?"

"You have your place back. Are you staying?"

He swallowed. "The trouble's over."

"I could still use the rent."

He moved his gaze from one sharp eye to the other. "Are you just saying that?"

"Why have an apartment if it's not producing income? Do you think I want someone I can't bully in your place?"

He smiled. "I don't think anyone like that exists."

"You'd be surprised. Take your Exi, for example."

"Exi?"

"She has smartly put me, my brother, and his entire security force in our places."

His throat hurt.

"If you don't win her back, you're the biggest fool who ever lived."

He cocked his jaw. "It's not that simple."

"Why not?"

"I need to make changes, and the biggest is about women and sex and … all that."

Her lips parted. "You're coming out of the closet?"

He canted his head. "I almost died in a gutter. My body all but shut down. Then things happened and I'm not sure I could touch someone if I wanted to. That way, I mean." He toyed with his thumbnail.

"Is this coming from Eddie Bressard?"

"No, before him. I'm just glad the physical is dead, or it might not be so easy."

Her expression held everything she didn't say. "And Exi?"

"Is Jeffrey in the picture?"

"Not even close."

He absorbed that. "I'll talk to her. When I figure out what to say."

"I never took you for a coward."

"You should've." He made his way up the stairs.

The disorder in his place suggested Exi left in a hurry. A plate and fork in the sink, a skillet on the stove. She'd left hand weights on the exercise mat, a towel over the universal weight machine. He lifted it and sniffed, but caught no scent of her. Just as well.

The sax left on the table caused a chest pang he rubbed as if it would go away. He walked over and pressed a key, then ran his finger over the mouthpiece and imagined her lips there. Had she played? Did it make her happy? That's all he'd wanted, to help her be herself and be happy that way.

He turned to the partly open door opposite the kitchen. Bracing himself to face the disaster he'd left in the studio, he pushed the door ajar and froze. On every wall multiple times, he stared at himself—as he'd never seen himself. Wonder and a kind of horror came over him.

She was a genius, this girl who did backflips in the park. But it killed him to realize what she did while he was gone. He'd consumed her. His whole body shook as he studied the expressions she'd captured. Moments he remembered, others that could only come from her imagination. He jammed his hand into his hair.

He owed her an explanation. The truth. Every bit of it. *God.* The word touched his tongue in a way it never had. A prayer. A plea. *Don't let me hurt her.*

He reached out to the canvas, his fingertips to the fingers she'd painted. He rested his forehead on the surface, breathing the latent scent of paint. He pressed his other palm to the wall as if her art might absorb him.

He stood so long the light changed. Finally he pushed off. He should call. That was the fair thing to do. Find out where she was and when—if—he could see her. But he went downstairs and petitioned the queen for her 1933 Rolls Royce Phantom II Continental Barker Sedanca.

Her eyes held a knowing glint. "You know where to find the keys."

It took a while to start, but the car slid out of its bay like the elegant craft it was. He drove to Flatbush and found only the freckled friend, Suz, at the apartment. When she got her mouth working, the information didn't surprise him as much as it might have. It felt right.

33

"It's almost five, Mom," Exi called into the office, happy they'd made it through the first day without trauma from the gunshot spoiling it for either of them. "Want me to bring you the cash drawer?"

"Please."

She went forward to lock up before exposing the cash but halted when Bo stepped inside. In jeans and T-shirt, mussed hair and stubble, he hardly fit the vintage Rolls parked in the loading zone at the curb. But her breath caught just the same. Bo Corrigan in her mother's flower shop, looking like every aching brushstroke she'd put to canvas. Time rolled backward.

"Exi?" Rhonda's speech might be slow, but she came out and read the situation with her eagle eye and lioness defenses.

Exi scratched her cheek. "You might want to run."

He shook his head.

Exi half turned. "Mom, this is Bo Corrigan. Bo, Rhonda Murphy."

"What … do you … want?"

"Some time with Exi."

"You've had … enough."

Heart hammering, Exi met his eyes, asking the same thing as her mom, only angrier. What did he want?

"Please, can we talk?"

She drew a ragged breath. "I need to carry the register drawer. Mom's wrist is still …" She waved a hand at the cast. Even with the injury it would be a toss-up which wounded woman had a better grasp on things. Exi removed the drawer and carried it to the office. Her mother followed her in and eyed her severely.

"I'll be okay." The waver in her voice cried *liar, liar.* "Dad's coming for you, right?"

Her mom nodded, then brushed a hand down her cheek as they met in the doorway. "Careful."

"You better believe it." They shared a staunch smile. "Lock up after me."

At the curb, Bo opened the shiny black car door. She slid into the sky blue seat and watched him close it. Because she couldn't help herself, she watched him walk around the hood and get in beside her. Then she looked down at her hands. "We can talk right here, then you can take me home. Since you already said good-bye."

His shoulders bowed. "I'm not here to hurt you."

"Oh, good." She avoided his eyes.

He drew a ragged breath. "Sorry is too small."

She held her tongue. She didn't want to hurt him either. She should get this over with. "Why did you go? Why did you leave without a word and ignore everything I said to you?"

"You know why. To keep you safe."

"John Helm kept me safe. You made me crazy."

"I thought …"

"What?" She folded her arms.

"That my luck was everyone else's curse. Barb, Grace, you. I didn't need Devin to say it."

"Bo …"

"I'm trying to believe it's not true, even though the pattern continued wherever I went."

"Partying?"

He swallowed. "When I left that party I was …"

"Injured, sick, dying?"

He slid her a look. "Pretty close. I ended up in a culvert so infected I almost shut down. My fault, I know."

He was breaking her heart confirming all she'd guessed. "How bad was it?"

"Bad enough Barb kept me company."

"What?"

He moistened his lips. "I don't know what was real. She just … talked to me. Such a nag it seemed real, saying I was stupid to be there, only I didn't have much choice by that point." His voice shook. "She was … not good to look at."

Horror swept over as she pictured the possibilities.

He pushed his hair back. "Then someone found me, and I went to this place."

Exi swallowed. "A geographical anomaly where no phones work?"

"Someone took my wallet, my phone, and my watch."

"And without them you had no idea who you were and how to get replacements?"

"I knew. I just thought it would be safer all around if I stayed silent. I didn't know you were calling and texting." He blew out a breath. "Okay, I guessed you would, but I thought you were better off giving up on me."

"Wow. That says a lot."

"Part of the time, a lot of it actually, I was too sick to think of anything. They kept me in the clinic and nursed me back to life."

A sobering and painful thought.

"Then they let me be part of what they do, and I felt like a different person. I felt like someone who does good in the world instead of the nothing I was."

Nothing? She stared.

"But then, other bad things happened to people I was with. One—" His breathing got shallow. "I don't know how it will go. I was hoping I could take you there. Unless you want to go home."

The smart part of her said run. The part that always won said, "I'll go."

His hand shook when he started the car. They drove from Flatbush to Hell's Kitchen. Bo parked Eileen's Rolls next to a van in the tiny walled parking lot connected to a building. To her surprise, he went to a side door and keyed in the code. He waved her inside a utility area.

She could hear voices from what turned out to be a cafeteria. It smelled of tomato sauce and garlic. As they entered, a cry went up, hoots and clapping. One youth shouted, "Hollywood!" But these people were rough. Even the youngest looked broken down somehow.

A hefty mocha-skinned woman rose from a nearby table. "So, Plato. Decided to show up?"

Hollywood, Plato, who was this man?

"Georgia, this is Exi. Can we see DeShawn?"

Her face clouded. "You know the way."

Exi didn't resist when he took her hand. She thought he might explain, but he said nothing until they reached what must be the clinic he mentioned. It was small, three cots with other medical equipment. On one lay a kid with skin like a pinto mustang. An IV gave him fluids. The oxygen cannula had come askew. He didn't move except for the shallow rise and fall of his chest and one hand twitching.

When Bo pulled the door wider and motioned her through, she saw an older woman with deeply creased skin beside the occupied cot. She set a prayer book aside and rose from the metal stool. "Ah, Beau. It's good to see you." She squeezed his hands with a look of incredible warmth and affection.

"Exi, this is Ann—Sister Ann."

She took the woman's outstretched hand, sensing strength and acceptance in its grip. "It's nice to meet you."

"The blessing is mine." Their eyes met with understanding.

Bo's voice graveled. "How is he?"

"No change. Doc Patel says all we can do is wait."

"I'm not good at that."

Amusement infused Sister Ann's smile. "So full of things you're not good at."

Bo pulled the stool up next to the bed. He sat and shook the kid's shoulder. "Hey, Sparky." His voice was thick. "All the grief you gave me? Who's the waa-waa baby now?"

Nothing. Exi pressed a hand to her mouth.

Bo's hand settled gently. "Come on, DeShawn. Find your way back. We need your example."

No response.

Bo adjusted the cannula. "All right, fine. But I'm taking your dog until you tell me otherwise." He fought emotion when Sister Ann squeezed his shoulder.

"It would do him good to keep hearing you. Come when you can?"

Bo's throat worked. "Okay." He got up. "Call me if things change."

"I will. You're also welcome, Exi."

"Thank you." She struggled to fit Bo into this place, and yet he did. In the hall, she said, "Is there really a dog?"

"Sheriff Shorty law dog. He found me. Ann and DeShawn pulled me out of the culvert. Who knows how they got me to the clinic."

"The dog lives here?"

"No, he's out there somewhere. DeShawn scrounges food for him from trash bins." As they passed through, Bo raised a hand to the crowded cafeteria.

A beautiful girl with milky skin underlaid by ocher hints of bruises intercepted them. When Bo paused, she petted his arm. "I thought you weren't coming back."

"I'll be around."

"But not staying?" She curled her fingers into his T-shirt sleeve and tugged.

"Misty, this is Alexis."

The girl released his sleeve, glared, and walked away. Exi looked from her back to Bo's face.

"Let's go." They left the cafeteria and went back through the utility area where they'd come in. "You should wait in the car while I find the dog."

"Why?"

"Part of Misty's story." He glanced down at her. "There's a drug dealer gunning for me."

Her jaw fell slack. "Bo." It was a nonissue, though, because he pushed through the door to the parking lot and there stood the mangiest dog she'd ever seen.

"Hey, Sheriff." Bo went to one knee and stroked the animal. Wiry hairs flew off. "You must be wondering what's going on."

The dog whined. Exi melted. It started with Bo's hand on that boy's chest, now this.

He held out the car key. "Can you open the back, please?" When she took the key, he lifted the dog.

"He'll shed in the car."

Bo winked. "I'll have it detailed."

There went her heart again. She opened the door, and he closed the dog in. Sheriff instantly started to howl, crashing around so that every surface bore his mark.

"Careful getting in."

She didn't have to be told. That dog would bolt with half a chance.

He started the engine. "Can we drop him at Eileen's before I take you home? It's a shorter drive."

"Yes. Of course." She didn't want to go home. "I want to know the rest." But Sheriff started barking, an ear-splitting clamor. She covered her ears and Bo looked pained.

He hollered, "It's because I'm taking him away from DeShawn."

"Or he hates cars."

"He got hit by a truck. But I can't risk something happening before DeShawn recovers."

"From what?"

"Wait until we're out of this noise."

"Should I go back there?" She thumbed toward the back seat.

"Would you?"

She crawled over the panel separating the front and back seats. What an incredible car. How would Eileen feel if the dog tore it up? She pulled him onto her lap. "Hey there, Sheriff. It's not so bad." He trembled so hard his fur flew off like Pigpen in the Peanuts cartoon. But he stopped barking. It took a while for her ears to recover. Then his odor overtook her senses. To top it off she saw something crawling on his skin.

"Um, Bo? He's going to need a bath. With vermin shampoo."

He looked at her in the rearview mirror. "He was treated for fleas at the vet."

"At least one didn't get the word. Dish soap and cider vinegar will do it. I'm sure Sondra has both."

"Great." He drove like the car was an extension of him. No wonder Devin said she should paint it. Too bad she wanted to paint Bo in it.

Finally they pulled into the garage. He closed the big door before she and Sheriff got out.

"Don't want him casing the hood before he's presentable."

She crooked a brow. "Presentable might stretch it—on a good day."

He pulled a slow smile that set her heart racing, then wrapped the dog in a plastic trash bag and lifted him. "That should control the situation."

"Sure." She led the way in.

Eileen's bedroom door was closed so they tiptoed past. Sondra's door was also closed, though a light shone underneath. Exi whispered, "I'll grab the soap and vinegar." Plastic-wrapped dog in arms, Bo climbed the stairs. She bit her lip to keep from laughing but tears were not far beneath.

Bo unwrapped the dog in his bathroom, less sanguine about this than he'd let on. Sheriff's whining echoed off the tiled walls and floor as he scrambled around as hyper as DeShawn … had been. Bo pressed his palms to his temples and pictured DeShawn on that path in the story about the wayward son, all jitters and swagger before he sees the father standing, arms outstretched. A noise half sigh, half groan came out of him. "If you're there," he rasped, "do it for him. I had my chance. DeShawn never did. Hold him. Hold him tight."

Sheriff pawed the crack under the door, trapped and aware of it. "Don't panic, foxhole buddy. This won't kill you." He grabbed the dog from the door when Exi came. He could smell the vinegar she'd mixed into shampoo in the plastic tumbler. He said, "I'd rather use the shower than the tub. I don't want fleas in the jets, alive or dead."

Snickering, she toed off her sandals. "Okay. Ready?"

They marshalled the dog into the shower and closed the door. The whine hit decibels his ears objected to. One of the shower heads had a retracting hose attachment. Sheriff's reaction when Bo turned on the water gave him the feeling neither his jeans nor her shorts would get through this dry.

Exi said, "You soak him and I'll suds him."

"Right." Every time the hose nozzle neared the dog, Sheriff charged, flipped, and twisted free.

Exi squealed when the spray shot her, then shoved the tumbler into a cubby and grabbed the dog. "Go. Just spray him."

With her arms around the dog, he aimed the nozzle until they were all soaked. Together they lathered and combed, then sprayed again. He turned off the water. Sheriff shook himself with remarkable violence. Bo pulled a towel down, tackled Sheriff, and wrapped him up.

Drenched, Exi sank down against the shower wall, breathing hard. "You sure show a girl a good time." She pushed wet hair off her face.

He'd never seen anything more gut-wrenchingly beautiful.

"Why did I take all my clothes home?" She asked it rhetorically, wringing water from her T-shirt.

He swallowed every response that came to mind. "I'll get you a guest robe." He pushed Sheriff out of the shower and grabbed his own towel, swabbing his hair and face. If not for the clear glass, he'd strip right here. Instead he shed the wet clothes in the closet, put on lounge pants, and went to the guest room for Exi's robe. He stopped when he saw the bed haphazardly made and it sank in she had slept here. While he'd been gone, she was in this room. It bent his mind.

Sheriff tore in, shook himself, and burrowed under the bed. At least he was clean. Bo grabbed the robe and tapped the bathroom door. Exi reached through the crack, and just like that his body responded. He'd been delusional to think otherwise—with her anyway. He pressed his forehead to the wall and stifled a groan. It didn't change what he knew.

He heard something running and realized she'd put her wet clothes and maybe his into the stacked washing machine he'd never used. Sondra did it all or sent it out. Toweling her hair, Exi came out. Her eyes were huge, with wet lashes clumped like starbursts. "You said you'd tell me the rest."

When he could get his breath, he motioned to the couch. "Want to sit?"

She curled into one end, plucking the robe over her knees and said, "What's wrong with DeShawn?"

"What isn't?"

"You said he found you."

"His first mistake."

"Bo."

"Okay." He sat on the other end of the couch facing her. He gave her DeShawn's background. Crack-addicted mother, abusive dad. "Maybe Grandma cared, but she died. The landlord kicked him out at thirteen, and he started traveling."

Her face showed his own puzzlement.

"That means homeless, going city to city, begging and stealing, and for most of them, using drugs they earn by going between dealers and customers."

"Oh," she breathed. "He can't have done it long."

"Four years."

"But you said …"

"He's seventeen. That's what crack and malnutrition do for you. And his own drug of choice, heroin."

"That's so sad."

"But he turned it around, coming to the mission." He explained DeShawn's limitations and challenges, his physical issues, his character and courage. "Man, that kid could talk. Drive you crazy talking. And forget thinking he'd sit still." His eyes teared up. "He called me his project. He'd found me and, like Sheriff, I was his responsibility." Bo ground a palm into his wet eyes and laughed. "Which mostly meant he gave me grief over everything."

Exi's face held the sorrow of what she'd seen at the clinic in contrast to his words.

"So, I helped prepare him for the GED. Then Ann asked me to help him get a job. It's a requirement in the program that they become self-sustaining." He stared at the couch cushion between them and told her how he'd turned the interview into an audition. "We drilled and rehearsed until I knew he could get it. And he did. I just didn't know what that would do to him."

He stood up and moved to the center of the rug, facing the wall. "That was the day the news broke about the task force arrests and showed my mug on the TV."

"They didn't know who you were?"

"They saw that stupid article a few days before. But with the TV news DeShawn saw the writing on the wall. That and some … phobia about holding a job, it was just too much. He gave me back the phone, watch, and wallet he'd lifted in the culvert. He'd listened to and read everything you and other people sent. It made him feel loved and missed. But he gave it back and … I didn't see it. I didn't see he was giving up."

Tears streamed. He didn't realize Exi had joined him until her hand was on his back. He almost begged her to take it off. "I need a shirt." Her hand slid off as he moved away. In his room, he pulled on a T-shirt and made himself go back. He'd promised her the truth.

She was standing where he left her, and now they were face-to-face. "I noticed he was missing. Luke and I searched." He fought his traitorous voice and won. "We found him in an alley, the needle in his arm, more dead than alive. Luke said it was over, that help would take too long for a street kid overdose. But I called John and a firetruck came." He buried himself in Exi's eyes. "I had to get as far from the kid as it was possible to get." His hands clenched. "He should never have entered my disaster of a life."

With her own eyes streaming, she shook his reality away. "That's not true."

"I was tired of being the Death Star."

"You're not. You don't hurt people."

She hadn't seen DeShawn in that alley. "I thought it would save him. It's not what I wanted, but that's what I thought. I sat on the bridge, but, before I let go I listened and read. And it was … so good. You were—are—so good." Again his voice tried to get away. "Ann told me to relieve people's concerns—though that wasn't exactly what she meant—so I texted everything I wanted people to know." He rubbed his face. "Then only one thing held me. When I thought it might hurt you, I just … couldn't let go."

"Thank God." Her voice was so small. She moved in and put her hands on his chest, still smelling faintly like wet dog. Even that endeared her. "Thank you for not leaving me, Bo. I could not have borne it if you jumped. I love you."

"Please don't." It drove the shaft deeper. "You're everything good and I want you that way."

Confusion clouded her. "I don't understand."

"Yes, you do. You know what I am, how I've been, the life I've led."

"You think I'm perfect?"

"Close enough."

"That's not true. Even if it were, it wouldn't matter."

"Exi." He gripped her wrists. "You have no idea. That party? I don't even know what I did or with whom."

"The condition you were in, probably way less than you think."

He shook his head. "My whole life is the prodigal son."

Her brow furrowed. "How do you know the prodigal son?"

"Devin's dad."

"My cousin Eddie?"

His mouth quirked. "Yeah, I guess." A holy trio.

"Then you know that son is welcomed with rejoicing. He's forgiven and restored."

"But the consequences remain. He can't undo what he did, how he was. I see things now that I didn't before."

"What things?"

He expelled a breath. "That girl in the cafeteria?"

"Misty?"

No surprise she'd filed it. "One of the things I did for the mission, the main thing really, was go out in the van overnight with another guy, Luke."

"The one you searched with."

"Yes. We took sandwiches to the street kids, tried to encourage them to consider the program. These two girls, Misty and Vi, they came in a lot. We'd talk but it never mattered. Luke told me Misty had tried the program then relapsed, and this dealer, Spider—her boyfriend—almost killed her. When he jacked her heart back up with cocaine, she thought that meant he loved her."

"No." Exi saw the obvious.

"It's how it is this … incestuous codependence. The whole community's that way. They expect to die young so what does anything matter? They live for the high. She couldn't live without it. But … she wanted to. I saw something in her that wasn't in the other girl. Vi just mouthed off. Misty … I don't know."

"It was you. It's how people are with you. They want to do what you want." He started to shake his head but she said, "I saw her, Bo. I know that look."

"One night I was sick of the games, the delusions, the lies they told themselves. When Misty and Vi got in, I laid it out. I told Misty she'd be safe with us if she didn't go back to Spider. She was too wasted to get it, but Vi did. And she went straight to Spider."

He told her how he found pregnant Misty gang raped and beaten. "I'm sorry," he said to the horror in her face. "But you have to understand."

She swallowed. "Then tell me."

"Luke and I took her to the clinic. Ann and Dr. Patel patched her up. When she got well enough, Misty thought we could start something. Georgia warned me. You know what she said?" His voice graveled. "Misty thought it would turn me on to hear what they did to her." His stomach clenched, but he went on.

"As horrifying as that was, I realized it's only degrees. How they treated her and how I've treated others, like Louisa, is just shades of the same thing. I didn't think—maybe didn't care—if they wanted more than I would give. You said it yourself. People want to give me what I want. They always have. And I was happy to take it all."

Exi's arms slackened in his grip. "That's not the same."

But he could see she got it. He released her. "Ann told me sex is sacred. That could not be farther from how I've treated it."

"Yes, it could. You don't hurt people for pleasure or power or terror. Misty's wrong. She might not know the difference but I do."

"Exi."

"The guy who hit me? He liked it. There's not one cell in you like that."

"There are other kinds of hurt, and to go through life not even seeing it? That's inexcusable."

"You think you're the only one? Everyone hurts someone."

He couldn't bear her eyes on him.

"Look at me." She made him. "I love you, Bo. I told you that. Now I've told you twice. I'll tell you every day for the rest of my life."

"Exi." He jammed his fingers in his hair.

"Did you look in that studio?" She waved at the doorway.

"Yes."

"Then you saw what I see in you. You saw what I know here"—she pointed to her temple—"and feel here"—she pressed a hand to her heart.

"It's not me."

"It's not the mask you wear, but it's you." She took his hands. "Marry me."

"What?" He huffed the word.

"You said it in your texts. What we have is real. It hit the first time we talked and don't pretend you didn't feel it. You said you're in love with me. That's what you wanted me to know when there was nothing left of you. Well, you're here, and I'm not letting go."

Heat coursed through him, burning the shame.

She stepped close again. "I'm not sure I can promise sacred sex, but covenant sex?"

His heart thumped. "I'm not sure I've had sober sex."

She gripped his shirt, eyes shining like supernovas. "We can fill out the forms and get a license in the morning, then be back in City Hall to get married the next day."

"Elope?" He could hardly think. "You wanted a Grace Evangeline wedding."

"Jeffrey wanted that."

"But this isn't even a church. Your faith—"

"It takes a year to go through that program. I want to do it and hope you do. But this is a binding covenant. We'll renew our vows when we've done the work."

"Exi …" He brought his hand to her cheek. Then his mouth was on hers, tasting what he thought he'd lost forever. He pressed his forehead to hers. "I don't know what to say."

"Whatever it is"—her hoarse voice shot hunger through him—"you could say it on one knee."

He felt his broken pieces coming together. This woman, this incredible, talented, sanctified woman wanted him, not for his fame or beauty, but him. If that wasn't God with arms outstretched …

He swallowed. "Not without a ring."

She bit her lip. "I'm not particular."

"I am." He took her hand and hurried down four flights of stairs. "Let's see if I can steal the car again."

As they moved quietly back toward the garage, Eileen called to them from her bedroom. He met Exi's eyes, then pushed open the door.

Eileen sat propped up in bed, a diminutive empress with a half-shaved head. "You might sneak by me once—with a whimpering dog—but not twice."

He walked to her bedside, kissed her brow and kept his mouth there. "I need the car to go buy Exi a ring."

"Oh." Her eyes filled with tears. "No need for that. We've had an account with Cartier for generations. It's all been handed down to me." She instructed him to open a wall safe and rattled off the combination. It took muscles to extract the enclosed chest. "Set it here on the bed."

He did and watched Exi's face as Eileen opened a complete tier of rings.

"Take your pick, dear. It would tickle me no end."

EPILOGUE

Alexis and Bo—scratch that—Beau Corrigan Wedding plan.

8:00 a.m. Apply for license and control yourselves for twenty-four hours.

Lexi watched Beau's face in the town car as he took a phone call and stilled. "Okay," he said low. "I'll get there as soon as I can." The hand with the phone fell to his thigh.

"What is it?" Her heart skipped.

"DeShawn is fading."

She drew a breath. "Tell the driver we're not heading for City Hall."

His brow furrowed. "Are you sure?"

"We can fill out forms anytime."

"They're not just forms."

"Beau, seriously. Tell him."

He gave the driver their new destination, then sank back in his seat. "Sorry."

"Don't. There's no need." Did he think she couldn't see his heart breaking? "This is what matters now." She hid the inner trembling. If the worst happened, would this death bring on more of the crazy thinking that drove him to the bridge? Please, no.

He pressed a hand to his eyes and said nothing, but when she slid her fingers into his, he butted his thumb against the vintage Cartier diamond as if reminding himself it was there, that he was the one who slid it on her finger when Eileen forced them to accept one from her collection. This exquisite ring from the twenties took her breath when Eileen pointed it out. Now it seemed he was clinging to that moment too.

They had talked long into the night. Somewhere in that discussion, he told her he was changing his name—well, the spelling. When he explained why, she got it. The mission impacted him so powerfully he saw himself the way Ann had mistaken it.

First it had been a role to hide behind, a way to pretend the woman didn't know him, but that alter-identity awakened something in his core. Eddie's prodigal son story drove it home. He told her Bo left the pigsty, but it was Beau the father welcomed. Her heart could hardly contain that joy. He hadn't been reduced. He'd been refined.

They entered through the front doors. This time no boisterous voices hailed him, only downcast murmurs. She ached for him, for them all. In the clinic, a slight yet vital-looking man attended DeShawn. Ann was also there, and both greeted Beau when he walked in. Exi held back while they talked, but she could see the youth on the cot was receiving palliative care, as Barb must have.

Dear God, don't let this break him.

He settled on the stool and took DeShawn's hand. No joking this time. He sat silent a long while, then leaned close and murmured, "You got this, kid. Nothing to it. The one who's waiting has open arms and unquenchable love. I got that on the best authority."

Ann's eyes warmed. "It seems DeShawn's project has come a long way."

Beau kept his eyes on the boy. "Long way still to go."

"Just remember those arms are for us all. No exceptions."

Beau drew a ragged breath. "Did he know?" He pressed DeShawn's hand between both of his and fought tears.

"I believe he did, and soon he'll have no doubt."

They kept a vigil, kids coming and watching, then making room. Georgia and the man named Luke came and stayed. No one asked

Beau to leave his place, but when DeShawn's spirit found the welcome he'd longed for in life, Beau rose. He held Ann a long time, then said, "Let me pay for whatever comes now. Can he have a grave to visit?"

"He can have whatever you provide."

Exi felt his sorrow when he took her hand to leave. Outside, he called for the car, then backed her into the wall. He clasped her head and kissed her like tomorrow might not come.

Forehead pressed to hers, he said, "I loved that kid. They're all trying so hard with such hideous stories and disabilities. It's a mystery they don't all give up."

"But they don't. And we can help."

"I don't want to buy more graves."

Her heart trembled. "If there are, it's not on you."

His kiss was so slow and deep she could hardly stand. He rasped, "I want you so much."

"To stop the hurt?"

He took a while to answer. "It would have been, before. It's probably part of it still. And maybe always will be." His lips moved to her neck. "But I'm in love with you, and that makes it so much more."

"Please tell me there's no part of you thinking crazy thoughts."

"Oh, I'm thinking crazy thoughts." His eyes heated. "But not about that black hole. I promise not to go there again. Eddie showed me a whole new paradigm. One where Barb wasn't shafted, where she's the lucky one."

Her spirit soared, and it must have shown because Beau reacted with a full-on heavy-metal kiss.

Breathing hard, he said, "I guess DeShawn's lucky too." His voice cracked but he found a smile. "The best part is imagining that kid yacking her ear off for a change." He actually laughed.

"Oh, Beau." She wrapped her arms around him. "I love you so much."

"Good. You can chalk that one off."

She searched him, puzzled.

"You said you'd tell me every day for the rest of your life."

She sank into his embrace. "Might be a thousand times a day."

If you end up with more than a day to plan—even for a sad reason—

make full use of the opportunity ... and resources.

Sitting in front of her cousin's wide-open cityscape with Grace, Cate, and Mia three days after the funeral, Exi sighed. "I really don't know what to wear. I'm not sorry everything fell through with Jeffrey, but I kind of regret not having a Mia gown."

Mia tapped her chin. "Oh, it could happen."

"In a week?"

"When you told me about your custom wedding plans, I envisioned your gown. I may even have drawn it." She winked. "With all the materials I keep on hand, it would just be measuring and sewing."

Exi gaped. "Seriously?"

"You could have it by Friday if I do it myself."

"You'd do that for me?"

Mia flipped her flaxen hair over her shoulder. "You know how you feel with a blank canvas and paint? That's how I am with a new dress design. I'm itching to make it. I sew all the prototypes before anyone else gets a work order."

Exi couldn't think what to say. "I'm ... I'm ..."

Mia leaned over the table. "So we're on?"

Tears stung. "Yes. Thanks! Wow." She looked at all of them. "It'll feel like a real wedding."

"It is real." Grace smiled. "Just not entirely complete until it's blessed."

She wiped the tears. "But that's coming. Beau's spending lots of time with Eddie."

Grace cocked an eyebrow. "You should hear Devin grumble. But he started it and really can't complain."

"Sure he can." Exi laughed. "It's what he does."

When they finished laughing at her husband, Grace touched her tablet. "If you're not expecting people to fly in, and you're using Eileen's house for the reception, with all her access to florists, caterers, and talent, there's really no holdup."

"You might want to specify no zombie madrigals," Cate warned cryptically, then explained about a certain Christmas party. "It's the one where Grace told Devin to find a different call girl."

"On another subject"—Grace fingered her earring—"do your parents understand about the church vows coming later? It's hard when your family's not onboard."

"My dad put the fear of God in Beau if he even thinks of shirking that, but he and Mom eloped right out of high school, so there's not much he can say."

"Then it's looking like a plan."

Her mind whirled. "It could work."

"Of course it could. I never plan a wedding that can't work. And I have to say this whole story would make a dynamite novel."

She gaped. "Oh. Wow. Do you mean that?"

"Unless you don't want me to. It just needed the right leading man."

Tears welled up. "I can't tell you how much I love him."

"Like you have to?" Grace smiled. "It's all over you."

"The glow is blinding." Mia pressed thumb and finger to her eyelids.

"No," Cate said, "that's her bling."

Grace lifted Exi's hand and studied the Cartier masterpiece. "What do bet Eileen had this planned from that first dinner invitation?"

Exi laughed. "From the cast party of your *Windows and Doors* anniversary. She admitted it."

"Took credit, more like."

Exi felt her heart grow three sizes. "I'm just so happy."

"Well, you should be," Grace agreed. "You're the bride."

Even a simple ceremony is cause for great rejoicing. Savor the moment.

Beau went weak when Exi arrived with her entourage at the Office of the City Clerk: Marriage Bureau in a drop-dead runway gown that made his mouth go dry and his blood heat up. Now he knew why Grace said nothing but his Armani tux would do. He locked onto Exi's eyes so full of love. If they weren't already doing this, he'd drop to his knees and beg—forget the paparazzi having a heyday.

Devin, Grace and Mattie, Eileen and Eddie, Exi's parents and her brother Sully, plus her star-struck friends, Suz and Treya, were here for the event. He'd come early to get a number before the waiting times got crazy, and when it came up, they went into a room with nothing special about it. He felt a pang for agreeing to this and swore the church part would be perfect. But no way was he waiting a year for what he wanted.

That thought froze him. "Exi."

She pivoted and searched him, seeing too easily what happened inside his head. "What?"

"I can't do this."

She squeezed his hands. "What do you mean?"

"This is me getting everything I want. Like always."

Her smile lit the room. "Um, that would be both of us."

He brought his mouth to her ear. "It shouldn't be tacky."

She giggled. "It's just the first step."

He held her face between his hands. "Are you really sure? I don't want you disappointed."

"You can't disappoint me."

There it was again, her unconditional love. Now he could tell Ann he got it. Determined to do this again with all the trappings, he promised everything he had to give. And she did too. The kiss was almost chaste, a brush of his lips on hers, the slightest hint, because he didn't want to go up in flames.

They walked out with cameras shooting them from every angle. He ignored all the shouted questions about his disappearance and let nothing into his mind but this moment. John let them into an SUV just in case word of this had reached Spider.

He'd think about that another day. As he helped Exi out of the SUV at Eileen's, the charter bus arrived. One after another, the kids, Luke, and Georgia disembarked. Georgia's hug went on so long it embarrassed him.

"Go in for the party, you guys," he told the ragtag crew. "Best behavior. This isn't my house." It was a testament to trust, letting them in there. If he was wrong, Liam, John, and his security crew were on hand. But he knew how much these young people wanted to make it in life. How could they, if no one believed?

He stood with Exi at his side as they all filed in.

Ann left the bus last, and when he worked out that Misty hadn't come, she said, "Spider heard about the baby and wants another chance. Misty swears he's sorry, he loves her, and it's going to work out."

His stomach felt sick.

"We don't win them all, Beau. We can only try."

He fought tears of anger and disbelief.

"But this is a day of celebration." Ann squeezed Exi's hands. "Life can be beautiful and should be lived to the utmost."

Then it was just the two of them. He stood a moment with his bride, letting all the bad flow away, determined to live to the utmost no matter what came.

She smiled. "Ready?"

"Yeah," he breathed, and they joined the revelers.

Inside, Sticks knelt and petted Sheriff. "He's so clean."

"And better stay that way." Eileen glided by on her brother's arm.

They had disposed of reception conventions, but that didn't mean the party wasn't fun. Actors and musicians performed famous love scenes and ballads on the staircase. Caterers carried courses of gourmet foods, wedding petit fours, and sparkling cider—in consideration of the sober kids. He feasted on Exi simply mingling.

At one point, her brother Sully, whose position on the task force made him privy to more than he would have liked, approached. "Congratulations." They shook hands. "And you know what we Brooklyn guys say. Hurt my sister, I'll kill you." His grip tightened.

"If I hurt your sister I'll do it myself." Truer than Sully knew.

Grace took his place. "I talked to Exi about making your story a novel."

He slid her a look. "Shades of Jeffrey?"

"Not even close." She laughed. "Devin said he'd write the screenplay. When I told the publisher, he floated it by a production company."

"Wouldn't Devin do that too?"

Her eyes got a mischievous glint. "Movie production company. The producer's highly motivated … with you locked in as lead."

He swallowed. "You know how I feel about Hollywood."

"And I see how you feel about these kids. Would it be the end of the world to make money on their behalf?"

He looked around the house. "Wouldn't that be a kick in the … derriere?"

"You discussing derrieres with my wife, Corrigan?" Devin came over.

"Only in the kicking sense."

Devin sipped from his flute. "Have to say I'm surprised you had it in you to propose marriage."

"Actually, Exi proposed to me, and Eileen took it from there."

"What?" Grace laughed. "That'll make an interesting twist in the novel."

"Everything just falls into your lap, doesn't it?" Devin growled.

Beau looked at his bride with adoration.

Grace fanned herself. "If you two don't quit, we're going to have to clear the room."

"Works for me. Or better yet …" He strode over with no intention of quitting anything. Exi took the hands he offered, and he led her up the stairs. His mouth covered hers on the second floor landing in sight of everyone, a stage kiss for the crowd. On the third landing, out of sight, their mouths started learning the language of love they would speak from now on. On the fourth, he lifted her into his arms, no longer prodigal but husband to this one love. In her eyes, he saw the man he could be, the person he would be and more … so help him God.

The End

Author's Note

Thank you so much for reading TOLD YOU TWICE. I wasn't sure what to expect when Bo stepped up for his story. I mean he had some serious issues, some damage, and a worldly nature he wasn't eager to shed. But I could feel that underneath his posturing, I'd find a noble soul. Just the one for Exi, whose strength everyone underestimated.

The street kid mission in this story is loosely based on the Covenant House ministry and many of the stories are tragically similar to what I've portrayed. For more about this organization go to: www.covenanthouse.org.

If you enjoyed the experience, I'd appreciate you helping others find out by leaving a review online. If you'd like to know more about what I'm writing, book launches or appearances, special deals and giveaways, you can sign up on my website kristenheitzmann.com or follow me on Facebook, Goodreads, Pinterest, and Twitter.

Happy reading. ☺

Coming next in the TOLD YOU series

Twice Take Two

A novella featuring Beau and Exi

Just when they thought they could relax and enjoy their relationship, movie making takes Beau and Exi to LA, where his roots come back to haunt. Can their fledgling marriage withstand more discord and danger?

Acknowledgements

What an honor it is to have wonderful people assisting my endeavors. Erin Healy, editor extraordinaire. Rel Mollet, amazing Aussie Virtual Assistant. Beta-readers who helped shape this story: Jessica Lovitt (brainstorming and myriad revisions!) James Heitzmann (always), Charlene Brown, David Ladd, and Bruce Basler.

Very special thanks to my art expert—and amazing talent—Charlene Brown. Check out the beauty she creates at charlenembrown.com.

Special thanks to cover design team: Jessica, Steve, and Chelsea. You guys rock!

And thank you reader friends who have been so supportive. I couldn't do this without you.

Praise for TOLD YOU SO

"A battle of wits quickly morphs into a battle of hearts—and, oh, what a glorious fall when love heals old wounds and lifts them all! *Told You So* is an engaging, rich, and compelling read masterfully executed in the talented Kristen Heitzmann's capable hands. Bravo!"

-VICKI HINZE, USA Today Bestselling Author

"Kristen Heitzmann has such a brilliant way of exploring the human psyche, penning romances that outshine and stand apart. Her latest release, *Told You So* is no exception. She took me deeper than I could ever have imagined, cutting away layer after layer until the characters were laid bare, and me right along with them. Readers will be captivated and mesmerized by Heitzmann's *Told You So.*"

-ELIZABETH GODDARD, award-winning author of the Mountain Cove romantic suspense series.

"Kristen Heitzmann's novel *Told You So* is a feast of delicious storytelling, from the page-turning banter of two people who couldn't be less alike, to an unexpected twist that will leave the reader breathless. I couldn't get enough of the characters or the world she's drawn. Heitzmann couldn't have written it any better. It's a must-read."

-RENE GUTTERIDGE, author of *Old Fashioned*

"Capturing a sassy, chick-lit essence, Kristen Heitzmann weaves a subtle suspense plot within this fun romantic comedy. The characters' insecurities, snobbish prejudices, and inadvisable tactics entwine readers within the laughter and pain Devin and Grace inflict upon each other—and themselves—before discovering their unusual, and oh-so-satisfying happy ever after. Loved it! Highly recommended!"

-SERENA CHASE, *USA Today*'s Happy Ever After blog, author of *The Ryn*

Books by Kristen Heitzmann

Told You Series

Told You So

Told You Twice

A Rush of Wings Series

A Rush of Wings

The Still of Night

The Breath of Dawn

Redford Series

Indivisible

Indelible

Diamond of the Rockies

The Rose Legacy

Sweet Boundless

The Tender Vine

The Michelli Family Series

Secrets

Unforgotten

Echoes

Standalone Titles

The Edge of Recall

Freefall

Halos

Twilight

Made in the USA
Columbia, SC
13 December 2020